PRAISE FOR THE CONTRIBUTORS

MARK BILLINGHAM
"Disturbingly original." —*Time Out*

LAWRENCE BLOCK
"One of the very best writers now working the beat."
—*Wall Street Journal*

ANDREW COBURN
"A natural storyteller." —*New York Times*

MICHAEL CONNELLY
"Connelly is a crime-writing genius."
—*Independent on Sunday*

JEFFERY DEAVER
"Teeth-chattering suspense." —*Daily Mail*

JOHN HARVEY
"One of the masters of British crime fiction."
—*Sunday Telegraph*

REGINALD HILL
"Clever, involving and admirably resolved." —*Guardian*

BILL JAMES
"Bill James is a frontrunner among those who have turned
the police procedural on its head." —*Sunday Times*

DENNIS LEHANE
"One of the greats of crime writing." —*Guardian*

MEN
FROM BOYS

MEN
FROM BOYS

Edited by

John Harvey

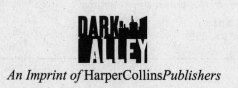

An Imprint of HarperCollins*Publishers*

A continuation of the copyright page appears on page ix.

This book was originally published in Great Britain in 2003 by William Heinemann, a division of The Random House Group Limited.

HarperCollins books may be purchased for educational, business, or sales promotional use. For information please write: Special Markets Department, HarperCollins Publishers Inc., 10 East 53rd Street, New York, NY 10022.

FIRST U.S. EDITION

Library of Congress Cataloging-in-Publication Data

Men from boys / edited by John Harvey.—1st ed.
    p. cm.
    ISBN 0-06-076285-3 (trade pbk.)
    1. Detective and mystery stories, American. I. Harvey, John, 1938–

PS648.D4M46 2005
813'.087208—dc22

                                                        2005040234

05 06 07 08 09 RRD 10 9 8 7 6 5 4 3 2 1

CONTENTS

Earlier versions of this book... First published by Scribner, an
(William Morrow & Co., New York, 2007) ... Imprint Simon & Schuster.
... reprinted by permission of the author.

"Resurrection" or Upon Jones... by Bill Murray... First
published as U.S. Schoolwork... from Survey Graphic...
Map of Canterbury... (Bristol Books, London, 1986)...
reprinted by permission of the author.

An original fairy tale wrought sent by Bill... appears in
the novel... first ever Routledge... (Routledge, London,
1996)... reprinted by permission of the author.

MEN
FROM BOYS

INTRODUCTION

It began with a simple enough idea: a book which would collect together stories by those writers in the crime and mystery area whose work I respect, admire and enjoy most. Simple? Well, no.

For one thing, the choice would be too vast, the book too large. But then, unbidden, the title leapt to mind: *Men from Boys*. And once it was there, lodged in my brain, it wouldn't leave. It was – it is – a kind of statement, a declaration, but also, and crucially, it provided a focus and a theme.

It also had the effect of cutting the number of writers I might have approached by half. No McDermid, no Fyfield, no Stella Duffy; no Grafton, no Paretsky, no Julie Smith. No Alice Sebold. No Suzanne Berne.

Just men.

Men writing, for the most part, about what it is to be a man.

To succeed; to fail. To open one's eyes.

What the majority of the pieces in the collection address, some directly, others more tangentially, are issues of self-knowledge, of accepting – or denying – certain responsibilities. What does it mean to be a father? What does it mean to be a son? What does it mean to be a man?

As the protagonist in Don Winslow's 'Douggie Doughnuts' comes to realise, there are things you do and things you don't do. Again and again – but never two ways the same – the people who inhabit these stories are having to determine what is right, what will give them dignity, what will earn them self-respect.

Some – the young men in Mark Billingham's 'Dancing Towards the Blade' or Michael Connelly's 'After Midnight', for instance – make their choices with their fathers' voices ringing in their ears; others have to contend with parents who are venal at best, incorrigibly corrupt at worst.

Little is perfect. In Daniel Woodrell's beautifully understated 'Two Things', the best a father can say of his relationship with his son is that it was 'something terrible I have lived through'. Andrew Coburn's marvellous novella takes us through three generations of an extended family whose members variously fall to sudden acts of violence or simple self-regarding avarice, and where the strength of purpose and single-mindedness of the father is passed on not to the son but to the daughter.

So did I achieve my aim to include all of those, now admittedly male, writers I revere? Of course not. No matter how many times I wrote and faxed, e-mailed and phoned, no matter how much pleading and cajoling I engaged in, there were some – a few – whose dance cards, for whatever reason, were regretfully too full. A pleasant diversionary party game might be to guess who these were. Just don't ask: I'll never tell.

But if all had accepted that would have simply meant a bigger book. There is no one here whose name I am not pleased and proud to include; no piece of work that has not earned its place.

The trouble with writing short stories, as James Ellroy has recently lamented, and as most of us I'm sure would agree, is that they take so damned long to write. For every earnestly crafted page, at least a chapter of a novel would likely come whizzing off the computer and with less heartache. 'There is no room for error in short stories,' says Annie Proulx. 'The lack of a comma can throw everything off.'

That's why we keep doing it, of course. Trying to. One reason, anyway. Testing ourselves, testing the skill. It certainly isn't, unless we're lucky enough to turn heads at *The New Yorker*, for the money.

'There's a joy', says Donald Westlake (and, yes, he'd be in here if I had my way), 'in watching economy of gesture when performed by a real pro, whatever the art.' He compares writing short stories with playing jazz: 'a sense of vibrant imagination at work within a tightly controlled setting'. He says it's what turns writers on. Readers too.

There's a real pleasure for me in the way the writers of these stories create worlds that are instantly recognisable and believable yet as widely apart as a deprived London housing estate and the trenches of the First World War, the claustrophobia of a late-night back-room poker game or a rundown jazz joint in Manhattan and the slow but irrevocable decay of the small New England town on which Don Winslow riffs so passionately. I'm in awe, too, of the way James Sallis leads us through a landscape delineated with absolute clarity, except that by kicking away the narrative props that we're used to, the scene takes on a bewildering half-amnesiac state which mirrors what is going on in the central character's mind.

The prospect of Bill James's lustful yet lethal Assistant Chief Constable Isles let loose in a posh private girls' school and of Brian Thompson's semi-retired geezers girding up their loins to take on the Russian mafia both fill me with delight, and I give myself up joyously to the promise of Dennis Lehane's 'Until Gwen', whose first sentence hurtles us along with dangerous expectation. 'Your father picks you up from prison in a stolen Dodge Neon with an eight-ball in the glove compartment and a hooker named Mandy in the back seat.'

And . . .

But enough from me. Enjoy. Read on.

John Harvey
London, January 2003

DANCING TOWARDS THE BLADE

Mark Billingham

He was always Vincent at home.

At school there were a few boys who called him 'Vince', and 'Vinny' was yelled more often than not across the playground, but his mother and father never shortened his name and neither did his brothers and sisters whose own names, in turn, were also spoken in full.

'Vincent' around the house then, and at family functions. The second syllable given equal weight with the first by the heavy accent of the elder members. Not swallowed. Rhyming with 'went'.

Vincent was not really bothered what names people chose to use, but there were some things it was never pleasant to be called.

'Coon!'

'Fucking coon . . .'

'Black coon. Fucking black bastard . . .'

He had rounded the corner and stepped into the passageway to find them waiting for him. Like turds in long grass. A trio of them in Timberland and Tommy Hilfiger.

Not shouting, but simply speaking casually. Saying what they saw. Big car. Hairy dog. Fucking black bastard . . .

Vincent stopped, caught his breath, took it all in.

Two were tallish – one abnormally thin, the other shaven-headed – and both cradling cans of expensive lager. The third was shorter and wore a baseball cap, the peak bent and pulled down low. He took a swig of Smirnoff Ice, then began to bounce on the balls of his feet, swinging the frosted glass bottle between thumb and forefinger.

'What you staring at, you sooty cunt?'

Vincent reckoned they were fifteen or so. Year eleven boys. The skinny one was maybe not even that, but all of them were a little younger than he was.

From somewhere a few streets away came the noise of singing, tuneless and incoherent, the phrases swinging like bludgeons. Quick as a flash, the arms of the taller boys were in the air, lager cans clutched in pale fists, faces taut with blind passion as they joined in the song.

'No one likes us, no one likes us, no one likes us, we don't care . . .'

The smaller boy looked at Vincent and shouted above the noise, 'Well?'

It was nearly six o'clock and starting to get dark. The match had finished over an hour ago but Vincent had guessed there might still be a few lads knocking about. He'd seen a couple outside the newsagent as he'd walked down the ramp from the tube station. Blowing on to bags of chips. Tits and guts moving beneath their thin, replica shirts. The away fans were long gone and most of the home supporters were already indoors, but there were others, most who'd already forgotten the score, who still wandered the streets, singing and drinking. Waiting in groups, a radio tuned to *5 Live*. Standing in lines on low walls, the half-time shitburgers turning to acid in their stomachs, looking around for it . . .

The cut-through was no more than fifteen feet wide and ran between two three-storey blocks. It curled away from the main road towards the block where Vincent lived at the far end of the estate. The three boys who barred his way were gathered around a pair of stone bollards, built to dissuade certain drivers from coming on to the estate. From setting fire to cars on people's doorsteps.

Vincent answered the question, trying to keep his voice low and even, hoping it wouldn't catch. 'I'm going home . . .'

'Fucking listen to him. A posh nigger . . .'

The skinny boy laughed and the three came together, shoulders connecting, forearms nudging one another. When they were still again they had taken up new positions. The three now stood, more or less evenly spaced across the walkway, one in each gap. Between wall and bollard, bollard and bollard, bollard and wall . . .

'Where's home?' the boy in the cap said.

Vincent pointed past the boy's head. The boy didn't turn. He raised his head and Vincent got his first real look at the face, handsome and hard, shadowed by the peak of the baseball cap. Vincent saw something like a smile as the boy brought the bottle to his lips again.

'This is the short cut,' Vincent said. 'My quickest way . . .'

The boy in the cap swallowed. 'Your quickest way home is via the airport.' The smile that Vincent had thought he'd seen now made itself very evident. 'You want the Piccadilly Line to Heathrow, mate . . .'

Vincent chuckled softly, pretending to enjoy the joke. He saw the boy's face harden, watched him raise a hand and jab a finger back towards the main road.

'Go round.'

Vincent knew what he meant. He could walk back and take the path that led around the perimeter of the estate, approach his block from the other side. It would only take a few minutes longer. He could just turn and go, and he would probably be home before they'd finished laughing.

'You heard.' The skinny boy leaned back against a bollard.

He could *easily* turn and go round . . .

'Now piss off . . .'

The edges of Vincent's vision began to blur and darken, and the words that spewed from the mouth of the boy with the shaven head became hard to make out. A distant rhythm was asserting itself and as Vincent looked down at the cracked slabs beneath his feet, a shadow seemed to fall across them. A voice grew louder, and it was as if the walls on either side had softened and begun to sway above him like the tops of trees.

The voice was one Vincent knew well. The accent, unlike his own, was heavy, but the intonation and tone were those that had been passed on to him and to his brothers and sisters. It was a rich voice, warm and dark, sliding effortlessly around every phrase, each dramatic sentence of a story it never tired of telling.

His father's voice . . .

Looking out from his bedroom window, the boy could see the coffee plants lying like a deep green tablecloth across the hillside, billowing down towards the canopy of treetops and the deep, dirty river beneath. If he raised his eyes *up,* he saw the mountain on the far side of the valley, its peaks jutting into the mist, the slopes changing colour many times a day according to the cloud and the position of the sun. Black or green or blood red. Other colours the boy had no name for.

A dozen views for the price of one, and he'd thought about all of them in the time he'd been away. He'd tried to picture each one during the bone-shaking, twelve-hour bus ride that had brought him home from school five days before.

'Hey! Stand still, boy. This is damn fiddly . . .'

Uncle Joseph, on his knees in front of him, his thick fingers struggling with the leather fastenings, as they had every morning since they'd begun. It was hard to tie the knots so that the strings of beads clung to the calves without slipping, but not so tightly that they would cut into the flesh.

When he'd finished with the beads on the lower legs, Uncle Joseph would move on to the thick bands of dried goatskin, each heavy with rows of bells and strapped around the thighs. These were expensive items, handmade like everything else. Lastly, Joseph would wrap the dark, highly polished belt round the boy's waist. On three out of the last four mornings, much to the boy's amusement, he'd sliced a finger on one of the razor-sharp shells sewn into the leather.

Behind him, Uncle Francis worked on attaching the beads that crossed his back and chest in an X, like brightly coloured bandoliers. Francis was always cheerful, and the boy imagined that he too looked forward to that moment when Joseph would cry out, curse and stick a bleeding finger into his mouth. It was always Francis and Joseph who dressed him. The rest of his uncles waited outside. He'd been amazed at quite how *many* uncles he had, when they'd gathered on the night after he'd got back; when the family committee had met to organise it all.

There had been lots to decide.

'Do we have drummers?'

'Of course. This is important. *He* is important . . .'

'Grade A. Definitely Grade A . . .'

'These drummers are not cheap. Their damn costumes alone are a fortune . . .'

'I think they should come *with* their costumes. It isn't fair. We shouldn't have to pay for the costumes separately . . .'

'We should have *lots* of drummers!'

And on and on, deep into the night, arguing and getting

drunker while the boy listened from his bedroom. Though he didn't understand everything, the passion in the voices of these men had caused excitement to swell in his chest. Yes, and an equal measure of dread to press down on it, like one of the huge flat stones that lay along the river bed at the bottom of the valley. He'd lain awake most of that night thinking of his friends, his age-mates in the other villages, wondering if they were feeling the same thing.

'All set, boy,' Uncle Joseph said.

Uncle Francis handed him the headdress, rubbed the back of his neck. 'Feeling fit?'

Outside, he was greeted with cheers and whoops. This was the last day of gathering and there was more noise, more gaiety than there had been on any day previously. This was the eve of it all: the final glorious push.

He took his place in the middle of the group, acknowledged the greetings of his brothers, of uncles and cousins whose names he could never remember. Though no one was dressed as extravagantly as he was, everyone had made the necessary effort. No man or boy was without beads or bells. The older ones were all draped in animal skins – monkey, zebra and lion. All had painted faces and strips of brightly coloured cloth attached to the edges of their leather vests.

A huge roar went up as the first drum was struck. A massive bass drum, its rhythm like a giant's heartbeat. The smaller drums joined then, and the whistles, and the yelps of the women and children, watching from the doorways of houses, waving the gatherers goodbye.

The boy cleared his throat and spat into the dirt. He let out a long, high note, listened to it roll away across the valley. The rhythm became more complex, more frantic, and he picked up his knees in time to it, the beads rattling on his legs and the shells clattering against the belt round his waist.

He began to dance.

The procession started to move. A carnival, a travelling circus, a hundred or more bare feet slapping into the dirt in time to the drummers. A cloud of dust rose up behind them as they picked up speed, moving away along the hard brown track that snaked out of the village.

The mottled grey of the slabs was broken only by the splotches of dogshit brown and dandelion yellow.

Vincent looked up from the floor of the walkway.

The eyes of the two taller boys darted between his face and that of their friend. It seemed to Vincent that they were waiting to be told what to do. They were looking for some sort of signal.

The boy in the cap raised his eyes up to Vincent's. He took a long, slow swig from his bottle, his gaze not shifting from Vincent's face. Then he snatched the bottle from his lips, wiped a hand across his mouth and glared, as if suddenly affronted.

'*What?*'

Vincent smiled, shook his head. 'I didn't say anything.'

'Yes you fucking did.'

The boy with the shaved head took a step forward. 'What did you say, you cheeky black fucker?'

The smaller boy nodded, pleased, and took another swig. Vincent shrugged, feeling the tremble in his right leg, pressing a straight arm hard against it.

'Listen, I don't want any trouble. I'm just trying to get home . . .'

Home.

Vincent blinked and saw his brother's face, the skin taken off his cheek and one eye swollen shut. He saw his mother's face as she stood at the window all the next afternoon, staring out across the dual carriageway towards the lorry park and the floodlights beyond. He saw her face when she turned finally, and spoke. 'We're moving,' she'd said.

One more blink and he saw the resignation that had returned to her face after a day doing the maths; scanning newspapers and estate agents' details from Greenwich and Blackheath. As the idea of moving *anywhere* was quickly forgotten.

'I've already told you,' the boy with the bottle said. 'If you're so desperate, just go round.'

Vincent saw the face of his father then. As it had been that day when his brother had come home bleeding, and then, as he imagined it to have been twenty-five years before. In a country Vincent had only ever seen pictures of.

The boy sat at the back of the house, beneath the striped awning that his father had put above his bedroom window. Rose rubbed ointment on to his blisters. They stared across the valley at the sun dropping down behind the mountain, the slopes cobalt blue beneath a darkening sky.

He knew that they should not have been sitting together, that his uncles would not have approved. Contact with young women was frowned upon in the week leading up to the ritual. He would regret it, his uncles would have said, in the days afterwards, in the healing time after the ceremony. 'Talk to young women . . .' Joseph had told him, 'let them smile at you now and shake their hips, and you will *pay*.'

He didn't care. He had known Rose since before he could walk and besides, Joseph, Francis and the others would be insensible by now. They had sat down around the pot as soon as they had finished eating supper. Talking about the day, filling in the elders on how 'the boy' was doing and getting slowly drunker. Sucking up powerful mouthfuls of home brew from the pot through long bamboo straws.

The boy had watched them for a while, no longer jealous,

as he would have been before. Once it was all over, he would have earned the right to sit down and join them.

'Fine, but not yet, you haven't,' Rose had said when he'd mentioned it to her.

It had been a hard day and the boy was utterly exhausted. He reckoned they had danced twenty miles or more, visited a dozen villages, and he had sung his heart and his throat out every step of the way. He was proud of his song, had been since he'd written it months before. Even Rose had been forced to concede that it was pretty good. He'd practised it every day, knowing there was prestige and status attached to the best song, the best performance. He'd given that performance a hundred times in the last week and now his voice was as ragged as the soles of his feet.

It had been a successful day too. Uncle Philip had not announced the final tally, but it had certainly been a decent haul. Relatives close and distant in each homestead had come forward dutifully with gifts: earthenware dishes piled high with cash; chickens or a goat from cousins; cattle from those of real importance. Philip had made a careful note of who'd given what, in the book that was carried with them as they criss-crossed the district, each village ready to welcome them, each able to hear them coming from a mile or more away.

Everyone had been more than generous. By sundown the following day, the boy would be a rich man.

'Are you scared?' Rose asked.

He winced as she dropped his foot to the floor. 'No,' he said.

The boy wasn't sure why he lied. Being frightened was fine, it was *showing* the fear that was unacceptable, that would cost you. He remembered the things that had scared him the most that day, scared him far more than what was to come the following afternoon. He had been sitting with the elders in the village where his father had been born. Squatting in the shade, stuffed full of roasted goat and green bananas, with barely the energy to nod as each piece of advice was given, each simple lesson handed out.

'You will not fear death . . .'

'You will defend your village against thieves . . .'

Then he'd been handed the baby.

'There are times when your wife will be sick, and you must look after yourself and your children.'

'You will learn to cook . . .'

'You will learn to keep a fire burning all day . . .'

They roared as the baby began to piss on his lap, told him it was good luck. They were still laughing as the boy danced his way out of the village. All he could think about, as he began his song again, was how being unafraid of death and of thieves sounded easy compared with taking care of children . . .

He thought about telling Rose this, but instead told her about what had happened in the first village they'd visited that day. Something funny and shocking. A distant cousin of his father's had been discovered hiding in the fields on the outskirts of the village. Trying to dodge the handover of a gift was a serious matter and not only had the offering been taken from him by force, but he had brought shame upon himself and the rest of his family.

'Can you believe it?' the boy said. 'That man was Grade A! Cowering in the tall grass like a woman, to avoid handing over a bowl. A *bowl* for heaven's sake . . .'

Rose pushed her shoulder against his. 'So, you think *you're* going to be Grade A? Grade B maybe? What d'you think, boy?'

He shrugged. He knew what he was hoping for. All he could be certain about was that this was the last time anybody would call him 'boy'.

*

The one with the bottle stood a foot or so forward from his two friends. He reached over his shoulder for the lit cigarette that he knew would be there, took three quick drags and handed it back. 'What team do you support anyway?'

'Fucking Man U, I bet . . .'

For a moment, Vincent thought about lying. Giving them their own team's name. He knew that he'd be caught out in a second. 'I don't follow a team.'

'Right. Not an *English* team . . .'

'Not any team,' Vincent said.

'Some African team, yeah? Kicking a fucking coconut around . . .'

'Bongo Bongo United FC!'

'"Kicking a coconut", that's classic . . .'

'Headers must be a nightmare, yeah?'

The skinny one and the one with the shaved head began to laugh. They pursed their lips and stuck out their bumfluffy chins. They pretended to scratch their armpits.

'You know what FC stands for, don't you? Fucking coon . . .'

Vincent looked away from them. He heard the monkey noises begin softly, then start to get louder.

'Look at him,' the one in the cap said. 'He's shitting himself.' He said something else after that, but Vincent didn't hear it . . .

Dawn, at the river, on the final morning.

Dotted for a mile or more along the flat, brown river bank were the other groups. Some were smaller than his own, while others must have numbered a hundred, but at the centre of each stood one of the boy's age-mates. Each ready to connect with the past, to embrace the future. Each asking for the strength to endure what lay ahead of him.

The boy was called forward by an elder. As he took his first steps, he glanced sideways, saw his age-mates along the river bank moving in a line together towards the water.

This was the preparation.

In the seconds he spent held beneath the water, he wondered whether a cry would be heard if he were to let one out. He imagined it rising up to the surface, the bubbles bursting in a series of tiny screams, each costing him grades.

He emerged from the river purified and ready to be painted with death.

The sun was just up but already fierce, and the white mud was baked hard within a minute or two of being smeared across his face and chest and belly. The mist was being burned away, and looking along the bank, the boy saw a row of pale statues. A long line of ghosts in the buttery sunlight.

He watched an old man approach each figure, as one now approached him. The elder took a mouthful of beer from a pumpkin gourd and spat, spraying it across the boy's chest. The beer ran in rivulets down the shell of dried mud, as prayers were said and his uncles stepped towards him.

The group that had been nearest to him jogged past, already finished, and he looked at his age-mate, caked in white mud as he was. The boy had known him, as he'd known most of them, for all of their sixteen years, but his friend was suddenly unrecognisable. It was not the mask of mud. It was the eyes that stared out from behind it. It was the eyes that were suddenly different.

The boy was nudged forward, was handed his knife, and the group began loping away in the same direction as his friend. Drumming again now, and singing, heading for the market place. All of them, all the ghost-boys, moving towards the moment when they would die and come back to life . . .

*

'Shut up!' Vincent shouted.

After a moment or two the skinny one and the one with the shaved head stopped making their monkey noises, but only after a half-glance in their direction from the one in the cap.

'Turn your pockets out,' he said.

Vincent's hands were pressed hard against his legs to keep them still. He slowly brought each of them up to his pockets, slipped them inside . . .

'Maybe we'll let you *pay* to go home. Let me see what you've got.'

Vincent's left hand came out empty. His right emerged clutching the change from his train ticket. He opened his hand and the one in the cap leaned forward to take a look.

'Fuck that, mate. Where's the notes?'

Vincent shook his head. 'This is all I've got.'

'You're a fucking liar. Where's your wallet?'

Vincent said nothing. He closed his hand around the coins and thrust his fist back into his trouser pocket.

The one in the cap took a step towards him. He was no more than a couple of feet away. 'Don't piss me about. I don't like it, yeah?'

He could easily turn and go round . . .

'Where's his phone?' the skinny one said.

'Get his fucking phone, man. They always have wicked phones.'

The one in the cap held out his hand. 'Let's have it.'

It suddenly seemed to Vincent that the phone might be the way out of it, his way past them. Handing it over, giving them something and then trying to get past was probably a good idea . . .

The mobile was snatched from his grasp the second he'd produced it. The one in the cap turned and swaggered back towards his friends. They cheered as he held it up for them to look at.

The three gathered round to examine the booty and Vincent saw a gap open up between the far right bollard and the wall. He thought about making a run for it. If he could stay ahead of them for just a minute, half a minute maybe, he would be virtually home. He reckoned he could outrun the two bigger ones anyway. Perhaps his mother or father, one of his brothers might see him coming . . .

He took a tentative step forward.

The one in the cap wheeled round suddenly, clutching the phone. 'Piece of cheap shit!' His arm snapped back, then forward and Vincent watched the phone explode against the wall, shattering into pieces of multi-coloured plastic.

The crack of the phone against the bricks changed something.

By the time Vincent looked again, the gap had been filled. The three stood square on to him, their bodies stiff with energy despite their efforts to appear relaxed. The space between them all was suddenly charged.

Vincent had no idea how he looked to them, what his face said about how he felt at that moment. He looked at *their* faces and saw hatred and excitement and expectation. He also saw fear.

'Last chance,' the one in the cap said.

The boy was stunned by the size of the crowd, though it was nothing unusual. He could remember, when he'd been one of the onlookers himself as a child, thinking that there couldn't possibly be this many people in the whole world. Today, as at the same moment every year, those that could not get a clear view were standing on tables and other makeshift platforms. They were perched on roofs and clustered together in the treetops.

He and his age-mates were paraded together, one final time, carried aloft like kings. His eyes locked for a few seconds with a friend as they passed each other. Their Adam's apples were like wild things in their throats.

While the boy moved on shoulders above the teeming mass of bodies, the dancing and the drumming grew more frenzied. Exhausted, he summoned the strength to sing one final time, while below him the basket was passed around and each relative given a last chance to hand over more money or pledge another gift.

Now, it was only the fizzing in the boy's blood that was keeping him upright. There were moments – a sickening wave of exhaustion, a clouding of his vision as he reached for a high note – when he was sure he was about to pass out, to topple down and be lost or trampled to death. He was tempted to close his eyes and let it happen . . .

At the moment when the noise and the heat and the *passion* of the crowd was at its height, the boy suddenly found himself alone with Joseph and Francis at the edge of the market place. There was space around him as he was led along a track towards a row of undecorated huts.

'Are you a woman?' Joseph asked.

'No,' the boy said.

The boy wondered if thinking about his mother and father made him one. He knew that they would be waiting, huddled together among the coffee plants, listening for the signal that it was over. Did wishing that he was with them, even for the few moments it would take to shake his father's hand and smell his mother's neck, make him less than Grade A?

'Are you a woman?' Francis repeated.

'No!' the boy shouted.

His uncles stepped in front of him and pushed open a door to one of the peat latrines. 'This will be your last chance,' Joseph said.

The boy moved inside quickly, dropped his shorts and squatted above the hole formed by the square of logs. He looked up at the grass roof, then across at his uncles who had followed him inside. He knew that they had sworn to stay with him until the final moment, but honestly, what did they think he was going to do? Did they think he would try to kill himself by diving head first into the latrine?

Did they think he would try to run?

Joseph and Francis smiled as the shit ran out of him like water. 'Better now than later,' Francis said.

The boy knew that his uncle was right.

He stood and wiped himself off. He felt no shame, no embarrassment at being watched. He was no more or less than a slave to it now.

A slave to the ritual.

The beer can hit him first, bouncing off his shoulder. It was almost empty, and Vincent was far more concerned by the beer that had sprayed on to his cheek and down his shirt. The can was still clattering at his feet when the cigarette fizzed into his chest. He took a step back, smacking away the sparks, listening to the skinny one and the one with the shaved head jabbering.

'I don't believe it, he's still fucking here . . .'

'Is he? It's getting dark, I can't see him if he isn't smiling . . .'

'He said he wasn't looking for trouble . . .'

'Well he's going to get a fucking slap.'

'He's just taking the piss now . . .'

'We gave the cunt every chance . . .'

'They're *all* taking the piss . . .'

'He's the one that's up for it, if you ask me. It's *him* who's kicking off, don't you reckon? He could have walked away and he just fucking stood there like he's in a trance. He's trying to face us down, the twat. Yeah? Don't you reckon?'

'Come on then . . .'

'Let's fucking well. Have. It.'

Vincent became aware that he was shifting his weight slowly from one foot to the other, that his fists were clenched, that there was a tremor running through his gut.

A hundred yards away, on the far side of the estate, he saw a figure beneath a lamp-post. He watched it move inside the cone of dirty, orange light. Vincent wondered if whoever it was would come if he shouted . . .

His eye darted back to the boy in the cap, and to the boy's hand, which tilted slowly as he emptied out what drink there was left in his bottle.

The noise in the market place died as each one stepped forward, then erupted again a minute or two later when the ritual had been completed.

It was the boy's turn.

The crowd had moved back to form a tunnel down which he walked, trancelike, his uncles slightly behind. He tried to focus on the two red splodges at the far end of the tunnel and when his vision cleared he saw the faces of the cutters for the first time. Their red robes marked them out as professionals – men who travelled from village to village, doing their jobs and moving on. They were highly skilled, and had to be. There were stories, though the boy had never seen such a thing happen, of cutters being set upon by a crowd and killed if a hand was less than steady; if a boy were to die because of one of them.

The boy stopped at the stone, turned to the first cutter and handed over his knife. He had sharpened it every day on the soft bark of a rubber tree. He had confidence in the blade.

In three swift strokes, the knife had sliced away the fabric of the boy's shorts. All he could feel was the wind whispering at the top of his legs. All he could hear was the roaring of the blood, loud as the river, inside his head.

He was offered a stick to clutch, to brace against the back of his neck and cling on to. This was the first test and with a small shake of the head it was refused. No Grade A man would accept this offer.

He was hard as stone . . .

His hands were taken, pressed into a position of prayer and placed against his right cheek. His eyes widened and watered, fixed on the highest point of a tree at the far end of the market place.

Repeating it to himself above the roaring of the river. Hard as stone . . .

The boy knew that this was the moment when he would be judged. This was everything – when the crowd, when his family would be watching for a sign of fear. For blinking, for shaking, for shitting . . .

He felt the fingers taking the foreskin, stretching it.

Focused on the tree . . . chalk-white ghost-boy . . . stiff and still as any statue . . .

He felt the weight of the blade, cold and quick. Heavy, then heavier and he *heard* the knife pass through the skin. A boom and then a rush . . .

This was when a Grade A man might prove himself, jumping and rubbing at his bloody manhood. The crowd would count the jumps, clap and cheer as those very special ones asked for alcohol to be poured into the wound . . .

The boy was happy to settle for Grade B. His eyes flicked to his uncle Joseph who signalled for the second cutter to come forward. The knife was handed across and, with three further cuts, the membrane – the 'second skin' – was removed.

A whistle was blown and the boy started slightly at the explosion of noise from the crowd. It was all over in less than a minute.

Everything took on a speed – underwater slow or blink-quick – a dreamlike quality of its own as the pain began . . .

A cloth was wrapped around the boy's shoulders.

He was gently pushed back on to a stool.

He lowered his eyes and watched his blood drip on to the stone at his feet.

There was a burning then, and a growing numbness as ground herbs were applied, and the boy sat waiting for the bleeding to stop. He felt elated. He stared down the tunnel towards the far side of the market place, towards what lay ahead.

He saw himself lying on a bed of dried banana leaves, enjoying the pain. Only a man, he knew, would feel that pain. Only a man would wake, sweating in the night, crying out in agony after a certain sort of dream had sent blood to where it was not wanted.

He saw himself healed, strutting around the market place with other men. They were laughing and talking about the different grades that their friends had reached. They were looking at women and enjoying the looks that they got back.

The boy looked down the tunnel and saw, clearer than anything else, the baby that he'd been handed the day before. He watched it again, happily pissing all over him.

He saw its fat, perfect face as it stared up at him, kicking its legs.

The skinny one and the one with the shaved head were drifting towards him.

Vincent knew that if he turned and ran they would give chase, and if they caught him they would not stop until they'd done him a lot of damage. He felt instinctively that he had a chance of coming off better than that if he stood his ground. Besides, he didn't want to run.

'I bet he's fucking carrying something,' the skinny one said.

The one with the shaved head reached into his jacket

pocket, produced a small plastic craft knife. 'Blacks always carry blades . . .'

Vincent saw the one with the cap push himself away from the bollard he was leaning against. He watched him take a breath, and drop his arm, and break the bottle against the bollard with a flick of his wrist.

Vincent took a step away, turned and backed up until he felt the wall of the block behind him.

Hard as a stone . . .

'Stupid fucker.'

'He can't run. His arse has gone . . .'

'I bet he's filling his pants.'

Vincent showed them nothing. As little as his father had shown when the blade sang against his skin. He tensed his body but kept his face blank.

'Three points in the bag, lads,' the one with the broken bottle said. 'Easy home win . . .'

Vincent had learned a lot about what you gave away and what you kept hidden. They could have his phone and whatever money they could find. He would give them a little blood and a piece of his flesh if it came to it, and he would try his hardest to take some of theirs.

Vincent looked down the tunnel and saw them coming. He would not show them that he was afraid, though. He would not give them that satisfaction.

He was Grade A.

POINTS

Lawrence Block

The Knicks were hosting a first-year expansion team at the Garden, and when the two men arrived, thirty minutes before game time, half the seats were empty. 'I'm afraid it's not going to be much of a game,' the younger man said, 'and it looks as though I'm not alone in that opinion. Last time I was here the Lakers were in town and there wasn't an empty seat.'

'We're early,' the older man said. 'They won't sell out tonight, but they'll come closer than you might guess. Remember, this is New York. A lot of guys don't even leave their desks until seven-thirty for a game that starts at eight.'

'That's me you're describing. Not tonight, but the Laker game? There were points on the board by the time I got to my seat. And it would have been the same story tonight if I hadn't put my foot down. Carrigan came into my office at half past six with something that had to be done and would only take me a minute, swear to God. "Not tonight," I told him. "I'm meeting my Dad."'

Anyone looking at them would have suspected they were father and son. The resemblance was unmistakable, in their faces and in their easy loose-limbed grace. Both were tall men, standing several inches over six feet. Both had been slim in their youth and both had thickened some around the middle with age, the father more than the son. The son was perhaps an inch taller than the father, a fact which had not gone unremarked at their meeting a few minutes earlier.

'You're taller,' Richard Parmalee had said. 'I don't suppose your pituitary gland kicked into overdrive when nobody was looking. Have you been taking growth hormone?'

The son, whose name was Kevin, shook his head and grinned.

'Then the odds are you're not taller,' the father said. 'So, I guess you've got lifts in your shoes . . .'

'Just insoles, but they don't make you any taller.'

'That's what I was afraid of. Well, where does logic inexorably lead us? I'm shrinking.'

'You look the same to me.'

'Hell, I'm not melting away like the Wicked Witch of the West. Everybody shrinks, starting around forty or forty-five, but it takes fifteen or twenty years before it's enough to notice. You're not even forty for another year and a half, so you've got a while before your cuffs start scraping the pavement.'

'That hasn't happened to you.'

'No, if I've lost half an inch that's a lot. It's enough to notice, but only just. And I only just noticed it myself within the past month or so. I knew it was something that happens to everybody, but I figured I was different, it wouldn't happen to me. Same as right now you're listening and nodding and telling yourself it won't happen to you.'

The younger man laughed. 'Got me. Exactly what I was telling myself.'

'And who knows? You might be right. You've got a few years and by then they may have something to prevent it. I wouldn't put it past them.'

As Richard Parmalee had predicted, there were a lot of late arrivals and most seats were occupied by game time. The Knicks, eleven-point favorites according to the line in the papers, jumped off to an early lead that opened up to twenty-two points at half-time.

'Well, it's not much of a game,' the son said. 'I was afraid of that.'

'No, but it's still fun to watch them. I remember coming here to see the Harlem Globetrotters when I was still in high school. They were playing an exhibition game against somebody, probably the Knicks. I couldn't believe the things they did. Now everybody does that, but without the clowning.'

'They're still around, the Globetrotters.'

'And they're probably as entertaining as ever, but less remarkable, because everybody plays like that. It's a completely different game than when I played it.'

'It looks completely different to me,' the son said, 'so I can only imagine the difference from your point of view.'

'In my day we played on our feet. Your generation played the game on your toes. And now it's a game played in the air.'

'It's true.'

'And I swear the rules are different.'

'Well, the three-point shot . . .'

'Of course, but that's not what I mean. They routinely commit what would have been a travelling violation, but you never see it called. If a guy's driving to the basket it doesn't seem to matter how many steps he takes.'

'I know. There's a rule, but I can't figure out what it is.'

'And they'll turn the ball over when they're dribbling. Double dribble, that used to be, and you lost possession. Not any more.'

'I like the three-point shot, though,' Kevin Parmalee said.

31

'Improves the game. No question. But only at the pro distance. The college three-pointer is too close.'

'It's ridiculous. And yet the college game's more fun to watch. It's not as good a game, but it's more exciting.'

They went on chatting comfortably until play resumed, then fell largely silent and watched the action on the court. The visitors narrowed the gap in the third quarter and with three minutes to play only six points separated the two teams. Then the Knicks surged, and led by fourteen when the buzzer sounded.

On their way out the son said, 'Well, they made a game of it. It was never close, but you wouldn't have known that from the fans.'

'They beat the spread,' the father said, 'and that wasn't a foregone conclusion. It could have gone either way until the final seconds.'

'You figure that many of the people here had money on the game?'

'Probably more than you'd think, but that's not the point. We're New Yorkers, Kev. When we root for a team, we don't just want to win the game. We want to beat the spread.'

'And we did, so hoorah for our side.'

'Amen. It was a good game.'

'And God knows the price was right.'

'You told me who gave you the tickets, but I forget. One of the senior partners?'

'No, one of Joe Levin's clients. He gave them to Joe, and Joe thought he could go and then couldn't, which was why the whole thing was as last-minute as it was.'

'Terrific seats.'

'Well, some corporation pays for them, and lists them as a business expense. So they didn't cost us anything and they didn't cost anybody else anything, either.'

'That's the way it ought to be,' Richard Parmalee said. 'I made a reservation at Keen's, not that I think we'll need one at this hour on a week night. That sound all right to you?'

'As long as it's on me.'

'Not a chance.'

'Hey, I asked you out, remember?'

'You got the tickets, I get the dinner check.'

'The tickets were free, remember?'

'So's the dinner, as far as you're concerned. You're not going to win this argument, Kevin, so don't even try.'

The headwaiter greeted the older man by name and showed them to a table in the grill room. Richard Parmalee ordered a single-malt scotch, neat, with water back. Kevin ordered a Mexican beer.

'I was reading an article on malt whisky,' he said, 'and halfway through I decided I owed it to myself to develop a taste for it. Then I remembered that I never liked hard booze, and I especially don't like the stuff you drink. Laphroiag?'

'No one ever mistook it for mother's milk,' the older man conceded. He took a small sip and savored it, as if tasting it for the first time. 'I'm not sure I like the taste myself,' he said. 'I appreciate it, but that's not the same thing, is it? All in all, I'd have to say you're better off with beer.'

'I'd probably be better off with orange juice.'

'Chock full of vitamin C. But you don't drink much, do you?'

'No.'

'I have a drink every day, but it's an unusual day when I have a second. Which I guess makes this an unusual day, come to think of it, because I had one at my club this afternoon, and here I am having a second. Two drinks in one day and only five or six hours apart at that.'

'I'll call AA.'

They ordered the same meal, steak and salad. The

restaurant's ceiling was festooned with white clay pipes, each reserved for a particular patron, and over coffee the father said, 'I almost asked him to bring my pipe.'

'That's right, you have a pipe here, don't you? I have a faint memory of you smoking it after dinner.'

'It must have been the first time I brought you here. After a game, I suppose.'

'St John's-Iona. St John's won, and if I worked at it I could probably remember the score. I was fifteen, and I remember deciding that when I grew up I'd have a pipe of my own here.'

'If you were fifteen then I would have been forty-one. So that may well have been the last time I smoked that pipe, because I was forty-two when I quit. Your grandfather was diagnosed with lung cancer, and I threw my cigarettes in the garbage. I had some pipes, although I rarely smoked them.'

'I don't think I ever saw you smoke a pipe aside from that one time right here.'

'As I said, I rarely did. But I threw them out along with the cigarettes. And I gave away all my lighters and cigarette cases, including a silver Ronson that my father had given me. I figured he'd given me plenty of other things, I didn't have to hang on to it for sentimental reasons. You've never smoked, have you?'

'Not tobacco.'

'Then what . . . oh, marijuana. Do you use it?'

'I did in college, and for a year or two after. I was never into it that much. Mostly just at parties. I haven't smoked it in years and I haven't even smelled it, except on the street. I don't go to that many parties and when I do there's never anybody lighting up a joint in the corner.'

'I suppose I assumed you tried it at college, although I can't remember giving much thought to the subject. It wasn't around when I was in college. Oh, it must have been, but I wasn't aware of it and certainly didn't know anybody who smoked it.'

'So you never tried it.'

'I didn't say that. Your mother and I both tried it a few times in, oh, it must have been 'Sixty-seven or -eight.'

'I was five years old. Were you and Mom hippies? You should have turned me on while you were at it.'

'Hippies,' the father said and shook his head. 'The first time we smoked nothing happened. Our friends, the people who turned us on, swore we were stoned, but if we were we didn't know it, so what good was that? The second time we both got high and it was very nice, though I can't say I remember what exactly was nice about it. But it was. And then we smoked once or twice after that, and one time your mother became very anxious and when it wore off we agreed this wasn't something we wanted to waste our time on.'

'Mom got paranoid?'

'That's as good a word for it as any, and how did we get on this? Pipes on the ceiling, we're a long way from pipes on the ceiling. But I had a hell of a time quitting cigarettes, so I don't think I'll call for my pipe and my bowl.'

'Did you smoke when you were playing basketball?'

'Not while I was out on the court. But that's not what you meant. Sure, I smoked. I was a kid and kids are stupid. I heard smoking would cut my wind, so I tried it and I didn't see any difference, so I decided they were full of crap. What did I expect, that the first cigarette I smoked would add three seconds to my time in the hundred-yard dash? Still, I was never that heavy a smoker when I was playing. After I graduated, that's when the habit took off.'

'Neither of the girls smoke,' Kevin Parmalee said.

'As far as you know.'

'Well, that goes without saying, doesn't it? There's no end

of things they don't do as far as I know, and God only knows what they do that I don't know, and I don't want to think about it.'

'Jennifer's more the athlete, isn't she?'

They talked about the girls. Kevin Parmalee's daughters, Richard's granddaughters. They agreed that Jennifer, the older of the two, had innate athletic ability, but lacked the desire to do anything with it. She had the height for basketball, the older man pointed out, and they talked about the emergence of that sport.

He said, 'You know how the college kids play a more interesting game than the pros? Well, I'll tell you something. The women's game is better than the men's.'

'College or pro?'

'Either one.'

'I know what you mean. But . . .'

'But it's impossible to give a damn which team wins.'

'I was about to say it was hard to get interested in it, but you just nailed it. That's exactly what it is. It's like watching golf, I get completely absorbed in it but I don't give a damn who wins. Why do you figure that is?'

'One of life's mysteries,' Richard Parmalee said. 'Here's another. Remember how the fans were cheering earlier, rooting for the Knicks to win by more than twelve points?'

'To beat the spread. Sure.'

'It meant something to the fans, whether or not they had bets down. We talked about that earlier. But what did it mean to the players?'

'I'm not sure I follow you. What did it mean to them?'

'Why did they knock themselves out? They couldn't have played any harder if the game was nip and tuck.'

'You think they had money on the game?'

'You wouldn't think they'd bother, the kind of salaries they make. Other hand, I don't suppose it's entirely unheard of. But I can't believe they all bet on the game and they were all playing their hearts out.'

'They're pros,' Kevin Parmalee said. 'Playing all-out is what they do.'

'They've been known to dog it from time to time. Maybe they were trying to beat the spread so it wouldn't look as though they were trying not to beat the spread.'

'In other words, if they dog it somebody might think they're shaving points. You think that goes on in the NBA?'

'Shaving points? I don't know. Again, with their salaries, how could you bribe them? Kev, I think you're probably right. They weren't even aware of the spread and they played hard because that's the way they play.' He picked up his coffee cup, set it down. 'When you played,' he said, 'were you ever approached?'

'Approached? Oh.'

'Were you?'

'God, why would anyone come to me? I was lucky to be on the team.'

'Don't sell yourself short. You were damn good.'

'I would have been okay somewhere else. I know, Duke was all my idea, but I've never been sorry I went. Even if I did ride the bench for four years. I never had more than eight minutes of playing time, so there were never any guys with bent noses trying to get me to dump games.'

'And your team-mates were too busy trying to get into the NBA.'

'Trying to get into the Final Tour. They knew they were going to get into the NBA.'

The waiter came and Kevin Parmalee put his hand over his cup. 'Just a half a cup for me,' Richard Parmalee said and was silent until the waiter withdrew. Then he said, 'I was approached.'

'Really?'

'Not by a guy with a bent nose. His nose was as straight as yours or mine, and you wouldn't have marked him as a gangster, not by his appearance or by his manner. Although I suppose that's exactly what he was.'

'And he wanted you to dump games?'

'Not to dump games. "I would never ask you to lose a game," he said. It was fine with him if we beat the other team. Just so we didn't beat the spread.'

'Did you report him?'

'No,' Richard Parmalee said. 'No, I didn't report him.'

'Oh.'

'I took the money,' he said and raised his eyes to meet his son's. 'And did what I could to earn it.'

'You shaved points.'

'I shaved points. If we were favored, and if Harold gave me the word, I did my best to see that we didn't cover the spread.'

'How did you do it? Miss shots that you could have made?'

'I missed shots. I don't know that I could have made them if I hadn't had a reason not to. Another way, I'd be wide open and I'd pass off instead of taking the shot. There are a million things you can do without being too obvious about it.'

'I can imagine.'

'I got five hundred dollars a game. And this was 1957 we're talking about. That was a lot of money in 1957.'

'Sure, it must have been a fortune.'

'When I graduated, my first job was as a management trainee with Kaiser & Ledbetter. Starting salary was five thousand dollars a year. And that wasn't bad money. That's what you paid a promising college graduate in a job with a future. So every time we didn't manage to beat the spread, I was making a tenth of a year's salary, and that's not counting taxes.'

'I guess you didn't declare the money that . . . Harold?'

'Harold. I never knew his last name, and no, I didn't declare it. He paid me in cash and I didn't know what the hell to do with it. It's funny. I was doing it for the money, but I didn't do anything with the money. I kept it in a cigar box and I kept moving the box around because I was afraid someone would find it.'

'You couldn't put it in the bank?'

'Kev, I didn't have a bank account. I lived at home with my parents. They gave me a scholarship to play basketball, but all that covered was tuition. I thought the extra money would come in handy, but I didn't spend a dime of it.'

'You saved it in a cigar box. What did it add up to, do you remember?'

'Forty-five hundred dollars, and how could I forget? He always paid me in twenty-dollar bills. Twenty-five of them at a time, so what does that come to? Two hundred twenty-five? Is that right? Well, it's close enough. Not enough bills to fill the cigar box, but a good-sized handful.'

'Nine games, that would have been.'

'Nine games,' the father said. 'Nine college basketball games and all I had to do was hold back a little bit, and how hard was that? And who did it hurt? I mean, who gave a damn if we beat St Bonaventure's by ten points or three points? The fans didn't care. The only people who got hurt were the ones who bet on us, and they were breaking the law in the first place by gambling on a basketball game. What the hell did I owe them?'

'It's not as though your team lost.'

'We did lose one game. We played Adelphi at home and we were favored, and Harold gave me the word. And I did what I could to keep up from getting too far ahead, and then in the third quarter Adelphi started playing way over their heads, and before I knew it they were out in front, and we never did catch up. Would they have beaten us anyway? The way they were playing I'm tempted to say they would have beaten the Knicks that night, but I don't know. Maybe yes and maybe no.'

'It must have been weird, watching the game slip away from you.'

'It was awful. I never played harder in my life than in the last five minutes of that game. We were all knocking ourselves out. I remember one shot that went around the rim and out, and the look on the face of the kid who put it up. I'd had my suspicions about him, and his expression confirmed it.'

'You know, I'd been thinking you were the only one doing it, but of course there must have been others.'

'And I never knew how many, or who they were. That one boy, on the basis of the look on his face, but which of the others? Not that I spent a lot of time thinking about it. And I certainly didn't let myself think about the consequences.'

'Of losing the game?'

'Of doing what I was doing and getting caught at it. It was a crime, you know.'

'I guess it must have been.'

'Oh, no question. There'd been some scandals a few years earlier. A fair number of young men had their lives ruined and a few went to prison for it. I didn't worry about it and it turned out there was nothing to worry about.'

'What happened to the money?'

'Nothing for a couple of years. Then when your mother and I got married, we had expenses. Young couples always do. So the money came in handy after all.'

'Did Mom know where it came from?'

'All she knew was that the bills got paid. Nobody knew that I shaved points. Until tonight, I never said a word about it to anyone.'

'It's hard to believe,' Kevin Parmalee said, after a moment. 'Not that you never said anything, but that you did it. It seems . . .'

'What?'

'Out of character, I guess.'

'It seemed that way to me at the time. I don't know that I can explain it. Maybe Harold was a persuasive guy, or maybe I was easily persuaded.'

'How come . . . no, never mind.'

'What?'

'I just wondered how come you decided to tell me.'

'I hadn't planned on it.'

'Really? Because I had the sense there was something.'

'There was, but it wasn't worth it.'

'Oh?'

'If I'd called for my pipe,' Richard Parmalee said, 'I could fuss with it, and tamp the tobacco down and relight it, and kill a surprising amount of time that way. Sometimes I think that was as much of an addiction as the nicotine. I went to the doctor about six weeks ago for my annual physical, which is a misnomer, because I'm doing well if I get around to it every other year. He called me two days later to tell me my PSA was a little high, if you know what that is.'

'I don't.'

'You probably will in a few years. I forget what it stands for, but it's a prostate test. A slight elevation could be the result of enlargement of the prostate, or a sign of the presence of a low-grade infection. Or it could be an indication of early stage prostate cancer.'

The two men looked at each other. 'So he sent me to a urologist,' Richard Parmalee went on, 'and he did his own examination and his own test, and put me on an antibiotic for a week in case it was an infection that was causing the high reading. And a week later he took blood for another test, and the result was still the same, so he had me come in for a biopsy.'

'Jesus.'

'It's a goddamn undignified procedure,' he said, 'but less painful than a sprained ankle, and you don't need an Ace bandage. You have blood in the urine for a few days afterward, and in the semen for up to a month. All of that's nothing compared to waiting for the lab results. I had the biopsy on a Tuesday and I didn't hear until the following Monday. Not to keep you in suspense, it came back negative. I haven't got cancer.'

'Thank God.'

'I suppose I could have said that right off,' Richard Parmalee said, 'but instead I let you wait and wonder for what, five minutes? If that. Well, that was to give you an idea. I had a full month to wait and wonder, and maybe you can imagine what that was like.'

'You never said anything.'

'There was nothing to say, not until I found out what I had or didn't have.'

'Did Mom know?'

'I told her the morning I went in for the biopsy. If it was just an infection, or a false positive, why put her through it? By the time I was ready to go in for the procedure, I figured she ought to know. And I was worn out keeping it to myself.'

'But you're all right?'

'I have to go in every six months,' he said, 'for a PSA, which just means they take some blood and send it to the lab. If there's no change, all I do is make another appointment. It's normal for the level to increase gradually with age. If that's all it does, that's fine. If there's a big increase, I get to have another biopsy.'

'Every six months for how long?'

'For as long as possible.'

'For as long as . . . oh, I get it. In other words, every six months for the rest of your life.'

'And I hope that's a long time. That's one of the things I found out while I was waiting. I didn't want it to be over. If I have to get a needle in my arm twice a year, well, that's a pretty small price to pay to stick around.'

'I'll say.'

'But from this point on my life is different. All of a sudden I'm an old man.'

'The hell you're an old man.'

'I was a kid with a basketball, and the next thing I know I'm an old fart with a prostate. Well, what's the difference? Either way you dribble.'

They laughed, the two of them, a little more heartily than the line warranted, and when the laughter stopped they were silent. Then the older man said, 'I knew I wanted to tell you. I wasn't in a rush, but it was something you ought to know. Then you called to say you had Knicks tickets, and while I was making dinner reservations I decided it would be the right time and place for this conversation.'

'I'll probably be a while taking it all in.'

'Oh, I'm sure of that. Intimations of mortality, and your own as well as mine. I'm in damn good shape, I'm happy to say, but in a sense I feel a good deal more vulnerable than I did a couple of months ago. But there's something I can't quite figure out. What made me tell you about my little arrangement with Harold?'

'Maybe you were stalling.'

'Stalling? Telling you the one thing to delay telling you the other? No, I don't think so. That would have been a reason for small talk, but I wasn't making small talk.'

'No.'

'And it's something I've been thinking about lately.

43

Would my life had been different if I'd told Harold thanks but no thanks.'

'How?'

'That's what I've been wondering. I did something that wasn't honest, and I kept it a secret. How did that affect the choices I made in life?'

'Maybe it didn't.'

'Maybe not,' Richard Parmalee said, 'but I'll never know, will I? The road not taken. Maybe it's made a difference, and maybe it hasn't.'

'Phil Carrigan called me in two, three weeks ago,' the son said. 'I'd knocked myself out for him, and he wanted to let me know how much he appreciated it. "Listen," he said, "I owe you a big one. And Lisa, I want to make it up to her for the extra hours you put in. Here's what you do, Kevin. Take the lovely lady to Lutéce. You can bill the client."'

'That's perfect.'

'Isn't it? His eyes, he was being magnanimous. Giving me something to show his appreciation of what I did for him. So I had his permission to stick it to the client for a couple of hundred dollars. That's his idea of a grand gesture and he really thought he was being generous. And maybe he was, because he could just as easily have taken his wife to Lutéce at the client's expense.'

'That's interesting. I'm not sure it fits with what we were talking about, but I'm not sure it doesn't either. How was the meal?'

'It was terrific, but I'm just as happy with a steak and salad, to tell you the truth.'

'You're like your old man. And it's time your old man headed home.'

He raised his hand for the check. 'I wish you'd let me get this,' the son said.

'Not a chance. I told you, you got the tickets.'

'And I told you they didn't cost me a cent.'

'And neither will dinner,' Richard Parmalee said. 'The hell, I'll bill it to a client.'

'Oh, right,' Kevin Parmalee said. 'That's just what you'll do.'

AFTER MIDNIGHT

Michael Connelly

He hated the job but loved the drive home at night. The streets were always empty and a lot of the time shiny from rain. Steam would rise like intrigue off the asphalt. Just like in the movies, the old black and whites his father liked to watch on the tube. It seemed as though the city did not even begin to cool off until this time, until after midnight. Cruising along the beach with the windows down he would always encounter stragglers. Girls older than he but still just girls, making their way home or to last call at the last bar on the circuit. Some would flag him down, ask for a ride. Sometimes he would stop and oblige, the thrill of being with a stranger smelling of beer and suntan oil in the dark overcoming the potential of danger – and embarrassment. They were always surprised at how young he was. How young he looked. Some of them even laughed, thought he was thirteen years old and out joyriding in a stolen car.

At the end of the beach cruise he would turn inland and head over the drawbridge and toward home. Toward a shower and bed, maybe a talk with the old man if he was still awake and sober.

It was coming over the drawbridge and heading home one

night when he encountered the running man. The boy had worked a double shift that day and was tired. It was a night for no riders. He had cruised the beach quickly and was heading west on Sunrise Boulevard. Close to home. He had just cleared the bridge but caught the traffic light by the closed gas station. He stopped at the deserted intersection and waited for the green. He knew no one would know the difference if he ran it but he waited for the green anyway. His father had taught him that the rules were in place whether anybody else was there to watch or not.

And that was when he saw him. A man running. A big man with a big beard and long hair. He cut across the dark parking lot behind the gas station. He came right out of the darkness and headed for the bridge. He was no jogger. He wasn't running for sport or fitness. The boy could tell that. The man was fully clothed – open lumberjack shirt over a T-shirt, jeans, work boots. No, he wasn't just running. He was running to something or away from something.

The boy studied the darkness from which the man had come. His eyes peered into the parking lot behind the gas station. Nothing moved there. Nothing was recognisable. Farther down the street he could see the dim glow of the Kwik Mart, but nothing else.

The traffic light turned green. Ready to dismiss what he had seen – maybe the guy was just trying to make last call at one of the beach bars – the boy turned to take a final glance at the running man. He immediately noticed that the man no longer wore the outer shirt. He had removed it while running. And at the moment the boy glanced back he also saw the running man slow his pace just long enough to shove the red lumberjack shirt into the hedge that lined the sidewalk before the bridge. He then kept going.

The light was still green. But the boy sat there in his beat-up Volkswagen and thought about what he had just seen. He had a decision to make. Pop the clutch, press the gas pedal and move on toward home. Or turn the car around and check it out. Why had the running man stuffed his shirt into that hedge?

The boy was on the edge of manhood. Not in physical size or development – he had always been small and was stopped regularly by police who thought him to be too young to be driving. But inside, in thinking about his life and his options and in the way he studied the girls that walked the beach road at night. Inside, where it counted. His father kept the chorus going, all the time chiding him for his mistakes. *It's time to be a man.*

The light turned yellow. As if he was out of time and desperate, the boy hit the gas and dragged the bug into a squealing U-turn. He drove back toward the bridge. The running man was gone now, having gone up and over the bridge, dropping down past the span toward the beach. The boy stopped at the curb near the hedge. He left the car running and got out. He went to the hedge and saw the spot where the branches had been freshly disturbed. He reached in for the shirt, the interior branches scratching at his arm.

As he pulled his arm back he felt something hard and heavy buried in the shirt. Slowly he unwrapped it and looked down at its contents. A blue steel revolver as shiny as the wet streets was in his hand. He felt a little thrill go through him, coming all the way up from his testicles.

A gun. The boy had never held one before, had never even seen one this close. His father had a rule, no guns. He picked it up with his hand and hefted its weight. It felt warm to him. He put his nose to the barrel and sniffed. A sharp, bitter odor invaded his nostrils. Was that gunpowder? Was the gun warm because it had been fired?

He quickly wrapped the gun in the shirt again and took it back to the car. He stuffed the shirt and gun into the glove box and closed it. He then pulled away from the curb and drove back over the bridge. It only took him a minute to catch up to the running man. He watched as the man stopped before he got to the beach and turned right into the street behind the big white hotel. The boy drove by, turned right on the beach road and then took the next right. He came to the same street the running man was on but a block further down. The boy dropped the clutch and slowed. He saw the running man was now walking. He finally came to a stop and then calmly stepped through the front door of a bar called The Pirate. It was a place the boy knew about from the outside. A rough place. Motorcycles always parked out front in a line. He knew that the men that came out of that bar had a habit of coming out mean.

The boy picked up speed and kept his car moving. He made his way back to Sunrise and once again headed west to the bridge and home.

But as he crested the bridge his eyes were greeted by all of the lights. Blue and red and yellow. Police lights, seemingly everywhere. A spotlight from a helicopter cutting through the parking lot behind the gas station. The traffic signal was red again. He slowed to a stop and looked back at the spot in the hedge. He could still make out the place where the manicured wall of leaves had been disturbed. He knew he had another choice to make.

A car pulled up next to him. A police car. Just as the boy turned to look the bright beam of a flashlight hit him full in the face. He could see nothing. A voice sounded from behind the light. 'Hey, kid, are you old enough to drive?'

'I'm sixteen,' he responded. 'I have a license.'

'Where are you going?'

'Home from work.'

'Pull into the gas station when the light changes.'

'Okay.'

He turned away but was still blind. He tried to focus on the traffic signal. When he finally could see it, it was green. He pulled forward and then turned left into the closed station. The patrol car followed him.

There were two of them. They got out simultaneously. One of them put his flashlight on the boy's face again.

'You've gotta be kidding me,' he heard one say.

He knew they were talking about his size. Barely five-four and a skinny frame. Barely a hundred pounds. He felt his face burning red in the bright beam of their scrutiny. 'I have a license,' he said again.

'Then let's see it,' said the one behind the beam.

The boy unsnapped a pocket and brought out his thin wallet. He took out the license and held it out. He noticed that his hand was shaking. The one with the light took the license and thankfully lowered his beam to look at it. He turned it over and studied the edge as if to check for counterfeiting. Other cops who had stopped him had done the same thing.

'Where are you coming from?' asked the other cop.

'Work. I'm a dishwasher at Bahia Mar. The banquet center.'

'Working late.'

'Yes. We had two banquets.'

'Busy night. You own this car?'

'Yes.'

He suddenly realised the registration was in the glove compartment. Along with the gun. 'What is everybody looking for?' he asked.

'Not what, who,' he said. 'We're looking for a scumbag. An armed robber.'

The boy thought about the gun in his glove box again. A tremor of fear went through his chest. He had touched the gun. He'd held it. Fingerprints. He knew about fingerprints from movies and TV. He and his father watched *Kojak* together every Sunday night.

'Does anybody know what he looks like?' the boy asked.

'Why, you seen somebody?'

The beam suddenly came back up to his face, blinding him again.

'Did you, kid? What did you see?'

The boy almost said not what, who. But he didn't think that would be received so well. The two policemen had tensed. They were keyed up about something. He thought about the gun again – remembered that it had been warm to his touch – and realised he could be in trouble. He chided himself for taking the gun. How stupid!

'Hey, kid, you still there?'

'Yes. I was just thinking. I saw a man running. Down near the beach.'

'Running? What did he look like?'

'I noticed because he was fully dressed but he was, you know, running.'

'Give us a description.'

'He was big. He –'

'You mean compared to you?'

'No, compared to anybody. He was tall. He had a beard and his hair was long.'

'White, black, brown?'

'White.'

'Okay, what else? What about the clothes?'

The clothes. He wasn't sure how to answer. Describe the man before or after he'd taken off the red shirt? He decided if there had been a robbery, the victim would have seen the red shirt.

'He had on blue jeans and a white T-shirt. And he had on a red lumberjack shirt – you know, like with a pattern.'

'If he had that on how do you know about the T-shirt?'

54

'The red shirt was open. Unbuttoned. I could see the T-shirt.'

The one without the flashlight peeled away and started talking into a radio mike attached to the shoulder of his uniform. He could hear him putting out the description and he wondered why they didn't already have it.

'That's a pretty good description, kid,' said the one with the flashlight. 'What were you doing that you saw this guy so well?'

The boy shrugged. 'I don't know. I saw him running. I thought it was strange because he was fully dressed. I saw where he went, too. He went into a bar. The Pirate.'

'Mendez, you hear this?'

'Let's go,' his partner answered.

'Okay, kid, let's get in the car.'

The boy was put in the back seat and then they took off for the bridge. The cop in the passenger seat announced their destination on the radio and asked for back-up. A minute later they were in front of The Pirate. Half a minute later the back-up car was there. And a third car was not long behind. By radio it was directed to the back of the bar.

The driver of the first car, the one called Mendez, turned round to look at the boy. 'You are going to stay here. We're going in. We're going to look for the guy. What we'll do is bring anybody we want to talk to outside. You watch through the window. If you see the guy, you give the nod. Okay?'

'I nod if I see him?'

'Right. Now sit tight.'

The cops got out and made their way around the line of motorcycles. They met the two uniformed men from the back-up car. The boy watched them talk for a few moments and then one opened the bar's door and they went in. The boy saw that the last cop to go in was holding his baton down at the side of his leg.

He waited for what seemed like an hour but was only a few minutes. When the bar's door opened next, it wasn't a cop who came out. It was a customer. A man with a white T-shirt and a black leather vest. He quickly moved to one of the motorcycles and carefully pushed it out into the street between the two patrol cars. He saddled it, kick-started the engine and took off. He never saw the boy watching and the boy wondered if he had snuck out of the bar or had been allowed to leave.

As he considered this the door to the bar opened again and the two officers from the back-up car escorted two men out. Both had beards and long hair, but neither was the running man the boy had seen. Then the other two cops came out with two more men. The boy now recognised the running man. They had him.

The cops instructed the four bearded men to face the front wall of the bar and put their hands against it. The men complied slowly, with the worn acquiescence of men who faced this sort of intrusion on a daily basis.

Mendez stood back while the other officers checked the men leaning against the wall for weapons. He turned and looked at the boy in the patrol car. The boy nodded and Mendez nodded back. He then surreptitiously pointed a finger at the first man in line and the boy shook his head. They repeated this until Mendez pointed at the third man in line and the boy nodded.

But just as he nodded, the third man turned his face from the wall and looked directly at the boy. Whether he understood or not that an identification was being made didn't matter. The boy was frozen to the bone. The man said something – just a couple of words – but the boy could not hear it because the windows of the car were up. Their eyes locked and held until Mendez barked a command at the man and he turned back to the wall. Mendez then came up behind

56

the man and pulled his arms off the wall and cuffed them behind the man's back. The man did not struggle as he did this. Again there was a casual acquiescence, as if what was being done to him had been done before. As if it was expected.

The officers told the other three men they could return to the bar. Mendez then pushed the running man toward the two officers from the back-up car and they walked him to their car. As they were pushing him into the back seat the man began to struggle for the first time. Not to get away but just to keep his head up. He looked over at the boy again and said the words again, this time exaggerating the movements of his mouth because he probably understood that the boy could not hear. He then relented and let them push his head down and then into the back of the car. The car took off quickly and the boy watched its blue light go on as it sped away.

Mendez stood on the street and spoke at length over his radio mike before he and his partner returned to the car in which the boy sat. Mendez got behind the wheel but turned to look back at the boy before turning the ignition. 'We got him, kid. Good job.'

'What did he say?'

'He didn't say anything but we don't need him to say anything. With your ID we've got him. The detectives are heading over here to search the joint for the gun. They find that and its bye-bye dirtbag. You did good.'

'What about the robbery? The victim. You need him to say he did it.'

'Actually, there are two victims. But we're not very likely to get that from either one.'

'They're afraid?'

'No, both got shot. During the robbery. One's dead and, last we heard, the other wasn't going to make it either.'

The boy felt the air go out of his lungs. Not because of

what Mendez said, though that certainly put a different inflection on things. But because he had suddenly realised what the running man had said before being put into the patrol car.

'He said, "You're dead." When he saw me. He said, "You're dead," didn't he?'

'Don't worry, it's bullshit. He was trying to intimidate you but he was too late. He's going to be in lock-up until you're an old man. He can't get to you.'

'What about his friends? Is he in a motorcycle gang or something?'

'Not hardly. He doesn't even have a bike. Why do you think he was running when you saw him?'

Mendez turned round and started the car.

'Let's go downtown now and see the detectives.'

He put it in drive and the car lurched forward. He reached over and punched his partner on the shoulder. 'We got it, McHugh. We got the arrest.'

McHugh didn't answer.

'What about my car?' the boy asked.

'What about it?' Mendez replied. 'It's in a safe place. Someone will take you back to it when you're finished with the detectives.'

'I need to call my dad.'

'We can do that at the station. First thing.'

Fifteen minutes later the boy was sitting at a desk in the detective bureau. Mendez handed him the phone and told him to dial nine first to get an outside line. Mendez said the boy could tell his father to come to the station if he wanted.

The boy dialed his home number but after ten rings the old man didn't pick up. He hung up. He thought it was strange that there was no answer. His father had not said anything about going out. If he had gone out for cigarettes or beer it seemed as though he would have done so earlier. The boy dialed the number a second time but once again got no answer. He hung up the phone.

'Pop's not there, huh?' Mendez said.

'No answer.'

'Okay, well, the lead detective on this case wants to talk to you so we're going to move you into one of the interview rooms and then he'll be in to see you as soon as he's free. We've got to get our paperwork done and then get back out on the street.'

He followed Mendez and McHugh to a small room with a table and two chairs. There was also a mirrored window that the boy figured led to a viewing room. He'd seen it on *Kojak* before.

They left him there and an hour drifted slowly by while the boy thought about what the running man had said before they shoved him into the patrol car. Then the door opened and a man wearing a suit stepped in. He had fiery red hair and a grim smile. He said his name was Sonntag and offered his hand. The boy said his own name as they shook and the detective, for just a moment, stopped shaking then started again. He then pulled out the chair and sat across from the boy.

'Where do you live, kid?'

He gave his address and watched the detective's face turn grimmer.

'What? What's wrong?'

'I need to some questions first. Who lives there with you? Your mom and dad?'

'Just my dad.'

'Where's your mom?'

'I don't know. She's been gone a long time. What does this have to do with anything? I saw a guy running. What does it matter where my mother is?'

'It doesn't. I'm just asking questions. Tell me about the man you saw running.'

The boy repeated the story he had told the first two cops. He added no new details, believing the less said with Sonntag the better. The detective asked no questions until the story was finished.

'And you are sure the man they took into custody was the man you saw running?'

'I don't know. I guess so.'

'You guess so?'

'Well, so far, I haven't gotten to look at him, except from the car.'

'We'll take care of that in a minute. Now you said you saw this running man coming from the direction of the draw-bridge, right?'

'Yes.'

'Did you see him on the bridge?'

The boy didn't know what to do. The one lie he had told had cascaded. Now he had to keep lying to stay clear. He wished he could talk to his father.

'You either saw him on the bridge or you didn't,' Sonntag said.

'I didn't. Can I use the phone again? I want to call my father.'

Sonntag stared at him a moment before speaking. 'Not yet. Let's get the story down first. So you didn't see him on the bridge but you're pretty sure he was coming from that direction.'

'Yes.'

'We're having trouble locating the weapon. Is it possible that he threw it into the river when he was coming over the bridge?'

'Yeah, I guess so. It's possible.'

'Did you see him do that?'

'No, I told you, I didn't see him on the bridge.'

The boy knew that Sonntag was trying to trick him, or get

him to agree to seeing something he didn't see. The boy sat frozen. He knew that now was the time to tell. Tell about the gun and try to explain it. But he couldn't.

'I want to talk to my father.'

Sonntag nodded like he understood and would arrange for the request right away. But that's not what he said when he opened his mouth. 'Your father's name is Edison Chambers, correct?'

'Yes, that's right,' the boy answered, his voice rising with suspicion. 'Is he here?'

'No, I'm afraid not. I feel awful about this, kid, but I have to tell you. It looks like your father was one of the people this dirt bag shot.'

The boy's mouth shot open. He felt the room and the bright lights crashing in on him. He heard Sonntag still talking.

'Edison Chambers. We got the ID from his wallet. He was in the store, getting a six-pack from one of the coolers in the back. He bent down to get it from the bottom and we guess the shooter didn't see him in there. He came in and went to the register. The woman there, he probably shot her first. That was when your father stood up. The shooter saw him then . . .'

Sonntag didn't have to finish. The boy leaned forward and put his face into his hands. In the blackness he heard the detective ask him if he had any other family living in the area.

'My aunt and uncle,' he said.

'We need to call them when we're finished here.'

'I want to go to my house.'

'We'll release you to your aunt and uncle and the three of you can decide.'

The boy didn't say anything. He didn't know what to say or to think. He suddenly flashed on the gun in the glove box. He wanted to get back to his car.

'We're setting up a line-up,' Sonntag said.

The boy straightened up. Tear trails marked both sides of his face. 'What do you mean?'

'We're putting the suspect in a line-up of men and we'll see if you can pick him out. Don't worry, he won't see you. You'll be behind a mirror.'

But he already did see me, the boy thought but didn't say. He just nodded his head. A plan was formulating. He concentrated on it instead of thinking about his father.

'You ready, then?' Sonntag asked.

'I guess so.'

'Okay, then. Let's do it and then we'll get your aunt and uncle on the phone. Let's go do this thing for your dad.'

The boy stood up and followed Sonntag through the door. He was taken to a dark room where a window looked into a well-lighted room. The far wall was white and spotless, except for the hash marks that marked feet and inches so an observer could gauge height. After a few minutes six men were led into the well-lit room in a line and they stood facing the boy against the wall.

'They can't see me?' he asked.

'No,' said Sonntag. 'It's one-way glass.'

The boy looked at the men in the line-up. Only two had beards. And one was the running man. He could tell. He was looking at the man who had killed his father. Thoughts blasted though him with sounds like waves crashing on the beach. He felt weak in the knees but strong in the heart. He felt a tear slide down his soft, whiskerless cheek. He wiped it away and heard the waves replaced by his father's voice. *Time to be a man*.

'Well,' Sonntag said, bending down close to the boy's ear to whisper. 'Which one?'

The boy didn't answer. He was working a plan out in his head.

'Pick him out, son,' said the detective.

The boy shook his head. 'No,' he said slowly. 'You don't have him. He's not there.'

The boy could literally feel the detective tense.

'What do you mean?'

'I mean the guy I saw isn't there.'

'Kid, come on. We're talking about your father.'

'I know. I want to get the right man and he's not there.'

Sonntag bent closer to him again to whisper, 'Don't be afraid. He can't hurt you. Just pick him out.'

'I'm not afraid. He just isn't there.'

'But one of those men over there is the one you picked out at the bar.'

'It was dark and I was sitting in a patrol car. I saw the beard and thought . . .'

'Thought what?'

'I thought it was him but it's not. You have the wrong guy.'

Sonntag exhaled loudly, angrily. His voice returned to normal volume. 'Let me tell you something, besides you we've got nothing. No weapon, no witness, no camera in the store. The guy you say you picked by mistake does have one thing, though. Gunshot residue on his hands. We know he fired a gun in the last few hours. But if we don't get an ID or recover that weapon and connect him to it, then guess what, he walks out of here like nothing ever happened. They'll have his beer waiting on the bar for him at The Pirate. So do me a favor and look again and pick him out.'

The boy shook his head. 'I can't. He's not there.'

'Well, kid, then I hope you can face your father's ghost. Let's go.'

Sonntag roughly clapped the boy on the shoulder and pushed him toward the door.

Twenty minutes later the boy sat on a bench in the front

lobby. His uncle was on the way. Sonntag had told him he had twenty-four hours to change his mind about the identification. That was how long they could hold the running man. After that they had to charge him or let him go. That was fine with the boy. Twenty-four hours was plenty of time to do what he needed to do.

His uncle wasn't happy to see him. He had been told by Sonntag about the failure to make an identification of the running man. 'He was your father but he was my brother,' the uncle said. 'If he was the guy you should've said it was the guy.'

'I would've, but they don't have him. They just wanted to arrest somebody, doesn't matter who.'

'That detective told me on the phone that they had the right guy. That it was you who messed it up.'

'He's wrong. Can you take me to my car?'

'You are supposed to come home with me. The police said you –'

'I am coming to your place but I can't leave my car in the middle of a gas station all night. I also need to go by the house to get some clothes. So drop me off at my car and I'll come by later.'

'Don't make it late.'

'It already is late.'

They said very little the rest of the way. They drove by the Kwik Mart where the shooting had taken place. There were still police cars and a white van in the parking lot. There was yellow tape all around.

'Is that where . . . ?' the uncle asked.

'Yeah.'

The boy looked away. In a few minutes they pulled into the closed gas station and the lights of his uncle's car washed across the boy's Volkswagen.

'Still there,' the uncle said.

'Yeah. Thanks for the ride.'

'We'll see you in a little while?'

'Yes.'

'Look, Bobby, I'm sorry. About your dad. My brother. You know. He wasn't the nicest guy to you, I know. But something like this . . . It shouldn't have happened, you know?'

'Yes, I know.'

He said goodbye and closed the door. After his uncle pulled away the boy looked around. The streets were dark and empty. The police were gone. He looked up toward the bridge and the hedge that ran alongside the sidewalk. No police, only darkness.

He thought about the plan and decided it was a good plan, a plan that would work. He went to his car and opened the passenger door. He punched the button on the glove box and the lid dropped open to reveal the red plaid shirt containing the gun was still in place. He pulled it out and held the bundle close to his chest. With his other hand the boy reached into the glove box for the Swiss Army knife he kept in there, mostly for emergencies, or if he needed to turn the fuel feed screw on the car's carburetor.

The boy closed the car door and headed on foot toward the bridge. He chose to stay off the sidewalk, walking instead in the dark shadows along the hedge line.

Three days later the boy found the story on the second page of the metro section. It wasn't a long story but he didn't care about its placement or importance in the newspaper. He cared about its contents.

DOUBLE-MURDER SUSPECT FATALLY WOUNDS SELF

A man the police said was the primary suspect in a convenience store robbery that left two dead was killed himself yesterday when he attempted to retrieve the hidden gun used in the crime.

Police said that Edward Togue, thirty-nine, was shot once in the upper body when he reached into a hedge lining the ramp of the Sunrise Boulevard drawbridge and attempted to withdraw a gun he had apparently hid there three days earlier. The gun's trigger apparently was snagged on a branch inside the hedge and was engaged when Togue pulled on the gun.

The weapon discharged once and the bullet struck Togue. He was fatally wounded and died at the scene.

Police termed the shooting accidental and said it also will serve to conclude the investigation into the Saturday night shooting at the Kwik Mart just three blocks from where Togue killed himself.

Police said the gun Togue was retrieving has been matched by ballistics analysis to the shooting in which a cashier and customer were killed during a robbery. Togue had been arrested shortly after that shooting and questioned by police but later released when no evidence could be found linking him to the shooting.

The boy stopped reading. The rest he knew. He folded the paper closed and put it aside. He went back to packing his clothing and other belongings into boxes. He didn't know if he would be able to fit everything into the bug but he was going to try. He was then going to get in the car and start driving. Not to his aunt's and uncle's home. He was just going to drive.

As he put some photos into a box he thought about what Sonntag had said about his father's ghost. The boy smiled. He knew the only spirit he needed to worry about now was the ghost of Edward Togue.

THE POKER LESSON

Jeffery Deaver

> *Poker is a game in which each man plays his own*
> *hand as he elects. No consideration should be*
> *expected by one player from another.*
>
> John Scarne

'I want into one of your games,' the boy said.

Sitting hunched over a hamburger in Angela's Diner, Keller looked up at the blond kid, who stood with his hip cocked and arms crossed, trying to be cool but looking like an animal awkwardly trying to stand on its hind legs. Handsome enough even though he wore black-rimmed nerd glasses and was pale and skinny.

Keller decided not to ask the kid to sit down. 'What games?' He ate more of his burger and glanced at his watch.

The kid noticed the move and said, 'Well, the one that's starting at eight tonight, for instance.'

Keller grunted a laugh.

He heard the rumble of one of the freight trains that bisected this neighborhood on the north side of town. He had a fond memory of a diesel rattling bar glasses six months ago just as he laid down a flush to take a fifty-six thousand three hundred and twenty dollar pot away from three businessmen who were from the South of France. He'd won that pot twenty minutes after the first ante. The men had scowled French scowls but continued to lose another seventy thousand over the course of the rainy night.

'What's your name?'

'Tony Stigler.'

'How old're you?'

'Eighteen.'

'Even if there *was* a game, which there isn't, you couldn't play. You're a kid. You couldn't get into a bar.'

'It's in Sal's back room. It's not in the bar.'

'How do you *know* that?' Keller muttered. In his late forties, the dark-complected man was as strong and solid as he'd been twenty years ago. When he asked questions in this tone you stopped being cute and answered straight.

'My buddy works at Marconi Pizza. He hears things.'

'Well, your buddy oughta watch out what he hears. And he *really* oughta watch who he *tells* what he hears.' He returned to his lunch.

'Look.' The kid dug into his pocket and pulled out a wad of bills. Hundreds mostly. Keller'd been gambling since he was younger than this boy and he knew how to size up a roll. The kid was holding close to five thousand. Tony said, 'I'm serious, man. I want to play with you.'

'Where'd you get that?'

A shrug. 'I got it.'

'Don't give me any *Sopranos* crap. You gonna play poker, you play by the rules. And one of the rules is you play with your own money. If that's stolen you can hike your ass outa here right now.'

'It's not stolen,' the kid said, lowering his voice. 'I won it.'

'At cards,' Keller asked wryly, 'or the lottery?'

'Draw and stud.'

70

Keller enjoyed a particularly good bite of hamburger and studied the boy again. 'Why my game? You got dozens you could pick.'

The fading city of Ellridge, population two hundred thousand or so, squatted in steel-mill territory on the flat, gray Indiana river. What it lacked in class, though, the city more than made up for in sin. Hookers and lap dance bars, of course. But the town's big business was underground gambling – for a very practical reason: Atlantic City and Nevada weren't within a day's drive and the few Indian casinos with licensed poker tables were filled with low-stakes amateurs.

'Why you?' Tony answered. ''Cause you're the best player in town and I want to play the best.'

'What's this, some John Wayne gunfighter bullshit?'

'Who's John Wayne?'

'Christ . . . You're way outa our league, kid.'

'There's more where this came from.' Hefting the wad. 'A lot more.'

Keller gestured at the cash and looked around. 'Put that away.'

The kid did.

Keller ate more burger, thinking of the times when, not much older than this boy, he'd blustered and lied his way into plenty of poker games. The only way to learn the game poker is to play – for money – against the best players you can find, day after day after day. Losing and winning.

'How long you played?'

'Since I was twelve.'

'Whatta your parents think about what you're doing?'

'They're dead,' he said unemotionally. 'I live with my uncle. When he's around. Which he isn't much.'

'Sorry.'

Tony shrugged.

'Well, I don't let anybody into the game without somebody vouches for them. So –'

'I played in a couple games with Jimmy Logan. You know him, don't you?'

Logan lived up in Michigan and was a respected player. The stakes tended to be small but Keller'd played some damn good poker against the man.

Keller said, 'Go get a soda or something. Come back in twenty minutes.'

'Come on, man, I don't want –'

'Go get a soda,' he snapped. 'And you call me "man" again I'll break your fingers.'

'But –'

'Go,' he muttered harshly.

So this's what it'd be like to have kids, thought Keller, whose life as a professional gambler over the past thirty years had left no room for a wife and children.

'I'll be over there.' Tony nodded across the street at the green awning of a Starbucks.

Keller pulled out his cell phone and called Logan. He had to be cautious about who he let into games. A few months ago some crusading reporters'd gotten tired of writing about all of Ellridge's local government corruption and CEO scandals so they'd done a series on gambling (THE CITY'S SHAME was the yawner of a headline). The police were under pressure from the mayor to close up the bigger games and Keller had to be careful. But Jimmy Logan confirmed that he'd checked the boy out carefully a month or so ago. He'd come into the game with serious money and had lost bad one day but'd had the balls to come back the next. He covered his loss and kept going; he walked away the big winner. Logan had also found out that Tony's parents'd left him close to three hundred thousand dollars in cash when they'd died. The money had been in a trust fund but had been released on his eighteenth birthday, last month.

With this news Keller's interest perked up.

After the call he finished his lunch. Tony delayed a defiant half-hour before returning. He and his attitude ambled back into the diner slowly.

Keller told him, 'Okay. I'll let you sit in tonight for a couple hours. But you leave before the high-stakes game starts.'

A scoff. 'But –'

'That's the deal. Take it or leave it.'

'I guess.'

'Bring at least ten thousand. . . . And try not to lose it all in the first five minutes, okay?'

The moments before a game begins are magic.

Sure, everyone's looking forward to lighting up the sour-smooth Cuban cigars, arguing about the Steelers or the Pistons or the Knicks, telling the jokes that men can tell only among themselves.

But the anticipation of those small pleasures was nothing compared with the one overriding thought: *Am I going to win?*

Forget the talk about the loving of the game, the thrill of the chase . . . those were all true, yes. But the thing that set real gamblers apart from dilettantes was their consuming drive to walk away from the table with more money than they sat down with. Any gambler who says otherwise is a liar.

Keller felt this rush now, sitting in the pungent, dark back room of Sal's Tavern, amid cartons of napkins, straws and coffee, an ancient Pabst Blue Ribbon beer sign, a ton of empties growing mold, broken bar stools. Tonight's game would start small (Keller considered it penny ante, despite the ten-large admission price) but would move to high stakes later in the night, when two serious players from Chicago arrived. A lot more money would change hands then. But the electric anticipation he felt with big stakes wasn't a bit different from what he felt now or if they'd only been playing for pocket change. Looking over the bare wood table, seeing the unopened decks of the red and blue Bicycle cards stacked up, one question sizzled in his mind: *Am I going to win?*

The other players arrived. Keller nodded a greeting to Frank Wendall, head of bookkeeping at Great Lakes Metal Works. Round and nervous and perpetually sweating, Wendall acted as if they were about to be raided at any minute. Wendall was the smart boy in Keller's poker circle. He'd drop lines into the conversation like, 'You know, there're a total of five thousand one hundred and eight possible flushes in a fifty-two-card deck but only seventy-eight possible pairs. Odd but it makes sense when you look at the numbers.' And he'd then happily launch into a lecture on those numbers, which'd keep going until somebody told him to shut up.

Squat, loud, chain-smoking Quentin Lasky, the owner of a chain of body shops, was the least educated but the richest man in the room. People in Ellridge must've been particularly bad drivers because his shops were always packed. Lasky played ruthlessly – and recklessly – and would win and lose big.

The last of the group was the opposite of Lasky. Somewhere in his late sixties, lean, gray Larry Stanton had grown up here, worked for another local manufacturer all his life and then retired. He was only in Ellridge part of the year; winters he spent in Florida. A widower, he was on a fixed income and was a conservative, cautious player, who never won or lost large sums. Keller looked at the old guy as a sort of mascot of the game.

Finally the youngster arrived. Trying to be cool but obviously excited to be in a serious game, Tony stepped into the room. He wore baggy slacks, a T-shirt and a stocking cap, and he toted a Starbucks coffee. Such a goddamn teenager, Keller laughed to himself.

Introductions were made. Keller noticed that Stanton seemed troubled. 'It's okay. I checked him out.'

'Well, it's just that he's a little young, don't you think?'

'Maybe you're a *little* old,' the kid came back. But he smiled good-naturedly and the frown that crossed Stanton's face slowly vanished.

Stanton was the banker and took cash from everybody and began handing out chips. Whites were one dollar, red were five, blue ten and yellow twenty-five.

'Okay, Tony, listen up. I'll be telling you the rules as we go along. Now –'

'I know the rules,' Tony interrupted. 'Everything according to Hoyle.'

'No, everything according to *me*,' Keller said, laughing. 'Forget Hoyle. He never even heard of poker.'

'Whatta you mean? He wrote the rules for all the games,' Lasky countered.

'No, he didn't,' Keller said. 'That's what people think. But Hoyle was just some Brit lawyer in the seventeen hundreds. He wrote this little book about three bullshit games: whist, quadrille and piquet. Nothing else, no Kankakee, pass the garbage, put-and-take stud or high-low roll 'em over. And try going into the MGM Grand and asking for a game of whist. . . . They'll laugh you out on your ass.'

'But you see Hoyle books everywhere,' Wendall said.

'Some publishers kept the idea going and they added poker and all the modern games.'

'I didn't know that,' Tony said distractedly. He shoved his geek glasses higher on his nose and tried to look interested.

Keller said sternly, 'Sorry if we're boring you, kid, but I got news: it's knowing everything about the game – even the little shit – that separates the men from the boys in poker.' He looked over carefully. 'You keep your ears open, you might just learn something.'

'How the hell can he hear anything even *if* he keeps his ears open?' Lasky muttered and glanced at the boy's stocking cap. 'What're you, some kind of fucking rapper? Lose the hat. Show some respect.'

Tony took his time removing the hat and tossing it on the counter. He pulled the lid off his Starbucks cup and sipped the coffee.

Keller examined the messy pile of chips in front of the boy and said, 'Now, whatever Jimmy Logan told you about playing poker, whatever you think you know from Hoyle, forget about it. We use the big boys' rules here, and rule number one: we play fair. Always keep your chips organised in front of you so everybody at the table knows how much you've got. Okay?'

'Sure.' The kid began stacking the chips into neat stacks.

'And,' Wendall said, 'let's say a miracle happens and you start to win big and somebody can't see exactly how many chips you have. If they ask you, you tell them. Down to the last dollar. Got that?'

'Tell 'em, sure.' The boy nodded.

They cut for the deal and Wendall won. He began shuffling with his fat fingers.

Keller gazed at the riffling cards in pleasure, thinking: *There's nothing like poker, nothing like it in the world.*

The game went back nearly two hundred years. It started as a Mississippi river boat cheaters' game to replace three-card monte, which even the most gullible slickers quickly learned was just a scam to take their money. Poker, played back then with only the ten through the ace, seemed to give them more of a fighting chance. But it didn't, of course, not in the hands of expert sharks (the innocents might've been more reluctant to play if they'd known that the game's name probably came from the nineteenth-century slang for wallet, 'poke', the emptying of which was the true object of play).

'Ante up,' Wendall called. 'The game is five-card draw.'

There are dozens of variations of poker games. But in Keller's games, five-card draw – 'closed poker' or 'jackpot' were the official names – was what they played, high hand the winner. Over the years he'd played every kind of poker known to man – from California lowball draw (the popular poker game west of the Rockies) to standard stud to Texas Hold 'Em. They were all interesting and exciting in their own ways but Keller liked basic jackpot best because there were no gimmicks, no arcane rules; it was you against the cards and the other players, like bare-knuckle boxing. Man to man.

In jackpot, players are dealt five cards and then have the option of exchanging up to three in hopes of bettering their hands. Good players, like Keller, had long ago memorised the odds of drawing certain combinations. Say, he was dealt a pair of threes, a jack, a seven and a two. If he decided to keep the pair and the jack and draw substitutes for the other two, he'd have a one in five chance of getting another jack to make a two-pair hand. To draw the remaining threes in the deck – to make four of a kind – his chances dropped to one in one thousand and sixty. But if he chose to keep only the pair and draw three new cards, the odds of getting that four of a kind improved to one in three hundred and fifty-nine. Knowing these numbers, and dozens more, were what separated amateur players from pros, and Keller made a very good living as a pro.

They tossed in the ante and Wendall began dealing.

Keller focused on Tony's strategy. He'd expected the kid to play recklessly but on the whole he was cautious and seemed to be getting a feel for the table and the players. A lot of teenagers would've been loud and obnoxious, Keller supposed, but the boy sat back quietly and just played cards.

Which wasn't to say he didn't need advice.

'Tony, don't play with your chips. Makes you look nervous.'

'I wasn't playing with them. I –'

'And here's another rule – don't argue with the guys giving you rules. You're good. You got it in you to be a great player – but you gotta shut up and listen to the experts.'

Lasky grumbled, 'Listen to him, kid. He's the best. I figure I bought his friggin' Mercedes for him, all the money I lost here. And does he bring it into my shop to get the dings out? Hell, no. . . . Call you.' He shoved chips forward.

'I don't get dings, Lasky. I'm a good driver. Just like I'm a good poker player. . . . Say hi to the ladies.' Keller laid down three queens and took the nine hundred dollar pot.

'Fuck me,' Lasky snapped angrily.

'Now there's *another* rule,' Keller said, nodding at the body-shop man, then turning to Tony. 'Never show emotion – losing *or* winning. It gives your opponent some information they can use against you.'

'Excuse me for breaking the rules,' Lasky muttered to Keller. 'I meant to say fuck *you*.'

Twenty minutes later Tony'd had a string of losses. On the next hand he looked at the five cards he'd been dealt and, when Stanton bet ten dollars, shook his head. He folded without drawing any cards and glumly toyed with the lid of his Starbucks cup.

Keller frowned. 'Why'd you fold?'

'Losing streak.'

Keller scoffed. 'There's no such thing as a losing streak.'

Wendall nodded, pushing the cards toward Tony to deal. The resident Mr Wizard of poker said, 'Remember that.

78

Every hand of poker starts with a fresh shuffle so it's not like blackjack – there's no connection between hands. The laws of probability rule.'

The boy nodded and, sure enough, played his way through Stanton's bluff to take an eight hundred and fifty dollar pot.

'Hey, there you go,' Keller said. 'Good for you.'

'So, what? You in school, kid?' Lasky asked after a few lackluster hands.

'Two cards,' the boy said to Keller, then dealing. He replied to Lasky, 'Been in computer science at the community college for a year. But it's boring. I'm going to drop out.'

'Computers?' Wendall asked, laughing derisively. 'High-tech stocks? I'll take craps or roulette wheel any day. At least you know what the odds are.'

'And what do you want to do for a living?' Keller asked.

'Play cards professionally.'

'Three cards,' Lasky muttered to Keller. Then to Tony he gave a gruff laugh. 'Pro card playing? Nobody does that. Well, Keller does. But nobody else I know of.' A glance at Stanton. 'How 'bout you, Grandpa, you ever play pro?'

'Actually, the name's Larry. Two cards.'

'No offense, *Larry*.'

'And two cards for the dealer,' Keller said.

The old man arranged his cards. 'No, I never even thought about it.' A nod at the pile of chips in front of him – he was just about even for the night. 'I play all right but the odds're still against you. Anything serious I do with money? I make sure the odds're on my side.'

Lasky sneered. 'That's what makes you a man, for Christ's sake. Having the balls to play even *if* the odds're against you.' A glance at Tony. 'You look like you got balls. Do you?'

'You tell *me*,' the boy asked and laid down two pairs to win an eleven hundred dollar pot.

Lasky looked at him and snapped, 'And fuck you *too*.'

Keller said, 'Think that means yes.' Everyone at the table – except Lasky – laughed.

The play continued with a series of big pots, Lasky and Tony being the big winners. Finally Wendall was tapped out.

'Okay, that's it. I'm out of here. Gentlemen . . . been a pleasure playing with you.' As always, he pulled a baseball cap on and ducked out the back door, looking hugely relieved he'd escaped without being arrested.

Keller's cell phone rang and he took the call. 'Yeah? . . . Okay. You know where, right? . . . See you, then.' When he disconnected he lit a cigar and sat back, scanned the boy's chips. He said to Tony, 'You played good tonight. But time for you to cash in.'

'What? I'm just getting warmed up. It's only ten.'

He nodded at his cell phone. 'The big guns'll be here in twenty minutes. You're through for the night.'

'Whatta you mean? I want to keep playing.'

'This's the big time. Guys I know from Chicago.'

'I'm playing fine. You said so yourself.'

'You don't understand, Tony,' Larry Stanton said, nodding at the chips. 'The whites go up to ten bucks each. The yellows'll be two fifty. You can't play with stakes like that.'

'I've got . . .' He looked over his chips. '. . . almost forty thousand.'

'And you could lose that in three, four hands.'

'I'm not going to lose it.'

'Oh, brother,' Lasky said, rolling his eyes. 'The voice of youth.'

Keller said, 'In my high-stakes game, everybody comes in with a hundred large.'

'I can get it.'

'This time of night?'

'I inherited some money a few years ago. I keep a lot of it

in cash for playing. I've got it at home – just a couple miles from here.'

'No,' Stanton said. 'It's not for you. It's a whole different game with that much money involved.'

'Goddamn it, everybody's treating me like a child. You've seen me play. I'm good, right?'

Keller fell silent. He looked at the boy's defiant gaze and finally said, 'You're back here in a half-hour with a hundred Gs, okay.'

After the boy left, Keller announced a break until the Chicago contingent arrived. Lasky went to get a sandwich and Stanton and Keller wandered into the bar proper for a couple of beers.

Stanton sipped his Newcastle and said, 'Kid's quite a player.'

'Has potential,' Keller said.

'So how bad you going to hook him? For his whole stake, the whole hundred thousand plus?'

'What's that?'

'"Rule number one is we play fair"?' Stanton whispered sarcastically. 'What the hell was *that* all about? You're setting him up. You've been spending most of the game – and half your money – catching his draws.'

Keller smiled and blew a stream of cigar smoke toward the ceiling of the bar. The old guy was right. Keller'd been going all the way with losing hands just to see how Tony drew cards. And the reconnaissance had been very illuminating. The boy had his strengths but the one thing he lacked was knowledge of the odds of poker. He was drawing blind. Keller was no rocket scientist but he'd worked hard over the years to learn the mathematics of the game; Tony, on the other hand, might've been a computer guru, but he didn't have a clue what his chances were of drawing a flush or a full house or even a second pair. Combined with the boy's atrocious skills at bluffing, which Keller'd spotted immediately, his ignorance of the odds made him a sitting duck.

'You've also been sandbagging,' Stanton said in disgust.

Score another one for Grandpa. He'd spotted that Keller had been passing on the bet and folding good hands on purpose – to build up Tony's confidence and to make him believe that Keller was a lousy bluffer.

'You're setting him up for a big hit.'

Keller shrugged. 'I tried to talk him into walking away.'

'Bullshit,' Stanton countered. 'You take a kid like that and tell 'em to leave, what's their first reaction? To stay. . . . Come on, Keller, he hasn't got that kind of money to lose.'

'He inherited a shitload of cash.'

'So you invited him into the game as soon as you found that out?'

'No, as a matter of fact, he came to *me*. . . . You're just pissed 'cause he treats you like a has-been.'

'You're taking advantage of him.'

Keller shot back with, 'Here's my real rule number one in poker: as long as you don't cheat you can do whatever you want to trick your opponents.'

'You going to share that rule with Tony?' Stanton asked.

'I'm going to do better than that – I'm going to give him a first-hand demonstration. He wants to learn poker? Well, this'll be the best lesson he ever gets.'

'You think breaking him and taking his tuition money's going to make him a better player?' Stanton asked.

'Yeah, I do. He doesn't want to be in school anyway.'

'That's not the point. The point is you're an expert and he's a boy.'

'He claims he's a man. And one of the things about being a man is getting knocked on your ass and learning from it.'

'In penny ante, sure. But not a game like this.'

'You have a problem with this, Grandpa?' Angry, Keller

82

turned ominously toward him.

Stanton looked away and held up his hands. 'Do what you want. It's your game. I'm just trying to be the voice of conscience.'

'If you play by the rules you'll always have a clear conscience.'

A voice called from the doorway, Lasky's. He said, 'They're here.'

Keller slapped Stanton on his bony shoulders. 'Let's go win some money.'

More cigar smoke was filling the back room. The source: Elliott Rothstein and Harry Piemonte, businessmen from the Windy City. Keller'd played with them several times previously but he didn't know much about them; the two men revealed as little about their personal lives as their faces shared what cards they held. They might've been organised crime capos or they might have been directors of a charity for orphans. All Keller knew was they were solid players, paid their losses without griping and won without lording it over the losers.

Both men wore dark suits and expensive, tailored white shirts. Rothstein had a diamond pinkie ring and Piemonte a heavy gold bracelet. Wedding bands encircled both of their left ring fingers. They now stripped off their suit jackets, sat down at the table and were making small talk with Stanton and Lasky when Tony returned. He sat down at his place and pulled the lid off his new Starbucks, nodding at Rothstein and Piemonte.

They frowned and looked at Keller. 'Who's this?' Rothstein muttered.

'He's okay.'

Piemonte frowned. 'We got a rule, we don't play with kids.'

Tony laughed and shoved his nerd glasses high on his nose. 'You guys and your rules.' He opened an envelope and dumped out cash. He counted out a large stack and put some back into his pocket. 'Hundred large,' he said to Stanton, who gave a dark look to Keller but began counting out chips for the boy.

The two new players looked at each other and silently decided to make an exception to their general rule about juveniles in poker games.

'Okay, the game is five-card draw,' Keller said. 'Minimum bet fifty, ante is twenty-five.'

Piemonte won the cut and they began.

The hands were pretty even for the first hour, then Keller began pulling ahead slowly. Tony kept his head above water, the second winner – but only because, it seemed, the other players were getting bad hands; the boy was still hopeless when it came to calculating the odds of drawing. In a half-dozen instances he'd draw a single card and then fold – which meant he was trying for a straight or a flush, the odds of doing that were just one in twenty. Either he should've discarded three cards, which gave him good odds of improving his hand, or gone with a heavy bluff after drawing a solo card, in which case he probably would've taken the pot a couple of times.

Confident that he'd nailed the boy's technique, Keller now began to lose intentionally when Tony seemed to have good cards – to boost his confidence. Soon the kid had doubled his money and had close to two hundred thousand dollars in front of him.

Larry Stanton didn't seem happy with Keller's plan to take the boy but he didn't say anything and continued to play his cautious, old-man's game, slowly losing to the other players.

The voice of conscience. . . .

As the night wore on, Lasky finally dropped out, having lost close to eighty thousand bucks. 'Fuck, gotta raise the price for ding-pulling,' he joked, heading for the door. He glanced at the duo from Chicago. 'When you gentlemen leave, could you bang inta some parked cars on the way to the expressway?' A nod toward Keller. 'An' if you wanta fuck up the front end of *his* Merc, I wouldn't mind one bit.'

Piemonte smiled at this; Rothstein glanced up as if the body-shop man were speaking Japanese or Swahili and turned back to his cards to try to coax a winning hand out of them.

Grandpa too soon bailed. He still had stacks of chips left on the table – but another rule in poker was that a player can walk away at any time. He now cashed in and pushed his chair back glumly to sip coffee and to watch the remaining players.

Ten minutes later Rothstein lost his remaining stake to Tony in a tense, and long, round of betting. 'Damn,' he spat out. 'Tapped out. Never lost to a boy before – not like this.'

Tony kept a straight face but there was a knowing look in his eye that said, *And you didn't lose to one now – I'm not a boy*.

The game continued for a half-hour, with big pots trading hands.

Most poker games don't end with dramatic last hands. Usually players just run out of money or, like Grandpa, get cold feet and slip away with their tails between their legs.

But sometimes there *are* climactic moments.

And that's what happened now.

Tony shuffled and then offered the cut to Keller, who divided the deck into thirds. The boy reassembled the cards and began dealing.

Piemonte gathered his and, like all good poker players, didn't move them (rearranging cards can telegraph a lot of information about your hand).

Keller picked up his and was pleased to see that he'd received a good one: two pairs – queens and sixes. A very winnable one in a game this size.

Tony gathered his five cards and examined them, not revealing any reaction. 'Bet?' he asked Piemonte, who passed – chose not to bet at this time.

To open the betting in draw poker a player needs a pair of jacks or better. Passing meant that either Piemonte didn't have that good a hand or that he did but was sandbagging – choosing not to bet to make the other players believe he had weak cards.

Keller decided to take a chance. Even though he had the two pairs, and *could* open, he too passed, which would make Tony think his hand was poor.

A tense moment followed. If Tony didn't bet, they'd surrender their cards and start over; Keller would swallow a solid hand.

But Tony glanced at his own cards and bet ten thousand.

Keller's eyes flickered in concern, which a bluffer would do, but in his heart he was ecstatic. The hook was set.

'See you,' Piemonte said, pushing his chips in.

So, Keller reflected, the man from Chicago'd probably been sandbagging too.

Keller, his face blank, pushed out the ten thousand, then another stack of chips. 'See your ten and raise you twenty-five.'

Tony saw the new bet and raised again. Piemonte hesitated but stayed with it and Keller matched Tony's new bet. As dealer, he now 'burned' the top card on the deck – set it face down in front of him. Then he turned to Piemonte. 'How many?'

'Two.'

Tony slipped him the two replacement cards from the top of the deck.

Keller's mind automatically began to calculate the odds. The chances of getting three of a kind in the initial deal were very low so it was likely that Piemonte had a pair and a 'kicker', an unmatched card of a high rank, probably a face card. The odds of his two new cards giving him a powerful full house were only one in one hundred and nineteen. And if, by chance, he *had* been dealt a rare three of a kind at first, the odds of his getting a pair, to make that full house, were still long: one in fifteen.

Filing this information away, Keller himself asked for one card, suggesting to the other players that he was going for either a full house or a straight flush – or bluffing. He picked up the card and placed it in his deck. Keller's mouth remained motionless but his heart slammed in his chest when he saw he'd got a full house – and a good one, three queens.

Tony himself took three cards.

Okay, Keller told himself, run the numbers. By taking three cards the boy signaled that he'd been dealt only one pair. So in order to beat Keller he'd have to end up with a straight flush, four of a kind or a full house of kings or aces. Like a computer, Keller's mind went through the various odds of this happening.

Based on his calculations about the boy's and Piemonte's draws, Keller concluded that he probably had the winning hand at the table. Now his goal was to goose up the size of the pot.

The boy shoved his glasses up on his nose again and glanced at Piemonte. 'Your bet.'

With a cautious sigh, the player from Chicago shoved some chips out. 'Twenty thousand.'

Keller had sat in on some of the great games around the country – both as a player and an observer – and he'd spent hundreds of hours studying how bluffers behaved. The small things they did – mannerisms, looks, when they hesitated and when they blustered ahead. What they said, when they laughed. Now he summoned up all these memories and began to act in a way that'd make the other players believe that he had a bum hand and was going for a bluff. Which meant he began betting big.

After two rounds, Piemonte finally dropped out, reluctantly – he'd put in close to sixty thousand dollars – and he probably had a decent hand. But he was convinced that Keller or Tony had a *great* hand and he wasn't going to throw good money after bad.

The bet came around to Keller once more. 'See your twenty,' he said to Tony. 'Raise you twenty.'

'Jesus,' Stanton muttered. Keller shot him a dark look and the old man fell silent.

Tony sighed and looked again at his cards, as if they could tell him what to do. But they never could, of course. The only answers to winning poker were in your own heart and your mind.

The boy had only fifteen thousand dollars left on the table. He reached into his pocket and took out an envelope. A hesitation. Then he extracted the rest of his money. He counted it out. Thirty-eight thousand. Another pause as he stared at the cash . . .

Go for it, Keller prayed silently. Please . . .

'Chips,' the boy finally said, eyes locked in Keller's, who looked back both defiant and nervous – a bluffer about to be called.

Stanton hesitated.

'Chips,' the boy said firmly.

The old man reluctantly complied.

Tony took a deep breath and pushed the chips on to the table. 'See your twenty. Raise you.'

Keller pushed ten thousand dollars forward – a bit dramatically, he reflected – and said, 'See the ten.' He glanced at all he had left. 'Raise you fifteen.' Pushed the remaining chips into the center of the table.

'Lord,' Piemonte said.

Even gruff Rothstein was subdued, gazing hypnotically at the massive pot, which was about four hundred and fifty thousand dollars.

For a moment Keller *did* feel a slight pang of guilt. He'd set up his opponent psychologically, calculated the odds down to the last decimal point – in short, he'd done everything that the youngster was incapable of. Still, the boy claimed he wanted to be treated like man. He'd brought this on himself.

'Call,' Tony said in a whisper, easing most of his chips into the pot.

Stanton looked away, as if avoiding the sight of a roadside accident.

'Queens full,' Keller said, flipping them over.

'Lookit that,' Piemonte whispered.

Stanton sighed in disgust.

'Sorry, kid,' Keller said, reaching forward for the pot. 'Looks like you . . .'

Tony flipped over his cards, revealing a full house – three kings and a pair of sixes. 'Looks like I win,' he said calmly and raked the chips in.

Piemonte whispered, 'Whoa. What a hand. . . . Glad I got out when I did.'

Stanton barked a fast laugh and Rothstein offered to Tony, 'That was some fine playing.'

'Just luck,' the boy said.

How the *hell* had that happened? Keller wondered, frantically replaying every moment of the hand. Of course, sometimes, no matter how you calculated the percentages, fate blindsided you completely. Still, he'd planned everything so perfectly.

'Time to call it a night,' Piemonte said, handing his remaining chips to Stanton to cash out and added humorously, 'Since I just gave most of my fucking money to a teenager.' He turned to Rothstein. 'From now on, we stick to that rule about kids, okay?'

Keller sat back and watched Tony start organising the chips in the pile. But the odds, he kept thinking . . . He'd calculated the odds so carefully. At least a hundred to one. Poker is mathematics and instinct – how had both of them failed him so completely?

Tony eased the chips toward Stanton for cashing out.

The sound of a train whistle filled the room again. Keller sighed, reflecting that *this* time it signified a loss – just the opposite of what the urgent howl had meant at the game with the Frenchmen.

The wail grew louder. Only . . . Focusing on the sound, Keller realised that there was something different about it this time. He glanced up at the old man and the two players from Chicago. They were frowning, staring at each other.

Why? Was something wrong?

Tony froze, his hands on the piles of his chips.

Shit, Keller thought. The sound wasn't a train whistle; it was a siren.

Keller pushed back from the table just as the front and back doors crashed open simultaneously, strewing splinters of wood around the back room. Two uniformed police officers, their guns drawn, pushed inside. 'On the floor, now, now, now!'

'No,' Tony muttered, standing and turning to face the cop nearest him.

'Kid,' Keller whispered sternly, raising his hands. 'Nothing stupid. Do what they say.'

The boy hesitated, looked at the black guns and lay down on the floor.

Stanton slowly got down on his knees.

'Move it, old man,' one of the cops muttered.

'Doing the best I can here.'

Finally on their bellies and cuffed, the gamblers were eased into sitting positions by the cops.

'So what'd we catch?' asked a voice from the alley as a balding man in his late fifties, wearing a gray suit, walked inside.

Detective Fanelli, Keller noted. Hell, not him. The cop had been Jesus Mary and Joseph enthusiastic to purify the sinful burgh of Ellridge for years. He scared a lot of the small players into not even opening games and managed to bust about one or two big ones a year. Looked like Keller was the flavor of the week this time.

Stanton sighed with resignation, his expression matching the faces of the pro players from Chicago. The boy, though, looked horrified. Keller knew it wasn't the arrest; it was that the state confiscated gambling proceeds.

Fanelli squinted as he looked at Rothstein's and Piemonte's driver's licenses. 'All the way from Chicago to get arrested. That's a pain in the ass, huh, boys?'

'I was just watching,' Rothstein protested. He nodded at the table, where he'd been sitting. 'No chips, no money.'

'That just means you're a loser.' The detective then glanced at Piemonte.

The man said a meek, 'I want to see a lawyer.'

'And I'm sure a lawyer's gonna wanta see you. Considering how big his fee's gonna be to try and save your ass. Which he ain't gonna do, by the way. . . . Ah, Keller.' He shook his head. 'This's pretty sweet. I been after you for a long time. You really oughta move to Vegas. I don't know if you follow the news much but I hear gambling's actually legal there. . . . And who's this?' He glanced at Stanton. He took Stanton's wallet from one of the uniformed cops and looked at his license. 'What the hell're you doing in Ellridge when you could be playing mahjong in Tampa with the ladies?'

'Can't afford the stakes down there.'

'The old guy's a wise ass,' the skinny detective muttered to the other cops. He then looked over Tony. 'And who're you?'

'I don't have to tell you anything.'

'Yeah, you do. This ain't the army. That name rank and serial number crap doesn't cut it with me. How old're you?'

'Eighteen. And I want a lawyer too.'

'Well, Mr I-Want-a-Lawyer-Too,' Fanelli mocked, 'you only get one after you've been charged. And I haven't charged you yet.'

'Who dimed me out?' Keller asked.

Fanelli said, 'Wouldn't be polite to give you his name but let's just say you took the wrong guy to the cleaners last year. He wasn't too happy about it and gave me a call.'

Keller grimaced. Took the wrong guy to the cleaners last year . . . Well, that shortlist'd have about a hundred people on it.

Looking down at the stacks of chips in front of where Tony'd been sitting, Fanelli asked, 'Pretty colors, red, blue, green. What're they worth?'

'The whites're worth ten matchsticks,' Rothstein said. 'The blues're –'

'Shut up.' He looked around the room. 'Where's the bank?'

Nobody said anything.

'Well, we *will* find it, you know. And I'm not going to start in here. I'm going to start out front and tear Sal's bar to fucking pieces. Then we'll do the same to his office. Break up every piece of furniture. Toss every drawer . . . Now, come on, boys, Sal doesn't deserve that, does he?'

Keller sighed and nodded to Stanton, who nodded toward the cupboard above the coffee machine. One cop took out two cigar boxes.

'Jesus our Lord,' Fanelli said, flipping through them. 'There's gotta be close to a half-million here.'

He glanced at the table. 'Those're your chips, huh?' he said to Tony. The boy didn't answer but Fanelli didn't seem to expect him to. He laughed and looked over the players. 'And you call yourselves men – letting a boy whip your asses at poker.'

'I'm not a boy.'

'Yeah, yeah, yeah.' The detective turned back to the boxes one more time. He walked over to the officers. They held a brief, whispered conference, then they nodded and stepped out of the room.

'My boys need to check on a few things,' Fanelli said. 'They've got to go corroborate some testimony or something. That's a great word, isn't it? "Corroborate".' He laughed. 'I love to say that.' He paced through the room, stopped at the coffee pot and poured himself a cup. 'Why the hell doesn't anybody ever drink booze at high-stakes games? Afraid you'll get a queen mixed with a jack?'

'As a matter of fact,' Keller said, 'yeah.'

The cop sipped the coffee and said in a low voice, 'Listen up, assholes. You especially, junior.' He pointed a finger at Tony and continued to pace. 'This happened at a . . . let's say a difficult time for me. We're concerned about some serious crimes that happen to be going down in another part of town.'

Serious crimes, Keller was thinking. Cops don't talk that way. What the hell's he getting at?

A smile. 'So here's the deal. I don't want to spend time booking you right now. It'd take me away from those other cases, you know. Now, you've lost the money one way or the other. If I take you in and book you the cash goes into evidence and when you're convicted, which you *will* be, every penny goes to the state. But if . . . let's just say *if* there was no evidence, well, I'd have to let you off with a warning. But that'd work out okay for me because I could get on to the other cases. The important cases.'

'That're being corroborated right now?' Tony asked.

'Shut up, punk,' the detective muttered, echoing Keller's thought.

'So what do you say?'

The men looked at each other.

'Up to you,' the cop said. 'Now what's it going to be?'

Keller surveyed the faces of the others around him. He glanced at Tony, who grimaced and nodded in disgust. Keller said to the detective, 'We'd be happy to help you out here, Fanelli. Do our part to help you clean up some – what'd you call it? Serious crimes?'

Stanton muttered, 'We have to keep Ellridge the show-place that it is.'

'And the citizens thank you for your efforts,' Detective Fanelli said, stuffing the money into his suit pockets.

The detective unhooked the handcuffs, stuffed them in his pockets too and walked back out into the alley without another word.

The players exchanged looks of relief – all except Tony, of course, on whose face the expression was one of pure dismay. After all, he was the big loser in all this.

Keller shook his hand. 'You played good tonight, kid. Sorry about that.'

The boy nodded and, with an anemic wave to everyone, wandered out the back door.

The Chicago players chattered nervously for a few minutes, then nodded farewells and left the smoky room. Stanton asked Keller if he wanted another beer but the gambler shook his head and the old man walked into the bar. Keller sat down at the table, absently picked up a deck of cards, shuffled them and began to play solitaire. The shock of the bust was virtually gone now; what bothered him was losing to the boy, an okay player but not a great one.

But after a few minutes of playing, his spirits improved and he reminded himself of another one of the Rules According to Keller: smart always beats out luck in the end.

Well, the kid'd been lucky this once. But there'd be other games, other chances to make the odds work and to relieve Tony, or others like him, of their bankrolls.

There was an endless supply of cocky youngsters to bleed dry, Keller reckoned and placed the black ten on the red jack.

Standing on the overpass, watching a train disappear into the night, Tony Stigler tried not to think about the money he'd just won – and then had stolen away from him.

Nearly a half-million.

Papers and dust swirled along the road bed behind the train. Tony watched it absently and replayed something that Keller had said to him.

It's knowing everything about the game – even the little shit – that separates the men from the boys in poker.

But that wasn't right, Tony reflected. You only had to know one thing. That no matter how good you are, poker's always a game of chance.

And that's not as good as a sure thing.

He looked around, making sure he was alone, then reached into his pocket and extracted the Starbucks cup lid. He lifted off the false plastic disk on the bottom and shut off a tiny switch. He then wrapped it carefully in a bubble-wrap envelope and replaced it in his pocket. The device was his own invention. A miniature camera in the sipping hole of the lid had scanned each card whenever Tony'd been dealing and the tiny processor had sent the suit and rank to the computer in Tony's car. All he had to do was tap the lid in a certain place to tell the computer how many people were in the game, so the program he'd written would know everyone's hand. It determined how many cards he should draw and whether to bet or fold on each round. The computer then broadcast its instructions to the earpiece of his glasses, which vibrated according to a code, and Tony acted accordingly.

'Cheating for Dummies', he called the program.

A perfect plan, perfectly executed – the only flaw being that he hadn't thought about the goddamn police stealing his winnings.

Tony looked at his watch. Nearly 1 a.m. No hurry to get back; his uncle was out of town on another one of his business trips. What to do? he wondered. Marconi Pizza was still open and he decided he'd stop by and see his buddy, the one who'd tipped him to Keller's game. Have a slice and a Coke.

Gritting footsteps sounded behind him and he turned, seeing Larry Stanton walking stiffly down the alley, heading for the bus stop.

'Hey,' the old guy called, noticing him and walking over. 'Licking your wounds? Or thinking of jumping?' He nodded toward the train tracks.

Tony gave a sour laugh. 'Can you believe that? Fucking bad luck.'

'Ah, raids're a part of the game, if you're playing illegal,' Stanton said. 'You got to build 'em into the equation.'

'A half-million dollar part of the equation?' Tony muttered.

'That part's gotta sting, true,' Stanton said, nodding. 'But it's better than a year in jail.'

'I suppose.'

The old man yawned. 'Better get on home and pack. I'm

going back to Florida tomorrow. Who'd spend the winter in Ellridge if they didn't have to?'

'You have anything left?' Tony asked.

'Money? . . . A little.' A scowl. 'But a hell of a lot less than I *did*, thanks to you and Keller.'

'Hold on.' The boy took out his wallet and handed the man a hundred dollars.

'I don't take charity.'

'Call it a loan.'

Stanton debated for a moment. Then, embarrassed, he took the bill and pocketed it. 'Thanks . . .' He shoved the cash away fast. 'Better get going. Buses stop running soon. Well, good playing with you, son. You've got potential. You'll go places.'

Yeah, the boy thought, I sure as hell *will* go places. The smart ones, the innovators, the young . . . we'll always beat people like you and Keller in the end. It's the way of the world. He watched Grandpa limp away, old and broke. Pathetic, the boy thought. Shoot me before I become him.

Tony pulled his stocking cap on, stepped away from the railing and walked toward his car, his mind already thinking of who the next mark should be.

Twenty minutes later the gassy municipal bus vehicle eased to the curb and Larry Stanton climbed off.

He walked down the street until he came to a dark intersection, the yellow caution light blinking for traffic on the main street, the red blinking for that on the cross. He turned the corner and stopped. In front of him was a navy-blue Crown Victoria. On the trunk were words: *Police Interceptor*.

And leaning against that trunk was the lean figure of Detective George Fanelli.

The cop pushed away from the car and walked up to

Stanton. The two other officers from the bust early that night were standing nearby. Both Fanelli and Stanton looked around and then shook hands. The detective took an envelope out of his pocket. Handed it to Stanton. 'Your half – two hundred and twenty two thousand.'

Stanton didn't bother to count it. He put the cash away.

'This was a good one,' the cop said.

'That it was,' Stanton agreed.

He and the vice cop ran one of these scams every year when Stanton was up from Florida. Stanton'd work his way into somebody's confidence, losing money in a couple of private games and then, on high-stakes night, tip the cops off ahead of time. Fanelli'd blame the bust on some anonymous snitch, take the bank as a bribe and release everybody; poker players were so happy to be able to stay out of jail and keep playing that they never complained.

As for Stanton, the gaff like this had always suited him better than gambling.

I play all right but the odds're still against you. Anything serious I do with money? I make sure the odds're on my side.

'Hey, Larry,' one of the cops called to Stanton. 'Didn't mean to be an asshole when I collared you. Just thought it'd be more, you know, realistic.'

'Handled it just right, Moscawitz. You're a born actor.'

Stanton and the detective walked past the unmarked squad car and continued down the dirty sidewalk. They'd known each other for years, ever since Stanton had worked as head of security at Midwest Metal Products.

'You okay?' Fanelli glanced down at Stanton's limp.

'I was racing somebody on a jet ski up at Lake Geneva. Hit a wake. It's nothing.'

'So when're you going back to Tampa?'

'Tomorrow.'

'You flying down?'

'Nope. Driving. He pulled keys out of his pocket and opened the door of a new BMW sports car.

Fanelli looked it over admiringly. 'Sold the Lexus?'

'Decided to keep it.' A nod toward the sleek silver wheels. 'I just wanted something sexier, you know. The ladies in my golf club love a man in a sports car. Even if he's got knobby knees.'

Fanelli shook his head. 'Felt bad about that kid. Where'd he get the money to sit in on a high-stakes game?'

'Tuition money or something. He inherited it from his folks.'

'You mean we just dipped an orphan? I'll be in confession for a month.'

'He's an orphan who cheated the pants off Keller and everybody else.'

'What?'

Stanton laughed. 'Took me a while to tip to it. Finally figured it out. He must've had some kind of electronic shiner or camera or something in his coffee cup lid. He was always playing with it on the table, moving it close to the cards when he dealt – and the only time he won big was on the deal. Then after the bust I checked out his car – there was a computer and some kind of antenna in the back seat.'

'Damn,' Fanelli said. 'That was stupid. He'll end up dead, he's not careful. I'm surprised Keller didn't spot it.'

'Keller was too busy running his own scam, trying to take the kid.' Stanton told him the pro's set-up of Tony.

The detective laughed. 'He tried to take the boy, the boy tried to take the table and it was us old guys who took 'em both. There's a lesson there someplace.' The men shook hands in farewell. 'See you next spring, my friend. Let's try Greenpoint. I hear they've got some good high-stakes games over there.'

'We'll do that.' Stanton nodded and fired up the sports car.

He drove to the intersection, carefully checked for cross traffic and turned on to the main street that would take him to the expressway.

CHANCE

John Harvey

The second or third time Kiley went out with Kate Keenan, it had been to the theatre, an opening at the Royal Court. Her idea. A journalist with a column in the *Independent* and a wide brief, she was on most people's B list at least.

The play was set in a Brick Lane squat, two shiftless young men and a meant-to-be fifteen-year-old girl: razors, belt buckles, crack cocaine. Simulated sex and pain. One of the men seemed to be under the illusion, much of the time, that he was a dog. At the interval, they elbowed their way o the bar through louche suits and little black dresses with tasteful cleavage, New Labour voters to the core. 'Challenging,' said a voice on Kiley's left. 'A bit full on,' said another. 'But relevant. Absolutely relevant.'

'So what do you think?' Kate asked.

'I think I'll meet you outside.'

'What do you mean?'

She knew what he meant.

They took the tube, barely talking, to Highbury and Islington, a stone's throw from where Kate lived. Across the road she turned towards him, a hand upon his arm. 'I don't think this is going to work out, do you?'

Kiley shrugged and thought probably not.

Between Highbury Corner and the Archway, almost the entire length of the Holloway Road, there were only three fights in progress, one between two women in slit skirts and halter tops, who clawed and swore at each other, rolling on the broad pavement outside the Rocket while a crowd bayed them on. Propped inside a telephone box close by the railway bridge, a man stared out frozen-eyed, a hypodermic needle sticking out of the scabbed flesh of his bare leg. Who needs theatre, Kiley asked himself?

His evenings free, Kiley was at liberty to take his usual seat in the Lord Nelson, a couple of pints of Marston's Pedigree before closing, then a slow stroll home through the back-doubles to his second-floor flat in a shabby terraced house among other shabby houses, too far from a decent primary school for the upwardly mobile middle-class professionals to have appropriated in any numbers.

Days, he sat and waited for the telephone to ring, the fax machine to chatter into life; the floor was dotted with books he'd started to read and would never finish, pages from yesterday's paper were spread out across the table haphazardly. Afternoons, if he wasn't watching a film at the local Odeon, he'd follow the racing on TV – Kempton, Doncaster, Haydock Park. *Investigations*, read the ad in the local press, *Private and Confidential. All kinds of security work undertaken. Ex-Metropolitan Police.* Kiley was never certain whether that last put off as many potential clients as it impressed.

Seven years in the Met, two seasons in professional soccer and then freelance: Kiley's CV so far.

The last paid work he'd done had been for Adrian Costain, a sports agent and PR consultant Kiley knew from one of his earlier lives. Kiley's task: babysitting an irascible yet

charming American movie actor in London on a brief promotional visit. After several years of mayhem and marriages
to Meg or Jennifer or Julia, he was rebuilding his career as a
serious performer with a yearning to play Chekhov or
Shakespeare.

'For Christ's sake,' Costain had said, 'keep him away
from the cocaine and out of the tabloids.'

It was fine until the last evening, a celebrity binge at a
Members Only watering hole in Soho. What exactly went
down in the small men's toilet between the second and third
floors was difficult to ascertain for certain, but the resulting
black eye and bloodied lip were front-page juice to every
picture editor between Wapping and Faringdon. Today the
UK, tomorrow the world.

Costain was incandescent.

'What did you expect me to do,' Kiley asked, 'go in there
and hold his dick?'

'If necessary, yes.'

'You're not paying me enough, Adrian.'

He thought it would be a while before Costain put work
his way again.

He put through a call to Maggie Hambling, a solicitor in
Kentish Town for whom he sometimes did a little investi-
gating, either straining his eyes at the local land registry or
long hours hunkered down behind the wheel of his car,
waiting for evidence of some small near-lethal indiscretion.

But Maggie was in court and her secretary dismissed him
with a cold promise to tell her he'd called. The connection
was broken almost before the words were out of her mouth.
Kiley pulled on his coat and went out on to the street; for
early December it was almost mild, the sky opaque and
indecipherable. There was a route he took when he wanted to
put some distance beneath his feet: north up Highgate Hill,
past the spot where Dick Whittington was supposed to have

turned again, and through Waterlow Park, down alongside the cemetery and into the Heath, striking out past the ponds to Kenwood House, a loop then that took him round the side of Parliament Hill and down towards the tennis courts, the streets that would eventually bring him home.

Tommy Duggan was waiting for him, sitting on the low wall outside the house, checking off winners in the *Racing Post*.

'How are you, Tommy?'

'Pretty fine.'

Duggan, deceptively slight and sandy-haired, had been one of the best midfielders Kiley had ever encountered in his footballing days, Kiley on his way up through the semi-pro ranks when Duggan was slipping down. During Kiley's brace of years with Charlton Athletic, Duggan had come and gone within the space of two months. Bought in and sold on.

'Still like a flutter,' Kiley said, eyeing the paper at Duggan's side.

'Academic interest only nowadays.' Duggan smiled. 'Isn't that what they say?'

The addictions of some soccer players are well documented, the addiction and the cure. Paul Merson. Tony Adams. Stories of others running wild claim their moment in the news, then fade. But any manager worth his salt will know the peccadilloes of those he might sign: drugs, drink, gambling, having at least one of his team-mates watch as he snorts a line of cocaine from between the buttocks of a four hundred pounds an hour whore. You look at your need, your place in the table, assess the talent, weigh up the risk.

When Tommy Duggan came to Charlton he was several thousand in debt to three different bookmakers and spent more time with his cell phone than he did on the training ground. Rumour had it, his share of his signing-on fee was lost on the back of a spavined three-year-old almost before the ink had dried on the page.

Duggan went and Kiley stayed: but not for long.

'Come on inside,' Kiley said.

Duggan shrugged off his leather coat and chose the one easy chair.

'Tea?'

'Thanks, two sugars, aye.'

What the hell, Kiley was wondering, does Tommy Duggan want with me?

'You're not playing any more, Tom?' Kiley asked, coming back into the room.

'What do you think?'

Watching *Sky Sport* in the pub, Kiley had sometimes glimpsed Duggan's face, jostling for space among the other pundits ranged across the screen.

'I had a season with Margate,' Duggan said. 'After I come back this last time from the States. Bastard'd shove me on for the last twenty minutes – "Get among 'em, Tommy, work the magic. Turn it round."' Duggan laughed. 'Every time the ball ran near, there'd be some donkey anxious to kick the fuck out of me. All I could do to stay on my feet, never mind turn round.'

He drank some tea.

'Nearest I get to a game nowadays is coaching a bunch of kids over Whittington Park. Couple of evenings a week. That's what I come round to see you about. Thought you might like to lend a hand. Close an' all.'

'Coaching?'

'Why not? More than a dozen of them now. More than I can handle.'

'How old?'

'Thirteen, fourteen. Best of them play in this local league.

Six-a-side. What d'you think? 'Less your evenings are all spoken for, of course.'

Kiley shook his head. 'Can't remember the last time I kicked a ball.'

'It'll come back to you,' Duggan said. 'Like falling off a bike.'

Kiley wasn't sure if that was what he meant or not.

There were eleven of them the first evening Kiley went along, all shapes and sizes. Two sets of dreadlocks and one turban. One of the black kids, round-faced, slightly pudgy in her Arsenal strip, was a girl. Esther.

'I ain't no mascot, you know,' she said, after Duggan had introduced them. 'I can run rings round this lot.'

'My dad says he saw you play once,' said a lad whose mum had ironed his David Beckham shirt straight from the wash. 'He says you were crap.'

'Your dad'd know crap right enough, wouldn't he, Dean,' Duggan said. 'Living with you.'

The rest laughed and Dean said, 'Fuck off,' but he was careful to say it under his breath.

'Okay, let's get started,' Tommy Duggan said. 'Let's get warmed up.'

After a few stretching exercises and a couple of circuits of the pitch, Duggan split them up into twos and threes practising basic ball skills, himself and Kiley moving between them, watching, offering advice.

No more than twenty minutes or so of that and their faces were bright with sweat under the floodlights.

'Now,' Duggan said, 'let's do a little work on corners, attacking, defending, staying alert. Jack, why don't you send a few over, give us the benefit of that sweet right foot.'

Kiley was sweating like the rest, feeling his forty years. Either his tracksuit had shrunk or he'd put on more weight than he'd thought. The first corner was struck too hard and sailed over everyone's heads, but after that he settled into something of a rhythm and was almost disappointed when Duggan called everyone together and divided them into teams.

Like most youngsters they had a tendency to get drawn out of position and follow the ball, but some of the passing was thoughtful and neat, and only luck and some zealous defending prevented a hatful of goals. Dean, in his Beckham shirt, hand forever aloft demanding the ball, was clearly the most gifted but also the most likely to kick out in temper, complain loudly if he thought he'd been fouled.

When he slid a pass through for Esther to run on to and score with a resounding drive, the best he could muster was 'Jammy cow!'

Game over, kids beginning to drift away, Duggan offered to buy Kiley a pint. There was a pub on the edge of the park that Kiley had not been into before.

'So what did you think?' Duggan asked. They were at a table near the open door.

'About what?'

'This evening, you enjoy it or what?'

'Yeah, it was okay. They're nice enough kids.'

'Most of them.'

Kiley nodded. The muscles in the backs of his legs were already beginning to ache.

'You'll come again, then?'

'Why not? Not as if my social calendar's exactly full.'

'No girlfriend?'

'Not just at present.'

'But there was one?'

'For a while, maybe.'

'What happened?'

Kiley shrugged and supped his beer. 'You?' he said.

Duggan lit a cigarette. 'The only women I meet are out for a good time and all they can get. Either that or else they've got three kids back home with the babysitter and they're looking for someone to play dad.'

'And you don't fancy that?'

'Would you?'

Kiley wasn't certain; there were days – not so many of them – when he thought he might. 'No,' he said.

Without waiting to be asked, Duggan fetched two more pints. 'Where d'you meet her anyway?' he said. 'This ex of yours.'

'I was working,' Kiley said. 'Security. Down on the South Bank. She'd just come out from this Iranian movie.'

'She's Iranian?'

'No. The film was Iranian. She's English. Kate. Kate Keenan.'

'Sounds Irish.'

'Maybe. A generation or so back maybe.'

'You're cut up about it,' Duggan said.

'Not really.'

'No, of course not,' Duggan said, grinning. 'You can tell.'

Kate's column in the *Indi* questioned the morality of making art out of underclass deprivation and serving it up as a spectacle for audiences affluent enough to afford dinner and the theatre, and then a taxi home to their three-quarters of a million plus houses in fashionable Islington and Notting Hill.

Under Duggan's watchful eye and with Kiley's help, the six-a-side team won their next two games, Dean being sent off in the second for kicking out at an opponent in retaliation and then swearing at the referee.

Margaret Hambling offered Kiley three days' work checking up on a client who had been charged with benefit fraud over a period in excess of two years.

'Come round my gaff, why don't you?' Tommy Duggan said one night after training. 'See how the other half lives.' And winked.

Drained by two lots of child support, which he paid intermittently but whenever he could, Duggan had sold his detached house in Totteridge and bought a thirties semi-detached in East Finchley, half of which he rented out to an accountant struggling with his MBA.

In the main room there were framed photographs of Duggan's glory days on the walls and soiled grey carpet on the floor. Clothes lay across the backs of chairs, waiting to be washed or ironed. On a table near the window were a well-thumbed form book, the racing pages, several cheap ballpoints, a telephone.

'Academic?' said Kiley, questioningly.

Duggan grinned. 'Man's got to have a hobby.'

He took Kiley to a Hungarian restaurant on the high street where they had cherry soup and goulash spiced with smoked paprika. A bottle of wine.

'Good, uh?' Duggan said, pushing away his plate.

'Great,' Kiley said. 'What's the pitch?'

Duggan smiled with his eyes. 'Just a small favour.'

The casino was on a narrow street between Soho and Shaftesbury Avenue, passing trade not one of its concerns. Instead of a bouncer with overfed muscles, Kiley was greeted at the door by a silvered blonde in a tailored two-piece.

'I'm here to see Mr Stephen.'

'Certainly, sir. If you'll come this way.' Her slight accent was Scandinavian.

Mr Stephen's name wasn't really Stephen. Not originally, at least. He had come to England from Malta in the late Fifties when the East End gangsters were starting to lose their grip on gambling and prostitution up West; had stood his ground and received the razor scars to prove it, though these had since been surgically removed. Now gambling was legal and he was a respectable businessman. Let the Albanians and the Turks fight the Yardies over heroin and crack cocaine, he had earned his share portfolio, his place in the sun.

The blonde handed Kiley over to a brunette who led him to a small lift at the far side of the main gaming room. There was no background music, no voice raised above the faint whirring of roulette wheels, the hushed sounds of money being made and lost.

Kiley was glad he'd decided to wear his suit, not just his suit but his suit and tie.

'Have you visited our casino before?' the brunette asked him.

'I'm afraid not, no.'

One of her eyes was brown and the other a greyish green.

When he stepped out of the lift there was an X-ray machine, the kind you walk through in airports; Kiley handed the brunette his keys and small change, and she gave them back to him at the other side.

'Mr Kiley for Mr Stephen,' she said to the man at the end of the short corridor.

The man barely nodded; doors were opened and closed. Stephen's inner sanctum was lined with books on two sides, mostly leather-bound; screens along one wall afforded high-angle views of the casino's interior. Stephen himself sat behind a desk, compact, his face the colour of walnut, bald head shining as if he had been recently buffed.

A few days before, Kiley had spoken to one of his contacts at Scotland Yard, a sergeant when he and Kiley had served together, now a detective superintendent.

'The casino's a front,' the superintendent told him.

'Prestige. He doesn't lose money on it exactly, but with all those overheads, that area, he'd make more selling the site. It's the betting shops that fetch in the money, one hundred and twenty nation wide. That and the fact he keeps a tight ship.'

'Can you get me in to see him?' Kiley had asked.

'Probably. But nothing more. We've no leverage, Jack, I'm sorry.'

Now Kiley waited for Stephen to acknowledge him, which he did with a small gesture of a manicured hand, no suggestion that Kiley should take a seat.

'Tommy Duggan,' Kiley said. 'He owes you money. Not a lot in your terms, maybe, but . . .' Kiley stopped and waited, then went on, 'He says he's been threatened. Not that you'd know about that directly, not your concern, but I imagine if you wanted you could get it stopped.'

Stephen looked at him through eyes that had seen more than Kiley, far more, and survived.

'Do you follow soccer at all, Mr Stephen?' Kiley asked.

No response.

'With some players it's speed, with others it's power, sheer force. Then there are those who can put their foot on the ball, look up and in that second see the perfect pass and have the skill to make it, inch perfect, thirty, forty yards crossfield.'

Something moved behind the older man's eyes. 'Liam Brady,' he said. 'Rodney Marsh.'

'Right,' said Kiley. 'Hoddle. LeTissier. Tommy, too. On his day Tommy was that good.'

Stephen held Kiley's gaze for a moment longer, then slipped his wristwatch free and placed it on the desk between them. 'Your Tommy Duggan, he owes close to one hundred thousand pounds. Each time the hands of that watch move round, he owes more.' He picked up the watch and weighed it in the palm of his hand. 'You tell him if he makes payments, regular, if the debt does not increase, I will be patient. Bide my time. But if he loses more . . .'

'I'll tell him,' Kiley said.

Stephen set the watch back on his wrist. 'Do you gamble, Mr Kiley?'

Kiley shook his head.

'In gambling, there is only one winner. In the end.'

'Thanks for your time,' Kiley said.

Almost imperceptibly Stephen nodded and his eyes returned their focus to the screens on the wall.

'Good evening, sir,' said the brunette in the lift. 'Good evening, sir,' said the blonde. 'Be sure to come again.'

'Jack, you're a prince,' Duggan said, when Kiley recounted the conversation.

Kiley wasn't certain what, if anything, he'd achieved.

'Room for manoeuvre, that's what you've got me. Pressure off. Time to recoup, study the field.' He smiled. 'Don't worry, Jack. Nothing rash.'

There was a message from Kate on his answerphone. 'Perhaps I was a little hasty. How about a drink, Wednesday evening?'

Wednesday was soccer training. Kiley called back and made it Thursday. The wine bar at Highbury Corner was only a short walk from Kate's house; from there it was only two flights of stairs to her bed.

'Something on your mind, Jack?'

There was and then there wasn't. Only later, his head resting in the cleft between Kate's bare calf and thigh, did it come back to him.

'He'll carry on gambling, won't he?' Kate said, when she had finished listening.

'Probably.'

'It's an illness, Jack, a disease. If he won't get proper help, professional help, there's nothing you can do.'

114

He turned over and she stroked his back and when he closed his eyes he was almost immediately asleep. In a short while she would wake him and send him home, but for now she was comfortable, replete. Maybe, she was thinking, it was time for another piece on gambling in her column.

Duggan had returned from his second spell in the States with a ponytail and a fondness for Old Crow over ice and down home butt-dirty country music, bluegrass and pedal-steel and tales of love gone wrong. Nothing flash, no rhinestones, the real thing.

Back in England, the ponytail lasted until the first time he watched Seaman run out at Highbury and realised how affected it looked; he toned down his new-found love of bourbon but still listened to the music whenever he could. In a music store off Upper Street, less than a week ago, he'd picked up a CD by Townes Van Zandt, *A Far Cry from Dead*. Country blues with a twist.

> *Sometimes I don't know where this dirty road is*
>   *taking me*
> *Sometimes I can't even see the reason why*
> *I guess I'll keep on gamblin', lots of booze and lots*
>   *of ramblin'*
> *It's easier than just a-waitin' round to die*

Playing it was like pushing your tongue against an abscessed tooth.

He had seen Van Zandt in London in 'ninety-seven, one of the last gigs he ever played. Standing sweating in the Borderline, a crowded little basement club off Charing Cross Road, he had watched as Van Zandt, pale and thin and shaking, had begun song after song, only to stop, mid-verse, forgetting the words, hearing another tune. His fingers failed

115

to grip the neck of the guitar, he could scarcely balance on the stool. Embarrassed, upset voices in the crowd began to call out, telling him to take a break, rest, telling him it was okay, but still he stumbled on. Dying before their eyes.

Two days before, Duggan had placed the first instalment of his payback money on a four-horse accumulator and, on the small betting shop screen, watched the favourite come through on the inside in the final race and leave his horse stranded short of the line.

Flicking the remote, he played the song again.

The money from the recording, some of it at least, would go to Van Zandt's widow and their kids. Duggan hadn't seen either his daughter or his two sons in years; he didn't even know where one of the boys was.

There were some cans of lager in the fridge, the tail end of a bottle of scotch; when he'd finished those he put on his coat and followed the familiar path to the Bald-Faced Stag.

Ten minutes short of closing, a motorbike pulled up outside the pub. Without removing his helmet, the pillion rider jumped off and went inside. Duggan was standing at the bar, drink in hand, staring up aimlessly at the TV. The pillion rider pulled an automatic pistol from inside his leather jacket, shot Duggan twice in the head at close range and left.

Duggan was dead before he hit the floor.

Several evenings later Kiley called the kids around him behind one of the goals. In the yellowing light, their breath floated grey and clear. He talked to them about Tommy Duggan, about the times he had seen him play; he told them how much Duggan wanted them to do well. One or two had tears in their eyes, others scuffed their feet in the ground and looked away.

'Who cares?' Dean said when Kiley had finished. 'He was never any bloody good anyway.'

Without deliberation, without meaning to, Kiley hit him: an open-handed slap across the face which jolted the boy's head back and round.

'You bastard! You fuckin' bastard!'

There were tears on his face now and the marks left by Kiley's hand stood out livid on his cheek.

'I'm sorry,' Kiley said. Some part of him felt numb, shocked by what he'd done.

'Fuck you!' the boy said and turned on his heel for home.

Dean lived in one of the flats that bordered Wedmore Street, close by the park. The man who answered the door was wearing jeans and a fraying Motorhead T-shirt, and didn't look too happy to be pulled away from whatever was playing, over-loud, on the TV.

'I'm Jack Kiley,' Kiley said.

'You hit my boy.'

'Yes.'

'You've got some balls, showing up round here.'

'I wanted to explain, apologise.'

'He says you just laced into him, no reason.'

'There was a reason.'

'Dean,' the man called back over his shoulder, 'turn that fuckin' thing down.' And then, 'All right, then, let's hear it.'

Kiley told him.

The man sighed and shook his head. 'That mouth of his, I'm always telling him it's going to get him into trouble.'

'I should never have lost my temper. I shouldn't have hit him.'

'My responsibility, right?' Dean's father said. 'Down to me.'

Kiley said nothing.

'What you did, maybe knock a bit of sense into him.'

'Maybe,' Kiley said, unconvinced.

117

'There's nothing else?'

'No.' Kiley took a step away.

'Tommy Duggan, what happened to him. It was wrong.'

'Yes.'

'Now that he's, you know, you think you might take over the team, the coaching?'

'For a bit, maybe,' Kiley said. 'It was Tommy's thing really, not mine.'

'Yeah. Yeah, that's right, I suppose.'

The door closed and Kiley took the stairs two at a time.

When he phoned Kate, she began by putting him off, a piece to finish, an early start, but then, hearing something in his voice, she changed her mind. 'Come round.'

The first glass of wine she poured, Kiley finished almost before she had started hers.

'If you just wanted to get drunk you could have done that on your own.'

'That's not what I wanted.'

He leaned against her and she held him, her breath warm on the back of his neck. 'I'm sorry about your friend,' she said.

'It's a waste.'

'It always is.'

After a while, Kiley said, 'I keep thinking there was something more I could've done.'

'It was his life. His choice. You did what you could.'

It was quiet. Often at Kate's there would be music playing but not this evening. From the hiss of tyres on the road outside it had started to rain. At the next coaching session, Kiley thought, he would apologise to Dean again in front of everyone, see if he couldn't get the lad to acknowledge what he'd said was wrong: start off on a new footing, give themselves a chance.

THE BOY AND MAN BOOKER

BOOKER

Reginald Hill

Boy Ansell awoke, had no idea where he was except that it wasn't his flat and for a moment felt afraid.

Then he remembered and joy washed away his fear.

Cautiously he raised his head from the soft bank of pillows. A slight muzziness, nothing more. It was true what they said, the best champagne leaves little trace of its passage and last night he had drunk nothing but the best.

He slipped his hand under the pillow. Another moment of panic, then his fingers touched paper. It was there, but he needed to see it. He groped for an unfamiliar light switch. A golden glow touched his surroundings like sunlight. A hotel room. But what a room! You could fit all of his Brighton flat in here. Furnished in the stately home neo-classical style with a sky-blue ceiling from whose lofty rococo cornice gilded cherubim looked down on acres of thick white carpet, it was probably costing his publishers more for one night here than a whole week at the kind of dump they used to put him in.

But they could do better.

They *would* do better now that he had this to wave at them.

He read the magic words on the piece of paper.

Pay David Boyd Ansell the sum of fifty thousand pounds . . . for and on behalf of MAN BOOKER . . .

Fifty thousand. With the kind of sales now in prospect, he could afford to smile at this paltry sum. It would, after all, buy him only five or six months in a room like this. He might even never bother to cash the cheque but keep it framed on his study wall.

Or better still, cash it but keep a convincing photocopy framed.

He swung his legs to the floor and viewed himself in a heavy gilt mirror nicely placed to catch the wide expanse of the king-sized bed. No sign that he'd had company last night. Not that it hadn't been there for the asking, he told himself complacently as he turned his face slowly from left to right profile. Boy David they called him, and even in his mid-thirties his face and figure still retained enough of the youthful perfection of Michelangelo's statue to justify the sobriquet. So pussy galore on offer. But at some point during all the back-slapping, cheek-pecking, body-hugging, champagne-swilling celebration, he had decided that this was a triumph he wanted to snuggle up with alone.

Molly had seen him safely back, he dimly recalled. Molly who was so sensitive to all his needs. Molly who, his sensual sensors told him, would not herself be averse to adding the remaining ninety per cent to the ten per cent of him she already had. But *never sleep with your agent* was the only useful bit of literary advice he'd ever been given.

Happily no one had ever said anything against sleeping with your agent's secretary.

If Toni had been around last night, now that might have been different. Timid little Toni, a real country mouse, still wide-eyed and tremulous at finding herself in the big city, might have seemed an impossible challenge to some. But the Boy's motto, as he boasted to his intimates, was *Vidi, vici, veni.* I saw, I conquered, I came. And as soon as he set eyes on this fresh young thing, a mouse in manner but a shapely pussycat in form, he'd known he had to have her.

It had taken him a mere ninety minutes from the first time he got her alone. Molly had sent her down to Brighton with a bunch of contracts for him to sign. She claimed she'd posted the originals to him weeks back. Well, she might have done. He wasn't responsible for the vagaries of the postal service. Now his signature was a matter of urgency, so shy little Toni got a day trip to Brighton. Tense at first, she soon relaxed under the glow of his famous charm. He could see she was ripe for plucking. It was in the stars, written there as reliably as a Fascist train timetable, a judgement confirmed when the phone rang and it turned out to be Molly with the news that her Booker mole had just given her the nod that Boy was on the shortlist. Pop! went the bubbly, and not long after, pop! went everything else, and as he put her on to the London train a couple of hours later, he was already looking forward to the next time.

But there hadn't been a next time. Enquiring after Toni when he turned up at Molly's office a couple of days later, he was told that family illness required her presence at home in the Midlands. Then, in the weeks that followed, he'd been swept up in a whirl of pre-Booker publicity, cashing in on being on the shortlist. You had to do it, Molly explained. Literary prizes were a lottery. Being odds-on favourite was no guarantee of success. Indeed, given the self-regarding vanity of some of the plonkers who did the judging, it could be counter-productive!

But this time they had been unable to resist the overwhelming evidence. In his mind he savoured the chairman's words once more.

'This was a shortlist of the highest standard. Each of these novels deserves superlative praise. Yet in the end we had no difficulty in choosing our winner. *The Accelerant* is a profound and moving modern fable. Superficially the story of a sexual predator who claims he never sleeps with any woman unless certain she wants to sleep with him, and who uses that certainty to justify all the short cuts both moral and chemical which he takes, at a deeper level this is a powerful parable of political degeneration, mapping the path from idealistic, altruistic beginnings to ruthless and bloody dictatorship, both in its blatant forms in Africa, the Middle East and South America, and in its subtler manifestations in our own Corridors of Power. Covering four continents and two decades, this is not easy material to deal with. But David Boyd Ansell has such a sharp eye for detail, such a keen ear for nuance, such a fine sense of balance and proportion that he keeps everything under perfect control. Truly here is a writer we can rely on to keep his head while all around are losing theirs . . .'

And so on, and so on. He'd stifled a small yawn at this point, ironically underlining on all the TV close-ups his indifference to such paeans. But oh! how the memory of them warmed his being like the memory of good sex.

He stood up, made the long journey to the window and drew the heavy damask curtains. Autumn sunlight streamed in, strong enough to make him blink. The view it lit up was undistinguished, anonymous rooftops mainly. But at least he could see a fair chunk of sky. London hotels charged for sky by the square inch.

A telephone rang. He found it, said, 'Yes?'

It was Molly.

'Good morning, Boy,' she said breezily. 'Just checking you're conscious and mobile.'

Sometimes her breeziness irritated him.

'Why shouldn't I be?' he said. 'I've been up for ages.'

'Excitement kept you awake, eh? That's good. We need to

be bright-eyed and bushy-tailed for the press call.'

'The what?'

'Come on, Boy, wake up, do! At last we're an overnight success and that means we've got a busy day. Conference suite, second floor, 11 a.m. Pics and a few questions from the mob, then an hour for *The Times* supplement piece. One o'clock we lunch with the Japs. This afternoon, there's a couple of telly things, then this evening *Front Row*. I'll give you a knock at quarter to. Don't wear that houndstooth shirt, by the way. You may not have time to change after lunch and it can look funny on the box. And dump that grotty leather jacket. We need to show the world that being a successful author doesn't have to mean dressing like Worzel Gummidge. Bye.'

She really did go too far sometimes. And what was all this *we* stuff? Okay, in the five years since he'd used her, his sales had risen steadily, but what real part had she played in his success other than fielding the bids for his books? By rights, all this media crap should be the responsibility of those nice young publicists from his publishers, sexy young Emma, for instance, whom he'd teased to distraction on the last tour. Or roly-poly Clare with the huge knockers from the tour before. Molly needed to be reminded exactly who she was. It wasn't just a question of responsibilities, it was also a question of manners. He didn't expect deference, just a modicum of respect. But his appearance on the Man Booker shortlist, far from screwing him up a notch or two in Molly's estimation, seemed to have been the signal for a marked increase in that offhand deprecatory familiarity which she liked to think of as her trademark. In the past he'd heard her refer to her distinguished client list as *my performing fleas*. Up till now, like the other fleas, so long as she did the job, he'd opted to grit his teeth and affect amusement. Now, though, he was past all that. Yes, it was time for a serious talk. Or perhaps more than just a talk. There was that flash Yank who'd assured him he could get double his American advance, no sweat, and that was before he'd joined the Booker pantheon. Maybe it was time to part company completely. He pictured doing it over a candle-lit dinner in a room like this. Good food, fine wine, soft music. Then, just as she was relaxing into the certainty of at last enjoying that part of him she'd clearly so long desired, he'd reveal that the only hard and pointed bit of his anatomy she was about to get was the elbow!

He was brought out of this pleasing fantasy by a gentle tap at the door.

He went to open it.

A large trolley stood there. It bore an elegant coffee pot, two plates covered with silver domes, a selection of breakfast cereals, a fresh grapefruit, a basket of croissants, a jug of orange juice, a bottle of champagne in an ice bucket and a vase of orchids. Pushing it was a dark-haired young woman in a fetching black skirt and bolero jacket.

'Good morning, Mr Ansell,' she said with a smile. 'Your breakfast.'

'Thank you,' he said. 'Did I order this?'

He couldn't recall filling in a breakfast card last night. Such trivialities had not been on the agenda.

'Compliments of the management, sir. And may I add my personal congratulations?'

She pushed the trolley into the room alongside the table in the window bay.

Then, running what looked like an appreciative eye over his classical features and an even more appreciative one over his pyjama'd torso, she said, 'Don't let it get cold, sir. Enjoy your breakfast.'

And left.

Nice arse. Reminded him of Toni. Or perhaps it was just

association of ideas. They all had nice arses.

Missed chance there, old son, he told himself. Should have asked her if she'd like to stay and serve me.

Still, there were other appetites which the smell of the fresh croissants had awoken.

He seized the handle of one of the silver domes and lifted it.

To his surprise, instead of the expected bacon, eggs, etc., he found himself looking at a white envelope with his name typed on it.

He picked it up and tore it open.

It contained a single sheet of paper.

He began to read what was typed upon it. After a few moments, he sat down on an elegant chaise longue and began to read again.

And so at last the Boy Wonder has scrambled to the top of the dung-heap!

Or to change my metaphor, the croaking frogs have gathered to cast their vote and once again come up with King Log.

What interests me is, as you listened to that etiolated idiot singing your praises last night – 'such a sharp eye for detail, such a keen ear for nuance, such a fine sense of balance and proportion. Truly here is a writer we can rely on to keep his head while all around are losing theirs . . .' – how much of this crap did you believe? One per cent? Ten per cent? Fifty per cent?

Not all of it?

Surely even you cannot believe all of it?

Or if you allowed the intoxication of the occasion to delude you into believing it last night, surely now in the cold light of morning you blush with embarrassment as the words come back to you? Or perhaps laugh with manic glee at the thought of how much wool you have pulled over all those stupid sheep eyes?

I should like to think so. I should like to believe that you are completely aware that you have done an emperor's-new-clothes job on the baa-ing classes, and that your sharp eye for detail and keen ear for nuance have left you gently amused at the yawning emptiness of it all.

But somehow I doubt it. I think it would take a very loud explosion indeed to blast such self-awareness into that classical head of yours which resembles Michelangelo's statue in one respect at least – it's as hard and dense as marble.

Talking of large explosions, I assume if you're reading this, you lifted the larger of the two plate covers first.

Enjoy your breakfast, Boy.

For a few seconds indignation overcame all other emotions. Then his gaze went to the breakfast trolley and fastened on the second silver dome.

'Oh shit!' he said.

Five seconds later he was running down the corridor. He didn't stop till he'd put several other rooms and a right angle between himself and his own door. None of the few people he met showed much interest in the rapid passage of a man in pyjamas which said something for the class of guest you still got at an old-fashioned five-star hotel. He came across a cleaner talking into a telephone. He took it off her without apology and barked into it, 'Security. Get Security to the fifth floor.' From the look on the woman's face, he saw that she thought this was a good idea too.

Half an hour later he was sitting in the manager's office, wrapped in one of the luxurious bath robes which you would be billed for if you 'accidentally' removed it, drinking coffee laced with whisky, when Molly came in, looking anxious. 'Boy, are you all right? I went up to your room but it's like a war zone up there. What's going on?'

He told her the tale and her thin intelligent face was expressing just the right mixture of concern for his safety and admiration for his sang-froid, which was becoming *plus froid* with each telling, when the door opened to admit a small man wearing a grey suit and an expression that said *I may be tiny but I'm important.*

In his hand he held a transparent plastic bag.

'Mr Ansell,' he said. 'Commander Hewlitt, Special Branch. The bomb squad chaps found this.'

He held up the bag. It contained a white envelope and a sheet of typewritten paper.

Boy peered close and said, 'Yes, that's it. The letter I told your people about.'

'No, sir,' said Hewlitt. 'The bomb squad passed that letter straight out to us in case things went wrong and it got destroyed. It's on its way to the lab now for examination. This letter they found on a plate under the other lid.'

'I don't understand,' said Boy, peering once more at the plastic bag. 'Are you sure there hasn't been a mistake? It looks like the same letter.'

'It is, sir. Except for one word in the penultimate sentence. *Large* has become *small.*'

Molly got there before he did. 'You mean, whichever lid Boy lifted first, he was going to find a letter making him think there could be a bomb under the other one?'

'Exactly, madam. The bomb people are checking the rest of the room but I don't think they'll find anything. So, a silly time-wasting jape.'

'It didn't feel like a jape to me!' said Boy indignantly.

'No, sir. Which is why we take such things seriously. Do

you have any idea who might have perpetrated it? I gather from the letter that you won some kind of award last night?'

'Yes, the Man Booker.'

'Man Booker? That would be for a book, then? You are a writer?'

Molly tried unconvincingly to turn an involuntary guffaw into a fit of coughing.

He glowered at her and snapped, 'Yes, I'm a writer.'

'There would be other contestants for this award?' said Hewlitt. 'Good losers, would you say? Or might one of them have been disappointed enough to seek a stupid revenge?'

'I shouldn't imagine so . . .'

Then he hesitated. Why wouldn't he imagine so?

'Yes, sir?' prompted Hewlitt.

'Look, I'm not accusing anyone, you understand. But one of the writers on the shortlist's an Irishman and you know what they're like with bombs. Then there's that gay Australian, I wouldn't put anything past him. And that little shit from up north, I expect this kind of thing passes for sophisticated humour up in Heckmondwyke.'

'You could be right, sir. I must enquire next time I visit my mother. Perhaps you could give me their names. And were there any other contestants?'

'Nominees,' corrected Ansell. 'It wasn't a game show. Yes, two more, but they are both women.'

'And that puts them out of the running, does it, sir?'

'Well, yes, I think it does, in most cases anyway. Though I say it myself, I get on rather well with women, which is perhaps another reason why some men might feel threatened enough to play a stupid practical joke. Can I go back to my room now?'

'Yes, sir. I'm sure they'll be finished up there now. We'll need a formal statement at some point . . .'

'But later, please, commander,' said Molly. 'Mr Ansell has a press conference in a few minutes. Boy, can you make it? In the circs, I don't think they'll mind hanging around a little while.'

'If they do mind, they can sod off,' said Boy, finishing his coffee and rising.

As he went through the door, Molly shouted after him, 'And remember. Not the houndstooth!'

She'd definitely have to go.

The press conference went very well. All the papers were represented, even the grotties. WRITER WINS MAN BOOKER was a yawn to most tabloids, but PRIZEWINNNER IN BOMB SCARE was worth a couple of paras. The revelation that in fact there wasn't any bomb rather took the gilt off the gingerbread, but Boy's relaxed, self-deprecating narrative plus his undeniably striking profile gave them the chance to present him as a uniquely British hero of a type not very common in these Americanised days.

He played up the image, interrupting some tabloid chick to protest that he was here to talk about his book, not about something as trivial as a threat to his life.

'Okay.' The hack yawned. 'So where did you get the idea for *The Accelerant* from?'

He winced for the benefit of the broadsheets, then gave his usual bland answer and saw her eyes glaze. The truth would have woken her up. He imagined telling it.

'It was this old varsity chum of mine, Piers, actually. He was a med student and with his help, we were into all kinds of shit back in those days. But most of it was targeted on keeping you going, whether it was doing exams or disco dancing till you dropped. As far as seduction juice went, I never really got much beyond slipping in an extra finger of gin with the old orange. I ran into Piers again a year or so back. Consultant at one of the big teaching hospitals. Like old friends often do on meeting, we quickly regressed to our early relationship, and one night after a few jars, he told me about this stuff he sometimes used just to help things along a bit, as he put it. When I realised what he was talking about, I was shocked. More than shocked. Horrified. When he saw this, he justified himself by asking what was the difference between getting a girl legless so you could screw her and slipping her a few drops of some harmless drug which left her without a hangover and next to no memory of what had taken place? I said the difference was about ten years in clink, and quite right too. He got quite heated, assuring me he never used it except when convinced the girl was as eager as he was.

'"You know how they can be," he said. "Positively gagging for it, but that doesn't mean they're not going to keep you waiting till you've gone through all the usual run-up rituals. Now, I don't mind that normally, but sometimes you just don't have the time. That's when an accelerant comes in useful. That's how I look on it, you see. Just an accelerant."

'And that's where I got the idea from. I'd been planning this political novel whose theme was the old one of ends justifying means and the consequent corruption. What I needed to make it fresh and immediate was an in-your-face analogy which would provide the page-turning dynamic to draw in the mass market. And here it was. My theme and my title. *The Accelerant.* I used it. It worked. And that's why I'm here, answering your stupid questions, with the Booker prize in my pocket.'

One day he might talk to them like that. One day when his bank balance was bigger than his life expectancy. But not yet.

So he gave them the usual line and when the bomb threat

questions started up again, he reverted to modest hero mode with only token resistance.

'You knocked 'em in the aisle,' said Molly afterwards. 'Hold back on the personal details with *The Times*. They've got an exclusive on the literary career, but I think we can do a hot deal with one of the tabs for the childhood trauma stuff. You did have childhood trauma, didn't you, Boy.'

'By the bucket load,' he said.

'Good. I'll bring him up to you soon as he arrives. By the way, you should find a few hundred books in your room waiting to be signed. Why don't you make a start on them?'

Signing books was a pain even though he'd reduced his official signature to a single undulating scrawl. And it was worse when you didn't have a skivvy at hand to open the volumes at the title page and stack them to one side as they were done. But it was a necessary evil and he set to with a will, determined to get as many as possible out of the way.

As many as possible turned out to be five.

When he opened the sixth, he found the title page had already been written on.

Still with us, Boy? Not to worry. Just another couple of signatures, then you won't have to worry about signing any more. Ever.

He looked at the tower of books and was tempted to kick it over. But why risk losing your leg for a gesture?

He left the room and went in search of a telephone.

Commander Hewlitt arrived just as the bomb people gave the all clear. They seemed pretty phlegmatic but the commander sounded definitely pissed off. 'False alarms like this tying up large numbers of highly trained personnel are a serious offence, sir. Up to seven years' imprisonment.'

'Is that all? I'd cut his balls off, whoever's responsible,' said Boy.

'Yes, sir. Now a few more questions, then a formal statement . . .'

Once more Molly protested that the pressure on her client's time was too intense to allow diversion, but this time Hewlitt was adamant.

When Molly continued arguing, Boy snapped, 'For God's sake, cancel the *Times* guy. Cancel the Jap lunch too. In fact, cancel everything. God knows what other little surprises this joker has got ready for me. If he's for real, I don't want to be about. And if it's just a pathetic game, soon the sympathy will start running out and I'll just look a laughing stock, which is probably what he wants anyway.'

'So what will you do, sir?' asked Hewlitt.

'I'll go home to Brighton and get on with my work, Commander, in the hope that you will get on with yours and catch the idiot behind these pranks.'

'Probably a good idea, sir,' said Hewlitt. 'But if we could just have that statement first . . .'

Two hours later Ansell climbed out of the elegant Mercedes his publishers had provided, said a curt thank you to the driver and went into his flat. Four years ago, when he bought it, the price had seemed exorbitant even though he'd picked it up at the bottom of a slump. Sea here was like sky in London, you paid through the nose for the privilege of viewing what God had provided free. Now it was worth possibly double the money. Before Booker, he'd played with the notion that if he won, he might sell up and use some of his new earning power to buy something in town. But to get what he had in Brighton in any reasonably central location was going to cost an arm and a leg, and after today's experience, he was no longer sure he wanted to be so near the rotten heart of things, particularly if arms and legs were literally what he might have to pay.

He glanced at his answer machine, which formed the base of a four-foot-high resin copy of Michelangelo's *David* with a telephone as a *cache sexe*. Some slight adjustment to the face made the personal resemblance even stronger, but the phone made it a joke instead of a vanity.

Some adjustment had been necessary to the crotch too, but that was for the lucky ones to find out.

The answer machine registered lots of messages, which was only to be expected.. Everybody loves a winner, he told himself with that cynicism only winners can afford. But it would be nice to relax with a large G and T and let this torrent of praise wash away the day's less pleasant memories.

First things first, though, especially in matters of relaxation. He headed to the bathroom. When the bullets start flying, keep a tight ass, was a piece of veterans' lore he recalled reading somewhere. Perhaps Mailer in *The Naked and the Dead*. Or Kate Adie anywhere. He seemed to have been keeping a tight ass all day. No smart alec reporter was going to be able to remark slyly that Boy Ansell reacted to threats against him by spending an unconscionable time on the loo. But now it was time to let go.

It was worth waiting for, till on the sixth sheet of toilet paper he found the message.

> *What a lucky Boy it is, then! One sheet the less and what worlds away. By such delicate chains do our lives hang.*

He read it again. Unnecessarily. He'd got the message first time. This was an exercise in humiliation. He was meant to go scuttling off to summon the bomb squad once more, this time to work over an unflushed lavatory.

He looked up at the old-fashioned high-level tank from

which a thin golden chain ran down to a metal ball, enamelled to look like planet earth (another of his jokes).

'Sod you!' he said.

And not giving himself time to reflect, he stood up, took the world in his hand, and pulled.

Water rushed and bubbled, the pan emptied. He stood there defiantly till the roar of the tank refilling died to a trickle then a drip. Finally, silence.

'Sod you,' he said again, this time in triumph.

He went back into his living room. The phone rang.

He sat down, unhooking the receiver from the Boy David's crotch.

'Ansell.'

'Boy, it's Molly. Just checking you got home safely.'

He thought of telling her about the latest incident, decided the absurdity outweighed the heroics, and said, 'No problem.'

'Oh good. I'm sorry it turned into such a trying day for you when you should have been simply enjoying your astounding triumph.'

His famous ear for nuance had always been able to spot a put-down at twenty paces. 'Astounding?' he said. 'To whom?'

'To you, I mean. Not to me, of course. But I can't believe that you in your heart of hearts really expected it. Did you?'

'Well, yes, in a way, I always hoped – look, what are you trying to say? That I didn't deserve it?'

He heard her laugh. 'I'm happy to debate *expected* with you, Boy. But I'm sure neither of us has any delusions about *deserved*.'

He opened his mouth, closed it again. He had misheard, he thought. Or was misinterpreting what he'd heard. Don't rush in with a hasty response. Keep control. Don't lose your head. Wasn't that one of the things he was famous for in his writing?

He said, 'You know me, Molly. No vanity. I never went around saying I thought I ought to win the Booker, but now that I have done, I'm certainly not about to quarrel with the verdict of such a distinguished panel of experts.'

'Experts?' She laughed again. 'If your claim to fame rests on being chosen by that bunch of self-regarding prancers, better forget it, darling.'

What had got into her? Not him, perhaps that was the trouble. Or could it be that, pissed off at having to cancel all that carefully organised publicity stuff today, she'd dived into a bottle and was now letting her resentment show? Whatever, it gave him the perfect cue for cutting the cord. And without the expense of a good dinner.

He said mildly, 'If you think so poorly of my books, perhaps it would be better for us both if you no longer had the disagreeable task of trying to sell them.'

See if that shocked her into sobriety.

It didn't.

'Oh, come on, Boy,' she said long-sufferingly. 'What I think about your books is neither here nor there. But surely even you won't grudge me a share of your success, after all the hard work I've put in.'

'All the hard work . . .?' he echoed in genuine puzzlement. 'You mean selling them to publishers who were gagging for them? Or ferrying me around to media events which, incidentally, is a task perhaps better left to my publisher's PR professionals who know how to treat a star.'

That set her laughing again. God, she must be really rat-arsed!

'Jesus, Boy, haven't you caught on yet that when you've got a tour coming up, the girls in the publicity department start going sick in droves? Given a choice between you and King Kong, they'd all be packing their jungle kit. That's why I took over myself, to preserve the peace. So I reckon that the time I spend on that, plus the work I've had to put in on your scripts, makes earning my ten per cent the hardest graft I've ever done.'

'On my scripts? My editor never has to do a thing with them. He says they're among the cleanest scripts he's ever seen. And I've heard you say so yourself.'

'Yeah, yeah, that's for Big Ears and Noddy out there, Boy, that's for the image. Come on, surely it must occur to you to wonder sometimes how your four hundred pages of waffly rambling turn into two fifty of crisp prose? With the spelling correct and the punctuation in the right place? Or perhaps you never read the finished product? Probably wise.'

Suspicions were swirling in his mind like storm clouds, but he wasn't ready yet to admit the tempest blast while he still had some shred of vanity to shelter behind. 'I don't get you. You said . . . you seemed to be saying that you expected me to win last night. That must mean . . .'

'It means that I'd called in more favours than you'd find at a gypsy's wedding, not to mention rattling a whole catacomb of skeletons in judges' cupboards. But that won't keep me awake nights, that's par for the course in the glitzy world of awards. What really bothers me, Boy, is one of the judges said to me afterwards, you needn't have bothered with all the pressure, darling, we all actually thought it was by far the best book. You see what this means? I've created a monster and no one else seems able to spot the stitching!'

Now the tempest broke.

'You bitch!' yelled Boy. 'It was you, wasn't it? These stupid jokes. It was you, trying to humiliate me.'

'Well done, Boy. I wondered how long that famous eye for detail and ear for nuance were going to take to get you there. Yes, indeed. And I actually got to the hotel early enough to see you sprinting down the corridor in your jim-jams. *A writer we can rely on to keep his head . . .* yes, even if it means running around half naked in public! God, you looked terrified!'

'Not so terrified I didn't pull the loo chain just now,' he snarled, defensive despite himself.

'Well done. On the other hand, sometimes a bit of real humiliating fear's not a bad thing, you know. Being brave kills more people than terror, I'd say. Though terror can leave permanent scars on the vulnerable and sensitive.'

'Well, it's not going to leave any scars on me,' he said. The famous control was back. For all he knew she was getting all this down on tape. He mustn't lose his head. 'You're the only one who's going to suffer damage here. We're finished, Molly. And by the time my lawyers are through, I doubt if you'll see a penny of my future earnings. I can't imagine what you thought you were playing at. Such silly pranks. A woman of your age!'

'What's my age got to do with it?'

'I understand strange changes often take place with the menopause. I advise you to see a doctor. Or a psychologist. There's been some good work done on sexual frustration, they tell me.'

'Frustration . . .? You mean I'm not getting enough generally? Or not getting enough of you?'

'You said it,' he replied equably. 'And it's too late now. I'm not in the therapy business.'

'Oh Boy, Boy.' She sighed. 'That sharp eye, that keen ear, and you never caught on during our years together that I'm gay? And here's me thinking it must be that which was protecting me. But now I think about it, you'd probably have regarded it as a challenge, wouldn't you? Get me up to your flat, bucketfuls of boyish charm, rather less of cheap bubbly, then an irresistible offer to let me find out what I'd been missing. You like a challenge, don't you? Toni must have seemed a challenge.'

'Toni?' He laughed triumphantly. 'Is that what this is really about? Young Toni? Now I begin to see things clearly. You found out. It wasn't me you were jealous of, it was her! Grooming her as a little bit on the side, were you? And then you found out she preferred the real thing. So you sacked her and thought you'd play your stupid pranks on me. And I used to think you were a sophisticated woman. I hope you had the decency to give her a good reference. I certainly would! Where is she now?'

'She's safe,' said Molly calmly. 'Recovering. It's going to take a long time, they say. Oh, I warned her that you'd probably have a go at her some time, told her to take no notice and eventually your vanity would make you give up on the grounds that if you hadn't tried anything, you couldn't have been rejected. I never dreamt you'd sink so low, Boy. What did you spike her drink with? Rohypnol, like the guy in your lousy book? Write about what you know, isn't that the advice they dish out on creative writing courses?'

Boy was genuinely horrified. Who the hell did this ancient dyke think she was, taking the moral high line with him? What did she know about good old-fashioned straight sex between a man and a woman? He could look back over a long line of willing and enthusiastic partners, most of whom came back for more, hence his initial revulsion at Piers's confession. Okay, he'd repressed his true feelings in the interests of research but that was the price an artist sometimes had to pay. Practical experience was important and eventually he'd got a sample of the stuff from Piers who, like his victims, was in no position to resist. First of all he tried it out on himself. Result, irresistible drowsiness and when he recovered, a memory gap whose edges were as fuzzy as candy floss. Next had been a woman he was in an intermittent sleeping arrangement with. When she woke up, she'd been apologetic, putting her retreat from full consciousness down to not counting the vodka martinis. After that, he'd only used it a couple of times, certainly not more than three or four, and always in the kind of situation described by Piers where it was merely accelerating the inevitable.

And that's how it had been with Toni. He'd soon seen that a couple of glasses of celebratory champagne weren't going to be enough. She was naïve, she was nervous, but beneath it all, she was ready, he was certain of that. A light lunch in his flat – one of his famous aphrodisiac salads – another bottle of bubbly, a shot of armagnac, and by two o'clock, two thirty at the latest, they'd have been in bed.

The problem was there was this Yankee journalist, nine out of ten attractive and desperate for an interview, who was lunching him at the Grand at one. He contemplated standing her up, but with news of the Booker nomination to drop casually into the conversation, this was too good an opportunity to be missed.

But so was Toni.

It was a situation tailor-made for the Accelerant. So tailor-made that he'd genuinely forgotten that he'd used it and when he did remember, the only regret he felt was that she might not be able to share completely his own delightful memories. He'd kissed her on the forehead as he put her on her train, still apologising for her silliness in letting a little champagne turn her so woozy, and promised himself that next time he would make sure there wasn't any need to rush.

'You still there, Boy? Guilt got your tongue?'

There was a strong temptation to justify himself, but with this bitch, that could be hugely dangerous. *Just keep your head*, he told himself. *Be very careful what you say.*

'Yes, I'm still here,' he said. 'It's simple incomprehension that's reduced me to silence.'

'Come on, Boy! Give it up! Okay, you probably told

yourself all you were doing was speeding up the inevitable, you weren't giving her anything she didn't really want. Just like your cardboard hero. And she wouldn't remember anyway. But she really didn't want it, Boy. And she does remember. In nightmares, in panic attacks. Oh yes, she remembers. It's going to take her a long time to forget.'

'I've no idea what you're talking about,' he said calmly. 'What I do know is, if you repeat any of these monstrous calumnies in public, I shall be obliged, albeit reluctantly, to seek protection from the Law.'

'Ah yes. The Law. That was my first reaction. Call in the police. But Toni got hysterical when I suggested it and Maggie, her sister, said no, it wasn't the way. Interesting woman, Toni's sister. Member of a club I go to. It was her got me to take on Toni in the first place, so we both feel responsible. Now Maggie, she's quite different from Toni. None of her hang-ups. Action woman, looks at life straight on, bags of self-confidence and common sense. Well, I imagine you need all that when you're an officer in the Ordnance Corps. And like a lot of soldiers, she doesn't have much faith in civil justice.'

'No, she wouldn't,' sneered Boy. 'Even in this enlightened age, military dykes can't have very good career prospects. I can see why she'd want to steer clear of the cops.'

'Now I'd never have thought of that, Boy. Must be that famous artistic sensitivity of yours. But don't misunderstand me, just because she's a military dyke, as you put it, doesn't mean she can't pass for normal in the dusk with the light behind her. Or even at dawn. In fact, you can judge for yourself. It was her who served your breakfast this morning. Anyway, we both agreed, no police, unless of course you agreed to plead guilty at the trial and save Toni the trauma of giving evidence?'

'Trial?' He laughed. 'Molly, don't be ridiculous. We both know there isn't going to be a trial. My conscience is clear. I have done nothing wrong except spend a pleasant hour in bed with a willing and enthusiastic young woman.'

Put that on your tape and play it! he told himself gleefully.

'Willing and enthusiastic? Yes, I can see you smiling at the jury and urging them to ask themselves, why would someone as attractive as I am need to resort to foul play to get my end away? You really do think of yourself as the Boy David, don't you? One whirl of your slingshot and the whole world's at your feet. And if they're not worshipping, unconscious will do.'

'Molly, I think you've had some kind of breakdown,' he said with avuncular concern. 'I think you need help. I'm sorry I can't give it, but I advise you to look for someone who can in the near future. No more pranks, please, or I definitely will call in the Law. My solicitor will be in touch anyway about terminating our agreement. I'll instruct him to be generous. Despite everything, I'm grateful for what you've done for my career.'

That would sound well on the tape, if there was a tape.

'That's kind of you, Boy. And don't think I don't recognise your good qualities too. For instance, it was brave of you to pull the loo chain. And you often said things that made me laugh. Okay, they were usually a bit sour and cynical, but they genuinely amused me. Which is why I'm putting in this effort to get you to see reason and face up to things like a man. A grown man, I mean. Okay, it'll be painful and when it's over, you won't be the famous Boy Ansell any more. But you can't stay like that for the rest of your life anyway. You've got to grow up some time. Might even help your writing. So let's talk a bit longer and see if we can't come to some resolution which makes sense to all of us.'

She sounded so genuinely concerned that despite himself he felt touched. But the crack about his writing was the last straw. Who the hell did she think she was, a stringy middle-aged literary leech talking like this to a man with a Booker cheque in his wallet?

He said, 'Molly, there's nothing left to say. I'm going to ring off now.'

She said, 'Boy, don't hang up. I'm warning you, don't hang up. Please.'

But of course he did.

Though perhaps, as he did so, because he was after all a good if somewhat overrated writer and deserving of at least a third of the praise heaped upon him, perhaps his keen ear for nuance detected that there was more of appeal than threat in Molly's words.

Then perhaps his sharp eye for detail reminded him that Toni's sister was an officer in the Ordnance Corps.

And perhaps there was even time for his fine sense of balance and proportion to register that there was something not quite right about the set of the shoulders on Michelangelo's statue, as if someone had been mucking about with the resin.

But there was no way even his brilliant mind could put all these things together in time to abort replacing the phone on the statue's crotch.

Which was when both Boy Davids lost their heads together.

LIKE AN
ARRANGEMENT

Bill James

Not everyone realised that the thing about Assistant Chief Constable Desmond Iles was he longed to be loved. Among those who did realise it, of course, a good number refused to respond and instead muttered privately, 'Go fuck yourself, Iles.' A very good number. On the other hand, there was certainly a young ethnic whore in the docks who worshipped the A.C.C. unstintingly, and he would have been truly hurt if anyone said it was because he paid well.

What Iles totally abominated was people who came to esteem him only because he had contributed or helped in some way: say a piece of grand, devastating violence carried out by the A.C.C. for them against one of their enemies. He despised such calculating, *quid pro quo*ism, as he called it. Once, he had told Harpur he utterly disregarded love that could be accounted for and reckoned up. Harpur felt happy the A.C.C. received from his docks friend, Honorée, and from Fanny, his infant daughter, the differing but infinite affection he craved. Also, Iles's wife, Sarah, definitely possessed some quaint fondness for him, quite often at least. She had mentioned this to Harpur unprompted in one of their quiet moments.

To Harpur, it seemed that much of Iles's behaviour could be explained by this need for completely spontaneous, instinctive, wholehearted devotion. Think of that unpleasant incident at the Taldamon School prize-giving, for instance. Although Iles would regard the kind of physical savagery he was forced into there as merely routine for him, it had made one eighteen-year-old girl pupil switch abruptly from fending off the A.C.C. sexually to offering an urgent come-on. This enraged Iles. He had been doing all he could to attract the girl, probably as potential stand-by in case Honorée were working away some time at a World Cup or Church of England Synod. Totally no go. And then, within minutes, the Taldamon girl suddenly changed and clearly grew interested in Iles, simply because he had felled and disarmed some bastard in the stately school assembly hall, and kicked him a few times absolutely unfatally about the head and neck where he lay on the floor between chair rows. Colin Harpur instantly knew the A.C.C. would regard this turnaround by the girl as contemptible: as grossly undiscerning about Iles, as Iles. That is, the essence of Ilesness, not simply his rabbit punching and kicking flairs, which could be viewed as superficial: as attractive, perhaps, but mere accessories to his core self. Harpur saw at the end of this episode that the A.C.C. wished to get away immediately from the girl and return to Honorée for pure, unconditional adoration even, if necessary, on waste ground.

It was some school: private, of course, and residential, and right up there with Eton and Harrow for fees. In fact, it cost somewhere near the national average wage to keep a child at Taldamon for a year, and this without the geology trip to Iceland, the horse riding and extra coaching in lacrosse and timpani. Harpur and Iles – Iles particularly – were interested in Taldamon because the police funded one of its pupils during her entire school career. This was an idea picked up from France. Over there, it had long been police practice to meet the education expenses for the child or children of a valuable and regular informant, as one way of paying for tipoffs. The scheme convinced Iles and others. It was considered less obvious – less dangerous – than to give an informant big cash rewards, which he/she might spend in a stupid, ostentatious way, drawing attention to his/her special income. That could mean the informant was no longer able to get close to villains' secrets because the villains would have him/her identified as a leak. It could also mean that his/her life was endangered. A child out of sight at a pricey school in North Wales would be less noticeable. Or this was the thinking.

They had put Wayne Ridout's daughter, Fay-Alice, into Taldamon, from the age of thirteen, and now here she was at eighteen, head prefect, multi-prizewinner, captain of lacrosse, captain of swimming and water polo, central to the school orchestra, destined for Oxford, slim, straight-nosed, sweet-skinned, and able to hold Iles off with cold, foul-mouthed ease until . . . until she decided she did not want to hold him off, following a gross rush of disgusting gratitude: disgusting, that is, as Harpur guessed the A.C.C. would regard it.

Harpur and Iles would not normally attend this kind of function. The presence of police might be a give-away. But Wayne had pleaded with Iles to come, and pleaded a little less fervently with Harpur, also. It was not just that Wayne wanted them to see the glorious results of their grass-related investment in Fay-Alice. Harpur knew from a few recent conversations with Wayne that he had felt down lately. Because of her education and the social status of Taldamon, Ridout sensed his daughter might be growing away from him and her mother, Nora. This grieved both, but especially Wayne. His wife seemed to regard the change in Fay-Alice as normal. Harpur imagined she probably saw it on behalf of the girl like this: when your father's main career had been fink and general crook rather than archbishop or TV game show host, there was only one way for the next generation to go socially – up and away. Regrettable but inevitable.

Wayne could not accept such sad distancing. He must reason that if he were seen at this important school function accompanied by an Assistant Chief Constable, who had on the kind of magnificent suit and shoes Iles favoured, and who behaved in his well-known Shah of Persia style, it was bound to restore Fay-Alice's respect for her parents. And it would impress the girl's friends and teachers. For these possible gains, Wayne had evidently decided to put up with the security risk in this one-off event. Harpur doubted Fay-Alice would see things as her father did and thought he and the A.C.C. should not attend. But Iles agreed the visit and addressed Harpur for a while about 'overriding obligations to those who sporadically assist law and order, even a fat, villainous, ugly, dim sod like Wayne'. The A.C.C. was always shudderingly eager to get among teenage schoolgirls if they looked clean and wore light summery clothes.

It was only out of politeness that Wayne had asked Harpur. As Detective Chief Superintendent, Harpur lacked the glow of staff rank and could not tog himself out with the same distinction as Iles. In fact, the A.C.C. had seemed not wholly sure Harpur should accompany him. 'This will be a school with gold-lettered award boards on the wall, naming pupils who've gone on not just to Oxbridge or management courses with the Little Chef restaurant chain, but Harvard, Vatican seminaries, even Time Share selling in Alicante. There'll be ambience. Does ambience get into your vocab at all, Harpur? I know this kind of academy right through, from my own school background, of course. I'd hate you to feel in any way disadvantaged by *your* education, but I ask you,

Col – do you think you can you fit into such a place as Taldamon with that fucking haircut and your garments?'

'This kind of occasion does make me think back to end of term at my own school, sir,' Harpur reminisced gently.

'And what did they give leaving prizes to eighteen-year-olds for there – knowing the two-times table, speed at dewristing tourists' Rolexes?'

'Should we go armed?' Harpur replied.

'This is a wholesome occasion at a prime girls' school, for God's sake, Col.'

'Should we go armed?' Harpur said.

Iles said, 'I'd hate it if some delightful pupil, inadvertently brushing against me, should feel only the brutal outline of a holstered pistol, Harpur.'

'This sort of school, they're probably taught never to brush inadvertently against people like you, sir. It would be stressed in deportment classes, plus during the domestic science module for classifying moisture marks on trousers.'

Iles's voice grew throaty and his breathing loud and needful: 'I gather she's become a star now as scholar, swimmer, musician and so on, but I can remember Fay-Alice when she was only a kid, though developing, certainly . . . developing, yes, certainly, *developing*, but really only just a kid . . . although . . . well, yes, *developing*, and we went to the Ridout house to advise them that she should –'

'There are people who'd like to do Wayne. He's helped put all sorts inside. They have brothers, colleagues, sons, fathers, mothers. Perhaps the word's around he'll be on a plate at Taldamon, ambience-hooked, relaxed, unvigilant.'

'A striking-looking child, even then,' Iles replied, 'despite Wayne and his complexion. A wonderful long, slender back, as I recall. Do *you* recall that, Harpur – the long slender back? Do you think of backs ever? Or was it the era when you were so damn busy giving it to my wife you didn't have time to notice much else at all?' Iles began to screech in the frenzied seagull tone that would take him over sometimes when speaking of Harpur and Sarah.

Harpur said, 'If we're there we ought at least to –'

'I mean her back in addition to the way she was, well –?'

'Developing.'

This long back Fay-Alice unquestionably still had, and the development elsewhere seemed to have continued as it generally would for a girl between thirteen and eighteen. A little tea party had been arranged on the pleasant lawns at Taldamon before the prize-giving, out of consideration for parents who travelled a long way and needed refreshment. It was June, a good, hot, blue-skied day. 'Here's a dear, dear acquaintance of mine, Fay-Alice,' Wayne said. 'Assistant Chief Constable Desmond Iles. And Chief Superintendent Harpur.'

Iles gave her a true conquistador smile, yet a smile which also sought to hint at his sensitivity, honour, beguiling polish and famed restraint. Fay-Alice returned this smile with one that was hostile, nauseated and extremely brief but which still managed to signal over her teacup, *Police? So how come you're friends of my father, and who let you in here, anyway?* Was it just normal schoolgirl prejudice against cops or did she have some idea that daddy's career might be lifelong dubious – even some idea that her schooling and Wayne's career could be unwholesomely related? This must be a bright kid, able to win prizes and an Oxford place. She'd have antennae as well as the long back.

'Fay-Alice's prizes are in French literature, history of art and classics,' Wayne said.

'Won't mean a thing to Col,' Iles replied.

'I wondered if there'd been strangers around the school lately,' Harpur said, 'possibly asking questions about the programme today, looking at the layout.'

152

'Which strangers?' Fay-Alice replied.

'Strangers,' Harpur said. 'A man, or men, probably.'

'Why would they?' the girl asked.

'You know, French lit. is something I can't get enough of,' the A.C.C. said.

'Mr Iles, personally, did a lot with education, right up to the very heaviest levels, Fay-Alice,' Wayne said. 'Don't be fooled just because he's police.'

'Yes, why are you concerned about strangers, Mr Harpur?' Nora Ridout asked.

'Are you two trying to put the frighteners on us, the way pigs always do?' Fay-Alice said.

'I recall Alphonse de Lamartine and his poem "The Lake",' Iles replied.

'Alphonse is a French name for sure,' Wayne said. 'There you are, Fay-Alice – didn't I tell you, Mr Iles can go straight to it, no messing? Books are meat and drink to him.'

Iles leaned towards her and recited: ' "Oh, Time, will you not stop a while so we may savour the swiftly passing pleasures of our loveliest days?" '

'Meat and drink,' Wayne said.

'Don't you find Lamartine's plea an inspiration, Fay-Alice?' Iles asked. 'Savour. A word I thrill to. The sensuousness of it, together with the tragic hint of enjoying something wonderful, yet elusive.' He began to tremble slightly and reached out a hand, as if to touch Fay-Alice's long back or some conjoint region. But moving quickly towards the plate of sandwiches on a garden table, Harpur put himself between the A.C.C. and her. He took Iles's pleaful, savour-seeking fingers on the lapel of his jacket. In any case, Fay-Alice had stepped back immediately she saw the A.C.C.'s hand approach and for a moment looked as if she was about to grab his arm and possibly break it in some kind of anti-rape drill.

'Or the history of art,' Wayne said. 'That's another terrific realm. This could overlap with French literature because while the poets were writing their verses in France there would be neighbours, in the same street most probably, painting and making sculptures in their attics. The French are known for it – easels, smocks, everything. It's the light in those parts – great for art but also useful when people wanted to write a poem outside. In a way it all ties up. That's the thing about culture, especially French. A lot of strands.'

'And you'll be coming home to live with Mother and Father until Oxford now, and in the nice long vacations, will you, Fay-Alice?' Iles asked.

'Why?' she replied.

Iles said, 'It's just that –'

'I don't understand how you know my father,' she replied.

'Oh, Mr Iles and I – this is a real far-back association,' Wayne said.

'But how exactly?' she asked. 'He's never been to our house, has he? I've never heard you speak of him, Dad.'

'This is like an arrangement, Fay-Alice,' Nora Ridout replied.

'What kind of arrangement?' Fay-Alice asked.

'Yes, like an arrangement,' Nora Ridout replied.

'A business arrangement?' Fay-Alice asked.

'You can see how such a go-ahead school makes them put all the damn sharp queries, Mr Iles,' Wayne said. 'I love it. This is what I believe they call intellectual curiosity, used by many of the country's topmost on their way to discoveries such as medical and DVDs. What they will not do, girls at this school – and especially girls who do really well, such as Fay-Alice – what they will not do is take something as right just because they're told it. Oh, no. Rigour's another word for this attitude, I believe. Not like rigor mortis but rigour in their thoughts and decisions. It's a school that teaches them how to sort out the men from the boys re brain power.'

'So, does the school come into it somehow?' Fay-Alice asked. 'Does it? Does it? How are these two linked with the school, Dad, Mum?' She hammered at the question, yet Harpur thought she feared an answer.

'Linked?' Iles said. 'Linked? Oh, just a pleasant excursion for Mr Harpur and myself, thanks to the thoughtfulness of your father, Fay-Alice.'

'A business or social arrangement?' Fay-Alice asked.

'No, no, not a business arrangement. How could it be a business arrangement?' Wayne replied, laughing.

'Social?' Fay-Alice asked.

'It's *sort* of social,' Wayne said.

'So, if it's friendship why do you call him Mr Iles, not Desmond, his first name?' Fay-Alice asked.

'See what I mean about the queries, Mr Iles? I heard the motto of this school is "Seek ever the truth", but in a classical tongue which provides many a motto around the country on account of tradition. You can't beat the classics if you want to hit the right note.'

The A.C.C. said, 'And I understand swimming has become a pursuit of yours, Fay-Alice. Excellent for the body. You must get along to the municipal pool at home. I should go there more often myself. Certainly I shall. This will be an experience – to see you active in the water, your arms and legs really working, wake a-glisten.' Beautifully symmetric circles of sweat appeared on each of his temples, each the size of a two-penny piece, although the group were still outside on the lawn and under the shade of a eucalyptus. 'The butterfly stroke – strenuous upper torso exercise, but useful for toning everything, don't you agree, Fay-Alice? Toning *everything*. Oh, I look forward to that. Wayne, it will be a treat to have Fay-Alice around in the breaks from Oxford.'

'Aren't you a bit old for the butterfly?' she said. 'I hate watching a heart attack in the fast lane, all those desperate bubbles and the sudden incontinence.'

Iles chuckled, obviously in tribute to her aggression and jauntiness. 'Oh, look, Fay-Alice –'

'We don't really need *flics* here, thank you,' she replied. 'So why don't you just piss off back to your interrogation suite alone and play with yourself, Iles?' Harpur decided that, even without pre-knowledge from its brochure, anyone could have recognised this as an outstandingly select school where articulateness was prized and deftly inculcated.

In the fine wide assembly hall, he appreciatively watched Fay-Alice on the platform stride out with her long back et cetera to receive prizes from the Lord Lieutenant. He seemed to do quite an amount of congratulatory talking to and hand shaking with Fay-Alice before conferring her trophies. All at once, then, Harpur realised that Iles had gone from the seat alongside him. For a moment, Harpur wondered whether the A.C.C. intended attacking the Lord Lieutenant for infringing on Fay-Alice and half stood in case he had to move forward and try to throw Iles to the ground and suppress him.

They had been placed at the end of a row, Iles to Harpur's right next to the gangway, Wayne and Nora on his left. To help keep the hall cool, all doors were open. Glancing away from the platform now, Harpur saw Iles run out through the nearest door, as if chasing someone, fine black lace-ups flashing richly in the sunshine. He disappeared. On stage, the presentations continued. Harpur sat down properly again. The A.C.C.'s objective was not the Lord Lieutenant.

After about a minute, Harpur heard noises from the back of the hall and, turning, saw a man wearing a yellow and magenta crash helmet and face-guard enter via another open door and dash between some empty rows of seats. At an elegant sprint Iles appeared through the same door shortly afterwards. The man in the helmet stopped, spun and, pulling an automatic pistol from his waistband, pointed it at Iles, perhaps a Browning 140 DA. The A.C.C. swung himself hard to one side and crouched as the gun fired. Then he leaned far forward and used a fierce sweep of his left fist to knock the automatic from the man's hand. With his clenched right, Iles struck him two short, rapid blows in the neck, just below the helmet. At once, he fell. Iles had been in the row behind, but now clambered over the chair backs to reach him. Harpur could not make out the man on the floor but saw Iles provide a brilliant kicking, though without thuggish shouts, so as not to disturb the prize-giving. Often Iles was damn fussy about decorum. He had mentioned his own quality schooling and this intermittent respect for protocol might date from then.

But because of the gunfire and activity at the rear of the hall, the ceremony had already faltered. Iles bent down and came up with the automatic. 'Please, do continue,' he called out to the Lord Lieutenant and other folk on the stage, waving the weapon in a slow, soothing arc, to demonstrate its harmlessness now. 'Things are all right here, oh, yes.' Iles was not big yet looked unusually tall among the chairs and might be standing on the gunman's face. A beam of sunlight reached in through a window and gave his neat features a good yet unmanic gleam.

Afterwards, when the local police and ambulance people had taken the intruder away, Harpur and Iles waited at the end of the hall while the guests, school staff and plat-form dignitaries dispersed. Wayne, Nora and Fay-Alice approached, Wayne carrying Fay-Alice's award volumes. 'Had that man come for me?' he asked. 'For me? Why?' He looked terrified.

'My God,' Nora said.

'Someone hired for a hit?' Wayne asked.

'I'd think so,' Iles said.

'All sorts would want to commission him, Wayne,' Harpur said. 'You're a target.'

'My God,' Nora said.

'Someone had you marked, Wayne,' Harpur said.

'He'd have gone for you in the mêlée as the crowd departed at the end of the do, I should think,' Iles said.

'But how did you spot him, Mr Iles?' Nora asked.

'I'm trained always to wonder about people at girls' school prize-givings with their face obscured by a crash helmet and obviously tooled up,' Iles said. 'There was a whole lecture course on it at Staff College.'

'Why on earth did he come back into the hall?' Nora asked.

'He would still have had a shot at Wayne, as long as he could knock me out of the way,' Iles said. 'He had orders. He's taken a fee, I expect. He'd be scared to fail.'

'Oh, you saved Daddy, Mr Iles,' Fay-Alice replied, riotously clapping her slim hands. 'An Assistant Chief Constable accepting such nitty-gritty, perilous work on our behalf, and when so brilliantly dressed, too! It was wonderful – so brave, so skilful, so selfless. I watched mesmerised, but *mesmerised,* absolutely. A privilege, I mean it. Thank you, Mr Iles. You so deserve our trust.' She inclined herself towards him, the long back stretching longer, and would have touched the A.C.C.'s arm. He skipped out of reach. 'We shall have so much to talk about at the swimming pool back home,' she said. 'I do look forward to it.'

'Let's get away now, Harpur,' Iles snarled.

'Yes, I must show you my butterfly, Mr Iles,' Fay-Alice said. 'Desmond.'

'Let's get away now, Harpur,' Iles replied.

UNTIL GWEN

Dennis Lehane

Your father picks you up from prison in a stolen Dodge Neon with an eight-ball in the glove compartment and a hooker named Mandy in the back seat. Two minutes into the ride, the prison still hanging tilted in the rear-view, Mandy tells you that she only hooks part-time. The rest of the time she does light secretarial for an independent video chain and tends bar two Sundays a month at the local VFW. But she feels her calling – her true calling in life – is to write.

You go, 'Books?'

'Books.' She snorts, half out of amusement, half to shoot a line off your fist and up her left nostril. 'Screenplays!' She shouts it at the dome light for some reason. 'You know – movies.'

'Tell him the one about the psycho saint guy,' your father says. 'That would put my ass in the seat.' Your father winks at you in the rear-view, like he's driving the two of you to the prom. 'Go ahead. Tell him.'

'Okay, okay.' She turns on the seat to face you and your knees touch, and you think of Gwen, a look she gave you once, nothing special, just looking back at you as she stood at the front door, asking if you'd seen her keys. A forgettable

161

moment if ever there was one but you spent four years in prison remembering it.

'. . . so at his canonisation,' Mandy is saying, 'something, like, happens? And his spirit comes *back* and goes into the body of this priest. But, like, the priest? He has a brain tumor. He doesn't know it or nothing but he does, and it's fucking up his, um –'

'Brain?' you try.

'Thoughts,' Mandy says. 'So he gets this saint in him and that *does it*, because like even though the guy was a saint, his spirit has become evil because his soul is gone. So this priest? He spends the rest of the movie trying to kill the Pope.'

'Why?'

'Just listen,' your father says. 'It gets good.'

You look out the window. A car sits empty along the shoulder. It's beige and someone has painted gold wings on the sides, fanning out from the front bumper and across the doors, and a sign is affixed to the roof with some words on it, but you've passed it by the time you think to wonder what it says.

'See, there's this secret group that works for the Vatican? They're like a, like a . . .'

'A hit squad,' your father says.

'Exactly,' Mandy says and presses her finger to your nose. 'And the lead guy, the, like, head agent? He's the hero. He lost his wife and daughter in a terrorist attack on the Vatican a few years back, so he's a little fucked up, but –'

You say, 'Terrorists attacked the Vatican?'

'Huh?'

You look at her, waiting. She has a small face, eyes too close to her nose.

'In the *movie*,' Mandy says. 'Not in real life.'

'Oh. I just, you know, four years inside, you assume you miss a couple of headlines, but . . .'

'Right.' Her face dark and squally now. 'Can I finish?'

'I'm just saying,' you say and snort another line off your fist, 'even the guys on Death Row would have heard about that one.'

'Just go with it,' your father says. 'It's not like real life.'

You look out the window, see a guy in a chicken suit carrying a can of gas in the breakdown lane, think how real life isn't like real life. Probably more like this poor dumb bastard running out of gas in a car with wings painted on it. Wondering how the hell he ever got here. Wondering who he'd pissed off in that previous real life.

Your father has rented two rooms at an EconoLodge so you and Mandy can have some privacy, but you send Mandy home after she twice interrupts the blowjob she's giving you to pontificate on the merits of Michael Bay films.

You sit in the blue-wash flicker of ESPN and eat peanuts from a plastic sleeve you got out of a vending machine and drink plastic cupfuls of Jim Beam from a bottle your father presented when you reached the parking lot. You think of the time you've lost and how nice it is to sit alone on a double bed and watch TV, and you think of Gwen, can taste her tongue for just a moment, and you think about the road that's led you here to this motel room on this night after forty-seven months in prison and how a lot of people would say it was a twisted road, a weird one, filled with curves, but you just think of it as a road like any other. You drive down it on faith or because you have no other choice and you find out what it's like by the driving of it, find out what the end looks like only by reaching it.

Late the next morning, your father wakes you, tells you he drove Mandy home and you've got things to do, people to see.

Here's what you know about your father above all else – people have a way of vanishing in his company.

He's a professional thief, consummate con man, expert in his field, and yet there's something far beyond professionalism at his core, something unreasonably arbitrary. Something he keeps within himself like a story he heard once, laughed at maybe, yet swore never to repeat.

'She was with you last night?' you say.

'You didn't want her. Somebody had to prop her ego back up. Poor girl like that.'

'But you drove her home,' you say.

'I'm speaking Czech?'

You hold his eyes for a bit. They're big and bland, with the heartless innocence of a newborn's. Nothing moves in them, nothing breathes, and after a while, you say, 'Let me take a shower.'

'Fuck the shower,' he says. 'Throw on a baseball cap and let's get.'

You take the shower anyway, just to feel it, another of those things you would have realised you'd miss if you'd given it any thought ahead of time, standing under the spray, no one near you, all the hot water you want for as long as you want it, shampoo that doesn't smell like factory smoke.

Drying your hair and brushing your teeth, you can hear the old man flicking through channels, never pausing on one for more than thirty seconds: Home Shopping network – zap. Springer – zap. Oprah – zap. Soap opera voices; soap opera music – zap. Monster truck show – pause. Commercial – zap, zap, zap.

You come back into the room, steam trailing you, and pick your jeans up off the bed, put them on.

The old man says, 'Afraid you'd drowned. Worried I'd have to take a plunger to the drain, suck you back up.'

You say, 'Where we going?'

'Take a drive,' your father says with a small shrug, flicks past a cartoon.

'Last time you said that, I got shot twice.'

Your father looks back over his shoulder at you, eyes big and soft like a six-year-old's. 'Wasn't the car that shot you, was it?'

You go out to Gwen's place but she isn't there any more, a couple of black kids playing in the front yard, black mother coming out on the porch to look at the strange car idling in front of her house.

'You didn't leave it here?' your father says.

'Not that I recall.'

'Think.'

'I'm thinking.'

'So you didn't?'

'I told you – not that I recall.'

'So you're sure.'

'Pretty much.'

'You had a bullet in your head.'

'Two.'

'I thought one glanced off.'

You say, 'Two bullets hit your fucking head, old man, you don't get hung up on the particulars.'

'That how it works?' Your father pulls away from the curb as the woman comes down the steps.

The first shot came through the back window, and Gentleman Pete flinched big-time, jammed the wheel to the right and drove the car straight into the highway exit barrier, air bags exploding, water barrels exploding, something in the back of your head exploding, glass pebbles filling your shirt, Gwen going, 'What happened? Jesus. What happened?'

You pulled her with you out the back door – Gwen, your

Gwen – and you crossed the exit ramp and ran into the woods and the second shot hit you there but you kept going, not sure how, not sure why, the blood pouring down your face, your head on fire, burning so bright and so hard that not even the rain could cool it off.

'And you don't remember nothing else?' your father says. You've driven all over town, every street, every dirt road, every hollow there is to stumble across in Stuckley, West Virginia.

'Not till she dropped me off at the hospital.'

'Dumb fucking move if ever there was one.'

'I seem to remember I was puking blood by that point, talking all funny.'

'Oh, you remember that. Sure.'

'You're telling me, in all this time, you never talked to Gwen?'

'Like I told you three years back, that girl got gone.'

You know Gwen. You love Gwen. This part of it is hard to take. There was Gwen in your car and Gwen in the corn stalks and Gwen in her mother's bed in the hour just before noon, naked and soft with tremors, and you watched a drop of sweat appear from her hairline and slide down the side of her neck as she snored against your shoulder blade and the top of her foot was pressed under the arch of yours and you watched her sleep, and you were so awake.

'So it's with her,' you say.

'No,' the old man says, a bit of anger creeping into his puppy-fur voice. 'You called me. That night.'

'I did?'

'Shit, boy. You called me from the pay phone outside the hospital.'

'What'd I say?'

'You said, "I hid it. It's safe. No one knows where but me."'

166

'Wow,' you say. 'I said all that? Then what'd I say?'

The old man shakes his head. 'Cops were pulling up by then, calling you motherfucker, telling you to drop the phone. You hung up.'

The old man pulls up outside a low-slung, red-brick building behind a tire dealership on Oak Street. He kills the engine and gets out of the car and you follow. The building is two stories. The businesses facing the street are a bail bondsman, a hardware store, a Chinese take-out place with greasy walls the color of an old dog's teeth, a hair salon called Girlfriend Hooked Me Up that's filled with black women. Around the back, past the whitewashed windows of what was once a dry-cleaner, is a small black door with the words True-Line Efficiency Experts Corp., stenciled into the frosted glass.

The old man unlocks the door and leads you into a ten-by-ten room that smells of roast chicken and varnish. He pulls the string of a bare light bulb and you look around at a floor strewn with envelopes and paper, the only piece of furniture a broken-down desk probably left behind by the previous tenant.

Your father crab-walks across the floor, picking up the envelopes that have come through the mail slot, kicking his way through the paper. You pick up one of the pieces of paper, read it:

Dear Sirs,

Please find enclosed my check for fifty dollars. I look forward to receiving the information packet we discussed as well as the sample test. I have enclosed a SASE to help facilitate this process. I hope to see you someday at the airport!
Sincerely,
Jackson A. Willis

You let it drop to the floor, pick up another one:

> *To Whom It May Concern:*
>
> *Two months ago, I sent a money order in the amount of fifty dollars to your company in order that I may receive an information packet and sample test so that I could take the US government test and become a security handler and fulfill my patriotic duty against them al Qadas. I have not received my information packet as yet and no one answers when I call your phone. Please send me that information packet so I can get that job.*
>
> *Yours truly,*
> *Edwin Voeguarde*
> *12 Hinckley Street*
> *Youngstown, OH 33415*

You drop this one to the floor, too, watch your father sit on the corner of the desk and open his fresh pile of envelopes with a penknife. He reads some, pauses only long enough with others to shake the checks free and drop the rest to the floor.

You let yourself out, go to the Chinese place and buy a cup of Coke, go into the hardware store and buy a knife with a quick-flick hinge in the hasp, buy a couple of tubes of Krazy Glue, go back into your father's office.

'What're you selling this time?' you say.

'Airport security jobs,' he says, still opening envelopes. 'It's a booming market. Everyone wants in. Stop them bad guys before they get on the plane, make the papers, serve your country and maybe be lucky enough to get posted near one of them Starbucks kiosks. Hell.'

'How much you made?'

Your father shrugs even though you're certain he knows

the figure right down to the last penny. 'I've done all right. Hell else am I going to do, back in this shit town for three months, waiting on you? 'Bout time to shut this down, though.' He holds up a stack of about sixty checks. 'Deposit these and cash out the account. First two months, though? I was getting a thousand, fifteen hundred checks a week. Thank the good Lord for being selective with the brain tissue, you know?'

'Why?' you say.

'Why what?'

'Why you been hanging around for three months?'

Your father looks up from the stack of checks, squints. 'To prepare a proper welcome for you.'

'A bottle of whiskey and a hooker who gives shitty head? That took you three months?'

Your father squints a little more and you see a shaft of gray between the two of you, not quite what you'd call light and it sure isn't the sun, just a shaft of air or atmosphere or something, swimming with motes, your father on the other side of it looking at you like he can't quite believe you're related.

After a minute or so, your father says, 'Yeah.'

Your father told you once you'd been born in New Jersey. Another time he said New Mexico. Then Idaho. Drunk as a skunk a few months before you got shot, he said, 'No, no. I'll tell you the truth. You were born in Las Vegas. That's in Nevada.'

You went on the Internet to look yourself up, never did find anything.

Your mother died when you were seven. You've sat up occasionally and tried to picture her face. Some nights, you can't see her at all. Some nights, you'll get a quick glimpse of her eyes or her jawline, see her standing by the foot of her bed, rolling her stockings on, and suddenly she'll appear whole cloth, whole human, and you can smell her.

Most times, though, it's somewhere in between. You see a smile she gave you and then she'll vanish. See a spatula she held, dripping with pancake batter, her eyes burning for some reason, her mouth an 'O', and then her face is gone and all you can see is the wallpaper. And the spatula.

You asked your father once why there were no pictures of her. Why hadn't he taken a picture of her? Just one lousy picture?

He said, 'You think it'd bring her back? No, I mean, do you? Wow,' he said and rubbed his chin. 'Wouldn't that be cool.'

You said, 'Forget it.'

'Maybe if we had a whole album of pictures?' your father said. 'She'd like pop out from time to time, make us breakfast.'

Now that you've been in prison, there's documentation on you, but even they'd had to make it up, take your name on as much faith as you. You have no social security number or birth certificate, no passport. You've never held a job.

Gwen said to you once, 'You don't have anyone to tell you who you are, so you don't *need* anyone to tell you. You just are who you are. You're beautiful.'

And with Gwen, that was usually enough. You didn't need to be defined – by your father, your mother, by a place of birth, a name on a credit card, driver's license, the upper left corner of a check. As long as her definition of you was something she could live with, then you could too.

You find yourself standing in a Nebraska wheat field. You're seventeen years old. You learned to drive five years ago. You were in school once, for two months when you were eight, but you read well and you can multiply three-digit numbers in your head faster than a calculator, and you've seen the country with the old man. You've learned people aren't that smart. You've learned how to pull lottery ticket scams and asphalt paving scams and get free meals with a slight upturn of your brown eyes. You've learned that if you hold ten dollars in front of a stranger, he'll pay twenty to get his hands on it if you play him right. You've learned that every good lie is threaded with truth and every accepted truth leaks with lies.

You're seventeen years old in that wheat field. The night breeze smells of wood smoke and feels like dry fingers as it lifts your bangs off your forehead. You remember everything about that night because it is the night you met Gwen. You are two years away from prison and you feel like someone has finally given you permission to live.

This is what few people know about Stuckley, West Virginia – every now and then, someone finds a diamond. They were in a plane that went down in a storm in 'fifty-one, already blown well off course, flying a crate of Israeli stones down the Eastern seaboard toward Miami. Plane went down in a coal mine, torched Shaft Number 3, took some swing shift miners with it. The government showed up along with members of an international gem consortium, got the bodies out of there and went to work looking for the diamonds. Found most of them, or so they claimed, but for decades afterward there were rumors, given occasional credence by the sudden sight of a miner still grimed brown by the shafts, tooling around town in a Cadillac.

You'd been here peddling hurricane insurance in trailer parks when word got around that someone had found one as big as a casino chip. Miner by the name of George Brunda, suddenly buying drinks, talking to his travel agent. You and

Gwen shot pool with him one night and you could see it in the bulges under his eyes, the way his laughter exploded – too high, too fast, gone chalky with fear.

He didn't have much time, old George, and he knew it, but he had a mother in a rest home, and he was making the arrangements to get her transferred. George was a fleshy guy, triple-chinned, and dreams he'd probably forgotten he'd ever had were rediscovered and weighted in his face, jangling and pulling the flesh.

'Probably hasn't been laid in twenty years,' Gwen said when George went to the bathroom. 'It's sad. Poor sad George. Never knew love.'

Her pool stick pressed against your chest as she kissed you and you could taste the tequila, the salt and the lime on her tongue.

'Never knew love,' she whispered in your ear, an ache in the whisper.

'What about the fairgrounds?' your father says as you leave the office of True-Line Efficiency Experts Corp. 'Maybe you hid it there. You always had a fondness for that place.'

You feel a small hitch. In your leg, let's say. Just a tiny clutching sensation in the back of your right calf, but you walk through it, and it goes away.

You say to your father as you reach the car, 'You really drive her home this morning?'

'Who?'

'Mandy?'

'Who's . . .?' Your father opens his door, looks at you over it. 'Oh, the whore?'

'Yeah.'

'Did I drive her home?'

'Yeah.'

Your father pats the top of the door, his denim jacket

flapping around his wrist, his eyes the blue of bullet casing. You feel, as you always have, reflected in them, even when you aren't, couldn't be, wouldn't be.

'Did I drive her home?' A smile bounces in the rubber of your father's face.

'Did you drive her home?' you say.

That smile's all over the place now, the eyebrows too. 'Define home.'

You say, 'I wouldn't know, would I?'

'You're still pissed at me because I killed Fat Fuck.'

'George.'

'What?'

'His name was George.'

'He would have ratted.'

'To who? It wasn't like he could file a claim. Wasn't a fucking lottery ticket.'

Your father shrugs, looks off down the street.

'I just want to know if you drove her home.'

'I drove her home,' your father says.

'Yeah?'

'Oh, sure.'

'Where'd she live?'

'Home,' he says and gets behind the wheel, starts the ignition.

You never figured George Brunda for smart and it was only after a full day in his house, going through everything down to the point of removing the dri-wall and putting it back, touching up the paint, resealing it, that Gwen said, 'Where's the mother stay again?'

That took uniforms, Gwen as a nurse, you as an orderly, Gentleman Pete out in the car while your father kept watch on George's mine adit and monitored police activity over a scanner.

The old lady said, 'You're new here and quite pretty,' as Gwen shot her up with Phenobarbitol and valium, and you went to work on the room.

This was the glitch – you'd watched George drive to work; watched him enter the mine. No one saw him come back out again, because no one was looking on the other side of the hill, the exit of a completely different shaft. So while your father watched the front, George took off out the back, drove over to check on his investment, walked in the room just as you pulled the rock from the back of the mother's radio, George looking politely surprised, as if he'd stepped into the wrong room.

He smiled at you and Gwen, held up a hand in apology and backed out of the room.

Gwen looked at the door, looked at you.

You looked at Gwen, looked at the window, looked at the rock filling the center of your palm, the entire center of your palm.

Looked at the door.

Gwen said, 'Maybe we –'

And George came through the door again, nothing polite in his face, a gun in his hand. And not any regular gun, a motherfucking six-shooter, like they carried in Westerns, long, thin barrel, a family heirloom maybe, passed down from a great-great-great-grandfather, not even a trigger guard, just the trigger, and crazy fat fucking George the lonely unloved pulling back on it and squeezing off two rounds, the first of which went out the window, the second of which hit metal somewhere in the room and then bounced off that and then the old lady went 'Ooof', even though she was doped up and passed out, and it sounded to you like she'd eaten something that didn't agree with her. You could picture her sitting in a restaurant, halfway through coffee, placing a hand to her belly, saying it: 'Ooof.' And George would come around to her chair, say, 'Is everything okay, Mama?'

But he wasn't doing that now, because the old lady went ass-over-tea-kettle out of the bed and hit the floor, and George dropped the gun and stared at her and said, 'You shot my mother.'

And you said, '*You* shot your mother,' your entire body jetting sweat through the pores all at once.

'No, you did. No, you did.'

You said, 'Who was holding the fucking gun?'

But George didn't hear you. George jogged three steps and dropped to his knees. The old lady was on her side, and you could see the blood, not much of it, staining the back of her white johnny.

George cradled her face, looked into it, and said, 'Mother. Oh, mother, oh, mother, oh, mother.'

And you and Gwen ran right the fuck out of that room.

In the car, Gwen said, 'You saw it, right? He shot his own mother in the ass.'

'He did?'

'He did,' she said. 'Baby, she's not going to die from that.'

'Maybe. She's old.'

'She's old, yeah. The fall from the bed was worse.'

'We shot an old lady.'

'We didn't shoot her.'

'In the ass.'

'We didn't shoot anyone. He had the gun.'

'That's how it'll play, though. You know that. An old lady. Christ.'

Gwen's eyes the size of that diamond as she looked at you and then she said, 'Ooof.'

'Don't start,' you said.

'I can't help it. Bobby, Jesus.'

She said your name. That's your name – Bobby. You loved hearing her say it.

Sirens coming up the road behind you now and you're looking at her and thinking this isn't funny, it isn't, it's fucking sad, that poor old lady, and thinking, okay, it's sad, but God, Gwen, I will never, ever live without you. I just can't imagine it any more. I want to . . . What?

And the wind is pouring in the car, and the sirens are growing louder and there are several of them, an army of them, and Gwen's face is an inch from yours, her hair falling from behind her ear and whipping across her mouth, and she's looking at you, she's seeing you – really *seeing* you; nobody'd ever done that; nobody – tuned to you like a radio tower out on the edge of the unbroken fields of wheat, blinking red under a dark-blue sky, and that night breeze lifting your bangs was her, for Christ's sake, her, and she's laughing, her hair in her teeth, laughing because the old lady fell out of the bed and it isn't funny, it isn't and you'd said the first part in your head, the 'I want to' part, but you say the second part aloud:

'Dissolve into you.'

And Gentleman Pete, up there at the wheel, on this dark country road, says, 'What?'

But Gwen says, 'I know, baby. I know.' And her voice breaks around the words, breaks in the middle of her laughter and her fear and her guilt and she takes your face in her hands as Pete drives up on the Interstate and you see all those siren lights washing across the back window like fourth of July ice cream and then the window comes down like yanked netting and chucks glass pebbles into your shirt and you feel something in your head go all shifty and loose and hot as a cigarette coal.

*

176

The fairgrounds are empty and you and your father walk around for a bit. The tarps over some of the booths have come undone at the corners and they rustle and flap, caught between the wind and the wood, and your father watches you, waiting for you to remember, and you say, 'It's coming back to me. A little.'

Your father says, 'Yeah?'

You hold up your hand, tip it from side to side.

Out behind the cages where, in summer, they set up the dunking machine and the bearded lady's chair and the fast-pitch machines, you see a fresh square of dirt, recently tilled, and you stand over it until your old man stops beside you and you say, 'Mandy?'

The old man chuckles softly, scuffs at the dirt with his shoe, looks off at the horizon.

'I held it in my hand, you know,' you say.

'I'd figure,' the old man says.

It's quiet, the land flat and metal-blue and empty for miles in every direction, and you can hear the rustle of the tarps and nothing else, and you know that the old man has brought you here to kill you. Picked you up from prison to kill you. Brought you into the world, probably, so eventually he could kill you.

'Covered the center of my palm.'

'Big, huh?'

'Big enough.'

'Running out of patience, boy,' your father says.

You nod. 'I'd guess you would be.'

'Never my strong suit.'

'No.'

'This has been nice,' your father says and sniffs the air. 'Like old times, reconnecting and shit.'

'I told her that night to just go, just get, just put as much country as she could between you and her until I got out. I told her to trust no one. I told her you'd stay hot on her trail even when all logic said you'd quit. I told her even if I told you I had it, you'd have to cover your bets – you'd have to come looking for her.'

Your father looks at his watch, looks off at the sky again.

'I told her if you ever caught up to her to take you to the fairgrounds.'

'Who's this we're talking about?'

'Gwen.' Saying her name to the air, to the flapping tarps, to the cold.

'You don't say.' Your father's gun comes out now. He taps it against his outer knee.

'Told her to tell you that's all she knew. I'd hid it here. Somewhere here.'

'Lotta ground.'

You nod.

Your father turns so you are facing, his hands crossed over his groin, the gun there, waiting.

'The kinda money that stone'll bring,' your father says, 'a man could retire.'

'To what?' you say.

'Mexico.'

'To what, though?' you say. 'Mean old man like you? What else you got, you ain't stealing something, killing somebody, making sure no one alive has a good fucking day?'

The old man shrugs and you watch his brain go to work, something bugging him finally, something he hasn't considered until now.

'It just come to me,' he says, his eyes narrowing as they focus on yours.

'What's that?'

'You've known for, what, three years now that Gwen is no more?'

'Dead.'

'If you like,' your father says. 'Dead.'

'Yeah.'

'Three years,' your father says. 'Lotta time to think.'

You nod.

'Plan.'

You give him another nod.

Your father looks down at the gun in his hand. 'This going to fire?'

You shake your head.

Your father says, 'It's loaded. I can feel the mag weight.'

'Jack the slide,' you say.

He gives it a few seconds, then tries. He yanks back hard, bending over a bit, but nothing. The slide is stone.

'Krazy Glue,' you say. 'Filled the barrel, too.'

You pull your hand from your pocket, open up the knife. You're very talented with a knife. Your father knows this. He's seen you win money this way, throwing knives at targets, dancing blades between your fingers in a blur.

You say, 'Wherever you buried her, you're digging her out.'

The old man nods. 'I got a shovel in the trunk.'

You shake your head. 'With your hands.'

Dawn is coming up, the sky bronzed with it along the lower reaches, when you let the old man use the shovel. His nails are gone, blood crusted black all over the older cuts, red seeping out of the newer ones. The old man broke down crying once. Another time he got mean, told you you aren't his anyway, some whore's kid he found in a barrel, decided might come in useful on a missing baby scam they were running back then.

You say, 'Was this in Las Vegas? Or Idaho?'

When the shovel hits bone, you say, 'Toss it back up here,'

and step back as the old man throws the shovel out of the grave.

The sun is up now and you watch the old man claw away the dirt for a while and then there she is, all black and rotted, bones exposed in some places, her ribcage reminding you of the scales of a large fish you saw dead on a beach once in Oregon.

The old man says, 'Now, what?' and tears flee his eyes and drip off his chin.

'What'd you do with her clothes?'

'Burned 'em.'

'I mean, why'd you take 'em off in the first place?'

The old man looks back at the bones, says nothing.

'Look closer,' you say. 'Where her stomach used to be.'

The old man squats, peering, and you pick up the shovel.

Until Gwen, you had no idea who you were. None. During Gwen, you knew. After Gwen, you're back to wondering.

You wait. The old man keeps cocking and recocking his head to get a better angle, and finally, finally, he sees it.

'Well,' he says, 'I'll be damned.'

You hit him in the head with the shovel and the old man says, 'Now, hold on,' and you hit him again, seeing her face, the mole on her left breast, her laughing once with her mouth full of popcorn, and then the third swing makes the old man's head tilt funny on his neck, and you swing once more to be sure and then sit down, feet dangling into the grave.

You look at the blackened shriveled thing lying below your father and you see her face with the wind coming through the car and her hair in her teeth and her eyes seeing you and taking you into her like food, like blood, like what she needed to breathe, and you say, 'I wish . . .' and sit there for a long time with the sun beginning to warm the ground and warm your back and the breeze returning to make those tarps flutter again, desperate and soft.

'I wish I'd taken your picture,' you say finally. 'Just once.'

And you sit there until it's almost noon and weep for not protecting her and weep for not being able to know her ever again, and weep for not knowing what your real name is, because whatever it is or could have been is buried with her, beneath your father, beneath the dirt you begin throwing back in.

THE RESURRECTION
OF BOBO JONES

Bill Moody

When Brew finally caught up with him, Manny Klein was inhaling spaghetti in a back booth at Chubby's, adding to his already ample girth with pasta and plying a green-eyed blonde called Mary Ann Best with tales of his exploits as New York's premier talent scout. As usual, Manny was exaggerating but probably not about Rocky King.

'The point is,' Manny said, mopping up sauce with a hunk of French bread, 'this time you've gone too far.' He popped the bread in his mouth, wiped his three chins with a white napkin tucked in his collar and gazed at Brew Daniels with the incredulous stare of a small child suddenly confronted with a modern sculpture. 'You're dead, sport. Rocky's put the word out on you. He thinks you're crazy and you know what? So do I.'

Mary Ann watched as Brew grinned sheepishly and shrugged. Nobody had ever called him crazy. A flake definitely, but with jazz musicians, that comes with the territory, where eccentric behavior is a byword, the foundation of legends.

Everyone knew about Thelonious Monk keeping his piano in the kitchen and Dizzy Gillespie running for president. And who hadn't heard about Sonny Rollins, startling passers-by with the mournful wail of his saxophone when he found the Williamsburg Bridge an inspiring place to practise after he dropped out of the jazz wars for a couple of years.

Strange perhaps, but these, Brew reasoned, were essentially harmless examples that if anything enhanced reputations and merely added another layer to the jazz mystique. With Brew, however, it was another story.

Begun modestly, Brew's escapades gradually gathered momentum and eventually exceeded even the hazy boundaries of acceptable behavior in the jazz world until they threatened to eclipse his considerable skill with a tenor saxophone. Brew had the talent. Nobody denied that. 'One of jazz's most promising newcomers,' wrote one reviewer after witnessing Brew come out on top in a duel with one of the grizzled veterans of the music.

It was Brew's off-stage antics – usually at the expense of his current employer – that got him into trouble, earned him less than the customary two weeks' notice and branded him a bona fide flake. But however outlandish the prank, Brew always felt fully justified even if his victims just as violently disagreed. Brew was selective but no one, not even Brew himself, knew when or where he would be inspired to strike next. Vocalist Dana McKay, for example, never saw Brew coming until it was too late.

Dana McKay is one of those paradoxes all too common in the music business: a very big star with very little talent, although her legions of fans don't seem to notice. Thanks to the marvels of modern recording technology, top-flight studio orchestras and syrupy vocal backgrounds, Miss McKay sounds passable on recordings. Live is another story. She knows it and the bands who back her know it, so when the musicians who hang out at Chubby's heard Brew had consented to sub for an ailing friend at the Americana, the smart money said Brew wouldn't last a week and Dana McKay might be his latest victim. They were right on both counts.

To Brew, the music was bad enough but what really got to him was the phoney sentimentality of her act: shaking hands with the ringsiders, telling the audience how much they meant to her – exactly the same way, every show, every night. Dana McKay could produce tears on cue. Naturally, Brew was inspired.

The third night, he arrived early, armed with a stack of McDonald's hats and unveiled his brainstorm to the band. They didn't need much persuading. Miss McKay had, as usual, done nothing to endear herself to the musicians. She called unnecessary rehearsals, complained to the conductor and treated everyone as her personal slave. Except for the lady harpist, even the string section went along.

Timing was essential, so on Brew's cue, at precisely the moment Miss McKay was tugging heartstrings with a teary-eyed rendition of one of her hits, the entire band donned the McDonald's hats, stood up with arms spread majestically and sang out, 'You deserve a break today!'

When the thunderous chorus struck, Miss McKay never knew what hit her. One of the straps of her gown snapped and almost exposed more of her than planned. She nearly fell off the stage. The dinner-show audience howled with delight, thinking it was part of the show. It got a mention in one of the columns but Miss McKay was not amused.

It took several minutes for the laughter to die down and by that time she'd regained her composure. She smiled mechanically and turned to the band. 'How about these guys, folks? Aren't they something?' Her eyes locked on Brew grinning innocently in the middle of the sax section. She fixed him with an icy glare and Brew was fired before the midnight show. He was never sure how she knew he was responsible but he guess the lady harpist had a hand in it.

Brew kept a low profile for a while after that, basking in the glory of his most ambitious project to date, and made ends meet with a string of club dates in the Village. It wasn't until he went on the road with Rocky King that he struck again. Everyone agreed Brew was justified this time but for once, he picked on the wrong man.

Rocky King is arguably the most hated bandleader in America, despite his nationwide popularity. Musicians refer to him as a 'legend in his own mind'. He pays only minimum scale, delights in belittling his musicians on the stand and has been known on occasion physically to assault anyone who doesn't measure up to his often unrealistic expectations. A man to be reckoned with, so when the news got out, Rocky swore a vendetta against Brew that even Manny Klein couldn't diffuse – and he'd got Brew the job.

'C'mon, Manny,' Brew said. 'Rocky had it coming.'

Manny shook his head. 'You hear that, Mary Ann? I get him the best job he's ever had, lay my own reputation on the line and all he can say is Rocky had it coming. Less than a week with the band, he starts a mutiny and puts Rocky King off his own bus forty miles from Indianapolis. You know what your problem is, Brew? Priorities. Your priorities are all wrong.'

Brew stifled a yawn and smiled again at Mary Ann. 'Priorities?'

'Exactly. Now take Mary Ann here. *Her* priorities are in exactly the right place.'

Brew grinned. 'They certainly are.' Mary Ann blushed slightly but Brew caught a flicker of interest in her green eyes. So did Manny.

'I'm warning you, Mary Ann,' Manny said. 'This is a dangerous man, bent on self destruction. Don't be misled by that angelic face.' Manny took out an evil-looking cigar, lit it and puffed on it furiously until the booth was enveloped in a cloud of smoke.

'Did you really do that? Put Rocky off the bus?' Mary Ann asked.

Brew shrugged and flicked a glance at Manny. 'Not exactly the way Manny tells it. As usual, he's left out a few minor details.' Brew leaned in closer to her. 'One of the trumpet players had quit, see. His wife was having a baby and he wanted to get home in time. But kind, generous Rocky King wouldn't let him ride on the bus even though we had to pass right through his home town. So, when we stopped for gas, I managed to lock Rocky in the men's room and told the driver he'd be joining us later. It seemed like the right thing to do at the time.'

'And what has it got you?' Manny said, emerging from the smoke, annoyed to see Mary Ann was laughing. 'Nothing but your first and last check, minus, of course, Rocky's taxi fare to Indianapolis. You're an untouchable now. You'll be lucky to get a wedding at Roseland.'

Brew shuddered. Roseland was the massive ballroom under the Musicians' Union and the site of a Wednesday-afternoon ritual known as cattle call. Hundreds of musicians jam the ballroom as casual contractors call for one instrument at a time. 'I need a piano player for Saturday night.' Fifty pianists or drummers or whatever is called rush the stage. First one there gets the gig.

'Did the trumpet player get home in time?' Mary Ann asked.

'What? Oh yeah. It was a boy.'

'Well, I think it was a nice thing to do.' She looked challengingly at Manny.

'Okay, okay,' Manny said, accepting defeat. 'So, you're the good Samaritan but you're still out of work and I . . .' He paused for a moment, his face creasing into a baleful smile.

'There is one thing . . . naw, you wouldn't be interested.'

'C'mon, Manny, I'm interested. Anything's better than Roseland.'

Manny shrugged. 'Well, I don't know if it's still going, but I heard they were looking for a tenor player at the Final Bar.'

Brew groaned and slumped back against the seat. 'The Final Bar is a toilet. A lot of people don't even know it's still there.'

'Exactly,' said Manny. 'The ideal place for you at the moment.' He blew out another cloud of smoke and studied the end of his cigar. 'Bobo Jones is there, with a trio.'

'Bobo Jones? *The* Bobo Jones?'

'The same, but don't get excited. We both know Bobo hasn't played a note worth listening to in years. A guy named Rollo runs the place. I'll give him a call if you think you can cut it. Sorry, sport, that's the best I can do.'

'Yeah, do that,' Brew said dazedly, but something in Manny's smile told Brew he'd be sorry. He was vaguely aware of Mary Ann asking for directions as he made his way out of Chubby's. So it had come to this. The Final Bar.

He couldn't imagine Bobo James there.

The winos had begun to sing.

Brew watched them from across the aisle. Two lost souls, arms draped over each other, wine dribbling down their chins as they happily crooned off-key between belts from a bottle in a paper bag. Except for an immense black woman, Brew and the winos were alone as the Seventh Avenue subway hurtled toward the Village.

'This city ain't fit to live in no more,' the woman shouted over the roar of the train. She had a shopping bag wedged between her knees and scowled at the winos.

Brew nodded in agreement and glanced at the ceiling

where someone had spray-painted *'Puerto Rico – Independencia!'* in jagged red letters. Priorities Manny had said. For once maybe he was right. Introspection was not one of Brew's qualities but maybe it was time. Even one-nighters with Rocky King was better than the Final Bar.

The winos finally passed out after 42nd Street but a wiry Latin kid in a leather jacket swaggered on to the car and instantly eyed Brew's horn. Brew figured him for a terrorist or at least a mugger. It was going to be his horn or the black woman's shopping bag.

Brew picked up his horn and hugged it protectively to his chest, then gave the kid his best glare. Even with his height, there was little about Brew to inspire fear. Shaggy blond curls over a choirboy face and deep-set blue eyes didn't worry the Puerto Rican kid, who Brew figured probably had an eleven-inch blade under his jacket.

They had a staring contest until 14th Street when Brew's plan became clear. He waited until the last possible second, then shot off the train like a firing squad was at his back. He paused just long enough on the platform to smile at the kid staring at him through the doors as the train pulled away.

'Faggot!' the kid yelled. Brew turned and sprinted up the steps, wondering why people thought it was so much fun to live in New York.

Outside, he turned up his collar against the frosty air and plunged into the mass of humanity that makes New York look like an evacuation. He elbowed his way across the street, splashing through gray piles of slush that clung to the curbs, soaked shoes and provided cabbies with opportunities to practice their favorite winter pastime of splattering pedestrians. He turned off 7th Avenue, long legs eating up the sidewalk, and tried again to envision Bobo James at the Final Bar, but it was impossible.

For as long as he could remember, Bobo Jones had been one of the legendary figures of jazz piano, one of the giants. Bud Powell, Monk, Oscar Peterson – hell, Bobo *was* a jazz piano. But Bobo's career, if brilliant, had also been stormy, laced with bizarre incidents, culminating one night at the Village Vanguard during a live recording session. Before a horrified opening-night audience, Bobo had attacked and nearly killed his saxophone player.

Midway through the first tune, the crazed Bobo had leapt wild-eyed from the piano, screamed something unintelligible and pounced on the unsuspecting saxophonist, who thought he had at least two more choruses to play. Bobo wrestled him to the floor and all but strangled him with the microphone cord. The saxophonist was already gagging on his mouthpiece and in the end suffered enough throat damage to cause him to switch to guitar. He eventually quit music altogether and went into business with his brother-in-law selling insurance in New Jersey.

Juice Wilson, Bobo's two-hundred-and-forty-pound drummer, had never moved so fast in his life unless it was the time he'd mistakenly wandered into a Ku Klux Klan meeting in his native Alabama. Juice dived over the drums, sending one of his cymbals flying into a ringside table full of Rotarians. He managed to pull Bobo off the gasping saxophonist with the help of two cops who hated jazz anyway. A waiter called the paramedics and the saxophonist was given emergency treatment under the piano while the audience looked on in stunned disbelief.

One member of the audience was a photographer for *Time* magazine, showing his out-of-town girlfriend the sights of New York. He knew a scoop when he saw it, whipped out his camera, and snapped off a dozen quick ones while Juice and the cops tried to subdue Bobo. The following week's issue ran a photo of Bobo, glassy-eyed in a straitjacket with the caption: 'Is This the End of Jazz?' The two cops hoped so because they were in the photo too and their watch commander wanted to know what the hell they were doing in a jazz club if they hadn't busted any dopers.

The critics in the audience shook their empty heads and claimed they'd seen it coming for a long time as Bobo was taken away to Bellevue. Fans and friends alike mourned the passing of a great talent but everyone was sure Bobo would recover. He never did.

Bobo spent three months in Bellevue, playing silent chords on the wall of his padded cell and confounding the doctors who could find nothing wrong with him, so naturally, they diagnosed him as manic-depressive and put him back on the street. With all the other loonies in New York, one more wouldn't make any difference.

Bobo disappeared for nearly a year after that. No one knew or cared how he survived. Most people assumed he was living on the royalties from the dozen or so albums he'd left as a legacy to his many fans. But then, he mysteriously reappeared. There were rumors of a comeback. Devoted fans sought him out in obscure clubs, patiently waiting for the old magic to return. But it seemed gone for ever. Gradually, all but the most devout drifted away, until, if the cardboard sign in the window could be believed, Bobo Jones was apparently condemned at last to the Final Bar.

Brew knew that much of the story but if he'd known the why of Bobo's downfall, he would have gone straight back to the subway, looked up the Puerto Rican kid and given him his horn. That would have been easier. Instead, he side-stepped a garbage can and pushed through the door of the Final Bar.

A gust of warm air, reeking of stale smoke and warm beer, washed over him. Dark, dirty and foul-smelling, the Final Bar is every Hollywood scriptwriter's idea of a Greenwich

Village jazz club. To musicians, it means a tiny, poorly lit bandstand, an ancient upright piano with broken keys and never more than seven customers if you count the bartender.

Musicians play at the Final Bar in desperation, on the way up. For Bobo Jones, and now perhaps Brew Daniels as well, the Final Bar is the last stop on the downward spiral to oblivion. But there he was, one of the legends of jazz. One glance told Brew all he needed to know. Bobo was down, way down.

He sat slumped at the piano, head bent, nearly touching the keyboard and played like a man trying to recall how he used to sound. Lost in the past, his head would occasionally jerk up in response to some dimly remembered phrase that just as quickly snuffed out. His fingers flew over the keys frantically in pursuit of lost magic. A forgotten cigarette burned on top of the piano next to an empty glass.

To Bobo's right were bassist Deacon Hayes and drummer Juice Wilson, implacable sentinels guarding some now-forgotten treasure. They brought to mind a black Laurel and Hardy. Deacon, rail-thin and solemn-faced, occasionally arched an eyebrow. Juice, dwarfing his drums, stared ahead blankly and languidly stroked the cymbals. They had remained loyal to the end and this was apparently it.

Brew was mesmerised by the scene. He watched and listened and slowly shook his head in disbelief. A knife of fear crept into his gut. He recognised with sudden awareness the clear, unmistakable qualities that hovered around the bandstand like a thick fog: despair and failure.

Brew wanted to run. He'd seen enough. Manny's message was clear but now, a wave of anger swept over him, forcing him to stay. He spun round toward the bar and saw what could only be Rollo draped over a bar stool. A skinny black man in a beret, chin in hand, staring vacantly at the hapless trio.

'You Rollo? I'm Brew Daniels.' Rollo's only response was to cross his legs. 'Manny call you?'

Rollo moved only his eyes, inspected Brew, found him wanting and shifted his gaze back to the bandstand. 'You the tenor player?' he asked contemptuously.

'Who were you expecting, Stan Getz?' Brew shot back. He wanted to leave, just forget the whole thing. He didn't belong here but he had to prove it. To Manny and himself.

'You ain't funny, man,' Rollo said. 'Check with Juice.'

Brew nodded and turned back to the bandstand. The music had stopped but Brew had no idea what they had played. They probably didn't either, he thought. What difference did it make? He tugged at Juice's arm dangling near the floor.

'Okay if I play a couple?' Brew asked.

Juice squinted at Brew suspiciously, took in his horn case and gave a shrug that Brew took as reluctant permission. He unzipped the leather bag and took out a gleaming tenor saxophone.

He knew why Manny had sent him down here. There was no gig. This was just a lesson in humility. It would be like blowing in a graveyard.

He put the horn together, decided against even asking anyone to tune up and blew a couple of tentative phrases. '"Green Dolphin Street", okay?'

Bobo looked up from the piano and stared at Brew like he was a bug on a windshield. 'Whozat?' he asked, pointing a long, slim finger. His voice was a gravelly whisper, like Louis Armstrong with a cold.

'I *think* he's a tenor player,' Juice said defiantly. 'He's gonna play *one*.' Bobo had already lost interest.

Brew glared at Juice. He was mad now and in a hurry. Deacon's eyebrows arched as Brew snapped his fingers for the tempo. Then he was off, on the run from despair.

Knees bent, chest heaving, body rocking slightly, Brew tore

into the melody and ripped it apart. The horn, jutting out of his mouth like another limb, spewed fire. Harsh abrasive tones of anger and frustration that washed over the unsuspecting patrons – there were five tonight – like napalm, grabbing them by the throat and saying, 'Listen to this, dammit.'

At the bar, Rollo gulped and nearly fell off the stool. In spite of occasional lapses in judgement, Rollo liked to think of himself as a jazz critic. He'd never fully recovered from his Ornette Coleman blunder. For seventeen straight nights, he'd sat sphinx-like at the Five Spot watching the black man with the white plastic saxophone before finally declaring, 'Nothin' baby. Ornette ain't playing nothing.' But this time there was no mistake. In a bursting flash of recognition, Rollo knew.

Brew had taken everyone by surprise. Deacon's eyebrows were shooting up and down like windshield wipers. Juice crouched behind his drums and slashed at the cymbals like a fencer. They heard it too. They knew.

Brew played like a back-up quarterback in the final two minutes of the last game of the year with his team behind seventeen to nothing. He ripped off jagged chunks of sound and slung them about the Final Bar, leaving Juice and Deacon to scurry after him in desperate pursuit. During his last scorching chorus, he pointed the bell of his horn at Bobo, prodding, challenging, until he at last backed away.

Bobo reacted like a man under siege. He'd begun as always, staring at the keyboard as if it were a giant puzzle he'd forgotten how to solve. But by Brew's third chorus, he seized the lifeline offered and struggled to pull himself out of the past. Eyes closed, head thrown back, his fingers flew over the keys, producing a barrage of notes that nearly matched Brew's.

Deacon and Juice exchanged glances. Where had they heard *this* before?

Rollo, off the stool, rocked and grinned in pure joy. 'Shee–it!' he yelled.

Bobo was back.

By the end of the first week, word had got around. Something was happening at the Final Bar and people were dropping in to see if the rumors were true. Bobo Jones had climbed out of his shell and was not only playing again but presenting a reasonable facsimile of his former talent, inspired apparently by a fiery young tenor saxophonist. It didn't matter that Brew had been on the scene for some time. He was ironically being heralded as a new discovery. But even that didn't bother Brew. He was relaxed.

The music and his life were, at least for the moment, under control. Mary Ann was a regular at the club – she hadn't signed with Manny after all – and by the end of the month, they were sharing her tiny Westside apartment.

But gnawing around the edges were the strange looks Brew caught from Deacon and Juice. They'd look away quickly and mumble to themselves while Rollo showed Brew only the utmost respect. Bobo was the enigma, either remaining totally aloof or smothering Brew with attentive concern, following him around the club like a shadow. If Brew found it stifling or even creepy, he wisely wrote it off as the pianist's awkward attempt at gratitude and reminded himself that Bobo had spent three months in a mental ward.

Of his playing, however, there was no doubt. For some unknown reason, Brew's horn had unlocked Bobo's past, unleashing the old magic that flew off Bobo's fingers with nightly improvement. Brew himself was as big a benefactor to Bobo's resurgence as his own playing reached new heights. His potential was at last being realised. He was loose, making it with a good gig, a good woman and life had never been sweeter. Naturally, that's when the trouble began.

They were curled up watching the late movie when Brew heard the buzzer. Opening the door, Brew found Bobo standing in the hall, half hidden in a topcoat several sizes too large, a stack of records under his arm.

'Got something for you to hear, man,' Bobo rasped, walking past Brew to look for the stereo.

'Hey, Bobo, you know what time it is?'

'Yeah, it's twenty after four.' Bobo was crouched in front of the stereo, looking through the records.

Brew nodded and shut the door. 'That's what I thought you'd say.' He went into the bedroom. Mary Ann was sitting up in bed.

'Who is it?'

'Bobo,' Brew said, grabbing a robe. 'He's got some records he wants me to hear. I gotta humor him I guess.'

'Does he know what time it is?'

'Yeah, twenty after four.'

Mary Ann looked at him quizzically. 'I'll make some coffee,' she said, slipping out of bed.

Brew sighed and went back to the living room. Bobo had one of the records on the turntable and was kneeling with his head up against the speaker. The record was one of his early ones with a tenor player called Lee Evans, a name only vaguely familiar to Brew.

Brew had studiously avoided the trap of listening to other tenor players except maybe for John Coltrane. No tenor player could avoid that, but his style was forged largely on his own. A mixture of hard brittle fluidness on up tempos, balanced by an effortless shifting of gears for lyrical ballads – a cross between Sonny Rollins and Stan Getz. But there was something familiar about this record, something he couldn't quite place.

'I want to do this tune tonight,' Bobo said, turning his eyes to Brew. It was the first time Bobo had made any direct reference to the music.

Brew nodded absently, absorbed in the music. What was it? He focused on the tenor player and only vaguely remembered Mary Ann coming in with the coffee. Much later the record was still playing and Mary Ann was curled up in a ball on the couch. Early-morning sun streamed in the window. Bobo was gone.

'You know, it's funny,' Brew told her later. 'I kinda sound like that tenor player, Lee Evans.'

'What happened to him?'

'I don't know. He played with Bobo quite a while but I think he was killed in a car accident. I'll ask Rollo. Maybe he knows.'

But if Rollo knew, he wasn't saying. Neither were Juice or Deacon. He avoided asking Bobo, sensing it was somehow a taboo subject, but it was clear they all knew something he didn't. It became an obsession for Brew.

He nearly wore out the records Bobo had left and, unconsciously, more and more of Lee Evans's style crept into his own playing. It seemed to please Bobo and brought approving nods from Juice and Deacon. As far as Brew could remember, he'd never heard Lee Evans until the night Bobo had brought the records but damned if he didn't sound very much the same. Finally, he could stand it no longer and pressed Rollo. He had to know.

'Man, why you wanna mess things up for now?' Rollo asked, avoiding Brew's eyes. 'Bobo's playin', the club's busy and you gettin' famous.'

'C'mon, Rollo, I only asked about Lee Evans. What's the big secret?' Brew was puzzled by the normally docile

Rollo's outburst and intrigued even more. However tenuous Bobo's return to reality, Brew couldn't see the connection. Not yet.

'Aw, shit,' Rollo said, slamming down a bar rag. 'You best see Razor.'

'Who the hell's Razor?'

'Wunna the players, man. Got hisself some ladies and he's . . . well, you talk to him, if you want.'

'I want,' Brew said, more puzzled than ever.

But Mary Ann was not so sure. 'You may not like what you find,' she warned. Her words were like a prophecy.

Brew found Razor off 10th Avenue.

A massive maroon Buick idled at the curb. Nearby, Razor, in an ankle-length fur coat and matching hat, peered at one of his 'ladies' from behind dark glasses. But what really got Brew's attention was the dog. Sitting majestically at Razor's heel, sinewy neck encased in a silver stud collar, was the biggest, most vicious-looking Doberman Brew had ever seen. About then, Brew wanted to forget the whole thing but he was frozen to the spot as Razor's dog – he hoped it was Razor's dog – bared his teeth, growled throatily and locked his dark eyes on Brew.

Razor's lady, in white plastic boots, miniskirt and a ski jacket, cowered against a building. Tears streamed down her face, smearing garish makeup. Her eyes were locked on the black man as he fondled a pearl-handled straight razor. Brew had never seen anyone so frightened.

'Lookee here, mama, you makin' old Razor mad with all this talk about you leavin', and you know what happen when Razor get mad right?' The girl nodded slowly as he opened and closed the razor several times before finally dropping it in his pocket. 'Aw right, then,' Razor said. 'Git on outta here.' The girl glanced briefly at Brew, then scurried away.

'Whatchu lookin' at, honky?' Razor asked, turning his attention to Brew. Several people passed by them, looking straight ahead as if they didn't exist.

Brew's throat was dry. He could hardly get the words out. 'Uh, I'm Brew Daniels . . . I play with Bobo at the Final Bar. Rollo said –'

'Bobo? Shee–it.' Razor slapped his leg and laughed, throwing his head back. 'Yeah, I hear that sucker's playin' again.' He took off the glasses and studied Brew closely. 'And you the cat that jarred them old bones. Man, you don't even look like a musician.'

The Doberman cocked his head and looked at Razor as if that might be a signal to eat Brew. 'Be cool, Honey,' Razor said, stroking the dog's sleek head. 'Well, you must play, man. C'mon, it's gettin' cold talkin' to these bitches out here. I know what you want.' He opened the door of the Buick. 'C'mon, Honey, we goin' for a ride.'

Brew sat rigidly in front, trying to decide who scared him more, Razor or the dog. He could feel Honey's warm breath on the back of his neck. 'Nice dog you got, Mr Razor,' he said. Honey only growled and Razor didn't speak until they pulled up near Riverside Park.

He threw open the door and Honey scrambled out. 'Go on, Honey. Git one of them suckers.' Honey barked and bounded away in pursuit of a pair of unsuspecting Cocker Spaniels.

Razor took out cigarettes from a platinum case, lit two with a gold lighter and passed one to Brew. 'It was about three years ago,' Razor began. 'Bobo was hot and he had this bad-assed tenor called Lee Evans. They was really tight. Lee was just a kid but Bobo took care of him like he was his daddy. Anyway, they was giggin' in Detroit or someplace, just before they was sposed to open here. But Lee, man, he had him some action he wanted to check out on the way so

201

he drove on alone. He got loaded at this chick's pad, then tried to drive all night to make the gig.' Razor took a deep drag on his cigarette. 'Went to sleep. His car went right off the pike into a gas station. Boom! That was it.'

Razor fell silent. Brew swallowed as the pieces began to fall into place.

'Well, they didn't tell Bobo what happened till an hour before the gig and them jive-ass, faggot record dudes said seein' as how they'd already given Bobo front money, he had to do the session. They got another dude on tenor. He was bad but he wasn't Lee Evans. At first, Bobo was cool, like he didn't know what was happening. Then all of a sudden, he jumped on this cat – scared his ass good, screamin' "You ain't Lee, you ain't Lee."' Razor shook his head and flipped his cigarette out the window.

Brew closed his eyes. It was so quiet in the car Brew was sure he could hear his own heart beating, as everything came together. All the pieces fell into place except one but he had to ask: 'What's this all got to do with me?'

Razor turned to him, puzzled. 'Man, you is one dumb honky. Don't you see, man? To Bobo, you is Lee Evans all over again. Must be how you blow.'

'But I'm not,' Brew protested, feeling panic rise in him. 'Someone's got to tell him I'm not.'

Razor's eyes narrowed, his voice lowered menacingly. 'Ain't nobody got to tell nobody nothin'. Bobo was sick for a long time. If he's playin' again 'cause of you, that's enuff. You,' he pointed a finger at Brew, 'jus' be cool and blow your horn.' There was no mistake. It was an order.

'But . . .'

'But nothin'. And if there's anything else goin' down, I'll hear about it. Who do you think took care of Bobo? You know my name, man? Jones. Razor Jones.' He smiled suddenly at Brew. 'Bobo is my brother.'

Razor started the car and whistled for Honey. Brew got out slowly and stood at the curb like a survivor of the holocaust. The huge Doberman galloped back obediently, sniffed at Brew and jumped in the car next to Razor.

'Bye,' Razor called, flashing Brew a toothy smile. Brew could swear Honey sneered at him as the car drove away.

The Final Bar was now the in place in the Village. Manny had seen to that, forgiving Brew for all his past sins and recognising Bobo's return, if artfully managed, would insure all their futures. Manny was pragmatic if nothing else. He was on the phone daily, negotiating with record companies and spreading the word that a great event in jazz was about to take place.

Driven by the memory of Razor's menacing smile, Brew played like a man possessed, astonishing musicians who came in to hear for themselves. He was getting calls from people he'd never heard of, offering record dates, road tours, even to form his own group. But of course Brew wasn't going anywhere. He was miserable.

'You sound great, kid,' Manny said, looking around the club. It was packed every night now and Rollo had hired extra help to handle the increase in business. 'Listen, wait till you hear the deal I've made with Newport Records. A live session, right here. The return of Bobo Jones. Of course, I insisted on top billing for you too.' Manny was beaming. 'How about that, eh?'

'I think I'll go to Paris.' Brew said, staring ahead vacantly.

'Paris?' Manny turned to Mary Ann. 'What's he talking about?'

Mary Ann shrugged. 'He's got this crazy idea about Bobo.'

'What's the idea? Brew, talk to me,' Manny said.

'I mean,' Brew said evenly, 'there isn't going to be any record. Not with me anyway.'

203

Manny's face fell. 'No record? Whatta you mean? An album with Bobo will make you. At the risk of sounding like an agent, this is your big break.'

'Manny, you don't understand. Bobo thinks I'm Lee Evans. Don't you see?'

'No, I don't see,' Manny said, glaring at Brew. 'I don't care if he thinks you're Jesus Christ with a saxophone. We're talking major bucks here. Big. Blow this one and you might as well sell your horn.' Manny turned back pleadingly to Mary Ann. 'For God's sake, Mary Ann, talk some sense to him, will you?'

Mary Ann shrugged. 'He's afraid Bobo will flip out again and he's worried about Bobo's brother.'

'Yeah, Manny, you would be too if you saw him. He's got the biggest razor I've ever seen. And if that isn't enough, he's got a killer dog that would just love to tear me to pieces.'

'What did you do to him? You're not up to your old tricks again?'

'No, no, nothing. He just told me, ordered me, to keep playing with Bobo.'

'So what's the problem?'

Brew sighed. 'Look, Manny, for one thing, I don't like being a ghost. And what if Bobo attacks me like the last time? He almost killed that guy. Bobo needs to be told but no one will do it and I *can't* do it. So it's Bobo, Razor or Paris. I'll take Paris. I've heard there's a good jazz scene there.'

Manny looked dumbly at Mary Ann. 'Is he serious? C'mon, Brew, that's ridiculous. Look, Newport wants to set this up for next Monday night and I'm warning you. Screw this up and I will personally see that you never work again.' He laughed then and slapped Brew on the back. 'It'll be all right, Brew. Trust me.'

*

204

But Brew didn't trust anyone and no one could convince him. Even Mary Ann couldn't get through to him. Finally, he decided to get some expert advice. He checked with Bellevue but was told the case couldn't be discussed unless he was a relative. He even tracked down the saxophonist Bobo had attacked but as soon as he mentioned Bobo's name, the guy slammed down the phone on him. In desperation, Brew remembered a guy he'd met at one of the clubs. A jazz buff, Ted Fisher was doing his internship in psychiatry at Colombia Medical School. Musicians called him Doctor Deep. Brew telephoned, explained what he wanted and they agreed to meet at Chubby's.

'What is this, a gay bar?' Ted Fisher asked, looking around the crowded bar.

'No, Ted, there just aren't a lot of lady musicians. Now look, I –'

'Hey, isn't that Gerry Mulligan over there at the bar?'

'Ted, c'mon. This is serious.'

'Sorry, Brew. Well, from what you've told me already, as I understand it, your concern is that Bobo thinks you're his former saxophone player, right?'

Brew looked desperate. 'I don't think it, I *know* it. Look, Bobo attacked the substitute horn player. What I want to know is what happens if the same conditions are repeated? Bobo's convinced I'm Lee Evans now, but what if the live recording session brings it all back and he suddenly realises I'm not? Could he flip again and go for me?' Brew sat back and rubbed his throat.

'Hmmm . . .' Ted murmured, staring at the ceiling. 'No, I wouldn't think so. Bobo's fixation, brought about by the loss of a close friend, whom he'd actually, though inadvertently, assumed a father-figure role for is understandable and quite plausible. As for a repeated occurrence, even in simulated, identical conditions, well, delayed shock would account for

205

the first instance, but no. I don't think it's within the realms of possibility.' Ted smiled at Brew reassuringly and lit his pipe.

'Could you put that in a little plainer terms?'

'No, I don't think it would happen again.'

'You're sure?' Brew was already feeling better.

'Yes, absolutely. Unless . . .'

Brew's head snapped up. 'Unless what?'

'Well, unless this Bobo fellow suddenly decided he . . . he didn't like the way you played. Brew? You okay? You look a little pale.'

Brew leaned forward on the table and covered his face with his hands. 'Thanks, Ted,' he whispered.

Ted smiled. 'Any time, Brew. Don't mention it. Hey, do you think Gerry Mulligan would mind if I asked him for his autograph?'

In the end, Brew finally agreed to do the session. It wasn't Manny's insistence or threats. They paled in comparison with Razor. It wasn't even Mary Ann's reasoning. She was convinced Bobo was totally sane. No, in the end, it was the dreams that did it. Always the dreams.

A giant Doberman, wearing sunglasses and carrying a straight razor in its mouth, was chasing him through Central Park. In the distance Razor stood holding his horn, laughing. Brew had little choice.

On one point, however, Brew stood firm. The Newport Record executives had taken one look at the Final Bar and almost cancelled the entire deal. They wanted to move the session to the Village Vanguard but Brew figured that was tempting fate too much. Through Mary Ann, Bobo had deferred the final decision to Brew and as far as he was concerned, it was the Final Bar or nothing. The Newport people finally conceded and set about refurbishing the broken-down club. Brew had to admit someone had really spent some money.

The club was completely transformed. It was repainted, new tables were added, blow-up photos of jazz greats were plastered on the walls and the sawdust floor was replaced with new carpeting.

When Brew and Mary Ann arrived, they were greeted at the door by Rollo, nattily attired in a tuxedo, collecting a hefty admission charge and looking as smart as any maître d' in New York. 'My man Brew.' He smiled, slapping Brew's palm. 'Tonight's the night!'

'Yeah, tonight's the night,' Brew mumbled as they pushed through the crowd. The club was jammed with fans, reporters and photographers. Manny waved to them from the bar where he was huddled with the Newport people. A Steinway grand had replaced the ancient upright piano and a tuner was making final adjustments as engineers scurried about running cables and testing microphones.

Brew suddenly felt a tug at his sleeve. He turned to see Razor, resplendent in a yellow velvet suit, sitting with a matching pair of leggy blondes. Honey hovered nearby. Razor flashed a smile at Mary Ann and nodded to Brew. 'I see you been keepin' cool. This your lady?'

Brew stepped around Honey, wondering if it were true that dogs can smell fear. 'Yeah. Mary Ann, this is Razor.'

Razor bowed deeply and kissed Mary Ann's hand, then stepped back to introduce the blondes. 'Say hello to Sandra and Shana.'

'Hi,' the blondes chorused in unison.

'What are you doing here?' Brew asked Razor.

'What am *I* doin' here? Man, this is my club. Didn't you know that?' He flashed Brew another smile. 'You play good now.'

In a daze, Brew found Mary Ann a seat near the

bandstand. As the piano-tuner finished, a tall man in glasses and the three-piece suit walked to the microphone and introduced himself as the Vice-President of Newport Records. He called for quiet, perhaps the first time it had ever been necessary at the Final Bar.

'Ladies and gentlemen, as you all know, we are recording live here tonight, so we'd appreciate your co-operation. Right now, though, let's give a great big welcome to truly, one of the giants of jazz, Mr Bobo Jones and his quartet.'

The applause was warm and real as they took the stand. Bobo, Deacon and Juice were immaculate in matching tuxes. Brew was dressed likewise but at the last minute had elected to opt for a white turtleneck sweater. Bobo bowed shyly as the crowd settled down in anticipation.

Brew busied himself with changing the reed on his horn and tried to blot out the image of Bobo leaping from the piano but there was nowhere to go. He rubbed his throat, tried to smile at Mary Ann as the sound check was completed. It was time.

They opened with one of Bobo's originals, simply titled 'Changes'. Bobo led off with a breathtaking solo introduction that dispelled any doubts about his return being genuine. Then, Deacon walked in, bass pulsing quietly, while Juice put the cymbals on simmer.

Brew decided that if he survived tonight, he'd just disappear. But now, locked into the music, his fingers flew over the horn in a blur while Deacon's throbbing bass and Juice's drums pushed and drove him through several choruses. Bobo, eyes closed, head back, nodded and passed the chords to Brew with love, till at last, Brew backed away and surrendered to Bobo.

Bobo spun out the old magic with a touch so deft he left the audience gasping for breath. This was the second coming of Bobo Jones. Rejuvenated and fresh lines flowed off his fingers effortlessly, transforming the mass of wood and metal and ivory into a total musical entity. Brew listened awestruck and nearly missed his entrance for the final cadenza.

He restated the plaintive theme, then made it his own, twisting, turning the melody before finally returning it safely to Bobo in its original form as the quartet came together for the final chord.

The applause that rang out and filled the room was deafening. But just as suddenly as it had erupted, it trailed off and lapsed into a tension-filled silence. Brew felt it then, his heart pounding, some murmuring as he caught a movement near the piano. He turned to see Bobo advancing toward him.

Brew stood frozen, staring hypnotically as Bobo stopped in front of him. As their eyes met in the hushed room, Bobo wiped away a tear, then suddenly grabbed Brew and hugged him close.

The audience began to clap again, only one or two people at first, gradually building in a crescendo, as Bobo whispered something in Brew's ear. No one heard what he'd said and it was later edited off the tape.

Brew wasn't sure he'd heard right at first. Bobo, face cracking into a huge grin, said it again. Brew smiled faintly, then threw his head back, laughing until tears came to his own eyes. Juice was laughing too and even Deacon smiled. Bobo went back to the piano and the rest of the evening went like a dream.

It was Mary Ann who finally remembered. Everyone was gone except for Manny who sat in a booth with them, calculating album sales and filling them in on the upcoming tour.

Brew sat slumped down while Mary Ann massaged his shoulders. The Newport people had been all smiles and had carted Bobo off to a celebration party. Brew had promised to join them later but for now he was content to bask in the luxurious feeling of freedom that washed over him in waves.

'What was it Bobo said to you? After the first number,' Mary Ann asked.

Brew grinned. 'Something I completely overlooked. "I knew all the time you wasn't Lee Evans, man,"' Brew said, imitating Bobo's hoarse whisper. '"Lee was a brother, and *you* sure don't look like a brother."'

Manny looked up puzzled, as Brew and Mary Ann both laughed. 'I don't get it,' he said. 'What's so funny about that?'

'Priorities, Manny. It's all a question of your priorities.'

PLASTIC PADDY

George P. Pelecanos

'I hate Arabs,' said Paddy.

A guy sat facing a good-looking blonde in a booth against the far wall. The guy was minding his own business. He and the girl were splitting a pitcher of draught and smiling at each other across the table. He would say something, or she would, and the other one would laugh. It looked like they were having a nice time. Paddy was staring at the guy like he wanted to kick his ass.

'How you know he's an Arab?' I said.

'Look at him,' said Paddy. 'Looks like Achmed Z-med, that guy on *T.J. Hooker.*'

'Adrian Zmed,' said Scott, the smart guy of our bunch.

'Another Arab,' said Paddy. This was five or six years after the Ayatollah, Nuke Iran and all that crap. Paddy was the only guy I knew who hadn't given that up.

Me and Paddy and Scott were in Kildare's, a pub up in Wheaton we used to drink at pretty regular. Wheaton was our neighborhood, not too far over the DC line, but a thousand miles away from the city, if you know what I mean. It was a night like most nights back then: a little drinking, some blow, then more drinking to take the thirst off the blow. Only this night ended up different than the rest.

I'd put the year at 1985, 'cause I can remember the bands and singers that were coming from the juke: Mr Mister, Paul Young, Foreigner, Wham . . . Hell, you could flush the whole Top Forty from that decade down the toilet and no one would miss it. Also, Len Bias was lighting it up for Maryland on the TV screen over the bar, so I know it couldn't have been later than 'Eighty-five. Maybe it was early 'eighty-six. It was around then, anyway.

Paddy was up that night, and not only from the coke. He always seemed angry at something back in those days, but we had chalked up his behavior to his hyped-up personality. Just 'Tool being Tool.'

O'Toole, I should say. Up until he was twenty-three, Paddy's name was John Tool. Most everyone who knew him, even his old man before he kicked, called him Tool. It was a nickname you gave to a fraternity brother or something, like Animal Man or Headcase, which was all right around the fellas, but didn't go over too good with the girls. Paddy liked it all right when he was growing up, but when he got to be a man he suddenly felt it didn't suit him. Still, he wanted a handle, something that could make him stand out in a crowd. He wasn't a guy you noticed, either for his character or his appearance. I think that's why he changed his name. That and his woman problem. He'd never had much success with the ladies and he was looking to change his luck.

What he told us was, he'd paid to have one of those family tree things done and found that he was all Irish on his mother's side. Turned out that his great-grandfather's name was O'Toole. A lightning-strike coincidence, he said, that Tool and O'Toole were so similar. So he made the legal switch, adding Paddy as his first name. He said he liked the way Paddy O'Toole 'scanned'.

It was around this time that he went Irish all the way. Started listening to The Chieftains and their kind. Became a Notre Dame fan, got the silver four-leaf clover charm on a silver-plated necklace, and had that T-Bird he drove, the garbage wagon with the Landau roof, painted Kelly green at the body shop where he worked. Then he fixed a 'Kiss Me, I'm Irish' sticker on the rear bumper, which totally fucked up what was already a halfway fucked-looking car.

Paddy began to drink more, too. I guess he thought that being a lush would admit him to the club. When he got really torched, he talked about his mother's cooking like it was special or something, and referred to his late father as 'Da'. His eyes would well with tears then, even though the old man had beat him pretty good when he was a kid. We thought it was all bullshit, and a little off, but we didn't say nothin' to him. He wasn't hurting anyone, after all.

We didn't say anything to his face, that is. Scott, the only one of us who had graduated from college, analysed the situation, as usual. Scott said that Americans who had that Irish identity thing going on were Irish the way Tony Danza was Italian. That most Americans' idea of Ireland was John Ford's Ireland, Technicolor green and Maureen O'Hara red and Barry Fitzgerald, Popeye-with-a-brogue blarney. And by the way, said Scott, John Ford was born in Maine. I didn't know John Ford from Gerald Ford, but it sounded smart. Also, it sounded like a lecture, the way Scott always sounded since he'd come back home with that degree. Scott could be a little, what do you call that, *pompous* sometimes, but he was all right.

So back to Kildare's. For years we had gone to this other joint around the corner, Garner's, made your clothes smell like Marlboro Lights and steak-and-cheese. But Paddy, who before he went Irish had never moved up off of Miller Lite, said the Guinness there was 'too cold', so we changed locals.

'Kildare is a county in Ireland,' said Paddy, the first time we went in there, like he was telling us something we didn't know, and Scott said, 'So is Sligo,' meaning the junior high school where all of us had gone. Paddy's mouth kind of slacked open then, like it did when he thought Scott was putting him on. I said, 'Dr Kildare,' just to hear my own voice.

Kildare's wasn't anything special. It was your standard fake pub, loaded with promotional posters and mobiles, courtesy of the local liquor distributors. The sign outside said 'A Publick House', like you could fool people into thinking Wheaton was London. I don't know, maybe the home-town rednecks bought into it, 'cause the joint was usually full. More likely they didn't care what you called it or what you dressed it up as. It was a place to get drunk. That was all anyone in these parts needed to know.

So the three of us were sitting at a four-top in the center of the room. I was hammering a Bud and Scott had a Michelob, another way he had of wearing his 'I went to college' badge. Paddy was on his third stout, and there was a shot of Jameson's set neat next to the mug. I didn't know how he afforded to drink the top-shelf stuff. He made jack shit at the body shop and went through a gram of coke every few days. But he still lived with his mother over on Tenbrook and it didn't look like he spent any money on clothes. I guess his paycheck went to getting his head up.

'I Want to Know What Love Is' was coming from the jukebox. Lou Gramm was crooning and I was thinking about my girl. I had met this fine young lady, Lynne, worked an aluminum siding booth up in Wheaton Plaza, who I thought might be the one. She had dark hair and a rack on her like that PR or Cuban chick, played on *Miami Vice*. I wanted to be with her but I was here. It was partly out of habit, and mostly because I knew Paddy would be holding. Also, Paddy had practically begged me to come. He didn't like to drink alone.

'You guys ready to do a bump?' said Paddy.

'Shit, yeah,' I said. I mean, what did he think? Hell, it was why I was sitting there.

'I gotta work tomorrow,' said Scott.

'What's your point?' said Paddy.

'It's a real job,' said Scott. At the time, Scott was putting in hours at a downtown law firm and studying for what he called the 'L-sats'.

Paddy looked over at the booth where the Arab dude sat, smiled kind of mean, then moved his eyes back to Scott. 'Like my job isn't real?'

'All I'm saying is, it's not the kind of job where you can just fall out of bed, stumble into a garage with a headache, and start banging out dings.'

'Oh, I get you. Big smart lawyer. What you makin' down at that law firm, Scott?'

'Nothing. It's an internship.'

'Better get in there refreshed in the morning, then. You wouldn't want to lose a gig like that.' Paddy turned his attention to me. 'Meet me in the head in a few minutes, Counselor. Okay?'

I had just dropped out of community college for the last time and had gotten this job at a local branch of a big television-and-stereo chain. The company called us 'Sales Counselors', like we were shrinks or something. Paddy thought it was a laugh.

'Okay,' I said.

'Watch this,' said Paddy, and he got out of his seat.

Paddy navigated the space between the floor tables and headed for the booth where the guy was drinking with the blonde. He walked right up to their table and bumped his thigh against it, hard enough to rattle their mugs and spill some of their beer. The guy looked up, not angry, just surprised. Paddy pointed his finger at the guy's face and said, 'Pussy.' Then Paddy made a beeline to the men's room, which was down a serpentine hall. The doorman, one of three cousins who owned the place, was standing nearby. He saw the whole thing.

'That was smooth,' said Scott.

The guy at the booth was staring at us, like, what's up with your buddy? Funny, with his face square on us, he did look like that Achmed Z-med dude. The blonde was busy mopping up the spilt beer with some napkins. I thought of going over to apologise, or shrugging to let them know that we were innocent in whatever had just happened, but I didn't, 'cause it would have been a betrayal of my friend. I just looked away.

'The lucky leprechaun's in rare form tonight,' said Scott. 'You guys drop me at my parents' place after this, okay?'

'Yeah, sure.'

'You want to get busted for something, that's up to you, but I got too much to lose.'

'I said we would.'

Scott's eyeglasses reflected neon from a Bud Light sign up on the wall. His hair was curly and short, and he was soft-featured and overweight. He had rose petal lips, like a girl's. Scott was one of those guys, you could tell what he was gonna look like when he got to be an old man, even when we were kids.

I pushed my chair away from the table, got up and walked towards the head. The doorman was giving me the fisheye, his arms folded across his chest. I didn't look at the Arab guy or the blonde.

I made it through the hall, black paneled walls lit by a red bulb, and knocked on the locked men's room door. Paddy opened up and I slid in. The room held a toilet, a stand-up urinal and a sink, all on the same wall. The toilet didn't have a door on it or nothin' like that, so if you had to take a shit you did it in front of strangers. There was a casement window by the toilet, always cranked open some to let out the smell. Everything was filthy in here. Paper towels overflowed the plastic trashcan by the sink and were crumpled like dirty white carnations on the tiled floor.

'Here you go, Counselor,' said Paddy. He held a small amber vial in one hand and a black screw-on top in the other. Inside the top a small spoon dangled by a chain. He dipped the spoon into the vial and produced a tiny mound of coke that he held to my nose.

I could see that there wasn't hardly any coke left in the vial. I knew if I did one jolt I'd be hungry for it the rest of the night. Even if we could find someplace to cop, I didn't have the dough to buy any more, and I didn't know if Paddy did, either.

I was thinking of this as I pressed a forefinger to one nostril and snorted the mound into the other. A good cool ache came behind my eyes.

Paddy produced another mound and I did it up the other nostril the same way. He scraped out what was left in the vial and did that himself. He found some more in there somehow and rubbed that on his gums while I ran water from the faucet, wet my fingers, tipped my head back and let some droplets go down my nose. Then I took a leak in the stand-up head.

'Hurry up,' said Paddy. 'Everyone's gonna think you're in here suckin' my dick.'

'No they won't. 'Cause everyone knows you don't have one.'

'Axe your mama if I have one.'

'Look, you gonna be a good boy out there?'

'I was just fuckin' with that guy.'

'For what?'

'I don't know.'

I tucked myself back in and zipped up my fly. I was already speeding and there was a drip, tasted like medicine, back in my throat. I wished my girl was out there; I could break away with her if she was. But it wouldn't be cool to split now, seeing as Paddy had just got me lit up. And by the time I got to her place, I'd be crashing. I'd hang with Paddy for a while, cop some more someplace, then knock on Lynne's door later on.

We walked out into the hall. 'Every Time You Go Away' was playing in the house. I felt tall and funny. Our waitress was going to the girl's room and I reminded her to wash her hands. She edged by us in the narrow passageway without even giving us a smile.

Good as I felt, I had forgotten about the doorman. My stomach flipped some as I saw him standing by our table. Our bill was on the table and Scott was kinda slumped in his seat. We went there and Paddy spread his hands, like, what's going on?

'Pay your tab and get out,' said the doorman, pointing at the bill.

'We're not finished drinking,' said Paddy.

'You're finished,' said the doorman. 'Pay your tab and get out.'

'What, 'cause of *that* guy?' said Paddy, jerking his head toward the Arab and the blonde. 'He was bothering me. Sayin' shit, and stuff. I wasn't just gonna let it pass.'

'I saw the whole thing,' said the doorman. His face was ugly and it was stone. 'Pay up and get out. You're not welcome in here any more.'

The doorman was short and wore one of those Woody Allen hats to cover his hair plugs. Basically, he was an insecure guy who liked to act tough. We all knew he couldn't walk it, and he knew we knew, and it just made him more mean. He was not a physical problem, but the Harris Brothers, a couple of guys worked nights in the kitchen, were. They had been wrestlers at our old high school, and there was no love lost between them and Paddy.

We dropped some money on the four-top. Scott stood and put some green in, too. A few of the drinkers at the tables and booths were checking us out with anticipation, waiting to see what we would do.

I already knew we weren't going to do a thing. Paddy's face had gone pink and he was just standing there, sway-backed, staring at his shoes. He was a pale-skinned strawberry blond who could have been handsome if his features had been hooked up better. I couldn't say what made him unattractive exactly, but there was something off about his looks. Scott called him an inbred Redford.

The three of us walked out, slow enough to salvage some dignity. But we kept moving and we didn't give any more lip to the little doorman with the hair plugs. I locked eyes for a moment with the guy in the booth. He didn't smile or any-thing, but he wasn't gloating about us getting tossed, either. He handled it all right. It was us that came off looking like assholes.

Out in the lot, walking towards Paddy's T-Bird, Scott said, 'Say goodbye to Kildare's, boys. We'll never drink in there again.'

'No loss,' said Paddy. 'We'll just drink at Garner's.'

'Aye, Garner's,' said Scott. 'I don't think so, lads. The Guinness is too cold.'

'Big college smart-ass, now.'

'How green was my valley,' said Scott, with a lilt.

'Fuck you,' said Paddy.

'Suck *what*?' said Scott.

They went on like that until we dropped Scott at his

father's house on Gabel. I didn't get in on the conversation. I was too busy thinking of my next bump.

Paddy left rubber on the street, hard to do with that heavy car, as we drove away from Scott's. He said that he was tired of Scott, how he wasn't the same since coming back from that fancy school, how he only tolerated him 'cause Scott and me went back to elementary, all that.

'I ain't goin' drinking with him again,' said Paddy.

I didn't comment, thinking that they would kiss and make up and we'd be up at Garner's or someplace like it the next week. But it turned out Paddy was right.

We picked up a six of domestic in Four Corners and cracked a couple of cans straight away. Both of us had a terrific thirst. Paddy drove down University Boulevard, then cut a left on to Piney Branch Road and took it to New Hampshire Avenue. We listened to a tape Paddy'd made, a balladeer named Christy Moore. He had a nice voice, with those whistles and pipes and shit like that in the background, but it sounded like something my father listened to, Vic Damone with an accent. I really thought Paddy had taken this Mick thing too far.

I saw where he was going as he cut up New Hampshire. They had garden apartments up along there where I'd heard you could cop. It was just above Langley Park, not as dangerous as Langley with the El Salvies and those crazy-assed Jamaicans, but still kinda grim. All varieties of Spanish here and a lot of blacks. Not that I was scared of 'em or nothin' like that.

Paddy turned into the parking lot, found a spot, and cut the engine and the lights. We sat there killing the rest of our beers.

'Who we gonna see?' I said.

'Some girl,' said Paddy. 'This guy I know at work hooked it up.'

'You don't know her?'

'It's just a girl. Don't worry, nothing could happen. I called her before I met you guys and she said it was cool. She sounded all right.' Paddy grinned. 'I bet she's fine, too.'

The way he said fine, like 'foyne', I knew she was a black girl. Paddy had a thing for black chicks, though I don't think he'd ever had any. Except for that one time, when that girl down at Benny's Rebel Room jacked him off for forty-five bucks.

'What're we getting'?' I said.

'An eight-ball.'

'Shit, Paddy, c'mon.' I had, like, sixteen bucks in my wallet, and next to nothing in the bank.

'I got you, man.'

So he was dealing. Small time, but there it was. That's how Paddy always had coke. It was the first time he'd let me know, even if it was in a back-door way. Because I was still high and feeling bold, it excited me some that he had let me in on his action. Also, I was a little bit scared.

'This your regular connection?'

'Nah, uh-uh, he's out of town. This is a one-time deal.'

I looked up at the apartments and the grounds. Some of the balconies were sagging and fast-food trash was strewn about the lot. 'Maybe we oughta wait until your man gets back.'

'You wanna get high, don't you?'

'Well, yeah.' I was at that stage, I was hungry for more.

Paddy threw his head back to drain his can of beer. He lofted the can over his shoulder. It hit some dead soldiers on the floorboard and made a dull metallic sound. I killed mine and dropped the can between my feet.

We got out of the car and walked across the lot. There were a couple of guys wearing mustaches, sitting in a black, late-model Ford parked nearby. Their heads were moving to music; the bass was up so loud I could hear it behind the closed windows of their car. I didn't make eye contact with them or anything. I figured they were doing some blow. Hell, everyone was rocking it back then. They were a little old for it, but it wasn't any business of mine.

We went up a stairwell, one of those open-air jobs with cinderblock walls. Paddy stopped on the second-floor landing. It was dark when it should have been lit. Then I saw the busted-out light bulb hung in a cage. I wondered if the girl dealing the blow had deliberately broken the light, made it so you couldn't see her apartment too good from the parking lot. Paddy knocked on the door, waited, then knocked again.

In a little while, a girl's voice came forward, muffled over some music that was playing inside the apartment. Paddy put his face close to the door and said his name, and also the name of his co-worker at the body shop. The door opened and Paddy stepped inside. I followed him. The girl stepped back against the wall to let us pass.

The girl was black, on the short side, with all the woman parts in place, including her black girl's onion. She wore Jordache jeans and a jean shirt unbuttoned kinda low. I could see one of her tits hanging in a loose white bra. She caught me checking her out as I squeezed by. She didn't seem to care. It was hard to read anything in her hard, unfriendly face and dark, almond-shaped eyes. I didn't say 'hey' to her or smile or anything like it. She took a deep cokehead's drag off the cigarette she was holding and closed the door.

Paddy put out his hand. 'C'mon,' said the girl, ignoring his gesture. We followed her down a short hall.

The music got louder as we walked. It was rap music, some black guy shouting over hard chords of electric guitar. We entered a living-room/dining-room arrangement, two small rooms, really, separated by nothing, where all the curtains were drawn tight. The place stunk of cigarettes. Cigarette smoke hung in the room.

A light-skinned black dude sat on the couch, dragging on a smoke, Jonesing for the nicotine like the girl. On the table before the couch was a mirror holding a largish mound of coke heaped beside a single-edged blade. An ashtray sat beside the mirror and was filled with butts. The dude raised his head as we came into the room and sized us up the way guys do. The way he looked at us, you could tell he wasn't too impressed.

Another black guy, darker-skinned with ripped arms, sat at the dining-room table. He wore a sleeveless black T-shirt to show off his guns. He was rapping along to the guy shouting from the stereo. There was a large amount of cocaine on the table, along with a scale, a big mirror, some blades, plastic Baggies of various sizes, and snowseals. The snowseals were real, the pharmaceutical kind, not just paper ripped from magazines and folded to size.

The coke was a mountain. I mean, it was Tony Montana big. I'd never seen so much shit before in my life.

A stainless-steel pistol, a short-nosed revolver, sat on the table. The guy touched the grip, turning it just an inch so that the barrel pointed our way. He looked at us, and his eyes were laughing and bright. As the voice came from the stereo, he kept his gaze on us and shouted along: 'It's *like* that, and that's the way it *is*.'

It's real clear, even today, what I was thinking: *You just got your life started and this is how you die. All you want to do is get your head up, nothing more than that. You walk into the wrong apartment, there's guns, and you fucking die.*

'You got it?' said Paddy to the girl. I had to hand it to him. He was acting pretty cool. Knowing Paddy, he was trying to keep himself together to impress her. For a guy who got no

225

play, Paddy was an optimist. He always thought he had a chance.

The girl went and turned down the stereo to almost nothing. The guy at the table kept rapping to the song.

'An eight, right?' said the girl to Paddy.

'That's right, baby.'

I was thinking, *Nah, don't go there, Paddy. Don't put on that bullshit black-talk of yours, not here.* But she didn't even blink. She went down another hall and into a kitchen that was visible through a cut-out in the dining-room wall. I watched her ratfuck through the freezer section of the refrigerator.

The guy at the table stopped rapping and said, 'Y'all want a taste?'

Paddy smiled friendly and put up his hands. 'That's all right,' he said. I'd never seen him turn down a blast of coke.

'Ain't like I'm asking you to drink out the same bottle as me.'

Paddy chuckled unconvincingly. 'It's not that. I just don't want any right now.'

'Well, I'm a little surprised, 'cause you look like a pro. Don't you always check out what you're buyin'?' The guy glanced at the dude sitting on the couch, then back at us. 'C'mon over here and give it a road test.'

Paddy shrugged and moved over to the table. I stayed where I was.

The guy at the table dipped a blade into an open Baggie that held some coke. I wondered why he didn't take it off the Everest that was in front of him. He dumped some powder off the blade and tracked out four thick lines on the mirror without giving it any chop. He handed a short tube of plastic, the cut-down barrel of a Bic pen, to Paddy.

When Paddy leaned over the table to do his lines, his

four-leaf clover pendant fell out of his shirt and hung suspended between the zippers of his Member's Only jacket.

'Irish, huh?' said the guy.

Paddy said, 'All the way.' He did a line and made a show of rearing his head back to take it all in.

'They call me Carlos. What do they call *you*?'

'Paddy.'

'No last name?'

'O'Toole.'

'Wow. That damn sure *is* Irish.' Carlos's voice was almost musical. 'Been to the motherland?'

'Not yet.'

'Tell the truth, man: that can't be your real name, right?'

'I changed it,' said Paddy, real low. The room was quiet, but you could barely hear him. He bent forward and quickly snorted the other line.

'You're like, *fake* Irish, then. That's what you tellin' me?'

Paddy cleared his nostrils with a pinch of his fingers. His eyes narrowed some as he straightened his posture. 'I'm Irish.'

Paddy said it real strong, like he was looking to make something of it.

'*All* the way,' said the guy on the couch.

Carlos looked Paddy over real slow. Then Carlos smiled. 'Plastic Paddy,' said Carlos. The guy on the couch laughed.

Paddy's face grew pink, like it had gotten at Kildare's. The girl came back through the hall with a Baggie in her hand and stood near the table. The cigarette still burned between her fingers; it was down to the filter now. Paddy turned to me, his face flushed, and held out the tube. I waved the offer away with my hand.

'Take it,' said Paddy. He sounded kinda mad.

I was frozen. I didn't want any coke. I was thinking of my parents and my kid sister. I just wanted to get outside.

'What's the matter with your boy?' said Carlos. 'Can't he find his tongue?'

'Give it to me,' I said to Paddy. The sound of my own voice was a relief. I walked a few steps and took the Bic from Paddy's outstretched hand. I did the lines fast, one right behind the other, and dropped the plastic tube on the table.

'Here you go, ace,' said the girl, speaking to Paddy. She handed him a Baggie that I guessed she had gotten from the freezer. I could see grains of rice in there with the coke.

'This from the same batch I just did?' said Paddy.

'Yeah,' said Carlos. 'It's good, right?'

Good. It wasn't even close. I knew right away that this shit was wrong. A curtain had dropped throughout my body and everything had gotten pushed down into my bowels. I was speeding without the happiness and I had to take a dump. This was bullshit coke. They had stepped all over it with baby laxative and who knew what else.

Paddy had to be feeling the same way I was. He *knew* he was getting ripped off. It was like the guy was asking, 'You don't mind if I fuck you, do you?'

But Paddy didn't complain. He reached into his jeans and pulled out a roll of bills. He handed the bills to the girl, who counted out the money with dead eyes.

'Ain't you gonna weigh it out?' said Carlos, chinning in the direction of the Baggie. 'I got a scale right here.'

Paddy didn't answer. He rolled the Baggie tight and slipped it in the inside pocket of his Member's Only.

'You just gonna eyeball it, *huh*?' said Carlos.

'Let's go,' said Paddy. He turned and began to walk. I followed him back down the hall toward the front door. We heard the guy on the couch say 'Plastic Paddy' in the voice of a game show host, and then all of them laughed. I didn't care because it looked like we were going to get out of there alive. But I know Paddy must have been hurting inside,

228

'cause they'd ripped something out of him. Also, it was the second time he'd been shamed that night.

We took the stairwell down toward the lot. As we crossed the sidewalk, Paddy said, 'Fuckin' niggers,' and right about then the guys I'd noticed in the Ford came out of nowhere, holding guns on us, shouting at us to lock our hands behind our heads and drop to the asphalt and kiss it. I went down shaking, seeing other men running around in the dark, hearing their adrenalised voices and the screech of tires and the closing of heavy car doors.

As I hit the ground I lost control of everything and crapped my pants.

You know all those cop shows on TV, where the detectives convince the suspect to talk before the lawyer arrives? It's bullshit, the worst thing you can do. My father always told me that if I ever got jammed up just to keep my mouth shut and wait for the guys in the suits. Also, 'cause he figured I'd get DWI'd some day, he told me to refuse the breath tests and keep my piss inside me. Judging from what happened to Paddy, I don't think he ever had any guidance like that. Plus, they gave him some court-appointed attorney who didn't help his case. My lawyer was a heavy hitter, a friend of my Dad's, and he did me right.

Paddy did a few months' detention up at Seven Locks, and I got a community service thing where I had to wear a jumpsuit and pick up trash in Sligo Creek Park. Also, I was required to attend these classes at an old Catholic school on Riggs Road, where some horse-faced guy talked about the evils of alcohol and drugs, one night a week for six weeks. It was me and a bunch of losers, alkies and spentheads who'd flip the teacher the bird behind his back when they weren't drawing sword-and-sorcery artwork in their notebooks or scratching their initials into their desktops.

You'd think it was lucky we walked into that bust before something worse happened to us. That I might have looked around me in that rehab class, checked out the company I was keeping, and realised that I needed to turn my life around. But I guess I wasn't that smart.

Soon after those classes ended I started doing the occasional blast on weekends again, telling myself it was recreational. Then, big surprise, I began to hunt for it during the week. One night I got drunk and wanted it so bad that I went into a rough neighborhood down in Petworth, off Georgia Avenue in DC, where this guy in a bar had told me I could cop. I bought a half from some hard-looking black dudes and got knocked out with a lead pipe by the same dudes while I was walking back to my car. I woke up at the Washington Hospital Center, my face looking like a duck's. I never did another line. My father said that I had to fall down and hit my head to find out I wasn't normal, and I guess he was right.

Paddy went away after his jail time, to Florida or some shit, and after that I lost contact with him completely. Scott had this theory that Paddy had flipped on Carlos and them, and was probably too scared to stay in Maryland. As for Scott, him and me drifted apart.

I saw them both at the twentieth reunion for my high school, held a few years ago at some hotel up in Gaithersburg. Scott was heavy and bald and on his second wife. He mentioned his law firm and something about a new model Lexus he had his eye on. He didn't really need to boast like that, 'cause I could tell from his suit that he had done all right. But I noticed that most of the night he was standing by himself. Nobody from our high school days seemed to recognise him. Scott had money but he didn't have friends.

I caught glimpses of Paddy during the evening, standing near the cash bar or hanging around the buffet table, where most of the food had been picked clean. His image was fuzzy – I was too vain to wear my glasses to the reunion – but I knew from the way he was standing, sway-backed like he'd always been, that it was him. When I'd try to catch his eye, though, he'd look away.

Our paths crossed in the bathroom later that night. I was taking a leak in the urinal when Paddy walked in. I got a good look at him while I zipped up my fly. He was wearing an ill-fitting suit and a hat sat crookedly on his head. The hat was one of those plastic derbies, green and covered in cellophane, with shamrocks glued underneath the cellophane. Like something you'd win at a carnival. Paddy's face was puffy and there were gray bags under his unfocused eyes. He leaned against the wall and looked me up and down.

'Paddy,' I said. 'How you doin'?'

'Big store manager,' he said, drawing out the words. His lip was curled with contempt.

I figured that someone at the reunion must have told him that I was managing a Radio Shack. But I was doing better than that. I had been promoted to Merchandising Director and I was in charge of four stores. Hell, I was knocking down close to forty-two grand a year.

I didn't correct him, though. I just went to the sink and washed my hands. I washed them real good before I left the room.

Paddy had been my bud for a long time, so I felt kinda bad for a couple days after, seeing him like that. He had taken a long fall. Or maybe, I don't know, he'd just kept moving sideways. Anyway, I haven't seen him since, and that suits me fine.

It's not like I'm denying who I was. I do think about those nights with Paddy and I know we had some laughs. But for the life of me I can't tell you what it was we were laughing about. I mean, I used to love to get my head up.

But now I can't remember what was so great about it. Mostly, when I think about it, it seems like it was all a waste of time.

SHADOW ON THE WATER

Peter Robinson

We were meant to be getting some sleep, but how you're supposed to sleep in a cold, muddy, rat-infested trench, when the uppermost thought in your mind is that you're going to be shot first thing in the morning is quite beyond me.

Albert Parkinson handed around the Black Cats to the four of us who clustered together for warmth, mugs of weak Camp coffee clutched to our chests, almost invisible to one another in the darkness. 'Here you go, Frank,' he said, cupping the match in his hands for safety, even though we were well below ground level. I thanked him and inhaled the harsh tobacco, little realising that soon I would be inhaling something far more deadly. Still, we needed the tobacco to mask the smell. The trench stank to high heaven of unwashed men, excrement, cordite and rotting flesh.

Now and then, distant shots broke the silence, someone shouted a warning or an order, and an exploding shell lit the sky. But we were waiting for dawn. We talked in hushed voices and eventually the talk got around to what makes heroes of men. We all put in our two-penn'orth, of course, mostly a lot of cant about courage, patriotism and honour, with the occasional begrudging nod in the direction of folly

235

and luck, but instead of settling for a simple definition, Joe Fairweather started to tell us a story.

Joe was a strange one. Nobody quite knew what to make of him. A bit older than the rest of us, he already had a reputation as one of the most fearless lads in our regiment. It never seemed to worry him that he was running across no man's land in a hail of bullets; he seemed either blessed or indifferent to his fate. Joe had survived Ypres one and two, and now here he was, ready to go again. Some of us thought he was more than a little bit mad.

'When I was a kid,' Joe began, 'about eleven or twelve, we used to play by the canal. It was down at the bottom of the park, through the woods, and not many people went there because it was a hell of a steep slope to climb back up. But we were young, full of energy. We could climb anything. There were metal railings all along the canal side, but we had found a loose one that you could lift out easily, like a spear. We always put it back when we went home so nobody would know we had found a way in.

'There wasn't much beyond the canal in those days, only fields full of cows and sheep, stretching away to distant hills. Very few barges used the route. It was a lonely, isolated spot, and perhaps that was why we liked it. We used to forge sick notes from our mothers and play truant from school, and nobody was ever likely to spot us down by the canal.

'Not that we got up to any real mischief, mind you. We just talked the way kids do, skimmed stones off the water. Sometimes we'd sneak out our fishing nets and catch sticklebacks and minnows. Sometimes we played games. Just make-believe. We'd act out stories from *Boy's Own*, cut wooden sticks from the bushes and pretend we were soldiers on patrol.' Joe paused and looked around at the vague outlines of our faces in the trench and laughed. 'Can you believe it?' he said. 'We actually *played* at being soldiers. Little did we know . . .

'One day, I think it was June or July, just before the summer holidays, at any rate, a beautiful, sunny, still day, the kind that makes you believe that only good things are going to happen, my friend Adrian and me were sitting on the stone bank dipping our nets in the murky water when we saw someone on the other side. I say *saw*, but at first it was more like sensing a presence, a shadow on the water, perhaps, and we looked up and noticed a strange man standing on the opposite bank, watching us with a funny sort of expression on his face. I remember feeling annoyed at first because this was our secret place and nobody else was supposed to be there. Now this grown-up had to come and spoil everything.

' "Shouldn't you boys be at school?" he asked us.

'There wasn't much we could say to that, and I dare say we just fidgeted and looked shifty.

' "Well," he said. "Don't worry, I won't tell anyone. What are you doing?"

' "Just fishing," I said.

' "Just fishing? What are you fishing for? There can't be much alive down there in that filthy water."

' "Minnows and sticklebacks," I said.

' "How old are you?"

'We told him.

' "Do your parents know where you are?"

' "No," I said, though I remember feeling an odd sensation of having spoken foolishly as soon as the word was out of my mouth, but it was too late to take it back.

' "Why do you want to know?" Adrian asked him.

' "It doesn't matter. Want to play a game with me?"

' "No, thanks." We started to move away. Who did he think he was? We didn't play with grown-ups; they were no fun.

'"Oh, I think you do," he said and there was something about his voice that made the hackles on the back of my neck stand up. I glanced at Adrian and we turned to look across the canal to where the man stood. When we saw the gun in his hand, both of us froze.

'He smiled, but it wasn't a nice smile. "Told you so," he said.

'Now, I looked at him closely for the first time. I was just a kid, so I couldn't say how old he was, but he was definitely a grown-up. A man. And he was wearing a sort of uniform, like a soldier, but it looked shabby and rumpled, as if it had been slept in. I couldn't see the revolver very clearly, not that I'd have had any idea what make it was, as if that even mattered. All that mattered was that it was a gun and that he was pointing it at us.

'Then, out of sheer nerves I suppose, we laughed, hoping maybe it was all a joke and it was just a cap gun he was holding. "All right," Adrian said. "If you really want to play . . ."

'"Oh, I do," the man said. Then he pulled the trigger.

'It wasn't as loud as I had expected, more of a dull popping sound, but something whizzed through the bushes beside me and dinged on the metal railing as it passed by. I felt deeply ashamed as the warm piss dribbled down my bare legs. Thankfully, nobody seemed to notice it but me.

'"That's just to show you that it's a real gun," the man said, "and that I mean what I say. Do you believe me now?"

'We both nodded. "What do you want?" Adrian asked.

'"I told you. I want to play."

'"Look," I said, "you're frightening us. Why don't you put the gun away? Then we'll play with you, won't we, Adrian?"

'Adrian nodded. "Yes."

'"This?" The man looked at his revolver as if seeing it for

the first time. 'But why should I want to put it away?"

'He fired again, closer this time, and a clod of earth flew up and stung my cheek. I was damned if I was going to cry, but I was getting close. I felt as if we were the only people for hundreds of miles, maybe the only people in the whole world. There was nobody to save us and this lunatic was going to kill us after he'd had his fun. I didn't know why, what made him act like that, or anything, but I just knew he was going to do it.

'"Don't you like this game?" he asked me.

'"No,' I said, trying to keep my voice from shaking. 'I want to go home."

'"Go on, then," he said.

'"What?"

'"I said go on."

'"You don't mean it."

'"Yes, I do. Go."

'Slowly, without taking my eyes off him, I backed up the bank towards the hole in the railings. Only when I got there, and I had to turn to squeeze through, did I take my eyes off him. As soon as I did, I heard another shot and felt the air move as something zipped by my ear. "I've changed my mind," he said. "Come back."

'Knowing, deep down, that it had been too good to be true, I slunk back to the bank. The man was muttering to himself, now, and neither Adrian nor I could make out what he was saying. In a way, that was even more frightening than hearing his words. He was pacing up and down, too, staring at the ground, his gun hanging at his side, but we knew that if either of us made the slightest movement, he would start shooting at us again.

'This went on for some time. I could feel myself sweating and the wetness down my legs was uncomfortable. Apart from the incomprehensible muttering across the water, everything was still and silent. No birds sang, almost as if they knew this was death's domain and had got out when they could. Even the cows and sheep were silent, and looked more like a landscape painting than real, living creatures. Maybe a barge would come, I prayed. Then he would have to hide his gun and we would have time to run up to the woods. But no barge came.

'Finally, he came to a pause in his conversation with himself, at least for the time being. "You," he said to Adrian, gesturing with his gun. "You can go now."

'"I don't believe you mean it," Adrian said.

'The man pointed the gun right at him. "Go. Before I change my mind and shoot you."

'Adrian scrambled up the grassy bank. I could hear him crying. I had never felt so alone in my life. Inside, I was praying for the man to tell Adrian to come back, the way he had with me. I didn't want to die alone by the dirty canal. I wanted to go home and see my mum and dad again.

'This time my prayers were answered.

'"Come back," he said. "I've changed my mind."

'"Are you going to shoot us?" I asked, when Adrian once again stood at my side, wiping his eyes on his sleeve.

'"I don't know," he said. 'It depends on what they tell me to do. Just shut up and let me think. Don't talk unless I ask you to."

'*They?* What on earth was he talking about? Adrian and I looked at one another, puzzled. There was nobody else around. Who was going to tell him what to do? You have to remember we were only kids, and we didn't know anything about insane people hearing voices and all that.

'"But *why*?" I asked. "Why are you doing this? We haven't done you any harm."

'He didn't say anything, just fired a shot – pop – into the bushes right beside me. It was enough. Then he started

240

talking again, and I think both Adrian and me now had an inkling that he was hearing the voices in his head, and that maybe he was having a conversation with the mysterious "they" he had mentioned.

'"All right," he said, the next time he calmed down. He pointed the gun at me. "What's your name?" he asked.

'"Joe," I said.

'"Joe. All right, Joe. You can go. What's your friend's name?"

'"Adrian."

'"Adrian stays."

'I stood my ground. "You're not going to let me go," I told him. "You'll only do the same as you did before."

'That made him angry and he started waving the gun around again. "Go!" he yelled at me. "Now! Before I shoot you right here."

'I went.

'Sure enough, when I got to the hole in the fence, I heard him laugh, a mad, eerie sound that sent a chill through me despite the heat of the day. "You didn't think I meant it, did you? Come back here, Joe."

'Somehow, the use of my name, the sound of it from *his* lips, on *his* breath, was worse than anything else. For a moment, I hesitated then I slipped through the hole in the railings and started running for my life.

'I knew that there was a hollow about thirty feet up the grassy slope, and if I reached it I would be safe. It was only a quick dash from there to the woods.

'I heard him shout again. "Joe, come back here right now!"

'I ran and ran. I heard the dull pop of his revolver and sensed something whiz by my right side and thud into the earth. My heart was pumping for all it was worth and the muscles on my legs felt fit to burst.

'But I made it. I made it to the hollow and dived into the

dip in the ground that would protect me from any more bullets. I heard just one more popping sound before I made my dash for the woods and that was it.'

Here, Joe paused, as if recounting the narrative had left him as out of breath as outrunning the lunatic's bullets. From our trench, we could hear more shots in the distance now and a shell exploded about two hundred yards to the west, lighting up the sky. Further away, somewhere behind our lines, a piper played. I handed around my cigarettes and noticed Jack Armstrong in the subdued glow of the match. Face ashen, eyes glazed, lips trembling, the kid was terrified and it was my guess that he'd freeze when the command came. I'd seen it happen before. Not that I blamed him. I sometimes wondered why we didn't all react that way. There but for the grace of God . . . I remembered Harry Mercer, who had tried for a Blighty in the foot and ended up losing the entire lower half of his left leg. Then there was Ben Castle, poor, sad Ben, who swore he'd do it himself before the Germans did it to him, and calmly put his gun in his mouth and pulled the trigger. So who were the heroes? And why?

'What happened next?' asked Arthur. 'Did you run and fetch the police?'

'The police? No,' said Joe. 'I don't really remember what I did. I think I just wandered around in a daze. I couldn't believe it had happened, you see, that I had been so close to death and escaped.'

'But what about your friend? What about Adrian?' Arthur persisted.

Joe looked right through him, as if he hadn't even heard the question. 'I waited until it was time to return home from school,' he went on, 'and that's exactly what I did. Went home. The piss stains on my trousers and underwear had dried by then, and if my mother noticed the next time she did the washing then she didn't say anything to me about it. We went on holiday the next day to stay for a week with my Aunt Betty on the coast near Scarborough. Every day I scoured my dad's newspaper when he'd put it aside after breakfast, but I could find no reference to the lunatic with the gun. I even started to believe that it had all been a figment of my imagination, that it hadn't happened at all.'

'But what about Adrian?' Arthur asked.

'Adrian? I had no idea. That whole week we were with Aunt Betty I wondered about him. Of course I did. But surely if anything had happened it would have been in the papers? Still, I knew I had deserted Adrian. I had dashed off to freedom and hadn't given him a second thought once I was in the woods.'

'But you must have seen him again,' I said.

'That's the funny thing,' Joe said. 'I did. It was about two days after we got back from our holiday. I saw him in the street. He started walking towards me. I was frightened because he was a year older than me, and bigger. I thought he was going to beat me up.'

'What did he do?' Arthur asked.

Joe laughed. 'That's the funny thing,' he said. 'Adrian walked up to me. I braced myself for an assault, and he said, "Thank you."

'I wasn't certain I'd heard him correctly, so I asked him to repeat what he'd said.

'"Thank you," he said again. "That was a very brave thing you did, dodging the bullets like that, risking death."

'I was stunned. I didn't know what to say. I must have stood there looking like a complete idiot, with my mouth hanging open.

'"Had he gone?" he asked me next.

'"Who?" I replied.

'"You know. The lunatic with the gun. I'll bet he'd gone when you came back with the police, hadn't he?"

243

'Now I understood what Adrian was thinking. "Yes," I said. "Yes, he'd gone."

'Adrian nodded. "I thought so. Look, I'm sorry," he went on, "sorry I didn't hang around till you got back with them, to help you explain and all, but I was so scared."

'"What happened?" I asked.

'"Well," Adrian said, "as soon as you made it to the woods, he ran off down the canal bank. He must have known you'd soon be back with help, and he didn't want to hang around and get caught. I probably stood there for a few moments to pull myself together, then I headed off in the same direction you did. I just went home as if I'd been to school and didn't say a word to anyone. I'm sorry," he said again. "I should have stuck around when you came back with the police."

'"It's all right," I said. "They didn't believe me. They thought I was just a trouble-maker. One of them gave me a clip around the ear and they sent me home. Said if anything like that ever happened again they'd tell my mum and dad."

'Adrian managed to laugh at that. I was feeling so relieved I could have gone on all day making things up. How I went back to try and rescue Adrian by myself and found the man a little further down the bank. How I carried the loose railing like a spear and threw it at him across the canal, piercing him right through the heart. Then how I weighted his body with stones and dropped it in the water. But I didn't. It was enough that I was exonerated in Adrian's eyes. Good enough that I was a *hero*.'

Joe began to laugh and it sounded so eerie, so *mad*, that it sent shivers up our spines. Jack Armstrong started crying. He wasn't going anywhere. And Joe was still laughing when the black night inched towards another grey dawn and the orders came down for us to go over the top and take a godforsaken blemish on the map called Passchendaele.

CONCERTO FOR VIOLENCE AND ORCHESTRA

James Sallis

To the memory of Jean-Patrick Manchette

It is a beautiful fall day and he has driven nonstop, two days
chewed down to the rind and the rind spit out, from New
York. He should be tired, exhausted in fact, spent, but he
isn't. Every few hours he stops for a meal, briefly trading the
warm vinyl Volvo seat for one not unlike it in a string of
Shoneys, Dennys and Union 76 truckstops. On the seat and
the floorboard beside him are packets of water crackers,
plugs of cheese, bottles of selzer and depleted carry-out cups
of coffee, wasabi peas. In the old world he drove away from,
tips of leaves had gone crimson, bright yellow and orange,
gold. Now he is coming into the desert outside Phoenix, the
nearest thing he ever had to a home. Crisp morning air rushes
into open windows. He passes an ostrich farm, impossibly
canting stacks of huge stone like primitive altars out among
the low scrub and cholla, a burning car at roadside with no
one nearby. On the radio a song he vaguely remembers from
what he thinks of as Back Then plays. He is happy.
Strangely, this has nothing to do with the fact that soon he

will be dead or that within the past month he has killed four people.

Pryor was the one who told him about it. There were these small rooms behind the huge open basement area used for church dinners, summer Bible School, youth meetings, evenings of amateur entertainment where groups of teenagers blackened faces with burnt cork and donned peculiar hats for minstrel shows, nerdish young men in ill-fitting suits and top hats urged objects from thin air and underscored the tentativeness of it all by transforming silk handkerchiefs to doves, sponge balls to coins, and where the church's music director in his hairpiece trucked out again and again, relentlessly, his repertoire of pantomime skits: a man flying for the first time, a foreigner confronted for the first time by jello, a child on his first fishing trip forced to bait his own hook. (Is there something intrinsically funny about firsts?)

In the ceiling of one of those rooms was a small framed section, like a doorway. You could drag the table beneath, Pryor said, place a chair on the table, reach up and push the inset away. Then you could climb up in there. And if you kept going, always up, along stairways and ladders and catwalks, in and out of cramped crawl spaces, eventually you'd arrive at the steeple, where few before had ever ventured. A great secret, Pryor intimated. The whole climb was probably the equivalent of three floors at the most. But to Quentin's eyes and imagination then, the climb seemed vast, illimitable, and he felt as though he might be ascending into a different, perhaps even a better, world.

It would not take much, after all. For it to be a better world.

Pushing the door out of its frame and pulling up from the chair, legs flailing, Quentin found himself in a low chamber much like a closet turned on its side. He couldn't stand erect,

248

but the far end of the chamber was unenclosed, and he passed through into an open, vaultlike space with a narrow walkway of bare boards nailed to beams. The nailheads were the size of dimes. Four yards or so further along, this walkway turned sharply right, fetching up rather soon at the base of a stairway steep and narrow as a ladder. The last few yards indeed *became* a ladder. Then he was there. Alone and far above the mundane, the ordinary, all those lives in their suits and cars and their cluttered houses with pot roasts cooking in ovens and laundry drying on lines out back. Quentin had seen *Around the World in Eighty Days* half a dozen times. This must be what it was like to go up in a balloon, float free, feel the ground surrender its claim on you. He was becoming David Niven.

Meanwhile he'd given no thought to Pryor, who seemed to have failed to follow, if indeed Pryor had begun at all.

Sunday School teacher Mr Robert, however, had been giving them both thought. He'd only a quarter-hour past dismissed the boys and now took note of their absence from services. So it was that, shortly after attaining his steeple, Quentin found himself being escorted down the aisle alongside Pryor and deposited in a front pew as Brother Douglas paused dramatically in his sermon, light fell like an accusing finger through stained-glass windows illustrating parables and the entire congregation looked on.

He was caught that time, but never again.

The steeple became Quentin's special place. Just as other children spend hours and whole days of their lives sunk into books, board games or television, so Quentin spent his in the steeple, there by speaker horns that had taken the place of bells, sandwiches and a thermos of juice packed away in his school lunch box. Since of all things at his disposal his parents were least likely to miss one can of it among many, the sandwiches were generally Spam, which Quentin liked with mayonnaise and lots of pepper, sometimes sliced pickles. The bread was white, the juice that in name only, wholly innocent of fruit, rather some marvelous, alchemical compounding of concentrates, artificial flavors and Paracelsus knows what else.

Sometimes up there in the steeple Quentin would pull himself to the edge and lie prone, propping elbows at the correct angle and sighting along an imaginary rifle as Jenny Bulow, Doug Prather or the straggling Dowdy family climbed from cars and crossed the parking lot below.

Years later, half a world away and more than once, Quentin would find himself again in exactly that same position.

But this has nothing to do with his life now, he always insisted – to himself, for few others knew about it. That was another time, another place. Another person, you might as well say. Quentin came home from that undeclared war and its long aftermath an undeclared hero even to himself, and after much searching (*You have no college? You* have *to have college!*) took a job at Allied Beverage, where he still works. Where he worked until last month, at least. He hasn't been in, or called, and doubts they've held the position for him. It's not as though they'd have much difficulty finding someone to take up his slack: keep track of health-care benefits, paid time off, excused absences, time and attendance, IRAs. Holidays the company loaded employees up with discontinued lines, champagnes no one asked to the prom, odd bottled concoctions of such things as cranberry juice and vodka, lemonade and brandy, licorice-flavored liqueurs. After work they'd all be out in the parking lot stowing this stuff in trunks. It would follow them home, go about its unassuming existence on various shelves and in various cabinets till, months or years later, it got thrown out. The company made little more ado over throwing away its people.

*

He pushed. Recently there'd been rain, and enough water remained to bear the body away. But you couldn't see the water. It looked as though the body were sliding on its back, on its own momentum, along the canal. Further on, an oil slick broke into a sickly rainbow. Food wrappers, drink containers, condoms, beer cans and unidentifiable bits of clothing decorated the canal's edge. Down here one entered an elemental world, cement belly curved like a ship's hold, walls to either side as far as one could see. Jonah's whale, what Mars or the moon might look like, a landscape even more basic than that stretching for endless miles around the city. Out there, barren land and plants like something dredged from sea bottoms. He looked up. Air shimmered atop the canal's cement walls, half a dozen palm trees thrust shaggy heads into the sky. The body moved slowly away from him in absolute silence. Out a few yards, it hit deeper water, an imperceptible incline perhaps, and picked up speed, began to turn slowly round and round. Water had soaked into the fabric of the man's cheap blue suit and turned it purple. Blue dye spread out like a stain in the water beneath him. When he looked up again, two kids were there on the wall, peering over. Their eyes went back and forth from the body to him. He waved.

He'd picked up a new car nearby, in one of those suburbs with walls behind which the rich live so safely, at a mall there. Tempted by a Lexus, he settled on a Honda Accord. That's what this country does, of course, it holds out temptation after temptation, forever building appetites that can't be assuaged. He didn't know if the Crown Vic was on anyone's list yet, but over the past few days he'd pushed it pretty hard. Probably time to change mounts. He left it there by the Accord. The whole exchange took perhaps five minutes.

For that matter, he had no reason to believe anyone might be on him, but one didn't take chances. Never move in straight lines.

He drove out of town, out into the desert, everything earth-colored so that it was difficult to say where city ended, desert began. But after a time, the walls, walls around individual houses, walls around whole communities, petered away. Lemon trees were in bloom, filling the air with their sweet sting. Bursts of vivid oleander at roadside. Imperial cactus.

The Accord handled wonderfully, a pleasure to drive. He settled back and, looking about, started to come to some sense of the life its owner lived. A small life, circumscribed, routine. Scattering bits of rainbow, a crystal key chain swung from the rear-view mirror. The compartment behind the gear shift held tapes of Willie Nelson, Johnny Mathis, Enya, Van Morrison. A much-thumbed copy of *Atlas Shrugged* on the floor. The owner had tossed empty water bottles behind his seat after screwing the tops back on, so that many of them had collapsed into themselves. There were a couple of bronchodilator inhalers in the glove compartment. Find yourself without one, tap the guy next to you and borrow his: everyone in the state carries them. Physicians used to send what were then called chest patients here for their health. They came, bringing their plants and their cars with them. Drive into Phoenix, the first thing you see's a brown film on the horizon. The city diverts water from all over to keep lawns and golf courses green, buys electric power at a premium to run the city's myriad air conditioners. Its children gulp for air.

On the rear floor there were two-hundred-dollar running shoes, in the back seat itself a sweatshirt and windbreaker from Land's End, a red baseball cap, a deflated soccer ball, a thick yellow towel. In the bin just fore of the gearshift he found the notice of a bank overdrawal that George Hassler (he knew the name from the registration) had crumpled and thrown there. Angrily?

America.

Was there any more alien a landscape than the one in which he found himself – this long, trailing exhaust of desert, mountains forever in the distance – anywhere? He drove across dry runnels marked Coyote Wash or Aqua Fria River, chugged in the new carapace past piles, pillars and ∏s of stone to challenge Stonehenge or Carnac, past crass billboards, cement oases of gas stations, fast-food stalls and convenience stores chock full of sugary drinks, salty snacks, racks of sunglasses, souvenir T-shirts, Indian jewelry. Past those regal cacti.

They stood like sentinels, in an endless variety of configurations, on hillside and plain, some of them over forty feet. Most never made it through their first year of life. Those that did, grew slowly. A saguaro could take a hundred and fifty years to reach full height; in another fifty years it died. Some would never develop arms, while others might have two or four or six all upraised like candelabra, or dozens of them twisted and pointing in all directions. No one knew why this happened. Shallow and close to the surface, root systems ran out as much as a hundred feet, allowing the plants rapidly to soak up even minimal rainfalls. As the cactus took on water, its accordionlike pleats expanded. Woodpeckers and other birds often made their way into it to nest. Some, particularly hawks and the cactus wren, preferred to nest at junctures of arm and trunk. Red-tailed hawks would build large platform nests there; they'd come back again and again, every year, till the pair stopped nesting altogether. Over a six-week period in May and June, brilliant flowers emerged atop mature cacti. These would bloom for twenty-four hours only, opening at night, closing for ever against the heat of day.

253

Lizards were everywhere and just as ancient. They scampered out from beneath tangles of cholla, crouched soaking up sun atop stones, skittered across the highway, minds clenched on memories of endless rain forests, green shade, green sunlight. Brains the size of bb shot enfolded dioramas, whole maps in stark detail, of worlds long gone, worlds long ago lost.

At a truck stop near Benson, Arizona, where the pie was excellent, a young man came up to say he'd seen him arrive in the Honda Accord. On one wall dinner plates with figures of wildlife hung among framed photographs of motorbikes and vintage automobiles; on the other, portraits of John Wayne, Elvis, Marilyn and James Dean. Out back, a crude hand-painted sign with the cameo of a Confederate soldier and the legend Rebel Café leaned against a crèche of discarded water heaters, stoves, sinks and minor appliances from which a rheumy-eyed dog peered out, as from an undersea grotto.

The young man wore an XXL purple-and-blue plaid shirt over a red T-shirt gone dull maroon, and well-used black jeans a couple of inches too long. The back half or so of the leg bottoms had been trod to shreds. Quentin's first thought as the young man approached was that he wore a baseball cap in the currently fashionable front-to-back style. But now he saw it was a skullcap. Knit, like those he'd seen on Africans.

'Had the Accord long?'

Quentin looked up at the young man. For all the alarm his question set off, this was obviously no cop. No more challenge or anxiety in those eyes than in Quentin's own. He approved, too, of the way the young man held back, staying on his feet, not presuming. Quentin nodded to the young man to join him. A corner booth. Nondescript beige plastic covering, blue paint above. Carpentry tacks stood out like a line of small brass turtles crossing the horizon.

'Had one myself,' the young man said. 'Accord, just like yours. Got off from work one day, came out and it was gone. First time I ever talked to police face to face.'

The waitress came to refill Quentin's coffee. He asked if the young man wanted anything. He shook his head.

'Same week, my apartment got broken into. Took the stereo, TV, small appliances, most of the clothes. Even hauled off a footlocker I'd had since college, filled with God knows what. I came home from a six-mile run, took one look around and said fuck it. Knew at some level I'd been *wanting* this to happen. Clear the decks. Free me to start over.'

Sipping his third cup of coffee, Quentin watched truckers as they bowed heads over eggs and ham, looking to be in prayer. From nearby booths drifted strains of pragmatic seductions, complaints about jobs and wives, political discussions. A hash of all the age-old songs.

In the car the young man fell asleep almost at once. He'd propped feet on his duffel bag; the world bucked up unseen, unfired upon, in the notch of his knees. Choppy piano music played on the local university station. Quentin hit Scan. Sound and world alike tilted all about him, falling away, rearranging itself. Rock, country, news, chatter. Stone, cactus, wildflowers, trailer park.

Awake now, Quentin's passenger said, 'Where are we?'

'Pretty much where we were before. It's only been a couple of hours.'

He thought about that.

'Damn.'

Roadside, an elderly Latino sold cabbage, cucumbers and bags of peppers out of the bed of his truck, the cover of which unfolded and sat atop rough wood legs to form a tent. A younger woman (daughter? wife?) sat on the ground in the shade of the truck, reading.

'Where we going?' Quentin's passenger said.

'East.'

Towards El Paso, one of America's great in-between cities. They ate in a truck stop on I-10 just outside Los Cruces, a place the size of a gymnasium smelling of onions, hot grease and diesel. Meat loaf was the daily special, with mashed potatoes and boiled cabbage on the side. Using his fork like a squeegee, Quentin's passenger scraped his plate clean, then caught up with a piece of bread what minuscule leavings remained.

Eschewing the Interstate, Quentin took the long way in, the back road as locals say, Route 28, skirting fields of cotton, chilis, onions and alfalfa, tunneling through the 2.7-mile green, cool canopy of Stahman Farm's pecan orchards, up past San Miguel, La Mesa, Chambertino, La Union. The sun was settling into the cleft of the mountains to the left, throwing out its net of evening to reel the world in. As they pulled onto Mesa, parking lots outside shops and offices were emptying, streets filling with cars, street lights coming on.

'You can let me out up at that corner,' Quentin's passenger said. 'Appreciate the ride. Looks like a good place, El Paso. For a while.' He leaned back into the window. 'They're all good places for a while, right?'

Dinner became caldo and chicken mole at Casa Herado, the rest of the evening a movie on the cable channel at La Quinta off Mesa on Remcon Circle.

In the space between seat and door on the passenger's side, Quentin found a well-worn wallet bound with rubber bands and containing a driver's license, social security card and two or three low-end charge cards for James Parker. Left behind, obviously, by his passenger. Had the young man stolen it, lifted it, liberated it? Much of the gypsy about him, no doubt about that. But mostly Quentin remembered the young man's remarks about becoming free, starting over.

By five in the morning, light in hot pursuit, Quentin was on Transmountain Road heading through Smuggler's Pass to Rim Road where, at one of the slumbering residential palaces there, he swapped the Honda for a Crown Vic. Some banker or real-estate salesman would greet the morning with unaccustomed surprise. Quentin hoped the man liked his new car. His own smelt faintly of cigars, spilled milk and bourbon. Wires had hung below the dash even before those Quentin tugged out and touched together. But when he goosed the accelerator in query, the car shuddered and roared to let him know it was ready.

Years ago in Texas, Quentin had witnessed an execution. The whole lethal injection thing was new back then and no one knew just how to proceed. Some sort of ritual seemed in order, though, so things were said by the warden, a grizzled, stoop-shouldered man looking twice his probable age, then by a tow-headed chaplain looking half his. It was difficult to find much to say. Casey Cortland had led a wholly unremarkable, all but invisible life before one warm Friday evening in the space of an hour killing his wife of twelve years, his ten-year-old son and eight-year-old daughter, and the lay minister of a local church. Cortland was brought in and strapped to a table. Beneath prison overalls, Quentin knew, he was diapered. Unlike the warden and chaplain, Cortland had no final words. When they injected the fatal drug, he seized: the IV line pulled out and went flying, dousing all those seated close by with toxic chemicals. State police took Quentin, who'd caught the spray directly in his eyes, to Parkland. Though basically unharmed, for several weeks he suffered blurred vision and headaches. Hours later on the prison parking lot Quentin reclaimed his Volvo, then I-30. Hour by hour, chunks of Texas broke off and fell away in his rear-view mirror. That night he had the dream for the first time. In the dream, along with an estimated half-million other viewers, he watched as Tiffany's father was eaten on camera, the mid-morning show live, producers and cameramen too stunned to shut it all down. Tiffany used to have a pair of earrings with the bottom half of a man hanging out of a shark's mouth. That's not what it was like. It wasn't like anything Quentin or other viewers had ever seen. Tiffany's father's legs rolled back and forth, feet pointing north-north-east, north-north-west, as the tiger chewed and pawed and pulled back its head to tear away chunks. There were sounds. Screams at first, then not so many. Gristle sounds, bone sounds. Growls. Or was it purring? Panels of experts, rapidly assembled, offered explanations of what this event said about society's implicit violence. Then Tiffany herself was there, sobbing into the microphone held close to her face like a second bulbous nose. Daddy only did it for her, she said. He did everything for her.

All that day off and on, Back Then as he now thought of it, Quentin had spent writing a letter he hoped might persuade Allied's insurance carriers to reconsider Sandy Buford's claim. Every two minutes the phone rang, people kept washing up from the passageway outside his cubicle, his boss broke in like a barge with queries re one or another file, the list of calls to return and calls to be made seemed as always to grow longer instead of shorter. Sandy had hurt his back on the job and now, following surgery, wasn't able to lift the poundage Allied's job description required. He was a good worker, with the company over fourteen years. But since the surgeon had released him and he couldn't meet the job's bottom line – even though Sandy's actual work from day to day didn't call for lifting – the insurance carrier had begun disallowing all claims, refusing payment to physicians, labs and physical therapists, and effectively blocking the company's efforts to re-employ him. Quentin's letter summarised the case in concise detail, explained why Allied believed the carrier's disallowment to be inappropriate and in error, and put forth a convincing argument (Quentin hoped) for re-evaluation.

Pulling out of the parking lot at 6.18, just a little over an hour late leaving, on the spur of the moment Quentin decided to swing by Sandy Buford's and drop off a copy of the letter, let him know someone cared. Quentin had called to let Ellie know how late he was running; she was expecting him home. But this would only take a few minutes.

Buford's address bore him to a sea of duplexes and shabby apartment buildings at city's edge. Many of them looked like something giant children, given blocks and stucco, might erect. Discarded appliances formed victory gardens in side and back yards. Long-dead cars and trucks sat in driveways, ancient life forms partially reconstructed from remains.

Quentin waded through front yards that may well have seen conga lines of children dancing their parents' preference for Adlai Stevenson over Ike (when had people stopped caring that much?) and climbed a stairwell where the Rosenbergs' execution could have been a major topic of discussion. One expected the smell of cooking cabbage. These days the smell of Quarter Pounders, Whoppers, Pizza Hut and KFC were far more likely, maybe a bit of cumin or curry mixed in.

Buford's apartment was on the third floor. There was music playing inside, sounded like maybe a TV as well, but no one responded to Quentin's knocks. Finally he pushed a copy of the letter, tucked into an Allied Beverage pay envelope, beneath it. He was almost to the second landing when he heard four loud cracks, like limbs breaking. Instinctively he drew back against the wall as two young men burst from the apartment nearest the stairwell. Both wore nylon stockings over their faces. Quentin moved forward, peered over the bannister just as one of them after pulling off his stocking glanced up.

That was the footprint he left.

Careful to give the two men ample time to exit, Quentin continued down the stairs. He was turning the corner on to Central in his Taurus when the first police cars came barreling down it.

A dozen blocks along, he began to wonder if those were the same headlights behind him. He turned on to Magnolia, abruptly into the parking lot at Cambridge Arms, pulled back out on to Elm. Still there. Same brilliance, same level, dipping a beat or so after he dipped, buoying up moments later. He pulled into a Sonic and ordered a drink. Drove on a half-mile or more before pulling up at the curb and getting out, motor left idling, to buy the early edition of tomorrow's newspaper. No lights behind him when he took to the street. Whoever it had been, back there, following him, was gone. If there'd been anyone. Only his imagination, most likely.

He said nothing of this to Ellie, neither as they had a pre-prandial glass of wine before the fireplace, nor as she pulled plates of flank steak, mashed potatoes and brussels sprouts, foil covered, from the oven, nor as, afterwards, they sat before the lowering fire with coffee. He spoke, instead, of the minutiae of his day. Office politics, the latest barge of rumor and gossip making its way upriver, cylinders banging, his concern over Sandy Buford. She shared in turn the minutiae of *her* day, including a visit to Dr Worrell.

Head against his shoulder, 12.37 when last he glanced at the clock bedside, Ellie fell fast asleep. Quentin himself was almost asleep when he heard the crash of a window downstairs.

*

The car hesitates, only a moment, though it must seem for ever, there at the lip.

He's not sure of any of this, of course. Not sure if it really happened, how it happened, where or when. More than once he's thought it might be only something suggested to him by a therapist; something he's read or seen on the dayroom TV whose eye is as bleary and unfocused as those of its watchers; something that he's imagined, a dream breaking like a whale from the depths of that long sleep. Yet it keeps coming back – like that other dream of a man being eaten by a tiger on live TV. Again and again in his mind's eye he *sees* it. It's as real as the plastic furniture, coffee makers and floor polishers around him – realer than most things in this world he's begun re-entering. But mind is only a screen, upon which anything may be projected.

Go on, then.

The car hesitates there at the lip.

With no warning a woman's nude body, pale as the moon, had stepped into his headlights on that barren stretch of road. Flying saucers might just as well have set down beside him.

He'd left Cave Creek half an hour past. No houses or much of anything else out here, no lights, headlights or other cars, this time of night at least, few signs of human life at all, just this vast scoop of dark sky above and, at the edge of his lights, vague huddled shapes of low scrub, creosote, cholla, prickly pear. Further off the road, tall saguaro with arms upraised – then the heavier darkness of sawtooth mountains.

Had he a destination in mind? Into Phoenix via some roundabout route to take dinner at a crowded restaurant perhaps, hopscotching over his isolation, his loneliness? Or, as he pushed ever deeper into the desert, did he mean to flee something else altogether, the dribble of headlights on gravel roads about him, high-riding headlights of trucks and SUVs behind, silhouettes of houses on hills half a mile away, himself?

His name was Parker.

He'd taken over a light-struck house with exposed beams and white shutters, leaving behind, at the apartment where he'd been staying, the pump of accordions through open windows, songs whose tag line always seemed to be *mi corazon*, afternoons filled with the sound of stationary racing motors from tanklike ancient Fords and Buicks being worked on in the parking lot. Coyotes at twilight walked three or four to the pack down the middle of streets. First night there, he'd sat watching a hawk fall from the sky to carry off a cat. The cat had come over to investigate this new person or say hello. It had leapt onto the half-wall facing his front door, ground to wall in that effortless, levitating way they have, here one moment, there the next. Then just as suddenly the hawk had appeared – swooping away with the cat into a sunset like silent bursting shells.

He remembered eating dinner, some pasta concoction he had only to pop into the microwave. Then he'd gone outside with a bottle of wine, watching day bleed away to its end, watching the hawk make off with the cat, watching as night parachuted grandly into the mountains. He'd gone in to watch part of a movie, then, bottle depleted, decided on a ride. In the car he found a tape of Indian flute music. Drove off, empty himself, into the desert's greater and somehow comforting emptiness.

Till the nude woman appeared before him.

Again: he has no idea how much of this is actual; how much remembered, suggested, imagined. Why, just returned from a turnabout trip to New York, and at that time of night, would he have driven off into the desert – driven anywhere, for that matter? What could have borne him off the highway on to that road, through fence breaks and boulders, up the bare mountainside, to its edge? What could the woman have been doing there, nude, in his headlights?

Seeing her, he swerves, instinctively left, away from the rim, but fetches up against a rise there and slides back, loose stone giving way at his rear when he hits his brakes.

The car rocks back.

In the moment before his windshield fills with dark sky and stars, he sees her there before the car, arms out like a bullfighter, breasts swaying. Braid of dark hair. In his rear-view mirror, a canyon of the sort Cochise and his men might have used, subterranean rivers from which they'd suddenly rise into the white man's world to strike, into which they'd sink again without trace.

Though the car's motor has stalled, the tape plays on as the flutist begins to sing wordlessly behind the breath of his instrument, providing his own ghostly accompaniment. A lizard scampers across the windshield. Music, sky and lizard alike go with him over the edge and down – down for a long time.

His name, the name of the person to whom this happens, is Parker.

Without thought, he left her there.

Acting purely on instinct, he was halfway across the roof before anything like actual thought or volition came, before the webwork of choices began forming in his mind. Never let the opponent choose the ground. Withdraw, lure the opponent on to your own, or at least on to neutral ground. By then years of training and action had broken over him like a flood. Four days later, on a Monday, Quentin stood looking down at two bodies. These were the men he'd seen fleeing the apartment below Sandy Buford's. For a moment it was Ellie's body he saw there on the floor of that faceless motel room. He knew from newspaper accounts that the two of them had spent some time at the house once he'd fled. He tried not to think how long, tried not to imagine what had happened there.

Surprisingly, as in the old days, he bore them no direct ill will. They were working men like himself, long riders, dogs let loose on the grounds.

Himself who, hearing the window crash downstairs, rolled from bed on to his feet and was edging out on to the roof even as footsteps sounded on the stairs. Then was up and over.

With small enough satisfaction he took their car, a mid-range Buick. A simple thing to pull wires out from beneath the dash, cross them. Somewhere in it he would find the map he needed, something about the car would guide him. He had that faith. Everyone left footprints.

Never blame the cannon. Find the hands that set elevation, loaded and primed it, lit the fuse. Find the mouth that gave the order.

They'd have to die, of course, those two. But that was only the beginning.

The world comes back by degrees. There are shapes, patterns of dark and light, motion that corresponds in some vague way to sounds arriving from out there. They knock at your door with luggage in hand, these sounds. While in here you have a great deal of time to think, to sink back into image and sensation in which language has no place. Again and again you see a sky strewn with stars, a lizard's form huge among them, a woman's pale body.

Constantly, it seems, you are aware of your breathing as an envelope that surrounds you, contains you.

For some reason flute music, itself a kind of breath, remains, tendrils of memory drifting through random moments of consciousness. Memory and present time have fused. Each moment's from a book. You page backward, forward, back again. All of it has the same import, same imprimatur.

Faces bend close above you. When you see them, they all look the same. You're fed bitter pastes of vegetables and meat. Someone pulls at your leg, rotates the ankle, pushes up on the ball of your foot to flex it. Two women talk overhead, about home and boyfriends and errant children, as they roll you side to side, wiping away excrement, changing sheets. One day you realise that you can feel the scratchiness, the warmth, of their washclothes.

The TV is left on all the time. At night (you know it's night because no one disturbs you then) the rise and fall of this voice proves strangely comforting. Worst is mid-morning when everything goes shrill: voices of announcers and game show hosts, the edgy canned laughter of sitcoms, commercials kicked into overdrive.

There are, too, endless interrogations. At first, even when you can't, even when it's all you can do to keep from drowning in the flood of words and you're wholly unable to respond, you try to answer. Further along, having answered much the same queries for daily generations of social workers, medical students and interns, you refuse to participate, silent now for quite a different reason.

The world comes back by degrees, and slowly, by degrees, you understand that it's not the world you left. Surreptitious engineers have sneaked in and built a new world while you slept. In this world you're but a tourist, a visitor, an impostor. They'll find you out, some small mistake you'll make.

Mr Parker, do you know where you are?

Can you tell me what happened?

Can you move your hand, feet, eyes?

Do you know who's President?

Is there anything you need?
'No.'

Here is what my visitor tells me.

We met, Julie and this Parker, just out of school, both still dragging along cumbersome ideals that all but dwarfed us. Once, she said, I told her how as a kid I'd find insects in drawers and cabinets lugging immense, stagecoach-like egg cases behind. That's what it was like.

We had our own concept of manifest destiny, Julie said. No doubt about it, it was up to us to change the world. We'd have long conversations over pizza at the Raven, beer at the Rathskeller, burgers at Maple Street Café. What could we do? Push a few books back into place and the world's shelves would be in order again? We fancied ourselves chiropractors of chaos and corruption: one small adjustment here, a realignment there, all would come straight.

Colonialism. Chile and the CIA. South Africa, Vietnam, our own inner cities, Appalachia. We imagined we were unearthing all manner of rare truth, whereas in truth, as immensely privileged middle-class whites, we were simply learning what most of the world had known for ever.

When I found out you were here, I had to come, she says. How long has it been? Twenty years?

She works as a volunteer at the hospital. Saw my name on the admissions list and thought: *Could it possibly be?*

Other things you begin to remember:

The smell of grapefruit from the backyard of the house across the alley from your apartment.

The rustle of pigeons high overhead in the topknots of palm trees.

Geckos living in a crack in the wall outside your window. By daylight larger lizards come out on to the ledge and rest there. Lizard aerobics: they push their bodies up on to extended legs. Lizard hydraulics: they ease back down.

Dry river beds.

Empty swimming pools painted sky-blue.

Mountains.

Even in the center of the city, you're always within sight of mountains. Mornings, they're shrouded in smog, distant, surreal and somehow prehistoric, as though just now, as slowly the earth warms, taking form. Late-afternoon sunlight breaks through clouds in fanlike shafts, washes the mountains in brilliance, some of them appearing black as though burned, others in close relief. Spectacular sunsets break over them at night – and plunge into them.

Sometimes you'd drive into the desert with burritos or a bottle of wine to witness those sunsets. Other times you'd go out there to watch storms gather. Doors fell open above you: great tidal waves of wind and lightning, the whole sky alive with fire.

This is when you were alive.

'You're going to be okay, Mr Parker.'

Her name, I remember, though I check myself with a glance at her nametag, is Marcia. On the margins of the nametag, which is the size of a playing card, she has pasted tiny pictures of rabbits and angels.

'The doctors will be in to speak with you shortly.'

I wonder just how they'll speak with me shortly. Use abbreviations, clipped phrases or accents, some special form of semaphore taught them in medical school? One rarely understands what they say in all earnest.

Marcia is twenty-eight. Her husband left her six months ago, she now lives in a garage apartment with an ex-biker truck driver named Jesse. To this arrangement Jesse has brought a baggage of tattoos (including two blue jailhouse tears at the edge of one eye) and his impression of life as a scrolling roadway, six hundred miles to cover before his day and daily case of beer are done. To this arrangement she's brought a four-year-old daughter, regular paychecks and notions of enduring love. Hers is the heavier burden.

I've paid attention, watched closely, hoping to learn to pass here in this new world. I know the lives of these others just as, slowly, I am retrieving my own.

Of course it's my own.

Marcia leans over me, wraps the bladder of the blood-pressure monitor about my arm, inflates it. 'It's coming back to you, isn't it?'

Some of it.

'No family that you know of?'

None.

'I'm sorry. Families are a good thing at times like this.'

She tucks the blood-pressure cuff behind its wall gauge and plucks the digital thermometer from beneath my tongue, ejecting its sheath into the trash can.

'Things are going to be tough for a while. Hate to think about your having to go it alone,' she says, turning back at the door. 'Need anything else right now?'

No.

I turn my head to the window. Hazy white sky out there, bright. Always bright in Phoenix, Valley of the Sun. Maybe when I get out I'll move to Tucson, always have liked Tucson. Its uncluttered streets and mountains and open sky, the way the city invites the desert in to live.

With a perfunctory knock at the door, Marcia re-enters. 'Almost forgot.' A Post-It Note. 'Call when you can, she says.'

Julie.

Back when we first met we'd walk, late afternoons, along Turtle Creek, downtown Dallas out of sight to one side,

Highland Park to the other, as Mercedes, Beamers and the bruised, battered, piled-high trucks of Hispanic gardeners made their ways home on the street. Just up the rise, to either side of Cedar Springs, bookstores, guitar shops and tiny ethnic restaurants straggled. Within the year, glassy brickfront office buildings took up residence and began staring them down. Within the year, all were gone.

She tells me this when she comes to visit.

Twenty years.

She never had children. Her husband died eight years ago. She has a cat. I've thought of you often, Julie says.

Tucked into a compartment in the driver's door Quentin found a rental agreement. When you need a car, rentals are always a good bet. You can identify them from the license plates mostly, and no one gets in a hurry over stolen rentals. The contract was with Dr Samuel Taylor, home address Iowa City, local address c/o William Taylor at an ASU dorm. Mr Taylor had paid by Visa. Good chance he was visiting a son, then, and that the car had been boosted somewhere in Tempe. Quentin called the rental agency, saying he'd seen some Hispanic teenagers who looked like they didn't belong in this car, noticed the plate, and was checking to see if it might have been reported stolen. But he couldn't get any information from the woman who answered the phone, and hung up when she started demanding his name and location.

A dead end.

He left his motel room (first floor rear, alley behind, paid for with cash) and went back to the Buick. He wasn't driving it, but he'd left it out of sight where he could get to it.

Neither of them had smoked. Radio buttons were set at three oldie stations, one country, one easy listening. The coat folded on the back seat he assumed to be Dr Taylor's; few enforcers (if that's what the two were) wore camel hair. Likewise the leather attaché case tucked beneath the driver's seat, which, at any rate, held nothing of interest. The paperback under the passenger's seat was a different matter. *Lesbian Wife*, half the pages so poorly impressed as to be all but unreadable. Tucked in between page 34 and 35 was a cash ticket from Good Night Motel.

Good Night Motel proved a miracle of cheap construction and tacky cover-up the builder no doubt charged off as architectural highlights. The clerk inside was of similar strain, much preoccupied with images on a six-inch TV screen alongside an old-style brass cash register. However he tried to direct them away, his eyes kept falling back to it.

'Look, I'm just here days,' he said, scant moments after Quentin tired of equivocations and had braced to drag him bodily across the desk's chipped formica. 'Never saw them. Might check at the bar.' And heaved a sigh as a particularly gripping episode of *Gilligan's Island* was left unspoiled?

In contrast to the inertial desk clerk, the barkeep was a wiry little guy who couldn't be still. He twitched, twisted, moved salt shakers, coasters and ashtrays around as though playing himself in a board game, drummed fingers on the bar top. He had a thin mustache and sharp features. Something of the rat about him.

Quentin asked for brandy, got a blank stare and changed his request to a draft with whiskey back. He put a fifty on the bar.

'I don't have change.'

'You won't need it.'

Quentin described the two men. The barkeep nudged a bin of lime wedges square into its cradle.

'Sure, they been in. Three, four nights this week. Not last night, though. One does shots, Jack Daniels. Other's a beer man. Friends of yours?'

'Purely professional. Guys have money coming, from an inheritance. Lawyers hired me to find them.'

'Sure they did.'

Quentin pushed the fifty closer. 'That covers the drinks. People I work for –'

'Lawyers, you mean.'

'Right. The lawyers. Been known to be big tippers.'

Another fifty went on the counter, closer to Quentin than to the bartender.

'Four blocks down, south corner, Paradise Motor Hotel. Saw them turn in there on my way home one night. Bottom-line kind of place, the Paradise. No bar, no place to eat. Gotta hoof it to Denny's a dozen blocks uptown. Or come here.'

Quentin pushed the second fifty on to the first.

'Freshen that up for you?' the barkeep asked.

'Why not?'

He waved away Quentin's offer of payment. 'This one's on me.'

Afterwards – it all happened quickly and more or less silently, no reason to think he'd be interrupted – Quentin searched that faceless motel room. Nothing. Sport coats and shirts hanging in the closet, usual toiletries by the bathroom sink, a towel showing signs of dark hair dye. Couple issues of *Big Butt* magazine.

Quentin went downstairs and across rippled asphalt to the office, set into a bottleneck of an entryway that let whoever manned the desk watch all comings and goings. Today a woman in her mid-twenties manned it. She looked the way librarians do in movies from the Fifties. This kind of place, a phone deposit was required if you planned to use it, and even local calls had to go through the desk. They got charged to the room. The records, of course, are private. Of course they are, he responded – and should be. Twenty dollars further on, they became less private. Another dour Lincoln and Quentin was looking at them. He wondered what she might do with the money. Nice new lanyard for her glasses, special food for the cat?

There'd been one call to 528-1000 (Pizza Palace), two to 528-1888 (Ming's Chinese) and three to 528-1433. That last was a lawyer's office in a strip mall clinging like a barnacle to city's edge, flanked by a cut-rate shoe store and family clothing outlet. Like many of his guild, David Cohen proved reluctant to answer questions in a direct, forthright manner. Quentin soon convinced him.

Bradley C. Smith was quite a different animal, his lair no motel room or strip-mall office but a house in the city's most exclusive neighborhood, built (as though to make the expense of it all still more evident) into a hillside. Location was everything. That's what real-estate agent Bradley C. Smith told his clients. But real estate was only one of Bradley C. Smith's vocations. His influence went far and wide; he was a man with real power.

But that power for many years now had insulated Bradley C. Smith from confrontation. That power depended on money, middle men, lawyers, enforcers, collectors, accountants. None of which were present when Quentin stepped into the powerful man's bathroom just as Bradley C. Smith emerged naked, flesh pale as a mushroom, from the shower.

There at the end, Bradley C. Smith tried to tell him more. Seemed desperate to tell him, in fact. That was what, at the end, Bradley C. Smith seized upon, holding up a trembling hand again and again, imploring with eyes behind which light was steadily fading.

Thing was, Quentin didn't care. Now he knew why the two killers had been dispatched to that apartment on Sycamore, now he had the other name he needed. Ultimately, those two had little to do with him, with his life, with the door he was pushing closed now. Soon they'd have nothing at all to do with it, neither those two, nor Bradley C. Smith, nor the other. Quentin walked slowly down the stairs, climbed into his stolen Volvo. Soon enough it would be over, all of it.

I fail to recognise myself in mirrors, or in Julie's memories, or in many of my own.

I remember riding in a car with a young man dressed strangely, in a plaid shirt that hung on him like a serape, black bell bottoms, an African skullcap. Remember finding a wallet bound with rubber bands once he'd gone.

I remember lying prone in a church steeple watching families come and go.

I remember a man drifting away from me in a culvert, blue dye coloring the water beneath him. Bodies below me on a motel room floor. Other bodies, many of them, half a world away.

As memory returns, it does so complexly – stereophonically. There is what I am told of Parker, a set of recollections and memories that seem to belong to him, and, alongside those, these other memories of bodies and cars, green jungles, deserts, a kind of double vision in which everything remains forever just out of focus, blurred.

I wonder if this might not be how the mind functions in madness: facts sewn loosely together, so that contrasting, contradictory realities are held in suspension, simultaneously, in the mind, scaffolds clinging to the faceless, sketchy edifice of actuality.

'I brought you some coffee. Real coffee. Figured you could use it. I've had my share of what hospitals call coffee.'

He set the cup, from Starbucks, on the bedside table.

'Thank you.'

'Don't mention it. City paid. You need help with that top?'

273

Parker swung his legs over the bed's edge and sat, pried off the cover. The detective remained standing, despite the chair close by.

Light-gray suit, something slightly off about the seams. Plucked from a mark-down rack at Mervyn's, Dillard's? Blue shirt that had ridden with him through many days just like this one, darkish red tie that from the look of deformations above and below the knot must turn out a different length most times it got tied. Clothes don't make the man, but they rarely fail to announce to the world who he thinks he might be.

'Sergeant Wootten. Bill.' He sipped from his own cup. 'You don't have kids, do you, Mr Parker?'

Parker shook his head. The sergeant shook his in turn.

'My boy? Sixteen? I swear I don't know what to make of him, haven't for years now. Not long ago he was running with a crowd they all had tattoos, you know? Things like beer can tabs in their ears, little silver balls hanging out of their noses. Then a month or so back he comes down to breakfast in a dark-blue suit, been wearing it ever since. Go figure.'

'What can I do for you, Sergeant?'

'Courtesy visit, more or less.'

'You realise that I remember almost nothing of what happened?'

'Yes, sir. I'm aware of that. Very little of what happened, and nothing from before. But paperwork's right up there with death, taxes and tapeworms. Can't get away from it.'

Holding up the empty cup, Parker told him thanks for the coffee. The sergeant took Parker's cup, slipped his own inside it, dropped both in the trash can by the door.

'I've read your statement, the accident reports, spoke with your doctors. No reason in any of that to take this any further.'

He walked to the window and stood quietly a moment. 'Beautiful day. Not that most of them aren't.' He turned back. 'Still don't have a handle on what happened out there.'

'Nor do I. You know what I remember of it. The rest is gone.'

'Could come back to you later on, the doctors say. They also say you're out of here tomorrow. Going home.'

'Out of here, anyway.'

'We'll need a contact address in case something else comes up. Not that anything's likely to. Give us a call.'

The sergeant held out his hand. Quentin shook it.

'Best of luck to you, Mr Parker.'

When he was almost to the door: 'One thing still bothers me, though. We can't seem to find any record of you for these past four years. Where you were living, what you were doing. Almost like you didn't exist.'

'I've been in Europe.'

'Well, that's it then, isn't it. Like I said: best of luck, Mr Parker.'

There was a time alone then, first in an apartment off Van Buren in central Phoenix where Quentin found comfort in the slam of car doors and the banging of wrenches against motors, in the rich roll of calls in Spanish across the parking lot and between buildings, in the pump and chug of accordions and conjunto bands from radios left on, it seemed, constantly; then, thinking he wanted to be truly alone, in an empty house just outside Cave Creek. Scouting it, he discovered credit-card receipts for two round-trip tickets to Italy, return date a month away. No neighbors within sight. He had little, few possessions, to move in. He parked the car safely away from the house.

There was a time, too, of aimless, intense driving, to Flagstaff, Dallas, El Paso, even once all the way to New

York, road trips in which he'd leave the car only to eat and sleep, as often as not selecting some destination at random and driving there only to turn around and start back.

He thought little about his life before, about the four men he had killed, still less about his present life. It was as though he were suspended, waiting for something he could feel moving towards him, something that had been moving towards him for a long time.

'Thanks for picking me up.'

'You're welcome. Guess I'd been kind of hoping you'd call.'

They pulled onto Black Canyon Freeway. Late afternoon, and traffic was heavy, getting heavier all the time, lines of cars zooming out of the cattle chutes. Clusters of industrial sheds – automotive specialty shops and the like – at roadside as they cleared the cloverleaf, then bordering walls above which thrust the narrow necks of palm trees and signage, sky beyond. The world was so full. Ribbons of scarlet, pink and chrome yellow blew out on the horizon as the sun began settling behind sawtooth mountains. Classical music on low, the age-old, timeless ache of cellos.

The world was so full.

'Had breakfast?' Julie asked.

Caught unawares, she'd thrown an old sweatshirt over grass-stained white jeans a couple sizes too large. Cheeks flushed, hair still wet from the shower. Nonetheless she'd taken time to ferret out and bring him a change of clothes. Her husband's, Parker assumed. They had the smell of long storage about them.

'Little late for that, don't you think?'

'Breakfast's a state of mind. Like so much of life. More about rebirth, things starting up again, knowing they can, than it is about time of day. It's also my favorite meal.'

'Never was much of a breakfast person myself.'

'You should give it a try.'

'You're right. I should.'

She nodded. 'There's a great café just ahead, breakfast twenty-fours a day, best in the valley. You got time?'

'I don't have much else.'

'Good. We'll stop, then. After that . . .You have a place to stay?'

'No.'

'Yes,' Julie said. 'Yes. You do.'

LIFE BEFORE THE WAR

John Straley

Afterward, when I was riding the train back to Anchorage, I noticed that the sky over the interior of Alaska was so vast it felt as if the top of my head was rising into the air. The few clouds around the top of Mount McKinley's twenty-thousand-foot summit seemed like wisps of inconsequential smoke. This is the mountain the Athabaskan people call Denali or 'The Great One', and I would not have argued with them.

Earlier in the day I hadn't noticed the mountain. I had been in a sour mood and it may have been because I was only serving a subpoena. The lawyer who had hired me to dump these papers had no understanding of Alaskan geography. He had called from Eugene, Oregon, and told me that cost was no object. His client wanted the papers served right away. He represented the wife in a divorce case and she knew her ex-husband was climbing McKinley. She wanted the papers dropped on him in the post-coital high he would be experiencing after he had summited North America's tallest peak.

The lawyer had no idea where I lived in relation to Mount McKinley. Through a friend of his, he knew I was in Alaska. That I lived in the southeastern panhandle of the state meant nothing to him. To ask me to serve papers on someone near Denali would be like hiring an investigator from Baltimore to drop papers on someone in Montreal. Denali was a hell of a long way away: almost a day of flying, one leg west to Juneau, then an hour and a half by jet to Anchorage, and then a train ride of some two hundred miles to the town of Talkeetna, which served as headquarters for the area climbers.

I told him all this. I told him I lived on an island on the Gulf of Alaska and that there were easier ways to get his papers served but he didn't listen. He had tried some Anchorage servers and apparently wasn't happy with their attitude so he settled on me and whatever expenses I wanted to rack up. His client was paying for it and she was not particular. She was going to nail her ex for all the legal expenses anyway so, in a sense, I would just be spending his money.

The money, what there would be of it, didn't matter much as I stood in front of Eagle's Nest bar in Talkeetna. I had the papers sitting in my pocket and they felt less like a paycheck than an overdue library book I needed to dump. The husband's name was Garth Holebrook; he was an anaesthesiologist from Portland. I had found him through talking to the kid who worked the desk at a flight service in Talkeetna. A plane had brought Dr Holebrook back from the base camp on the mountain and the kid knew that the climbers would be celebrating in the Eagle's Nest.

Where I live, it rains hard. Even in these early days of July the clouds can move in from the sea and curl against the mountains for weeks at a time. Living in southeastern Alaska is sometimes like living with a head cold. So for me the summer air in the northern interior has a biting narcotic thrill. The air is so dry and pure it can feel like a hit of cocaine. I looked through the one window into the bar to get a vague layout of where people were sitting, then I took a long breath in through my nose and walked into the clattering bar.

Serving court papers is a straightforward job. The server has no real authority other than his physical presence. The subpoena gains its authority from the judge. Once in the physical possession of the named recipient all arguments are channeled through the court. The server only has to identify the recipient and hand the papers over. The recipient doesn't have to be happy about it. They don't even have to hold them in their hands; they just have to acknowledge their receipt. Ripping them up in your face is acknowledgement enough. I keep a copy and take it back to the court, then I collect my hundred bucks and expenses.

My father had been a Superior Court judge. He had encouraged me to follow my sister's path into law school, but I never did. He could never understand that I liked this end of the law. I liked talking to people and I liked the physical authority which comes from wandering around in the real world. I liked living out from under the tangle of legal jargon. Serving subpoenas had always been enough for me. I was happy to leave the arguments to my sister and my good father.

Inside the bar six men and three women were sitting at one long table near the back. The climbers sat behind pitchers of beer looking drowsy and a little bit sad. All of these well-heeled adventurers had reverse racoon tans: weathered faces but pale around the eyes. The men had their fleece shirtsleeves rolled up to their elbows and their two-hundred-dollar sunglasses perched on their foreheads. I sat in a booth across the bar and looked over the top of the lunch menu toward the table where I was fairly certain my guy was sitting.

I had a description of him from the lawyer. Dr Holebrook

was forty-eight years old, had brown hair and brown eyes, was six foot three and weighed one hundred ninety pounds. He was sitting at the head of the table next to a blonde woman wearing a red beret and a white sleeveless undershirt. They were leaning toward one another, their heads almost touching, speaking softly.

I never drop papers on someone when it causes embarrassment, not if I can help it. I once had to serve papers on a Tongan prizefighter in Ketchikan. He was working for a logging outfit back in the days when logging camps were good places to hide out. He had a reputation for having a bad temper. I watched him for several days, in the bar or in the café early in the morning waiting for the rest of his crew to show up. He seemed like a friendly guy and was always in a conversation with the waitresses or someone at the counter. Finally I got him as he was coming out of the bathroom and he simply thanked me in a soft, almost feminine voice as he stuffed the papers in his sleeping-bag-sized cargo pockets.

Once I served a cab driver in Valdez and he started screaming so loudly he woke the neighbors. I was standing in his arctic entryway surrounded by boots and mismatched snowshoes. He had been hassled by everyone, he screamed. The police, the insurance company. He was sick of it, sick of everything. I didn't try to argue with him. He had a knife in his hand and I backed away slowly. Even with the knife, I wasn't afraid. His pride was just injured because I had gotten him out of bed in his dirty long underwear. He was sleepy and embarrassed but he still had enough sense not to kill the guy with the subpoena, for deep down he recognised me for what I was: the delivery boy.

My climber laughed and pushed back a bit in his chair. 'No. No. No. You don't understand. The gnostics were considered to be heretics. You see, they thought that everything in creation was corrupt.' The blonde woman's eyes glittered like chunks of ice and my climber gestured wildly around the bar.

'You see, it was a special knowledge that led a person toward God. This was before faith as we think of it. The gnostics believed divinity was a matter of knowledge.'

'So . . .' the woman said and she wobbled in her chair . . . 'you mean there was no God out here?' and she gestured toward the window, by which she meant the world, Mount McKinley, New York, Kosovo and Jerusalem.

Dr Holebrook was feeling the heady rush of late-afternoon drunken metaphysics. He would not be happy to have the subpoena from his ex-wife.

'There was no hippy, pantheist crap. The world was corrupt and the path to God was through knowledge alone. Knowledge you had to earn.'

He leaned back in his chair and stretched his arms back over his head. He had a certain self-satisfied countenance that made me almost certain that now was not a good time to interrupt him. He was in the throes of happy abstract musings, trying hard to impress this beautiful woman. It was not a good time to let him know that his ex-wife was going to bring him back into court to take possession of the Range Rover and a thousand more dollars a month in child support.

But we all have the same amount of time in a day and there wasn't enough in this particular one for me to wait much longer. I needed to catch a train. A couple of his drinking companions got up and left, saying something about grabbing a shower. I wanted to wait until he was a bit more alone before I dropped the paper on him. Ideally it would have been best to wait until the pretty blonde woman went for her shower. The combination of arrogance and flirting was a deadly one for the humiliation of a court order, but this woman was going to have to move along soon, or I was going to risk bruising the doctor's vanity anyway.

Holebrook leaned in close and poured himself and the blonde woman another beer from a fresh pitcher. I settled in. I would get him when he got up from the table. If they were walking out the door I'd ask him to step aside, catch him so the woman could walk easily ahead of us. I'd call his name, act like an old friend or a patient that he didn't quite recognise, wave her on as if it would just be a minute of inconsequential business and then I'd drop it on him.

I had another tonic water and lime. I hadn't had a drink in three years and I wasn't missing it. But even so, I felt foggy-headed and could feel the northern sunlight trying to pierce through the nail holes in the roof.

My father had been a climber of the old leather shoe and manila rope variety. He had done first ascents on six peaks in the southeastern panhandle. 'Nothing spectacular,' he often said dismissively. 'Just a walk up a steep hill nobody else had had a reason to take.' But he wasn't really dismissing his achievement, he was dismissing everybody else who hadn't done it.

He had taken me with him when I was twelve. It was only one time. I remember the approach up through the rainforest, hopping over the muddy little creeks and getting tangled in the brushy alder thickets along the rock slides. I remember my lungs burning before we even got to the alpine. I remembered the thrill of walking out into the alpine, and I would have been happy just sitting there all day. In the alpine the walking was clear and I could see the islands scattered out on the ocean below us. The steep pitch of the summit wasn't calling me. I rested there on my back in the grass and ate both my candy bars while my father scowled at his watch.

Later, up on the face, my legs gave out, and when my thigh muscles spasmed as if I were trying to peddle an antique sewing machine, my father tried to talk me through it. 'Focus,' he said. 'Feel your weight close in to the rock. Keep your three points anchored while you lift the fourth to the next higher point. Don't look down.'

He was trying to be calm, and in his own way he was trying to be gentle, but I could feel the irritation in his voice ease down on me as if it were an extra surge of gravity trying to strip me off the rock. When I looked down I felt the wooziness of vertigo and dread that seemed to be some kind of pre-falling sensation. My muscles were both clinging to the rocks and wanting to let go.

He virtually pulled me up the side of the mountain that day. I was shaking when I reached the summit, but I did not cry. The world, the forested islands and rumpled hills, circled our perch as if my father had created them all just for me. 'You did it, boy,' he said. 'You can think back on this day for the rest of your life and be proud.' But of course it didn't turn out that way.

My father's life was built on certainty. He knew we could make it up the mountain and we did. This is what my mother loved about him and what she always doubted about me. She said I was never going to be a climber. She said I was too fond of finding 'smoke's way' out of any difficult situation. She said this with what I later recognised was disdain, but for years I had honestly thought of it as a compliment.

The doctor stretched again. He and the blonde were the only two people at the table. He reached over and touched the side of her face, and then she got up from the table and walked over to the bathroom.

I tore the recipient's yellow copy from the subpoena, pushed the original for the court into my pocket and walked over to the edge of the table with the yellow copy in my hand.

'Dr Holebrook?' I asked. He looked up at me with a dreamy expectation as if he were waiting for me to compliment him on his climb.

'Yes,' he said, smiling.

'I've got some papers for you. They are from your wife's lawyers. If you have any questions about them, there's a number on the bottom you can call,' and I gave him the subpoena.

He reached up and took it, then laid the paper flat on the table. He stood up slowly, letting out his breath as if he were trying to think of the words to thank me for my long trip out to find him. Then he punched me in the mouth.

I don't know if Dr Holebrook had ever sucker-punched anyone before, but he definitely had a gift for it. The physics of a sucker punch are easy enough to understand. The more relaxed the recipient is, the more damage the blow inflicts. Getting in that first hard shot nine times out of ten ends whatever conflict there will be.

I thought of the beauty of this as I was lying on the floor. Blood was filling my mouth and as I leaned forward, first my lips and then my tongue pressed against the six teeth, three upper, three lower, which were folded back inside my mouth.

'You motherfucking lawyers,' he said, as he stood over me rubbing his right hand where the knuckles were bleeding.

'Noth uh law-uh,' I said as best I could through the blood and broken teeth. 'Youff . . . been . . . thirved,' I added with as much finality as I could muster, and I waved at the papers on the table.

The bartender was bending over me now. 'You want me to call the cops?' he asked and I waved him off. It would take too much time, I had a train to catch, and besides there was always the chance the cops would find some way to put me in jail for the whole thing.

The blonde woman was out of the bathroom and was wrapping a paper towel around the doctor's hand. I leaned up on one elbow. The bartender gave me a towel and some ice, and I held it to my face. My ears were ringing and my vision was a little bad, but I could see that the doctor was deciding what he should do next. It was clear I wasn't going to fight him and it didn't appear that anyone in the bar was going to be a sympathetic ear for the story of his ugly divorce. So he kicked me once in the ribs and walked out the door.

'Hey!' the bartender yelled. 'That's bullshit,' he said and went behind the bar reaching for the phone. 'That's just too fucking much.'

I pulled myself up and sat at the table. The doctor hadn't taken the papers but it didn't matter. He'd been served. I would mail the subpoena back to the court and they would take care of the rest. I had done my part here in Talkeetna in the shadow of the Great One.

I waited for the cops to come and start the whole new tangle of words that would eventually end in Dr Holebrook pleading to fourth-degree assault and enrolling in anger management classes. But here's the strange part. As I waited for all that to start, I was suddenly in a perfectly good mood. I was not anxious and I wasn't dreaming of somewhere else. I could see things in the room I hadn't noticed when I walked in: the dust motes floating on the shafts of light, the fine smear of a bruise across the bottom of the blonde woman's neck.

I've never been smacked like that before and I had always worried about what it would feel like. I realise now that I was having a light-headed shock reaction, but at the time I was surprised to be enjoying the emptiness in my head and the veil of blue lights drifting through my vision. I have been yelled at and threatened. I've been in loud little scuffles. I've even been shot with a high-powered rifle. But I had always avoided a sucker punch. Now my head was ringing like an empty wineglass and instead of being depressed about it I was exhilarated.

While the cops stood around in their creaking leather belts talking to me and taking pictures, I watched them with a mild disinterest. They brought the doctor back and talked to him outside by the cars, and now the doctor looked smaller, embarrassed, quite a bit deflated. It was beginning to dawn on him that the satisfaction he gained from punching me was going to be short-lived.

We were on opposite trajectories, of course. Later my bruises would be dark purple and I would long to eat a meal without wincing with pain. Later, too, my own anger would take hold, even to the point of filing a civil case of my own against Dr Holebrook to recover the cost of the dental reconstruction. But all of that was just another tangle of words which I wouldn't be entering for a few more weeks. Just then, I was happy. I had served the papers and I was going to be able to ride the train back south through the delirious sunshine toward the coast. I thought about the train ride and the doctor, and about what the old gnostics would have felt climbing up Denali, where there was no God in those muddy little streams, and none in the alpine either. And earlier in the day when Dr Holebrook had been laughing and celebrating at the top of North America's tallest peak, God would have only been that little thread of an idea the doctor had pinched between his thumb and forefinger but on which he could never quite gain purchase.

As I sat at the table in the bar I kept hearing a bell ringing and I felt as if some war was over. I couldn't remember my childhood, and that was fine. Everything that had ever happened to me seemed from another time anyway, a time before the war, when trouble was brewing but I hadn't been paying enough attention.

Now I seemed to be paying attention. When I walked across the little park to get on the train the cottonwood blooms drifted all around me, sparkling like planets and I held the frothy pink towel against my mouth. I thought about the doctor and I knew he was feeling bad. The thrill of his mountaineering accomplishment was gone now. He was feeling bad about being back in the world of lawyers and civil complaints. He was feeling bad about having to talk to the cops and he might even have been feeling bad about punching me in the mouth. But I didn't care. As I grabbed on to the handrail and swung up into the train I knew that I loved the poor son of a bitch who had clambered up those cliffs. I loved him like gravity, like sunlight, like a mountain.

GEEZERS

Brian Thompson

When his brother-in-law arrived, Harry Tolman was watching afternoon racing. From behind the curtains he studied Cliff locking the doors to his motor and then remembering his fags and having to open up again. Motor. Harry shrugged. Walk like that, talk like that: it was bred in the bone. Only the elderly said motor or fags these days. As if to prove his point an incautious movement of his arm produced that sudden jolt a junior doctor at the hospital had described to him as a deterioration of the brachial nerve. Or somesuch. He winced as he walked to let Cliffie in. The two men embraced without warmth.

'Let me say, straight off and before everything else, how choked everbody still is about Jean,' Cliff said. 'Even now, even after all this time.'

'Yeah, well.'

'I tried to put into words how we all felt at the funeral, Harry, but you were out with the fairies that day and no mistake.'

'If you say so,' Harry said. He walked into the kitchen to make a pot of tea.

Jean, through her brother Cliff, had been his last

connection to that wise-guy London thing and after she died he all too willingly let it drop. He had not been up the Smoke for a six-month and then only to drink at pubs where he knew he could not be recognised. Came home on the early evening train.

The seaside bungalow they stood in now was Jean's choice of a nice place to live, just as the perennials in the flower borders were hers. Harry ate from plates she had chosen, slept under the duvet she had selected from the catalogue. Her clothes were still in the wardrobe. That was the story. She was his woman, he was her man.

That was the story and what the neighbours had not seen with their own eyes they invented. Harry Tolman was that nice man at 32 whose wife had died so suddenly. Kept himself to himself, had an unexpectedly flat belly and strong forearms, looked sixty, could be younger, could be older. A former soldier, perhaps. Politely spoken, but with that characteristic cockney croak. A one-time market trader, maybe.

Cliffie drummed his fingernails on the kitchen worktop. 'Don't you want to know why I'm here?' he asked.

'Let me guess. You're in trouble.'

'Big time. But I mean big time.'

Harry smiled to himself. 'Now don't get me all excited, Cliff.'

'My hand to God,' his brother-in-law muttered.

'So? What do you want, money?'

'Be realistic,' Cliffie snapped, with enough sudden bitterness in his voice to make Harry glance up from the kettle and take notice. 'Would I ask you for money? Am I stupid?'

'Then it's business.'

'I am asking a favour of you.'

His nervousness was beginning to annoy Harry. When he saw that, Cliff ducked his head in acknowledgement. Licked his lips. 'This, then. You put your motor through the Tunnel, buzz off to France, drive to a meet with some lads we have business with there, deliver a certain package, money changes hands. And that's it.'

'What's in the package?' Harry asked.

But his brother-in-law had exhausted his small stock of guile for the moment and took his tea out on to the lawn, the set of his back and shoulders indicating a sour response to sea-breezes and distant gulls.

Harry joined him. 'So, what's in the package?' he repeated.

'I told you, it's a business thing,' his brother-in-law said far, far too lightly.

They walked down to the sea together, hands plunged in pockets. It was one of those calm spring days when the grey of the water stretched all the way to the horizon and then seemed to curl upwards into sky. There was nothing to look at and no trick of the imagination could invent France, less than thirty miles away.

'Come on, Harry, give me a break,' Cliffie mumbled after another few minutes of uncomfortable silence. 'I more or less told them you're the man for the job. I mean you wasn't named, I never named you, blah-blah-blah, but it's all down to me to see it right, see it goes off.'

'Is it drugs?'

Cliffie burst out laughing from pure nervous release. 'Drugs?' he cackled incredulously.

Harry threw his ice-cream cone into a wire bin and wiped his lips with the back of his hand. A total of eighteen years in prison, the last six in Parkhurst, had much altered his views on the life of crime. The sheer boredom of being banged up with other dreamers was worse than actual death: nowadays he lived on his pension and a little occasional delivery driving. In the old days he had a certain quiet class;

as, for example, tooling Fat Tony up to Birmingham along the M1 in a stolen Aston Martin, establishing what turned out to be an unshakeable alibi and, as Tony said admiringly, a land speed record.

'What do you drive now?' Cliffie asked, punting him a double voddie in the Carpenter's.

'Nothing fancy.'

'Good. That's good. Look, I don't want to put no pressure on you, Harry, but it's my arse if I cock this up.'

'How much is in it for me?'

'A grand,' Cliffie suggested, looking doubtful.

'And what's your end?'

'Jesus, Harry, you don't need to know all that. These guys I'm talking about – the geezers who want the job done – would have your balls off just for coughing in the wrong place. What I can tell you? Just that I'm bearing the heavy end of the load here, know what I'm saying?'

He glanced round the perfectly empty pub and then mouthed a single word: 'Russians.'

If he had said his principals were the Band of the Irish Guards Harry could not have been more surprised. He stared at his brother-in-law, his thinning hair and faintly blue lips, the over-expensive suit hanging from sagging shoulders.

'Who has the package now?'

'Not relevant. I bring it to you. Then you drive it over. You know, just dead casual. It'll be in the boot. A bit of cathedral bashing if you're asked where you're off to. Just a little spring break.'

'How big is this thing?'

Cliffie hesitated. He brushed his lapel distractedly. 'I need you to say yes before I go back to town. Then the final arrangements are made and then it goes down.'

'When?'

'When I tell you.'

Walking back up the road, Harry pointed out several plants he'd thought of growing in his own garden.

But Cliffie was jumpy. 'Nice, I'm sure, but I'm seeing Bungalow City here, Harry. And that's all I'm seeing.'

'Where d'you drink these days?' Harry asked him, far too casually.

'Some things don't change,' his brother-in-law said.

But then again, some things change very nicely. Where before there had been a timber yard opposite the Bear and Staff in Stockwell, there was now a supermarket and its generous car-park. Harry sat munching a salt-beef, watching the pub door through binoculars. Cliffie was presently with a heavy-looking blonde in her forties. Two nights running they parked up round the corner and then walked in single file into the green painted pub Harry remembered very well from the days of his pomp.

On the third night they were inside, presumably boring the arse off their chosen cronies, when a black Lexus pulled up and a huge guy got out to fetch Cliffie. The poor chump actually came to the kerb to talk to the passenger in the Lexus with a v and t in his hand, a reckless piece of bravado. The conversation was short and Cliffie was still making his points when the car pulled away into traffic. He stood there looking lost. Harry felt sorry for him.

Cliffie followed the Lexus and Harry followed after, tooling along listening to the BBC World Service, a bit of a thing with him in recent years. The meet took place in a furniture repository, very Russian in its forlorn dilapidations. Harry watched through glasses from the perimeter fence of a skip hire company.

The Lexus people carried out a white parcel wrapped in gaffer tape and stood it on end. One of them lifted the hem and showed Cliffie the nature of the goods. A peachy white

bum flared for the moment in the beams from passing cars.
There was some jolly laughter.

'Where was you last night?' Cliffie shouted. 'I told you to
stay by the phone.'

'Got the maps?'

'I said to stay by the phone. You can't mess with these
Russian geezers. Now listen. The goods are in the back of my
motor and I'm going to put them in yours. And then you're
going to drive to the spot marked X. Tomorrow. Have you
got that? Not the day after, not some time over the weekend.
Tomorrow.'

'Are the goods perishable?' Harry asked, just for the
pleasure of seeing his brother-in-law sweat. Then he relented
and put on his unlaced shoes. 'I'll give you a hand.'

'You stay right where you are. Here's the map. Read the
map.'

There really was a spot marked X. It lay less than a
hundred kilometres from the coast, close to the Rouen-Paris
motorway. Cliffie went over the plan, such as it was, again
and again, passed across two hundred in notes and (a
thoughtful touch) fifty in Euros for the petrol and a cup of tea
and that.

'You make the switch, right, and they'll give you a
grocery bag of dosh. Bank wrappers, all that.'

'Do I count it?'

'Don't worry,' Cliffie said bitterly. 'It'll all be kosher,
believe me. They are messing with people who could start a
third world war. They know that. You're just the bloody
messenger. They ain't going to cross nobody.'

'Well, give me a clue. How much dosh?'

'One hundred thousand in US dollars,' Cliffie said.
'Which is like chump change to these geezers. Soon as you
got it, you bell me, I'll meet you back here at the ranch.'

After he'd left, Harry walked into his garage via the door in the kitchen, opened the boot to his car and studied the package. He tore off some yards of tape, rolled back the fabric and touched a bare foot. It was warm. Just behind the ankle was an artery and he held his thumb to it. Whoever was inside the wrapping was drugged to the eyeballs, doubtless, but comfortable. In the circumstances. He went back to the kitchen, lit a small cigar and sat listening to the fridge.

Along that part of the French coast are dunes and marshes. Next to a rainswept golf course there is a lopsided clapboard property painted black, the kind of place only an Englishman would consider taking on as a commercial proposition. It is labelled MOT L. Derek Jukes greeted Harry like an old mate, which after all he had once been.

'How's Ricky?' Harry asked, out of courtesy.

'That little fairy! It was too quiet for him here. What it is, Harry, I've put you round the back, there's like a row of three but two is boarded up. It's the salt. Do you need to put the car under cover?'

'No, mate. I'll be out of here by three. Four at the latest.'

He passed across Cliffie's two hundred inside an Oxfam envelope.

'Good boy,' Derek said absently. 'I've had the old paraffin heater on all night. You'll find it warm enough.'

It was, in fact, stifling. Harry laid the package on the bed and cut it open with a Stanley knife. Inside was a girl in her early twenties. As he had imagined, she was naked and none too clean – the smell of her was overpowering enough to make him open the window. He checked her pulse. It was slow but regular.

Derek knocked at the door with a little tin box of works. He took in the situation at a glance, nodded, raised one of the girl's eyelids. 'She's only a kid,' he murmured.

'Safe to risk it?' Harry asked.

'Run the shower. She's going to be spewing her ring for an hour or so. Don't worry, mate. I am a former medical orderly of Her Majesty's Royal Air Force. You can't get better, this time of the morning. I take it what we have here is battlefield conditions.'

'You're a straight-up bloke, Derek,' Harry said.

'Not exactly, not as such.'

He took out the syringe and shooed Harry into the bathroom.

She was called Marika. Passing through international frontiers as a comatose parcel was a bit of a thing with her – she had been abducted by Cliffie's set of geezers three months earlier as part payment of a gambling debt incurred in Düsseldorf, where she had been unhappy, but not desperate, so to speak. This bold stroke had got up the nose of the Dusseldorf Russian, whose girl she had been, and so far three people had been killed in the ensuing business negotiations.

'Well, now it's all back to square one,' Harry suggested.

'You are crazy,' Marika observed with Slavic despair.

'You get to go home – Düsseldorf anyway – and the London geezers get their debt paid in cash. Where's the prob?'

'For something so simple they have to do me up like a turkey? Why not I fly to Düsseldorf? Why they need you?'

Harry considered. 'Because when they get you back, they're going to kill you.'

'For sure.'

All this while she sat on the bed naked, accepting little spoonfuls of a lightly boiled egg. She seemed to sense that Harry and naked women had not been strangers in the past: her movements and gestures were entirely unselfconscious.

'You don't want to know why they kill me?'

'I probably wouldn't be able to follow it in detail. A hundred thousand dollars has been mentioned, though.'

'Ha! And pigs might fly,' Marika said with a rare stab at idiom.

'Yes,' Harry said.

Derek poured them both a Stella. 'Look at it this way,' he said. 'Say the dosh exists. For a hundred grand I could lose you both in this country, no probs.'

'For a few months, maybe.'

'All right then, say it doesn't exist. You still get their car, whatever gear they have on them, their watches, wallets and all that – you're still coming out ahead on the day. And, put it this way, the more mess you make, the more it turns into a war-type situation where you and the kid become idle bystanders, mere nothings.'

'Making good sense now, Derek.'

'Or,' the former medical orderly and Brighton drag queen concluded, 'you could just knock her out again, deliver the goods and sod the lot of them.'

'What have you got in the way of weaponry?'

'Me?' Derek protested.

'Bloody hell,' Harry said.

They were going to have to do this work with a pistol that hadn't been fired since 1987 and five rounds of ammunition, arms that until last night had been under a floorboard in Harry's bungalow. He sighed.

'You know what this is all about? Honour. These geezers have seen too many films. The girl goes home in the most insulting way possible, done up like a turkey. It's a power thing, like I spit on your shoe, Düsseldorf. Yeah, Düsseldorf says, and I spit in your eye because there is no hundred thousand dollars. That is the bones of the plot, Derek.'

'You got five shots. You miss with two, that's three shots to off the boys who turn up. Which requires a cool head.'

303

In that instant they heard a distant and unmistakable report out in the marshes. M. Dieumegard, a retired lawyer from Soissons, was playing at duck-hunting with his Japanese pump-action. It was all very illegal, what he was doing, and he turned to greet the car with French plates with the faintly queasy feeling that he had been rumbled. Which he had. He surrendered the gun and nineteen cartridges, accepted a receipt for them scribbled on a pink slip, gave a false address and counted himself lucky. As the jovial plain-clothes policeman pointed out, the gun was in any case pretty useless. A duck would have to be sitting at the next barstool to be sure of being slaughtered.

'It was an impulse buy from a catalogue,' M. Dieumegard admitted gloomily.

Back to Marika, wearing some jeans and a white T-shirt Harry had purchased at a supermarket the moment they got off the ferry. No bra or knickers but a pair of what looked like red bowling shoes, two sizes too big.

'Now listen,' Harry said. 'I'm going to have a go at these people we've been talking about.'

'Impossible,' Marika cried.

'No, it's just ordinary common sense. But none of it need involve you. If you stay here, you should be safe for a week or so. So long as you don't go outside. And if there are any dollars, then I'll see you right.'

'They will kill you,' the girl said.

'Maybe.'

'I know. Because, if they were going to do business, then they wouldn't send old man like you. You and me both pffft. That is the plan.' She put her forefinger to her head and pulled the trigger.

Harry glanced at his watch. 'I'm taking Derek with me for company,' he said.

*

The meet had been arranged an hour after sunset, a time when the last tractor had grumbled away into the gloom. The spot was well chosen, for it lay upon a crossroads at least two kilometres from the nearest farmhouse. Harry's car was parked up on a little rectangle of ground where the local council kept their pile of gravel. There was also a very handy bottle bank on short stilts.

The Audi with German plates drove up at normal speed, turned left and disappeared into the night. Harry stared at the pistol in his lap, opened the car door and then drew it gently to without engaging the latch. The seat was pushed back as far as it would go, leaving his arms free of the steering wheel: other than these precautions he did not have the faintest idea what to do. Except smoke. He lit a rollie he'd made earlier.

When the boys came back it was from the direction they'd taken earlier. The lights were on main beam and raked the interior of Harry's car. The Audi slewed to a halt a hundred metres away.

'Yes. Get out of the car please,' a guy yelled from the driver's side.

'Let's get out together,' Harry yelled back.

The Mexican stand-off. A long-eared owl, a European rarity, flew through the Audi's beam and then veered indignantly away. After an uncomfortable pause three doors of the German car opened and the same number of men got out, each carrying an Uzi. Harry opened his own door and stood behind it, the pistol dangling in his right hand. The only good thing so far was that these guys were young.

'Where is your passenger?' one of them cried.

'I have a parcel in the boot,' Harry countered.

Every second that passed, he felt heartened. They were cocky wee sods, toting their own shooters at arm's length, chewing gum, acting up. Tarantino. They sauntered towards the car.

'Stay very still, old man,' one advised.

'No probs,' he said, trying to match the international tone.

'Stand away from the car.'

'I'm scared, boys.'

It got a laugh. They ambled a little closer.

'You are a dead man,' the smallest of the three suddenly decided.

Harry missed with the first shot, hit with the second as Derek let loose with the shotgun from underneath the commune's bottle bank. All three Russians fell, cursing. Harry fired twice more and jumped back into his car, reversing away in a shower of gravel and the smaller roadside weeds. Four more agonising minutes passed, punctuated by a final blast from the shotgun and then he saw the Audi speed away, Derek driving. The headlights blipped in a victory signal.

Bloody hell, he thought. This is too easy. It was only then that he realised that all along the Russians had been firing at him. He was sitting in a pool of blood. The old motor was handling a bit funny but he drove the back roads to the coast with what he liked to think of as professional calm, passing through village after village of shuttered houses and empty streets.

'They were after your tackle,' Derek murmured in the scorching heat of Cabin 7. The wound that had caused all the mess was inside his right thigh, high up. It had passed through the car door before hitting him, which accounted for what the ex-medical orderly called a rare bit of good luck but a nasty jag all the same.

'There was no money, of course.'

'Nah. We got the Audi, one of the guns, a laptop and a few hundred euros.'

'You are brave men,' Marika said, holding Harry's leg down while the wound was sutured.

'Was anyone killed?' he asked.

Derek tutted. 'And you a hardened criminal! These were kids sent on a man's errand, Harry. It's terrible, the things that happen nowadays. And d'you want to know what I think?'

They did.

It happened that the European Cup Final was held that year in Dortmund. The two Russian rivals who had started all these shenanigans met in an hospitality suite high up in the stands where they were photographed sharing a joke. One was toting a recent Miss Austria and the other one had girl-band superstar and Essex bimbo Robyn Nevill on his arm. The mood was cordial, fuelled by cocaine.

'So, how's your big boat?' one of them said in rapid Russian, referring to a monstrous white mini-liner presently moored in Monaco.

'It's good. How is your island?'

'Yeh, yeh, the island. It's good. But I tell you frankly, the Sicilians can be a pain in the arse about such matters. With them everything's a history thing.'

'History!' his rival repeated jovially, and they both laughed long and loud at the absurdity of the concept.

'These pumped-up clowns had very little sense of yesterday. They are villains with no need of the healing balm that memory provides the rest of us.'

So Derek, trying to teach Harry how to play golf. 'That, and the simple fact that they'd rather be pop stars or footballers than decent honest criminals. They are shoppers, is what they are. It's a bloody disgrace, Harry boy.'

'Grateful to you as ever, Derek.'

At that moment, Derek was fiddling about, moving

Harry's fingers this way and that on the golf club. It was, apparently, all in the grip. 'Heard from the girl?' he asked.

'What a romantic old queen you are, Dekker.'

Even Cliffie survived the adventure, though minus the toes on both feet, which he explained was just a bit of fun, just their way of marking his card. He walked a bit strange and his shoes cost a bloody fortune these days but all in all he counted himself a lucky man. He looked around the Carpenter's, where the whole scheme was first hatched.

'Don't you ever get tired of living down here?' he asked.

'No,' Harry said. 'It suits me. Jean liked it.'

'What a stroke you pulled, son,' Cliffie muttered. 'That kid owes you her life.'

Harry threw him a very sharp glance. 'Nice of you to say so,' he said with elaborate irony.

It passed clean over Cliffie's head. As Jean always said about her brother, he wasn't thick exactly but he never really got out of the playground. Mind, Harry thought, if he asks one more question about Operation Crossroads, I'm going to tear his lungs out. He watched indulgently as Cliffie reviewed all the possible things he might say next.

'I always loved her, you know. Jean, I mean.'

Harry touched him on the sleeve of his jacket and called for two more doubles. As happened once every three days or so, the fruit machine down at the far end of the bar paid a jackpot. Neither man looked up. Now there really was an activity designed for losers.

DOUGGIE DOUGHNUTS

Don Winslow

Doug Day don't have breakfast the morning of his father's wake.

He's too frickin' busy and besides, he don't have much money left. The factory's laid him off and the unemployment's run out and he was busy looking for a job when his father died but there ain't a lot of work out there and most of his time's been taken up trying to get his father buried.

Devon Day was a small-time thief and alcoholic who when he wasn't in the hole killed a lot of Bushmills, and the Bushmills finally paid him back in kind. He kicked out in a room over Chuck's Bar and Grill, and Pachetti's Funeral Home only agreed to take care of the body and have calling hours because they hope to get Chuck's business when *he* passes, so they do Chuck this favor and have calling hours for Devon.

'Could we do monthly payments?' Doug asked Tommy Pachetti Jr. They've known each other since junior high and play midnight hockey together at Ice World.

'Okay,' Tommy says, 'but this has to be like "no frills", okay, Doug?'

No frills is no shit, Doug thinks as he stands next to his father's cheap coffin, which Doug is not sure but thinks is made from plasterboard. Doug stands there to receive the callers who come to pay their respects and this is not exactly hard work because hardly anyone comes.

For one thing hardly anyone in Torrington, Connecticut had any respect for Devon. Second, any of the guys who did, like Dev's old cronies, are either dead or in the joint or just too down-and-out drunk in some shitty New England bar to know or care that Dev has checked out of his last SRO hotel. Third, there are a few guys – mostly hockey buddies of Doug's – who would have come except they know this thing is going to be very frigging depressing, which winter in Torrington already is without dragging your ass down to Pachetti's for a wake that is no frills.

It's one of those stone-gray New England Saturdays where it ought to snow but won't. It's just icy instead, so your car slips sideways every time you hit the brakes, which is often. And when you get out of your car the wind whips you in the face like it's saying *Fuck you – you're an asshole for living here.*

So all you're going to get by going out today is a head cold and a fender bender that won't meet the deductible, so a lot of people stay home for Devon's wake.

Edley Carpenter is there, though.

Edley also plays hockey at Ice World with Doug and figures he owes him the respect.

'Sorry for your loss,' Edley says after he walks past Devon's coffin without hardly looking at the body. 'Cold in here, isn't it?'

Doug nods.

Shit yes, it's cold in here, he thinks. He can practically see his own breath. Shit, he can practically see his *dad's* breath.

'Tell Tommy to turn the heat up,' Edley says.

'Well, this is sort of "no frills",' Doug says.

'Oh,' Edley says. He thinks about this for a second then says, 'They got any coffee, Doug?'

'I think that would be a frill.'

'Sure,' Edley says. From his mouth it comes out *Shoo-ah*. Edley's family having been in New England as long as Doug's, he's genetically incapable of pronouncing a terminal 'R'.

'Tommy should turn the heat up,' Edley says. He goes and sits in one of the metal folding chairs, because he doesn't know what else to do and otherwise Doug is just left standing there all alone in a cold room with just him and his dead father.

'You gonna play tonight?' Edley asks Doug.

'I dunno.'

And this is the truth because Doug hasn't really worked it out whether it's the right thing to do, to play hockey the same night your father has his calling hours.

'See how you feel,' Edley says.

'Yeah, see how I feel.'

Edley gets up and leaves as soon as Frank King comes in.

Frank King takes the accident of his surname as destiny.

He takes it real serious.

Why shouldn't he, Doug thinks, as King makes a royal entrance in his camel-hair overcoat, cashmere scarf and his usual two heelnippers behind him. He's got more money than probably most kings these days.

King takes a look at Dev in the coffin then comes over to Doug. 'Nice suit your father's wearing.'

Should be, Doug thinks. It's a three-hundred-fifty-dollar suit and Doug's going to be out on the street at the end of the month because Dev is getting buried in the rent money. Doug don't tell King that, though. All he says is, 'Thanks.'

'Your dad didn't have the jack for a suit like that,' King says.

'Yeah, I bought it,' says Doug.

'*You* don't have the jack for a suit like that.'

Even though at six-three Doug has five full inches on King, he feels like he's looking up at the man. Looking at his big shiny face and smelling his aftershave and the spray on his black hair. Looking at him like *what the fuck business is it of yours?*

King tells him. 'Your dad owes me money,' he says.

Which makes Doug laugh even though he don't mean to because it will piss King off. But anyway, Doug laughs, more like a chuckle, as he tilts his chin toward Dev's body, like, *so collect it*.

Then he's sorry he did that, because if anyone would take the clothes off a dead man, it would be Frank King. The man would do about anything to get his money, and Doug knows this because King *has* most of the money in north-west Connecticut.

King shakes his head, says, 'You're your father's heir, right, Douggie?'

Doug also has black hair except it's in a crew cut, and if anyone's paying attention they'd see it practically bristle. 'Don't call me that,' he says. 'My name is Doug.'

King's eyes go like frickin' death. 'But my point still pertains, doesn't it.'

'What point?'

'You inherited your father's entire estate,' King says.

Now Doug really laughs. Dev's entire estate consists of a hot plate that got maybe *warm* and one dollar and fifty-eight cents in wet change. And medical bills and a funeral bill. And Doug's already sold his 'eighty-six Charger and he's still way behind. So he says, 'Yeah, I got the whole thing, Mister King.'

'You can call me King.'

And the asshole *means* it.

314

'You inherit his assets,' King says, 'you inherit his debts.'

'I do?'

This is like, really bad and shocking news to Doug. This is something he did not know. But why not? In the world of shit storms, when it rains, it pours.

'How much did my dad owe you?'

King looks to Clark, standing behind him. Clark is King's accountant, which means basically he's a whiz at calculating compound interest. Clark makes a little show of looking into a little black notebook, although Doug knows that Clark has the exact figure in his head.

'Twelve thousand three hundred eighty-eight dollars,' he says.

'How much of that is interest?' Doug asks.

'Most of it,' King says.

'Growing every day,' says Whitey.

Whitey has the build of a dumpster and a soul to match. He got his tag because of his prematurely white hair. Guy's hair turned white when he was like twenty-eight or something. Which is like fifteen years ago, the same amount of time he's been working for King.

Collecting King's debts, Doug thinks, yeah, that would turn your hair white.

Doug does some quick math in his head and says, 'I can't make the next goddamn interest payment.'

Never mind the principal.

King nods like he's already figured that out. Then he asks, 'They got any coffee in this place, Douggie?'

'This is kind of a no frills deal.'

'Why don't you go get us some coffees?' King asks. He takes a five out of his pocket and hands it to Doug. 'Cream, two sugars for me. Black for Clark and Whitey.'

There's a 7-11 across the street, Doug thinks. He can be there and back in three minutes. He takes the five and says,

315

'I'll just bop across the street.'

'Go to Dunkin' Donuts,' King says. 'I like Dunkin' Donuts coffee.'

Dunkin' Donuts is seven cold, icy blocks away.

Doug stands there next to his father's coffin with the five-dollar bill in his hand wondering what is the right thing to do here.

King says, 'Okay, Douggie?'

Twelve thousand three hundred eighty-eight dollars, Doug thinks. It'll be twelve-nine by tomorrow.

'Okay, King,' Doug says.

Knowing, shit, this is what the rest of my life is going to look like. It's gonna suck. Major league suck. I'm nineteen years old and it's already frickin' over. He starts to put on his coat.

'And Douggie,' King asks, folding his body on to one of the metal chairs. 'Long as you're there, why don't you get us some doughnuts?'

This is how Doug gets the tag Douggie Doughnuts.

So now every morning at seven sharp Doug's at Dunkin' Donuts getting a cream two-sugars, two blacks and a half-dozen chocolate glazed. Then he shuffles across the icy sidewalks – which are getting more like tunnels lately what with the sooty snow piled up high on both sides – to the offices of King Real Estate which are in an old Victorian house on Main Street. Every morning Doug sets the cardboard tray down on the reception table, takes out the coffees, then goes in and sets the doughnuts down on a paper towel on the kitchen counter. Then he puts one of the doughnuts on a plate and takes it and the cream two-sugars into King's private office.

Same frickin' thing every morning – he knocks on the door and King yells, 'That you. Douggie Doughnuts?'

'Yeah.'

And he brings in the cream two-sugars and the doughnut and sets them on King's desk, and every morning King don't even look up from the papers he's working on but always asks, 'Cream, two sugars?'

Like Doug's some kind of idiot, he's been getting these coffees for like six weeks now and he still don't know King takes his coffee with cream and two sugars.

'Yeah,' Doug will say, then he goes out and pours rock salt on the sidewalk in front of the office, then takes a big ice chipper and scrapes ice off the sidewalk for a while, then he goes in and gets the garbage and takes it out, and then he checks with Whitey to see if anyone has anything for the gofer to go for.

And maybe they do and maybe they don't, but either way Clark reminds Doug how much he owes as of that morning, which is always more than he owed yesterday morning no matter how much garbage he takes out or ice he scrapes or how many doughnuts he fetches.

So Doug is stuck.

He can't get real work because King has him come in for the first two hours of the working day and the last two hours of the afternoon just so Doug *can't* get a normal job. And he can't get on a night shift anywhere because about half the nights King sends him on some dogshit errand just so he doesn't get any ideas about becoming independent. And when Doug tries to get a 'would you like fries with that' gig at Mickey D's, King puts the kibosh on it anyway.

'What are people going to think?' King asks him. 'They go in and see you with a paper cap on your dome shoveling out Egg McMuffins? What are they going to think about *me*?'

So King has Clark toss fifty or sixty bucks cash a week for Doug to eat on, and Doug can make it on this by getting the dollar special – two eggs, juice, toast and coffee – at Main Diner, the six-inch sandwich deal from Subway at lunch, and a bowl of chili with crackers back at Chuck's for supper. So Doug can eke it out on the fifty-sixty, problem is that Clark adds this money on to the debt so that every day Doug scrapes it out as King's slave he's deeper in the hole.

He even lives in one.

Camelletti lets him sleep on a cot in the basement boiler room at Ice World, in exchange for which Doug checks on the compressor and gives the hot water heater a smack with a ball bat once or twice a night to loosen up this rusty switch. Camelletti's good with this arrangement because Doug's been a rink rat since he was a little kid so he knows what there is to be done around the place. And if Doug sees something needs to be done, you can count on him he'll do it.

'Doug's nothin' like his old man,' Camelletti tells the guys at the diner who tell him he's nuts to have a Day living in his place of business.

'He'll steal the frickin' ice,' they tell him.

Camelletti don't think so, but anyway, what's he supposed to do? Let the kid freeze to death? Toss the kid out after midnight hockey, put him on the street? Don't Doug have it tough enough, what with being Devon's kid, and what with that prick Frank King doing him the way he's doing him?

Everyone in town with any *guize* knows what King is doing to Devon Day's kid, and they know why. One, he's making an example – you ain't going to welsh on a debt to King just by dying – and two, Frank is doing this for the same reason a dog licks his own balls – because he can.

Can turn a strong young man like Doug Day into Douggie Doughnuts.

There'll be a *lot* of people at Frank King's wake, Camelletti thinks, God speed the day. All of them smiling into their sleeves.

So at least Doug has a place to lie down and splash a little water on his face in the morning – from the janitor's sink in the mop room – but beyond that life is a little like his father's wake – no frills. And every day he sinks a little deeper into the hole.

'This isn't working out,' Clark says to him one morning after he drops off King's doughnuts.

That's no shit, Doug thinks.

'You know how much you owe now?' Clark asks.

'Kind of I've lost track.'

'Twenty-six nine,' Clark says.

Almost twenty-seven ger, Doug thinks. Might as well be twenty-seven mill, because either way I can't pay it.

'You remember Tommy LeClair?' Whitey asks.

Doug definitely remembers Tommy LeClair. Used to play hockey with Tommy until someone stove Tommy's right foot in with a tire iron. Tommy don't skate any more. Tommy don't do much of anything except chug pain pills and drag his foot around behind him, even with that special-built shoe the Goodwill people got for him.

'I remember Tommy,' Doug says, feeling like he's about to yank, happy for once he's got no breakfast in his stomach because if he did, it might be coming up.

'No one's talking about doing a Tommy on you,' Clark says. 'But this situation you're in. Well, it's just not working out.'

'You got to take some steps to help yourself,' Whitey says.

'Some positive steps,' Clark adds.

'What are you talking about?' Doug asks.

'How would you like King to forgive your entire debt?' Clark asks. 'Interest and principal?'

'How would I *like* that?'

'A second chance in life,' Whitey says.

Doug wasn't raised to believe in second chances. He grew up in a series of rooms over bars, so if he saw a guy get a second chance it was usually a second chance to get fucked.

'What do I got to do?' he asks.

A little favor, that's all.

A little favor.

Kill this guy.

'No frickin way,' Doug tells them.

No frickin' way.

There's things you do and things you don't do, Doug thinks as he tromps toward the warm air and hot coffee of Main Diner.

It's one of them north-west Connecticut mornings, cold as steel and twice as hard. A wind straight from the Arctic Circle bites into Doug's face. He's got his old peacoat on, and a knit watchcap pulled down over his ears, and his hands are shoved deep into his pockets and he's still frickin' freezing.

It's his feet.

Because what he's got on his feet are a pair of old Chuck Taylor hightop basketball shoes meant for banging hot asphalt in the summer. Sure, he's got wool socks on underneath, but one of them's got a hole in the heel and the other one a hole in the big toe and his feet feel like they're going to break off, but he'd get frostbite before he'd ask King for money to buy new socks.

Never mind winter boots.

Winter boots are going for fifty or sixty bucks a pair, even at Target out on the highway, and Doug don't see himself going without food for a week to get a pair of boots, and anyway winter has to end some time.

But right now it's definitely winter and he's cold and he's hungry, which makes him colder. I'm always frickin' hungry, he thinks, as he puts one foot after the other toward the diner. I'm always frickin' hungry and I'm always frickin' cold, except when I'm trying to sleep in the boiler room except the furnace is so frickin' hot, glowing red about five feet from the cot, that I'm lying there tossing around in my own sweat half the night. So you're either too hot or too cold but always too hungry, and you could put an end to all of that just by doing this little favor, but there's things you do and things you don't do.

And killing somebody is one of the things you don't do.

Maybe they ask me to join a crew, take down a truck or a warehouse, maybe drive a load of hijacked ciggies or something, maybe even help rough some guy up, start working off the debt, maybe that's something I think about and says yes to, but I ain't killin' nobody.

You go to hell for that.

So he tells them no, tells them the same thing every day for the next month and a half while the debt piles up like the dirty snow on the sidewalk.

Not that you can see the sidewalk. You can't. The actual concrete is buried under about fifteen layers of crusted snow and ice. Shit, half the time people don't even bother to shovel it, and you can only walk on it because people have trampled the snow into hard-packed little trails. Especially out front of the stores that have closed.

Which is most of them.

Doug walks down Main, he passes Stewart's Furniture: closed; Cristofaro's Plumbing and Hardware: closed; Kenyon's Department Store: closed. Doug remembers Kenyon's from when he was a little kid and would stand in front of the big window – boarded up now – and look at the Christmas display they did, with a big toy train running around the whole window case, and little mechanical elves and shit, and pretty clothes for pretty women draped over nice couches and chairs, and a big tree in the center, lit up with all them lights and ornaments and shit, and even though Doug knew he wasn't going to get *any* of that stuff or anything else for Christmas it was still nice to look through that window Christmastime.

Now that window is just a big sheet of plywood, and no one has shoveled the snow out in front.

Camelletti calls this a vicious circle.

'It's a vicious circle,' he tells the other guys having breakfast at the diner. Him and Arthur and Petit always have breakfast at the diner and sit in the same booth by the window. 'The factories shut down and some stores close. Some stores close, fewer people come downtown, more stores close. Maybe some company's looking at coming in, opening a factory, but they look downtown, see there's no stores and say what the hell we want to locate in a town where there's no stores and they don't shovel the snow? So more stores close . . .'

'So you're saying what?' Arthur asks. Arthur's is the diner's designated cynic. He reads the front section of the paper and writes letters to the editor. 'You're saying if we shovel the snow the factories will come back?'

This is the conversation Doug walks in on.

He comes through the door and the hot, stale air of the diner feels like heaven. He opens his peacoat to take in the warmth, shucks off his watch cap and plops down on a red vinyl stool at the counter.

For Doug the diner is the last best thing in town. It's a real diner, too, an old sheet-metal art-deco place that's been there since before World War Two. The diner serves real food, not that fancy ass shit they dish out in the yuppie places that have sprung up like mushrooms in the old Victorian houses where families used to live. Those places that cater to the people who drive their Beemers in from Danbury or Avon and plop down platinum cards for some dink piece of chicken on a bed of rice and some vegetable nobody ever heard of.

No, the diner serves *food*. Fried eggs and bacon and home-fried potatoes with little chunks of onion and red peppers in them, sprinkled with paprika and shiny with grease. The diner serves cheeseburgers and hot dogs with the buns still moist from the steamer, and you can dump as much relish and mustard and onions as you want, and that's lunch. The diner serves big bowls of chili with lots of hamburger in it and cheese if you want it, and that's supper, or there's hot open-faced turkey or roast beef sandwiches with mashed potatoes and thick, greasy gravy and green beans out of a can. The diner serves, for dessert, wedges of apple pie, peach pie, rhubarb pie with cheese or vanilla ice cream on top. The diner serves doughnuts, coffee cake, crullers and cinnamon rolls, the kind that leave your fingers sticky for the rest of the morning no matter how many times you wash your hands.

The diner serves coffee.

Not cappuccino, espresso, latte, decaf machiato with low-fat milk in breast-size mugs the color of nature – the diner serves coffee. Acid, bitter, loosen-your-bowels coffee, in white cups stained brown from generations of working men and women getting their morning will to go another day of making tools, making axes, making things from steel or iron that people use to make other things. Because that's what this town used to do – it made things. Not service or information or high-tech, it made things people put in their hands and held on to. That kind of coffee for that kind of town.

And the diner pours you your second cup before you finished your first, and you don't have to listen to no milk steamer hiss and bubble and you don't have to listen to some grunge-folk-rock singer whine about his daddy only sprung for a pre-owned Mercedes.

And the diner has milk and sugar in those old metal pitchers and bowls with hinged lids and a spoon stuck in the notch, and the coffee is hot, which is what you need on a morning like this, which is what Doug is thinking about when he comes in off the street, because that bottomless cup of coffee comes with the dollar breakfast.

Man, Doug can smell that breakfast.

He's had about thirty-seven minutes of sleep, what with tossing and turning next to the heat of the furnace and with thinking about King's offer, so he's tired and cold and hungry, and all that can be fixed by that dollar breakfast.

Doug gets the same thing every morning. Two eggs over easy, home-fried potatoes, rye toast, coffee. He'd like to get bacon with that, but bacon don't come with the special and he can't afford it. But anyway the eggs and toast taste real good and what he does is he dips the toast into the runny egg yolk and washes it down with the coffee. Saves the last slice of toast and spreads grape jelly on it, and though it isn't as sweet or sticky as a cinnamon roll it still does the trick.

So Doug comes in, nods a hello to Camelletti and Arthur and Petit, and says to Andy behind the counter, 'Breakfast special, please, Andy.'

The diner suddenly gets real quiet.

Camelletti and Arthur and Petit leave off the usual sports-economics-sex seminar and they all look at Andy kind of embarrassed like.

Doug wonders what's up.

Then Andy says, 'No more breakfast special.'

'What?'

'No more breakfast special,' Andy says, a little hostile, like he's covering up being embarrassed. He sees the look on Doug's face and says quietly, 'I'm losin' my ass here, Doug.'

'Yeah, but *shit*, Andy.'

'Shit *nothin'*, Douggie.'

Andy shrugs, which Doug understands as a rustbelt New England gesture which takes into it that the factories are shut down, the store windows are plywood, and the white-collar yuppies from the frickin' dot-com companies are buying three-dollar double-lattes in go-cups they can drink from while they drive to Danbury, and there ain't nothin' Andy can do about any of it, including that Doug's small thief alkie father died leaving him a ball and chain, and the jobs are gone for good and there ain't gonna be a diner for *anyone* to eat a dollar breakfast this time next year.

Doug gets all that

It's like, *www.gofuckyourself.com.*

The men in the diner are all staring out the window now because their table is stacked with plates shiny with grease, salt crystals sparkling like little diamonds, coffee cups sitting there waiting for the refill.

They've had *their breakfast, Doug thinks.*

Mine's in Mexico, or China or Korea or some place where the factories have moved, they don't have to pay minimum wage.

Some sunny, warm frickin' place.

'So what *can* I get for a buck?' he asks Andy.

'Toast, coffee,' Andy says.

Doug feels bad for him because Andy's a good guy. He needs to raise prices, he needs to raise prices is all. Doug looks up at the menu board behind the counter and sees that even at a buck for toast and coffee, Andy's cutting him a deal.

'You know what?' Doug says. 'Forget about it.'

He jams his watchcap back on and takes his coat off the hook.

Andy says, 'C'mon, Douggie, don't be that way.'

'I'm not being any way.'

'Have some coffee.'

'See you guys later.'

The wind smacks him in the face the second he steps out. He slogs down to Dunkin' Donuts and picks up the usual order. Ducks his head against the wind until he makes it to King Real Estate. Sets the doughnuts down on Clark's desk and says, 'I'll do it.'

'Do what?'

'Your little favor,' Doug says.

Kill this guy.

But, like, who?

'You don't need to know "who", yet,' Whitey tells him. 'First you need to know "how".'

He drives Doug out into the country, which doesn't take long because most of north-west Connecticut is second growth forest sprung up from what used to be farmland until even the New Englanders gave up trying to grow stuff on rocks.

Arthur has this theory that the famous New England dour personality is a product of the soil, or rather, the lack of it. 'Of course they got grouchy trying to farm this land,' he tells the other denizens of the diner. 'It costs fifty dollars to bury your cat, for Chrissakes.'

Anyway, a lot of what used to be fields is forest again, a lot of it turned into state parks, and that's where Whitey takes Doug, up Route 8 to Winsted, then east on Route 44 and north on 183, where they drive alongside the Farmington river through People's Forest.

People's Forest sounds Chinese, Doug thinks, although he doubts it really is, because there are exactly five Chinese people in the whole county and they run a restaurant out on 44 where they got a five dollar all-you-can-eat lunch buffet on Wednesdays that Camelletti always insists on going to.

'But the food is shitty,' Arthur argues, even though he agrees to go with him every week.

'Yeah, but there's lots of it,' Camelletti says.

'Yeah, but it's shitty.'

'Yeah, but it's five bucks.'

Doug has listened to them debate which is better – *more* shitty food for five bucks or *less* shitty food for five bucks – but for Doug the concept of shitty food is a non-starter.

Now he looks out the car window at the river below. It's pretty – all silver and black and white and dark gray as the water rushes through the ice and snow, and the trees in the background are dark-green.

It's only twenty minutes away from Torrington but he hasn't been here in years. His memories of the river are summer memories, when him and Edley and a couple of girls would come out and get sandwiches from the general store in the nearby village and then go out and sit at picnic tables on the river bank. In summer the river is slow and brown, not the fast black water cutting through the winter ice, and after they ate, him and Edley and the girls they'd toss inner tubes into the water and sit in them and float downstream to a little sandy beach off an eddy and they'd lie down in the sand and make out.

Those were good days.

Whitey turns right on to a dirt road that switchbacks uphill through a thick oak forest. He pulls over on a wide spot in the road next to a long, snow-covered meadow. 'We're here,' he says.

Doug gets out of the car.

The snow crunches under his feet.

'Aren't your feet cold?' Whitey asks, looking at Doug's Chuck Taylors.

'Yeah.'

'We gotta get you some decent frickin' shoes,' Whitey says.

Doug's noticed that Whitey and Clark have been treating him different since he agreed to do this favor for King. Not like he's an equal or anything like that, but their attitude has changed now he's agreed to kill this guy.

It's a fucked-up world, Doug thinks.

'We get back today,' Whitey says, 'we'll go to Payless Shoes.'

'Okay.'

'Get you some boots.'

Whitey opens the trunk, takes out a 9mm Berretta and a box of shells. He shakes a few of the rounds into his hand and loads the pistol. Then they walk across the meadow to an old gravel berm where the snow trucks used to take out gravel for the roads.

'You ever shot one of these things?' Whitey asks.

'I never shot anything.'

'Good, I won't have to unteach any bad habits,' Whitey says. He hands Doug the pistol. 'It's easy – you slide this back, you're ready to go. Then it's just like them computers they got these days. You just point and click.'

Doug raises the pistol, which feels heavy in his hand, and points it at the berm.

'You walk in,' Whitey says, 'pull the gun, point the gun, shoot the gun. Keep shooting until the *bang bang* becomes *click click*.'

'That easy, huh?'

'There's no skill in this, Doug,' says Whitey. 'You want skill, shoot a bow and arrow. That's what I do, I come up here during bow season and get me a deer. That's skill. This is just pulling the trigger. Try it.'

Doug raises the pistol again and shoots into the berm.

It feels great, he thinks, through the ringing in his ears, like each jerk of the trigger is getting something off his chest.

He can see how you could get to liking this.

Whitey sees the look in his eye and gives him this weird, almost embarrassed smile, like they're sharing some kind of dirty secret, like they're looking at some kind of sick porno or something and getting off on it.

'So it's simple, Doug,' Whitey says. 'You walk into this guy's office, guy'll probably be sitting behind his desk. You walk in, don't hesitate, just pull the gun and –'

'You sure the guy'll let me in?'

'He'll be expecting you.'

'But he won't be expecting . . .' Doug gestures with the pistol.

'No,' Whitey says. 'He'll be expecting, you know. . .'

Yeah, I know, Doug thinks.

He'll be expecting Douggie Doughnuts.

Doug don't eat breakfast that morning even though he's got money in his pocket.

He walks right past the diner in his new Merrell boots, not because he's pissed at Andy or nothing but because Whitey has told him that sometimes guys, especially their first time, throw up after they do it, right on the spot, and what's in the puke could be, believe it or not, evidence. Cops see like bacon, eggs, toast, home fries on the floor they're goin' straight to the diner and ask Andy who had breakfast in there that morning.

So Doug walks straight to Dunkin' Donuts, picks up his usual order and walks over to King Real Estate, not even feeling the cold because he's got them warm, fur-lined boots on and because this is his last morning doing this. Today he does this favor, then Clark gives him twenty k in cash, the keys to a clean car and a one-way air ticket, New York to Mexico, where he can stay until this whole thing cools down

– his debt forgiven and money in his pocket – and then come back.

Or not, whatever he wants.

Maybe not, Doug thinks as the heavy boots trod down the old, dirty snow. *Maybe I'll stay where it's warm all the frickin' time. Maybe I'll go south like the jobs did, and stay there, like the jobs did.*

He turns up the walk into the office.

Sets the cardboard tray down on the reception table, takes out the coffees, then goes in and sets the doughnuts down on a paper towel on the kitchen counter. He takes the pistol out of his pocket, pulls the slide back, and puts it back in his pocket. He slides the plastic glove onto his hand, then puts one of the doughnuts on a plate and takes it and the cream two-sugars to King's private office.

Knocks on the door.

King yells, 'That you, Douggie Doughnuts?'

'Yeah.'

Doug walks in, sets the coffee and doughnuts down on King's desk. He can smell the man's aftershave and his hair spray.

'Cream, two sugars?' King asks. Like usual, he don't even look up.

He don't see Doug take the pistol out of his pocket and point it at his head. He don't hear the *bang bang bang bang bang bang bang bang* as Doug empties the clip into him. Well, maybe he hears the first one, but he don't hear the second because the first goes right into his brain and turns the lights out.

Doug does feel the vomit building up in his stomach but he fights it down, drops the gun like Whitey told him to do, then walks out of the office.

Whitey's standing behind Clark's desk, gives Doug a nod of professional respect as Clark hands him the cash, the car keys and the tickets. Doug walks out of the house and, right to the plan, the stolen car is sitting out front, tank full of gas. Drive down to New York without stopping is the plan. Get on the plane to Mazatlan, enjoy himself while Clark and Whitey carve up King's business like the Christmas turkey.

Doug drives down Main Street past the boarded-up stores, past Stewart's Furniture, Cristofaro's Plumbing and Hardware, and Kenyon's Department Store where he used to look in the window at Christmas.

He pulls over beside Main Diner and parks.

Goes in, takes off his coat and hangs it up, sits on a red vinyl stool at the counter.

All the guys, Andy and Camelletti and Arthur and Petit just stare at him as he lays the twenty k in cash on the counter and says, 'Andy, I'll have two eggs over easy, home fries, rye toast, bacon, sausage and coffee, please.'

Andy sees the weird look in Doug's eyes and decides it ain't the time to ask any questions, so he just pours Doug a coffee into one of them stained white cups and then cracks the eggs on to the grill and starts shoving the home fries around with his old spatula.

Doug takes that first sip of coffee and it tastes great.

Hot and bitter going down, like coffee should be.

Andy sets the plate on the counter in front of Doug. The food is beautiful, the grease sparkling like a fresh field of snow in the sunlight.

'Thanks, Andy.'

'Sure. Anything else, Doug?'

'Yeah,' Doug says. 'Call the cops. I just killed Frank King.'

'Jesus, Doug, what happened?'

Doug looks at him, then at the guys sitting at the booth by

331

the window. He shrugs and says, 'He called me Douggie Doughnuts.'

Doug picks up his fork and digs into the food.

It's frickin' wonderful.

He's just finished eating when the cops come.

TWO THINGS

Daniel Woodrell

When she comes over it is in a rattly old thing. Color yellow, it got white ring tires that rime the way round and the exhaust has slipped loose and is dragging sparks from it. There are stickers from the many funny places she been to on the bumper and two or three of her ideas are pasted on the fenders. A band-aid that look just like a band-aid only it is a monster has been momma'd on to the hood like the rattly old thing got some child sore in the motor.

Now this official had mailed us a note that tell Wilma who is the woman who is my wife and me that this lady wants to visit. It seems she teach Cecil something useful at the prison.

The door flings out and she squats up out of the car coming my way. I have posted myself in the yard and she come straight at me smiling. Over her shoulder is a strap that holds up a big purse made of the sort of pale weeds they have in native lands I never saw.

She call me Mister McCoy right off like who I am is that clear cut. Her name Frieda Buell she go on then flap out a hand for me to shake. I give her palm a little rub and tell her she is welcome.

When I see that sits with her good I tell her to come into the house.

That is something she would love to do she tells me.

This is a remark I don't believe so I stand back and inventory her. She is young with shaggy blonde hair but she knows something about painting her face as she has done it smashing well. Her shirt is red and puffy and her shoes have heels that tell me walking is not a thing she practices over much. Her shiny pants is black and wetted on to her like my hot breath on a cold jewelry window.

The porch has sunk down so it hunkers a distance in front of the house. I ask her to be careful and she is. Inside I give her the good chair but I keep standing.

Right away I tell her I want to know what this about.

What it is about is a lulu. My son Cecil is a gifted man she says. He has a talent that puts a rareness to the world or something along those lines.

Cecil? Cecil a thief I tell her. And not that sly a one neither.

Once was she says. No more.

Always was I put in. My mind is made up on that. But what's got me puzzled is what is this rareness he puts to the world or whatever?

Poetry is her answer. She reach her hand that has been overdone with various rings into the big purse and pulls out a booklet. She says Cecil has written it and the critics have claimed him as a natural in ability.

I take the booklet in my hands. It is of thick dry paper and the cover says 'Dark Among the Grays' by Cecil McCoy. That is him all right I say. Tell me do this somehow line him up early for parole?

It could she says. She trying to face me bold enough but her eyes is playing hooky on her face and going places besides my own. She been teaching him for two years she says and what he has is a gift like she never seen before.

Gift I say. A gift is not like Cecil.

May I have the book she asks. I hand it to her. She opens it to a middle page. Like this, listen to this. She begin to read to me from what apparently Cecil my son has written out. The name of it is 'Soaring' and it is a string of words that say a bird is floating above the junk yard and has spotted a hot glowing old wreck below only the breeze sucks him down and he can't help but land in it. When she done reading the thing she look up at me like I should maybe be ridiculous with pleasure. I can't tell but that is my sense.

Is that one chapter or what I want to know.

She lets out one of them whistly breaths that means I might overmatch her patience. These are poems of his life on the street she tells me. But they are brimful of accurate thoughts for all. Yet grounded in the tough streets of this area.

They have junkyards everywhere is my comeback to her.

But the bird Mister McCoy. The bird is soaring over death which is an old car wreck. The poet is wanting to be that white bird winging it free above death. What it really signifies is that Cecil want to be let off from having to die. That is the point of it she says.

Now to me this point is obvious but I feel sad for a second about Cecil. Two things he never going to be is a white bird.

Read on I suggest.

She slides out a smile for me that lets me know I'm catching on. Then she turn the book to another page. This was in some big-time poetry magazine she says. Then she read. The words of this one are about a situation I recognise. The poet has ripped off his momma's paycheck to pay back some bad dudes he ain't related to.

Hold it there I ask her. That is a poem that actually happen several times lady. Cecil a goddamn thief.

No no no. He wants to make amends for it. He wants to overcome the guilt of what he done.

I tell her it would be in the hundreds of dollars to do that. Is these poems going to get him that kind of money? My question is beneath her. She won't answer it.

This poem has meanings for all the people she says. They look into it and see their selves.

That is nice and interesting I tell her but how come Wilma and me has to pay for this poem all alone? Everybody who looks in it and see their selves ought to pay some back to us.

This comment of mine puts pressure on her cool and she begins to pace about the room. The room is clean enough but the furniture is ragged. I have a hip weakness and janitor work pains it. Wilma has the job now.

The lady stops and looks out the window. Two cars is blocking traffic to say what's going on to each other. Horns are honking. People get hurt over things like that.

Mister McCoy do you love Cecil?

There was a time I answer. It was a love that any daddy would have. But that was way back. If I love Cecil now it is like the way I love the Korean conflict. Something terrible I have lived through.

He has changed Mister McCoy. He has got in touch with his humanity. If he had a place to live he could be paroled to start fresh.

I believe I will sit down. As I say it I drop to the three-legged chair by the door. I am thinking of my son Cecil. He was one of a whole set of kids Wilma and me filled out because we had only each other. He ate from the same pot of chili as the rest but he turned out different. His eyes were shiny and his nose turned up instead of being flat. The better he knows you the more relaxed he is about stealing you blind. Same pot of chili but different.

I don't believe we want to take him back I say.

338

But you are his family. There is no one else for him.

Family yes but main victims too lady. I reach up and pull the bridge from my mouth which leaves a bad fence of my teeth showing. See that I ask. Cecil did that. He wasn't but fifteen when he did that.

He has changed she says again. She says it like that settles it.

I don't believe it. He may well write out poems that say he sorry and guilty but I am leery of him. You listen to this lady. This porch right here. I was standing on this porch right here when it was less sunk and Cecil was out there in the street with a mess of boys. They were little but practicing to be dangerous some day. One of them picks up a stone and tosses it at the high up street light there. He misses it by a house or two. He ain't close. I stood there on the porch out of curiosity and watched. They all flung stones at the light but none was close to shattering it. Then Cecil pick up a slice of brick and hardly aims but he smash that light to bits. As soon as it left his hand I seen that his aim for being bad was awful accurate.

Well she says. He seems sensitive to her.

Oh he can do that lady. He could do that years ago.

You are a hard nut she tells me. He is lost without you. His parole could be denied.

Tell me why do you care? I ask her this but my suspicion is she would like to give Cecil lessons in gaiety.

Because I admire his talent Mister McCoy. Cecil is a poet who is pissed off at the big things in this world and that give him a heat that happy poets got to stand back from.

You want us to take him home because he pissed off? That ain't no change.

Artistically she goes, wheezing that putdown breath again.

Lady that ain't enough I tell her. Let me show you the door.

When we are on the porch she wants to shake hands again

but I don't chew my cabbage twice. I have been there so I lead her across the yard. Her cheeks get red. I look up and down the neighborhood and all the homes are like mine and Wilma's. The kind that if they were people they would cough a lot and spit up tangled stuff. Spit shit into the sink.

At her car she hands me the booklet. It is yours she says. Cecil insisted.

I take it in my hands. I say thank you.

She slips into the rattly old thing and starts the motor. A puff of oil smoke come out the back and there is a knocking sound.

I lean down to her window.

Look lady I say. Wish Cecil well but it is like this. He ain't getting no more poems off of us.

Her head nods and she flips her hand at me. The monster band-aid on the hood has caught my eye again. What kind of craziness is that about I wonder. I want to ask her but she shifts the car and pulls away. So I am left standing there alone to guess just what it is she believe that band-aid fix.

MY FATHER'S DAUGHTER

A STORY IN TWO PARTS

Andrew Coburn

PART ONE

'Truth has validity. Myth has muscle.'

Joseph Shellenbach

Hank West, womaniser, inveterate gambler and father of two, died as he had lived. On the edge. A razor passed so smoothly across his throat that he had no idea he'd been murdered.

He left behind a frayed wife, two adolescent sons and many debts. Jack, the elder son, had his father's dark hair, deep-set eyes and carefree ways. Edward, a year younger, blond and fair, with little definition to his face, resembled no one in particular. Jack had been his father's favorite. Edward seemed always in his mother's protective custody.

Distraught, drawing her sons to her, Milly West said, 'Who will take care of us?'

'I will,' Jack said.

Edward said, 'I'll help.'

They worked after-school jobs and their mother languished with the knowledge she would not last long. Jack came home late each evening from clearing tables at Lomazzo's Restaurant, where the waitresses were youngish and married.

With a peculiar hush about her, Milly West washed lipstick from his collars.

In private to Edward, she whispered, 'You're the younger, but it's Jack I worry about. You're the level-headed one. Are you listening, dear?'

Edward nodded, proud of the rating.

Later that evening, still carrying that peculiar hush, she spoke to Jack. 'You mustn't think of your father as any kind of hero. When he wasn't welshing on bets, he was chasing women, breaking up marriages. Others paid for his shenanigans.'

'Who killed him, Mom?'

'Could've been anybody.'

'But we should know.'

'It won't bring him back.'

Weather permitting, Milly West spent an hour each afternoon talking to her husband's headstone. On the last afternoon, braving a stiff breeze, she said, 'I'm not well, Hank. The boys don't know. Edward suspects but doesn't say anything. He's afraid of the truth, and Jack is too much wrapped up in himself to see. He's so much like you, Hank. That's not meant as a criticism. It's just the way you were and he is.'

She glanced away. Visitors to another grave were tidying up the site and lovingly positioning fresh flowers. She guessed they were father and daughter. When she returned her attention to the headstone, she was smiling. 'Here you are, Hank, lying cold-stone dead in the ground, but in the phone book you're quite alive and you still get mail. You never believed it, but see, there is life after death.'

The next day her breathing was bad. Feeling an unusual heaviness around her heart, she lay down on the couch, which was where Edward found her.

'What's the matter, Mom?'

She looked up at him with a smile so final Edward wanted to cry. She tried to raise her head but couldn't. No longer able to pump air, she gasped. No longer able to think, she drifted. No longer conscious, she died.

The boys grieved, each in his own way. At the funeral home Jack went out of his way to share memories of his mother. Edward, receiving condolences, was a thin-lipped collection of formalities.

At evening's end Edward leaned over the casket to give his mother a last look. Touching her chill hand told him the exact temperature of a grave. Jack, who played the piano by ear, could not take his eyes off his mother's face, the stillness of which suggested a sustained note of music pitched too high for human hearing, though a hound howling wouldn't have surprised him.

Later in the month Jack, a nonchalant student, graduated from Haverhill High. Edward, a fastidious one, had a year to go. They had no aunts or uncles and no grandparents. Their father had been an orphan and their maternal grandparents were long deceased.

With a hint of panic in his voice, Edward said, 'We're on our own.'

'Sooner or later,' Jack said, 'everybody's on his own. We're just starting sooner.'

'I don't want to quit school.'

'You don't have to.'

Jack worked two jobs, at Lomazzo's and at the Elite Bowling Alley, where he was the evening manager and a favorite among women bowlers, one of whom he had an affair with until her husband threatened him with bodily harm. Jack left Haverhill when Edward received a diploma, along with a scholarship to Bentley School of Accounting.

The brothers shook hands at the train station. Edward said, 'What if you get killed?'

'I won't,' Jack said and, smiling, boarded the train. 'Take care, kid.'

Jack spent three years in the army. Truman, then Eisenhower, was in the White House, and American troops were in Korea. Jack, however, spent the bulk of his service in Germany, where his buddies were college-educated draftees who included him in their bull sessions. With them, he sharpened his sense of the ridiculous and agreed that in a very large way soldiering was silly.

To Edward he wrote, 'No army camp is home, no bunk a bed, and my APO number is not an address. It's merely where I'm reachable. My uniform is not a suit of clothes. It's a body badge. It gives me certain privileges, some protection, but no rights.'

To a waitress at Lomazzo's: 'I still can't get used to saluting an officer. It's pretending the guy's a god when the odds are he's a horse's ass.'

Again to Edward: 'In the Bahnhof district every woman is available. The young ones are sweet and hard-working. The older ones have spooky eyes and look at you out of layers of makeup. They're the ones who've lost husbands, children, whole families in the war, which to us is just a historical event. They see us as brats worth no more than the military money in our pockets.'

Assigned to a supply depot and given responsibilities and a civilian assistant named Gretchen, Jack began dealing on the black market. Contraband included field jackets and overcoats, field phones and stopwatches, C rations and flashlights, tent stoves and electric pumps, wool blankets and sheets. Gretchen was his accomplice and, on his overnight passes, his bedmate.

To Edward: 'She's smart, university-educated, and she

speaks five languages and better English than I do. She adored her father, who was captain of a U-boat that lies somewhere at the bottom of the North Sea. Her mother hasn't been right since and Gretchen is sole support. I think I'm in love, kid.'

Edward wrote back that he had finished up early at Bentley and was working in the accounting department of the Haverhill National Bank. He did not mention that he was courting a co-worker named Marion, who some days seemed interested in him and other days not.

Marion was a year younger but seemed older. Her aloof bearing and the depth of her voice impressed people, Edward most of all. At times her reserve was impenetrable. Over spaghetti at Lomazzo's, a basket of bread and rolls separating them, he proposed. Moments passed.

'Did you hear me?'

'Yes.' She sprinkled grated cheese over her plate.

'Well?'

'My mother says to marry big or not at all.'

'I plan to make money,' he said with a sudden sense of himself. 'A lot of money.'

She twirled spaghetti around her fork, no loose ends. 'I'm a strong woman, Edward. Can you deal with that?'

'My mother was strong.'

'Really.' She tore bread and buttered a piece. 'Your brother used to work here, didn't he?'

'Yes. Did you know him?'

'Heard about him. Are you anything like him?'

'No.'

'Are you a virgin, Edward?'

He blushed.

'I thought so. I am too, more or less.'

He looked at her square in the face. 'Marion, what are your feelings for me?'

347

'I'm intrigued. You're the only person I know whose father was murdered.'

'That's it? That's all?'

'There must be more. Has to be. Otherwise I'm sure I wouldn't be here.'

'Then will you marry me?'

'I'll give it thought, Edward.'

They finished their dinner, their dessert, their coffee. When the check arrived, Edward produced a wallet branded with his initials, a birthday gift all the way from Germany. He scrutinised the check and paid it. The tip was a pittance. The waitress gazed down at them.

Marion rose stiffly and walked ahead of him. On the street she spun round. 'Don't ever embarrass me again.'

Less than a month before Jack was to return to the United States, he and Gretchen spent a weekend on the Belgian coast. Under a fleet of low-lying clouds they stood on a spit of sand and watched detonating waves diminish the beach. Dropping to one knee, Gretchen clamped a seashell to her ear and claimed she could hear two drowned sailors in quiet conversation.

'What are they talking about?' Jack asked with a grin.

She was slow to rise. Her eyes, which had filled, looked newly blue. 'What it would be like to live and breathe again.'

He guessed the image in her mind. 'I'm sorry,' he said, taking her hand.

'You lost yours too.'

'Your father was a hero. Mine wasn't.'

Hand in hand, they sauntered back to the hotel. In the small lobby, standing with a cane that twitched under his weight, an old man smiled at them and said something in French.

'What did he say?' Jack asked.

'Ah, to be our age again.'

In their warm room they made love twice, the second time with almost painful tenderness. Then they lay apart but wedded as if by an invisible ampersand. Jack whispered, 'Have you decided?'

'I can't leave my mother, you know that. But it's good you're going home. You take too many chances here.'

'You'll be all right? Financially?'

'More than all right.'

'I'll come back. I'll live here, Gretchen. We'll get married.'

'Every soldier says that.'

'But I mean it.'

Nudity made her a pale ghost. 'I love you, Jack.'

Sergeant stripes on his sleeves, Jack boarded the USS *General Blatchford*, which sailed out of Bremerhaven and docked eleven days later at Staten Island. Mustered out at Camp Kilmer, he flew from Idlewild to Logan, where he pumped hands with his waiting brother.

'You've gained weight, kid.'

'You haven't,' Edward said.

'We got different bones.'

'You got the better ones. Dad's.'

On the drive to Haverhill Jack said, 'What kind of car is this?'

'Pre-war Buick. A-one condition.'

'Radio work?' Jack reached over and turned it on. The singer was Dean Martin, the song 'That's Amore'.

'I'm doing good at the bank, Jack.'

'Knew you would. Good experience for when you come to work for me.'

'Yuh? What kind of work you talking about?'

'Haven't figured it out yet, but I got money. You banked it for me, didn't you?'

Edward handed over a passbook. 'Every cent.'

Jack checked the balance. 'I'm in business, kid. Only time will tell how big.'

Edward drove past Woolworths in downtown Haverhill and cruised up the hill past the Paramount Theater, the courthouse, the high school, with Jack gazing out at each.

'Good to be back. I missed you, kid.'

'You seemed to have had a good time over there.'

'I did.'

'What about that girl you told me about?'

'Gretchen? She's all woman. She'll keep.'

Edward drove past churches at Monument Square, hooked a left, then a right, and soon pulled up at the tenement house where, ground level, they had lived since boyhood. A light was on in the front window and someone was looking out.

'Who's that?'

'I've been waiting to tell you,' Edward said.

'So tell me.'

'I'm married.'

Jack laughed. 'Now tell me you're kidding.'

'Her name's Marion.'

Jack frowned. 'You do something like that not even asking me first? I can't believe it.'

Edward was silent.

Jack's frown vanished as if never there and his laugh was loud. 'Congratulations!'

Jack moved back into his old room, which was as he had left it, although Marion may have tidied it a little. The newlyweds had appropriated the marriage bed of Hank and Milly West. Edward, his bedroom converted into an office, supplemented his salary preparing tax returns.

From the start Jack aggravated Marion. When introduced, he had kissed her square on the mouth, a presumption she felt robbed her of rank. He exasperated her when he left his clothes around, and he infuriated her when he knocked on the bathroom door and asked how long she'd be.

In bed with Edward, she said, 'I don't like it when he walks around in his skivvies. That's disrespectful to me.'

'I'll speak to him.'

'You might as well know, I don't like the way he looks at me. That's disrespectful to you.'

'That's just Jack. He'd never do anything.'

'Don't be so sure. Another thing, I hate it when he calls you "kid". It belittles you.'

'He's being affectionate.'

'I'd call it condescending.'

The following evening she said to Jack, 'I'm sick of taking phone calls from women. I'm not your messenger.'

Jack, his dark hair slicked back, was dressed to go out. 'What's the matter?' he said with a grin. 'Jealous?'

She stiffened and glared. 'You think you're God's gift, don't you?'

'No, but I'm one hell of a guy. Obviously you've noticed.'

A deep whisper. 'You prick.'

'Ah, there's the real Marion,' he said. 'Has Edward met her yet?'

A few days later Edward said to Jack, 'What are we going to do?'

'Don't say another word. I'm moving out tomorrow.'

'You don't have to.'

'I already have another place. Not to worry, kid. I still love you.'

He moved to Haverhill's Bradford section, into a furnished flat on the first floor of the Bradford Manor. A nice neighborhood. A great address for his business card, his business unspecified, for he was still looking for one.

Evenings, when he wasn't with a woman, he was drinking at the bar in the Hotel Whittier, where the regulars were

World War Two veterans with past glories and limited futures. Some had known his father. Chuckie, whose face showed the clawmarks of time, said, 'You're the spit'n' image of him. Shame what happened to him.'

Jack, tasting his bourbon, said nothing.

'He's in a better place,' Chuckie pronounced, and others agreed.

Jack lit a cigarette. 'What makes you think so?'

'I figure he bluffed his way into heaven and right away asked for the best accommodations.'

'Here, here!' someone shouted from the end of the bar.

'Who killed him, Chuckie?'

'I could name a dozen guys might've. Who's to say?' Chuckie downed a shot of rye. 'Make sure what happened to him, Jack, doesn't happen to you.'

The Whittier was kitty-corner from the post office, where Jack posted his letters to Gretchen. In a hurried hand he told her he missed her mightily and hungered to be with her again, without giving any indication when that might be. He asked about the condition of Billie Holiday records he had left behind and in a postscript told her he was putting money into real estate.

Gretchen wrote unhurried letters without mentioning the stress from his departure and her sense of disconnection from much that was around her, especially at the supply depot. She merely mentioned that her ear for languages had landed her a job with her own government. She and her mother were moving to Bonn. Her letters ended with 'X's for kisses.

A year passed before she scheduled a transatlantic call to him. The time difference made her evening his afternoon. She said, 'I miss you, Jack.'

'I miss you, too.'

She hesitated. 'Have you met someone?'

He had met many women, none who counted. He said, 'No.'

Again she hesitated. 'Should I wait?'

'Yes,' he said.

His business card now listed him as a real-estate manager, though his sister-in-law called him a slumlord, for his rental properties were three-deckers verging on disrepair. His brother, who kept his books, defended him, but Marion would have none of it.

'Slumlord is what I said and slumlord is what I meant.' The three of them were eating at Lomazzo's. Her eyes went from Edward to Jack. 'You've had code violations. It was in the paper.'

'He's taken care of it,' Edward said.

With a smile, Jack said, 'You don't like me, do you, Marion?'

'I don't like your ways.'

Edward said, 'We're all family. So let's enjoy the meal.'

'Pass the Parmesan,' Jack said, and Marion did so with a grimace. He winked at her. 'You oughta loosen up.'

'Don't tell me what I ought to do.'

'Let's not fight,' Edward said.

Jack kept his eyes on her. 'How long you been married?'

She raised her chin. 'Figure it out yourself.'

'Time you got pregnant, isn't it?'

She started to speak, stopped and placed her napkin beside her plate. Rising stiffly, she peered down at her husband. 'I'll wait for you in the car.' Then she was gone.

'Jesus, Jack, that's a sore subject.'

'Sorry, kid. I didn't know.'

'I can't stay.'

Jack watched Edward stumble away and then returned to his dinner. A warm feeling came over him when a married waitress from the old days paused to chat, a hand high on her hip, the honest smell from her underarm endearing to him.

Edward joined his wife in the car. He spoke, but Marion did not respond until they were halfway home. Staring straight ahead, she said, 'Don't ever take his side against me again.'

'I didn't know I did.'

She stiffened into another silence, which lasted until they were home and slipping into bed, where Edward kept his distance, his eyes wide open in the dark. 'Do you have anything to say?' she asked.

'I'm sorry.'

'He's your brother, but it's not like you owe him anything.'

'He pays me well for the work I do for him.'

'He should, you're a good accountant. You have a future. He's never going to be anything but a slumlord.'

'You don't know Jack,' he wanted to say but kept quiet. He knew the Jack she didn't, the Jack who had looked out for him and never let anyone bully him. Now he was out of Jack's hands and in Marion's.

Marion said, 'What day is this?'

'Thursday.'

'If you want intercourse, I don't mind.'

Among Hungarian refugees trickling into Haverhill and occupying tenements owned by Jack were a plumber, an electrician and a clever handyman, each a godsend. Jack hired them at rates advantageous to him, paid them under the table and began buying more properties. The bank liked the way he did business and readily financed him. At the same time he began investing in electronics companies, especially those started along Route 128 by MIT grads.

At the Whittier bar Chuckie said, 'Whatcha doin', Jacko, buying up all of Haverhill?'

My Father's Daughter

Someone else said, 'What d'you think of the Russkies flyin' Sputniks over our heads? Ike should shoot 'em down.'

'We do that,' Jack said, 'you guys might be fighting World War Two all over again.'

'Hey, I'd do it, they raised me in rank.'

Chuckie said, 'You still got a gal in Germany waitin' for you, Jacko?'

'I guess you could say that,' Jack said. 'She's on hold.'

His letters to Gretchen were fragments and hers were less frequent. At the start of the new year she wrote, 'I feel naked. Writing is so personal, the mind exposing its wiring. How long have you been gone, Jack? Long enough to be a ghost?'

'I'm not a ghost,' he wrote back. 'Give me a little more time.'

In April she wrote, 'Time mocks us. The Swiss knew that when they added a cuckoo to the clock.' He chose to read little into that. Elsewhere in the letter she wrote, 'We desperately want to believe in the Cartesian split. It doubles our value.' He didn't know what the hell she was talking about and didn't ask.

He almost skipped the postscript, then glanced at it. 'How much of the world is womb? All of it, do you suppose?' He wondered whether she was herself.

He did not hear from her again until late August. 'My mother died Tuesday. The funeral was yesterday. Seeing her off, I realised death is the ultimate privacy. There was no way I could talk to her. I wonder, Jack, do the dead know they're gone?'

He immediately arranged for a transatlantic call. Two hours later he heard her voice and said, 'Why didn't you call me? I'd have flown right over.'

'I didn't see the need. I knew a long time ago you were never coming back.'

355

'Come here,' he said after a moment. 'Come to the States. Please, Gretchen.'

'I think it's too late for anything like that, don't you?'

'It doesn't have to be. Is there something you're not telling me?'

'What would that be, Jack?'

'I don't know.' He was frustrated. 'What's the problem?'

She was silent for so long he was uncertain she was still on the line. Then she spoke. 'Me, Jack. I'm the problem.'

He didn't understand and wasn't sure he wanted to. He told her he'd get back to her and he meant to. But he never did.

Jack joined the Rotary Club, lunched at Lomazzo's with people from city hall and accompanied a Haverhill delegation to Boston to shake hands with presidential candidate John F. Kennedy. He bet his brother, a Nixon supporter, fifty dollars that Kennedy would win. Close with money and cautious by nature, Edward lowered the bet to twenty-five.

At this time Jack began buying dilapidated downtown properties at auction, which Edward considered unwise speculation. A few years later President Kennedy was dead and Jack reported sizeable profits from properties taken over by the Haverhill Redevelopment Authority.

'Okay, you were right, I was wrong,' Edward said. Part of the breakfast crowd, they were in a booth in the Presto Diner, below the railway bridge. The 7.20 to Boston rumbled overhead. 'Unless you knew something I didn't.'

Jack blew smoke from a Pall Mall. 'When you hang around the right people, you hear things.'

Edward batted away the smoke. 'That your secret?'

'Little bit more to it than that, kid.'

'Do me a favor, Jack. Don't call me kid any more. Marion doesn't like it. Tell the truth, I don't either.'

'Right. Sorry. You're a man of means.'

Edward had on a new suit, one that now fit him. Rich food had extended his waistline. With Jack's backing and in a building Jack owned, he had left the bank and opened an accounting office.

Jack snuffed out his cigarette.

Edward exaggerated a cough. 'Thank God.' Then he said, 'Why can't you and Marion be friends?'

'Beats the hell out of me. Better ask her.'

'Maybe if you made the effort. If you were a little polite instead of always trying to get a rise out of her.'

'When she puts on that long face and looks down her nose at me, what am I supposed to do? Genuflect? That's your job, kid.'

The waitress freshened Jack's coffee. He plucked up the morning paper, which had lain unread near his elbow. Weeks had passed since Dallas, but Kennedy still dominated the news.

Sudden tears in his eyes, Jack tossed the paper aside. 'I wish *you* had won the bet. Then he'd still be alive.'

'I never felt the way you did about him,' Edward said sullenly. 'He was not a good president.'

'He had style. *Style*, kid. That's what he had.'

'So did Dad. But that didn't make him a good husband, did it?'

'Didn't make him a bad one. I was closer to Dad than you were, so maybe I knew him better.'

'And maybe you didn't know him at all. Mom told me things she never told you, the stuff he put her through. You want to hear some of it?'

'What's done is done.'

Edward was almost smiling. 'You never wanted to know. That's because you were his son, I was hers. Why don't you admit Dad got what he deserved?'

'Keep your voice down. Don't embarrass us.'

'You're just like him. You're all show, and you think you're the cat's miaow. Marion read you in a minute.'

Jack motioned for the check.

Edward's smile was perceptible. 'You still pretending you don't know who killed him?'

'I guess I always knew that,' Jack said quietly. 'What I don't know is whether you helped her.'

'I'll let you guess about that.' Edward reached for the check. 'This is on me.'

At Marion's urging, Edward bought a house on a residential street abutting Bradford Junior College, and Marion joined the Young Women's Republican Club of Greater Haverhill, faithfully attended the luncheon meetings and chaired one of the more visible committees. Her schedule was full. She took tennis lessons, participated in a new kind of exercise called aerobics and attended a book discussion group.

'You open a book, you open a door. Consider that a word to the wise, Edward.'

Edward worked twelve hours a day, more during tax time. He had added to his staff, moved to a larger office in his brother's building and was annoyed when Jack began charging him rent, which Marion maintained was a move to get back at her. She believed she was the cause of the brothers' unexpected coolness toward each other.

In the evening Edward stretched out to watch TV. His favorite programs, during which he usually dozed off, were *Andy Griffith*, *Hogan's Heroes* and *Bewitched*. Marion occasionally watched the news, though she angrily shut it off when footage showed hippies and the like protesting the war in South-east Asia, some by torching the American flag.

When tax season was over, Edward reluctantly consented to a short vacation. They flew to Aruba, checked into an extravagant hotel, feasted on ocean delicacies in one of the three dining rooms and spent hours on the beach, where they sipped alcoholic fruit drinks and took in the sunstruck sights, which included mature women with bare breasts. Edward was shocked.

'Don't be so provincial,' Marion murmured from behind outsize sunglasses. She was reading *The Valley of the Dolls*, a finger poised at the edge of the page.

'I'm trying not to look,' he said.

'Look all you want. Just don't gawk.'

'You'd think they'd be embarrassed.'

'They're European.'

Edward squinted. 'How do you know?'

'They don't worry about carrying an extra pound. And they don't shave under their arms.'

'I don't find that attractive.'

Putting the book aside, she glanced at him. 'You'd better rub more stuff on. You're starting to burn again.'

'I hate the smell of the stuff.'

'Do it anyway.'

He squirted lotion from a flask, applied it to the top of his hot shoulders and dropped back to doze off. Marion stretched her legs, her lengthy body well-oiled, her navel a minnow afloat in sweat. In passing, a French-speaking couple smiled appraisingly, which enlarged her sense of herself. A while later she and a muscular man with a close beard stared fully at each other in a shared moment of sensuality. Had Edward not been there, she'd have chatted with him.

Waking, Edward rubbed his eyes, glanced over at her and was aghast. 'What have you done?' In a panic, he searched here, there, for the top of her bathing suit. 'Where is it?' he demanded.

'Edward, relax!'

'How long has it been off?'

'Five minutes? Ten? What difference does it make?'

'For me, please. Cover up.'

'Do you see something wrong with them?'

'That's not the point.'

'What is the point?'

'You're not European.'

She slipped a hand behind her head, giving herself more relevance. Stubble shadowed her underarm. 'Pretend I am.'

'You're my wife.'

'Pretend I'm not,' she said with a smile and retrieved the top of her bathing suit.

'Thank God,' he murmured.

She was glad he didn't follow her down to the wet sand, where she stood somewhat majestically to welcome any eyes that might be on her. The gentle lap of waves gave her the sensation of someone breathing on her ankles. At home she fancied herself an artificial flower waiting to be real, but here the fancy was fact. She returned to Edward.

'What were you doing?' he asked.

'Getting my feet kissed.' She reached for her robe and tote bag. 'Shall we?'

During the short walk back to the hotel Edward was sullen, as if his honor had been sorely tested and his dignity lessened, but in their room he turned contrite. 'Marion, I'm sorry. I guess I just don't understand what was going on back there.'

'You should've been proud, not humiliated.' She stood with her robe open. 'Look at me, Edward. I'm in great shape, the best I'll ever be in. Why shouldn't I show off?'

With a half-nod, he sort of agreed.

She shucked her robe and both pieces of her bathing suit and posed. 'So what do you think, Edward?'

He shivered. 'You know what I think.'

'Then let's.'

'Now? We're all greasy.'

'So what?'

On the bed, fully engaged, slipping and sliding, she was all squishy arms and legs, while he, all frantic thrust and thump, tried to dig in, maintain a balance, lengthen his presence. At one point he pitched to one side. 'Stay with it,' she urged as he tried hard not to flounder. 'Go faster,' she commanded.

Instead he paused. 'Are you pretending I'm somebody else?' he asked.

'Do you mind?'

'Is it Jack?'

'He should be so lucky.'

With new resolve, he reasserted himself and held his place with the aid of her determined leg lock. Resuming his pace, he soon quickened it into what became a race where the winner would receive roses and kisses everywhere. In the fantasy he outdistanced all others, even himself.

Two days later they returned to Haverhill, Marion with a glorious tan, Edward with a sunburn, for which he consulted a doctor, who told him he should have known better and would have to suffer through it.

The telephone rang Sunday morning and woke Jack West and the young woman beside him. He reached over her, picked up the receiver and instantly recognised the voice on the other end. 'Gretchen!' he said. She wasn't calling from Germany but from New York. 'What are you doing in the States?'

The young woman slid out of bed, found something to slip on and with a look of understanding left the room.

Jack spoke into the phone. 'Is something wrong? . . . I can't hear you . . . Yes, of course I can. The Algonquin? I'll

361

catch a shuttle out of Boston . . . Gretchen, this is a wonderful surprise . . . What? Yes. See you in a few hours.'

The young woman lay in the embrace of hot bathwater. Looking in on her, he said, 'I'm sorry.'

'You know I don't demand anything from you.'

He knelt by the tub and sponged her shoulders. 'It's someone I knew a long time ago.'

She looked up with near-sighted blue eyes. 'You don't have to explain. I'll be out of the tub in a minute.'

He rose. 'I'll make it up to you, Sally.'

'You don't owe me a thing.'

Recklessly weaving in and out of lanes on Route 1A, he sped to Logan in record time. Inside the terminal he strode toward the ticket booth as if he were back in the army with a sergeant's *Hup! Hup!* keeping him in step. No delays. A shuttle got him to LaGuardia within the hour and a taxi delivered him to the Algonquin. The desk clerk rang Gretchen's room. Jack expected to go up, but she came down, stepping from the elevator with her hair shorter than he remembered, her face thinner, her whole appearance altered in some subtle way that disquieted him.

'Gretchen.'

He wanted to kiss her but managed only to brush her cheek when she moved her head. Suddenly he felt like a stranger.

'Hello, Jack.'

In the oak-paneled lounge, warm with voices, they sat in cushiony chairs at a small table.

She smiled. 'You haven't changed much. Still the handsome American.'

'It's been too long,' he said, and she seemed to nod. A waiter brought drinks, cognac for her, bourbon for him, which he needed. 'Something's wrong, isn't it?'

'What would that be, Jack?'

'Maybe you'll tell me.'

She tasted the cognac. 'I always wanted to see the Algonquin. I'm a fan of Dorothy Parker.'

The name meant nothing to him. He said, 'Are you ill?'

She glanced toward other tables, as if seeking faces of celebrities, interesting candidates available. A man whose gaunt good looks emanated an introspective air. An elegantly dressed woman who seemed a careful copy of an actress long dead.

'How bad?' Jack asked.

'How bad does it have to be?'

'You're not telling me anything. Am I supposed to guess?'

'That would be asking too much. I have something to show you.' She extracted a small photograph from her bag, passed it over and watched his expression slowly tighten. 'Is there any doubt?' she asked.

'How old is she?'

'Do the arithmetic.'

'Why didn't you tell me?'

'I didn't want you marrying me for only that reason and I knew you would have.'

He held on to the photo. It was precious and his now, and he continued to stare at it.

'Actually she's all you, isn't she, Jack? Physically, damn little of me.'

'What's her name?'

'Elsa. After my mother.'

Jack snared the waiter's eye. He wanted another bourbon and was silent until it arrived. 'Why did you wait till now to tell me?'

'I want you to acknowledge she's yours and I want you to adopt her. A lawyer here in the city has the papers for you to sign. Your State Department has made it possible.'

'The State Department, that's pretty high level. What's going on, Gretchen?'

She smiled ruefully. 'After you left, your intelligence people pulled me in. They knew about the black-marketing and held it over me. We both could've been prosecuted, but they gave me an option. While working for my government I went back on the payroll with yours.'

'You're a spy?'

'What's the harm? We're all on the same side against Communism, except Uncle Sam is paranoid and trusts nobody.'

He continued to stare at the photo, somewhat in wonder.

'I've never hidden you from her, Jack. She has a picture of you in your soldier suit and she's always known that some day she'd meet you.'

'Where is she now?'

'Private school. Switzerland.'

'When do I sign the papers?'

She touched his hand. 'Tomorrow at ten.'

They moved from the lounge to the dining room for early dinner, though neither seemed particularly hungry. Gretchen drank table wine with her Dover sole, which she didn't finish.

Jack scarcely touched his filet mignon but consumed another bourbon. The waiter asked if everything was satisfactory, and Jack nodded and ordered coffee. To Gretchen, he said, 'Are you in any danger?'

'None whatsoever.'

'Then it's your health.'

She shrugged. 'Nobody talks about cancer. So why should I?'

He was slow to speak. 'Incurable?'

'That's what they say. I can't give you the exact day or week, Jack, but I'm told I don't have long.'

He was shaking. When the coffee arrived, he wanted to

order another bourbon, but Gretchen whispered, 'Please. Don't.'

He stirred his coffee, though he had added nothing to it. Looking her full in the face, he said, 'I'm scared.'

'I know the feeling. I've gotten past it.'

'I don't know if I can.'

She made him stop stirring his coffee. 'You'll have to learn, Jack. You'll have to grow up.'

'You were always the more mature one, I remember that. You took care of me.'

'You were such a boy. But a lovable one.'

'And now I find out that after I left, you took the fall for us both.'

She consulted her watch, Swiss-made, one he had bought at the PX in Frankfurt. Her twenty-third birthday. He had thought her younger. 'I've booked you a room,' she said, and his eyes showed his dismay.

'Why can't we share yours?'

'I'm not the same woman, Jack. I don't have the same body. I may not even have the same soul.'

'Pretend we're old and gray. We'll just hold each other.'

When she did not respond, he said, 'Please.'

The room was small, the bed big. A low light was left burning because Gretchen did not like the dark, though he did not remember it a problem in the past. Her head lay snugged in the crook of his arm. Her hair smelled of hotel soap.

'Marry me,' he whispered.

'Too late, *Liebling*.'

'You never taught me German.'

'You never took the time to learn. You Americans expect everybody to speak English. Incidentally, your daughter speaks three languages, yours included.'

'When do I see her?'

'Arrangements have been made for her to come to you after the school year. I've written all the details out for you. Promise me you'll always look after her.'

'I swear.'

Her hand touched his cheek. 'I love you, Jack. I always have, and I don't trust any Americans, except you.'

'I've never known you to be cynical.'

'After what happened in Dallas, I thought the world would blow up. The assassination reeked of conspiracy.'

'I have too much on my mind to be bothered with that.' His free arm drew her closer and tightened, as if never to release her.

She squirmed. 'You're hurting me, Jack.'

'I'm sorry.'

'I'm glad my mother went first. It wouldn't have been right if I had.' She stretched her legs against his. 'You can turn the light out now. I feel safe.'

The morning was mild and brought with it the first tender leaves of spring, and the sudden appearance of a monarch that fluttered near Jack. He and the young woman stood outside a stately brick house on South Main Street, not far from his flat at the Bradford Manor. He was in the process of buying it, the papers soon to be signed. The young woman was surprised.

'Why all this?' she asked. 'Must be at least a dozen rooms in there.'

'You know why.' He had told her about his daughter and in the next breath had asked her to marry him. Now he was asking again. 'Please, look at me.' Then he noticed that something was different. 'Why aren't you wearing glasses?'

'Men don't make passes at girls who do. Dorothy Parker said that.'

The mention of the name brought him up short. Where had he heard it before and why did it give him a chill? He said, 'I'm well off, Sally. You'd never have to worry.'

'I know that.'

'Then what's the problem?'

'I know you don't love me.'

'How can you say that?'

'What you want, Jack, is a mother for your daughter. What is she – twelve, thirteen? I'm only seven years older.'

From tall shrubs came the berserk squawk of a jay. 'You'd be like a big sister. And we'd have children of our own.' As they approached the shrubs, the jay flew away. 'You'd like that, wouldn't you?'

'I seem to need you to tell me.' They passed a rose bush awaiting bloom. 'Tell me about her, Jack. Am I anything like her?'

'Who?'

'Gretchen.'

Something clicked. Stopping in his tracks, he asked, 'Who's Dorothy Parker?'

'She died recently. She was a brilliant woman.'

'So was Gretchen.'

They waited in the parlor of the Methodist minister who was to marry them. Sally wore a pearl choker Jack had bought her and a satiny blue dress on which he had fastened a corsage. He had on a three-piece suit with a boutonnière. Leaning toward her, he whispered, 'I'll be a good husband, I promise.'

'I know you will, Jack, and I love you.'

He glanced at his watch. 'Where the hell are they?'

The witnesses were late, Marion's fault, but they were on their way, though at the moment they were waiting for the lights to change.

Edward drummed his fingers on the steering wheel. 'Come on, come on,' he said, and red turned green as if so ordered.

Marion shook her head. 'I still say she's too young for him.'

'It's not that much of a difference. What's ten or so years?'

She removed a mirror from her purse and checked her face. 'And tell me something, Edward, how does he know that kid in Switzerland is his?'

'He showed me her picture. Couldn't be anybody else's.'

Marion impatiently shook her head. 'How gullible you men are. Over in Germany with all the GI's, you know what the women must have been like.'

'How would I know? I wasn't there.'

'Why not, Edward?' She tucked away the mirror and viewed him suspiciously. 'Shouldn't you have been in the army?'

'I had a college deferment. Then I married you.'

'Your lucky day.'

The minister was waiting for them at the door and accepted Marion's apology while Edward took the blame. In the parlor the minister arranged Jack and Sally in their places and Edward and Marion in theirs, and suddenly the air became solemn, the surroundings sacrosanct. The ceremony was the short version, which seemed to please Marion. The jewel-encrusted wedding band Jack fitted on Sally's finger impressed the minister, who in a resonating voice pronounced them man and wife.

Jack gave the bride a tender kiss and Edward followed with one on her cheek. Marion embraced her and kissed Jack on the mouth, so quickly he didn't have time to react.

At the curbing outside the minister's house she and Edward waved goodbye to the newlyweds, who were leaving in Jack's white Impala convertible with red leather upholstery and dual exhausts.

Marion made a face. 'In that car he must think he's still a kid. Did you see the gaudy ring he put on her finger? He must've paid plenty.'

'He always does.'

'You're his accountant. How much is he worth?'

'That's privileged, Marion, but his blue chips include Coca-Cola, Gillette, and Wells Fargo.'

'Maybe I should've married him, not you.'

'I'm doing all right.'

'You're doing fine, sweetheart. And you'll do even better.'

Destination Logan Airport, Jack drove in the slow lane of Route 1A with one hand on the wheel and his free arm round Sally. The roof was raised and the radio was tuned to a music station she had chosen. Her taste ran to rock while his remained loyal to the signature songs of Sinatra.

'I like him,' she said. 'Maybe in time I'll learn to like him more.'

'I'll give you all the time in the world.'

Their honeymoon plans, a Caribbean cruise, mandated a flight to Miami. Jack now had serious second thoughts.

'What if we went to New York City instead? Would you like that? We can stay at a great hotel and have breakfast in bed. We can catch a musical, see Ethel Merman. Ever see Yankee Stadium? We can do that.'

'You've already paid for the cruise.'

'Don't worry about it. Do you like Peggy Lee? We can find out what club she's singing at and go there. You look a little like her, did you know that?'

'With or without my glasses?'

'Makes no difference.'

'How do we get there?'

'We'll drive.'

'I can't keep up with you, Jack.'

He didn't hear her. He was looking for a way to get off Route 1A, to reach the Massachusetts Turnpike, a map already in his mind. Without thinking, he switched the radio from her station to his and then caught himself.

'It's all right,' she said and listened to Andy Williams crooning 'Moon River'.

'Sinatra's Tiffany,' Jack said. 'This guy's Woolworth's.'

'Do you think it will work for us, Jack? I so much want it to.'

'How can it not?'

'I'm afraid of your sister-in-law. I saw the way she kissed you.'

'Marion likes to cause trouble. Don't worry, Sal. She doesn't stand a chance.'

'Promise?'

'Promise.'

Under an untroubled sky and bursts of sunlight, they reached the Turnpike sooner than expected. Sinatra was singing 'Deep in a Dream'. Jack swayed his head. 'Lovely, lovely,' he said. The toll plaza loomed. 'Damn, I've got only hundred-dollar bills. You got anything small?'

She picked through her purse. 'Nickels, that's all. Jack, what are you doing?' He sped past a tollbooth without paying.

'Jack, you shouldn't have done that!'

Three miles down the Pike a state trooper, with siren shrieking and dome light flashing, caught up to them. The trooper, who was young and wore his visored cap in rigid military fashion, took his time stepping out of the cruiser and much more time ambling to and around the Impala. After giving Sally an insinuating once-over, he said to Jack, 'Forget something back there, asshole?'

Jack stiffened. 'What would that be, fuckface?'

The trooper reddened in the instant, drew his revolver and shot Jack in the throat. Then he shot Sally, but she, unlike Jack, lived to testify against him.

PART TWO

Some 90% of the universe is unknown.
Can we not say the same thing about ourselves?
                                          Joseph Shellenbach

On a sunlit pathway in the Common an old man bore his weight on a cane at every other step. Abruptly he stopped, stood straight and lifted the cane like a baton. The Boston Symphony Orchestra appeared full-blown before him, began to play resoundingly and continued even after the old man lowered the cane, opened his trousers and began to wet on the margin of the pathway. The slender dark-haired woman seated on a nearby bench noticed that the man resembled her uncle. Here her dream ended.

'What do you make of it?' she asked Dr Wall, whose dense hair capped a large head stuffed with other people's secrets, including some of hers.

'You tell me,' he said, as if all dreams, hers in particular, were self-evident.

'The obvious, I suppose. All that stuff I told you about. I was only a girl when I came to this country.'

Dr Wall's large eyes regarded her from shallow sockets. 'How old are you, Elsa?'

'You know how old I am. I'll be thirty soon.'

'Does that scare you?'

'Why should it?'

'You're not a girl any more. You're a mature woman, but you may not think like one. That could be a real problem. Is it, Elsa?'

'I'm paying you to tell me my problem, assuming I have one. Do I?'

'Since you're here, I presume you do, but I defer to your judgement. I certainly don't want to take your money under false pretences.'

She went silent and Dr Wall held his breath, for her visits meant much to him. Finally she said, 'I'm being unfair to you, aren't I? Forgive me.'

He let out his breath, visibly relaxed and remembered her first visit to his office. She looked younger than her years and could have been a college girl groping for eternal truths. The fall of her dark hair and the slimness of her figure entranced him. The father of three, he had conceived a fourth with his second wife in his arms and Elsa in his head.

'Well?' she said.

'Well, what?'

'Do you forgive me?'

'Nothing to forgive.' He doodled on a yellow notepad while considering his next question. 'How are you getting along with your aunt?'

'She's not my aunt by blood – and I see little of her.'

'Is that the way you want it?'

'It pleases us both.'

'But does that please your uncle?'

'Money pleases my uncle. I doubt very much my aunt does, though there's nothing he wouldn't do for her.'

'Does that disturb you?'

'My life disturbs me, Doctor. That's why I'm here. You're supposed to straighten me out.'

Dr Wall drew a small heart, which became a face when he added eyes, a nose and a smile. He had named his youngest child Eloise and had her picture on his desk. He said, 'Do you feel we're making progress?'

'Progress is a buzzword. Everything is buzz in this silly country. A movie actor for a president – you Americans aren't real.'

'What does that say about you, Elsa?'

'I'm not an American.'

'Your father was.'

'My father was a bedtime story. Mostly he was made up and now he's just a rumor.'

'I remember your telling me you loved him.'

'Surely I was fantasising. You must've seen that.'

Dr Wall doodled an oval into a face, minus the smile.

'How are you doing, Elsa? Are you in a relationship?'

'That's off limits. I no longer discuss that with you, Doctor.'

He raised his eyebrows. 'Why not?'

'You're in love with me. And that makes me nervous.'

He kept his composure, though his hand holding the pencil trembled. 'And what brought you to that conclusion?'

'It's obvious.'

'Not to me, I'm afraid,' he said and attempted a patronising smile, which she countered with a thin one.

'Am I embarrassing you, Doctor? Or should I call you Harvey now?'

'That wouldn't be entirely appropriate. Are you *trying* to embarrass me?'

'No, Doctor, merely trying to take control of my life. I've never actually had it.'

He viewed the wall clock with opposing emotions. Her

time with him had ticked away. 'Same time next week?'

She shrugged. 'Sure. Why change things now?'

His pencil hand still trembling, he watched her rise from the depth of her chair. Her blouse was blue, her skirt small. When she reached the door, he blurted out, 'Elsa!'

Surprised, she glanced back at him. 'What?'

'It's true. I am in love with you.'

'Don't worry,' she said, opening the door, 'your secret is safe.'

A taxi bore Elsa through Boston traffic to the steel and glass of the office tower where her uncle's lawyer was a partner in a venerable Yankee firm. He was also a family friend and Marion's confidant, though not always a trusted one. When Elsa was a girl he was Uncle Bob. Now he was Robert.

Robert, though busy, sent word that he would see her shortly. Waiting in plush surroundings, *Elle* and *Vogue* at her elbow, she was served coffee in bone china and scones on a crystal dish, and supplied with a napkin of Irish linen. Distant doors opened and closed. Men in tailored gray came and went. Two senior partners emerged from an elevator and in passing smiled at her. With her legs crossed and her skirt riding up, she felt like a racy magazine among sober volumes.

She had polished off the scones when a chic young woman briskly approached. 'Your uncle apologises for keeping you waiting. He shouldn't be much longer.'

'He's not my uncle,' Elsa said. 'Not any more.'

'Would you like more scones?' the young woman asked quickly.

'No, thank you.'

Twenty minutes later she was shown into Robert's expansive office of carved mahogany, glints of copper and brass, and paintings of hunting scenes. A figure rising from

376

behind a massive desk was silhouetted against a skyview of glass. A tailored length of manners and charm, Robert glided toward her with what Elsa saw as his ecclesiastical air.

'I feel like I'm being granted an audience. Do you have a ring for me to kiss?'

'You haven't changed, Elsa.'

She smiled into a precise face made more precise by round steel-rimmed glasses. His graying hair had a boyish cut. 'Nor you, Robert. Had you chosen the church, you'd be a bishop now, at least.'

He chose to ignore that. 'You look wonderful.'

'I knew you'd say that.'

'Then I'm glad I did.'

He guided her to a sitting area, where they sat in opposing wing chairs, she with her hands on her knees, as if she were thirteen again and listening to Robert summarise the legal document that made her real uncle her guardian.

'What can I do for you, Elsa?'

'How wealthy am I?'

He smiled. 'You're well off, you know that.'

'*How* well off?'

'Your uncle and I would need to sit down to figure it out. What's the problem, Elsa?'

'I think Uncle Edward has been stealing from me.'

He inclined his head. 'I don't understand.'

She spoke rapidly, the words rehearsed. Investment accounts she'd thought solvent were not, certain stocks had been sold without her knowledge and money her mother had left her was unaccounted for. She appreciated the record settlement Robert had negotiated for her father's wrongful death, but where had Uncle Edward invested it? Too much was up in the air.

Robert gave her a quiet look of dismay. 'Your uncle would never cheat you. He moves money around to keep it safe, his and yours. Besides, I look after your interests.'

'You look after his, not mine.'

'They're one and the same. Your uncle has always protected you, seen to your needs, your education. You've wanted for nothing.'

'I think he's forged my name to documents.'

'That's absurd.'

'I think the two of you are in it together. Or do I mean the three of you?'

Robert sighed heavily. 'I was wondering when you'd bring Marion into the mix. Can't you get over that? You're a big girl now.'

Her voice went cold. 'That's what you told me when I turned sixteen.'

'You've never forgiven me, have you, Elsa?'

'You once informed me I had nothing to forgive.'

'And I was right,' he said, his demeanor airtight. His armor was his suit, staid, boardroom.

'I plan to get my own lawyer,' Elsa said.

Nothing changed in his face. 'Why?'

'I'm taking a stand.'

'Against whom?'

'All of you.'

He rose smoothly from his chair, which told her the audience was over. On her feet, she needed a moment to maintain her balance. In one of the hunting scenes, hounds circling a wild boar appeared rabid. Robert walked her to the door.

'I understand you're seeing a psychiatrist.'

She threw him a look. 'How do you know that?'

'I see your checks.'

'I didn't know you went through them.'

'I browse.'

Opening the door, he stood by it. He was now fully his

legal self, cool-brained, his mistakes few if any. Elsa looked into baffling blue eyes that expressed only ambiguities. 'I expected more from you,' she said.

'I'm sorry.'

'I loved you, Robert.'

'I'm sorry about that too.'

A taxi took her through the heart of the city, through the crush of Kenmore Square, where traffic sounded like the Boston Symphony tuning up, and into Brookline to a shady side street and a brick house that rose unexpectedly above great growths of rhododendron and flowering pink almond. In the driveway a pigeon swirled up like a package coming apart. Elsa said to the driver, 'I used to live here.'

The driver, appreciative of the generous tip, said, 'That must've been grand.'

Approaching the front door, she heard Marion playing the piano, not very well, with a tendency to pound the keys. The playing stopped when Elsa rang the bell.

Marion seemed not at all surprised to see her. 'Come in, dear.' They sat in the sun room, by far the cheeriest room in the house, Elsa's favorite when she had lived there. Marion had a full-time maid now. The maid served tea and crustless sandwiches. 'Thank you, dear,' Marion said in the same tone she had greeted Elsa. Now in her fifties, Marion still had her looks, her figure and her inflated sense of self, which, in Elsa's estimation, rivaled Robert's.

Left to themselves, Elsa said, 'How long have you had her?'

'Juana? More than a month. She has many rough edges, but I'm smoothing them.'

'She's pretty.'

'Very.' Marion took a deliberate sip of tea. 'Are you still writing?'

'Yes.'

'Anything published?'

'Not yet.'

'Pity. With your Wellesley education, you'd think you'd be in print by now. Perhaps you should self-publish.'

'I don't think so,' Elsa said.

'Up to you, dear. Have you found a suitable man yet? I heard you have.'

'I know your tricks, Marion. You're fishing, pretending you know something you don't.'

'Do you really think I'm that devious?'

Elsa finished off a half-sandwich and, reaching for another, smiled. 'Yes.'

'We've had our differences, but don't you think it's time we put them aside? I certainly do.'

Elsa poured herself more tea. 'I'm not that scared and timid girl any more, Marion. Or that gullible young woman. I'm finally taking charge of myself.' She lifted her teacup. 'Why are you staring at me?'

'Sorry, dear, but it's amazing how much you resemble your father. When I first saw you I had my doubts, but surely that's his chin. So sad you never knew him.'

'I feel I do.' Elsa rose. 'Excuse me. I have to pee.'

Marion stiffened. 'Aren't you beyond that sort of talk?'

'What would you rather I say?'

'Let's not get into a pissing contest, dear. You know the way.'

Elsa could have used a downstairs bathroom but chose to mount the stairs, her fingers tapping the polished rail all the way to the top, where she turned left and glanced into Marion's bedroom. It was the master bedroom, but in the move from Haverhill to Brookline Marion had chosen it for herself, a knock needed for Uncle Edward to enter. Elsa remembered the room had always harbored an amorous smell, her uncle home or not, more so when he was not.

Toward the end of the passageway she entered a bedroom once hers and now one of the guest rooms, all traces of her gone, anything worth keeping she had taken with her, any reminders Marion had removed. In the bathroom, before using the john, she addressed the mirror in German: 'Do I know you?'

On Elsa's return to the sun room, Marion looked up with a faint smile and said, 'You haven't once asked about your uncle.'

'I was getting to it.' Elsa sat down, retrieved her teacup and crossed her legs. 'How's he doing?'

'Recovering beyond expectations. No stroke is going to keep him down.'

'Is he still in that nursing home?'

'Yes, dear. We chat by phone.'

'I plan to visit him.'

Marion shrugged. 'You don't seem to like us any more, dear.'

'He's been stealing from me.'

'That's ridiculous and cruel of you to say such a thing. You live wonderfully off the investments he's made for you.'

'No, Marion. I live off my father's money, plus my mother's – though I no longer know where much of it is.'

Marion's color sharpened. 'Let me set you straight, young lady. Your father walked a thin line. He was a manipulator, a conniver. Sure he made money, but your uncle made it grow.'

'How strange,' Elsa said glibly. 'All this time I thought Uncle Edward was just the bookkeeper.'

'He was the brains!' Marion immediately gathered herself. 'I'm not trying to take away anything from your father. All things considered, we got along quite well.'

Elsa rose to leave. 'I'll see Uncle Edward tomorrow.'

'Are you going to cause trouble?'

The maid reappeared. Elsa smiled at her.

'Juana, I don't believe I've introduced you to my niece. This is Miss West.'

'I'm not actually her niece,' Elsa said, still smiling. 'I'm my father's daughter.'

Barefoot in a terry robe, Marion poured herself a second glass of port, a self-imposed limit, just enough to give her a glow, and called out, 'Is it ready yet?'

Juana appeared at the top of the stairs. 'Yes, ma'am.' Marion, wineglass in hand, paused at the curve in the stairs. 'Is the phone plugged in?'

Juana reappeared. 'Yes, ma'am.'

'Thank you, dear. Thank you very much.' At the top of the stairs she said, 'What did you think of my niece?'

Juana, hesitating, pushed fallen locks of hair from her young face. 'She seem nice.'

'You work for your money, dear. Hers is a gift.'

Marion moved on. The master bathroom awaited her, womblike in its warmth, the air sultry. A bouquet of pink carnations topped a column of marble near the bidet. Marion dropped her robe and slipped into a sunken tub brimming with suds. Bubbles burst near her nose. After luxuriating for several minutes with her eyes closed, she stretched an arm and seized the phone, near which she had placed her glass of port. The call was to Haverhill. Extension 210, the rehab center.

'Edward?'

'Yes.'

'You sound better.'

'I'll be home sooner than expected.' He had lost the slur in his speech, though he still needed a walker and help getting in and out of bed.

'I had a visitor,' Marion said and took a slow sip of port. 'Your niece. Robert called me earlier, so I was expecting her.'

'Is there a problem?'

'Nothing Robert can't handle.'

'Ah, yes. Good old Robert.'

'Don't get touchy, Edward.' Marion raised a knee and soaped it with a sponge. 'I thought you'd gotten over that.'

'Tell me how, and I will.'

'I shouldn't have called. I've upset you.'

'Why did you call?'

'To prepare you, Edward. Elsa plans to visit you tomorrow.'

'Should I have Robert here to coach me?'

'Now you're being sarcastic.' Marion's other knee rose from the suds. 'That's not like you, Edward.'

'Are you in the tub?'

'How can you tell?'

'Your voice.'

She retrieved the wineglass. 'Different voices, different events. You know most of them.'

'But not all.'

'That keeps me a mystery. We friends again, pet?'

A minute or so later, after ringing off, she drained the wineglass, turned on the tap for more hot water and slid down to her chin. Her eyes closed, her head hot and turbulent with a kaleidoscope of thoughts, she luxuriated for twenty minutes more, was reluctant to rise and wasn't sure she would.

'Juana, where are you?' Juana was downstairs but heard the call and came up fast. The fluffy towels Marion wanted were right where Juana always left them, in plain sight and within easy reach. Juana moved them closer and retreated. 'Thank you, dear.'

Marion stepped from her bath and admired herself in the long panels of a mirror. How many women her age and even younger wouldn't kill to have a figure like hers? A hand on her hip, she turned sideways. Her bosom was a springy addendum, her buttocks a solid postscript.

'Wow!' she said aloud. If her own image excited her, what must it do to others? 'Juana, come in here and look at me.'

Elsa lived in a brownstone on Beacon Street, a fourth-floor condo with the Public Garden, the Common, the library and the theater district all within a stroll. She had converted a large bedroom into a reading room with two club chairs and three walls of books, as many in German as in English, some in French. A smaller room was her sanctuary for writing, her portable typewriter abandoned for a word processor, which Gordon had urged her to try.

Older than she by ten years and shorter by three inches, Gordon was her upstairs neighbor and a professor of humanities at Boston University. His usual attire was a blazer and bow tie. When carrying a book bag, he resembled a remarkably neat child. Sitting in one of her club chairs and sipping cappuccino, he said, 'Nothing to show me?'

He was a frequent reader of chunks of her writings. At present she was at the start of a novel in which she was the protagonist. Her purpose was to rescript her life and give herself better lines and a more forceful part, but today she had written nothing.

'Too busy seeing people,' she explained from deep within the matching chair, 'including my shrink.'

'Is the dear man helping you?'

'He's in love with me.'

'So am I, in my fashion.'

They exchanged smiles. Each was comfortable and caring with the other. When one had a cold, the other delivered soup.

Gordon appreciated her wit, she admired his learning. Sundays they brunched at the Ritz. Her company, he told her, gave him height. He escorted her to the theater and to the movies. Each wept when Debra Winger died in *Terms of Endearment*.

'Never *not* be in love with me,' she said.

'Not to worry.'

Studying her over the rim of his cup, he remembered when she moved in some seven years ago and answered his knock wearing a sleeveless top. He introduced himself with a bottle of wine. When she accepted it, he glimpsed hair in her underarms and thought her wonderfully natural. Now he thought of her as an indoor flower vulnerable to direct sunlight.

'More cappuccino?' she asked.

'I'm fine.' He squinted. 'But you're not.'

'Yes, I am. Would you like to hear some music?' Gordon knew the music she meant. Her mother had loved American jazz, and her father, she'd been told, had favored Sinatra and certain big bands. Their tastes dominated hers.

'No music,' he said. 'Tell me what's wrong.'

'Just the mood I'm in. One day carries no proof there'll be another. We take it on faith.'

'Certainties don't exist, you know that.'

'They did when I was little, very little.'

'Then you shouldn't have grown up.'

She frowned. 'Why did *you*?'

'Pure curiosity. Otherwise I wouldn't have.'

'I'm glad you did.' Her eyes filled.

'What's the matter?'

'I'm happy.'

'You don't look it.'

'Joy and sorrow,' she said. 'In German, they sound much closer. *Liebe und Leid*. Easy for one to bleed into the other, and they often do.'

He looked at his watch, time to leave. He had an early class in the morning. They carried their empty cappuccino cups into the kitchen, where he took hers, rinsed both out and placed them in the dishwasher. Then he smiled. 'I'd make a great spouse, wouldn't I?'

'I don't know what I'd do if I lost you, Gordon.' She walked him to the door and, opening it, kissed his cheek. 'Promise me something.'

'Anything.'

'Swear you won't get AIDS.'

Elsa rose early, ensconced herself at the word processor and composed the synopsis of a story she'd been mulling for some time. She printed it out, read it over slowly and shivered. An hour later, she met a friend for breakfast at the Parker House.

'Thanks for taking the time, Rachelle.'

The waiter served Elsa eggs Benedict, Rachelle only toast.

Elsa dug in. Rachelle, nibbling, said, 'I still hate you.'

They'd been roommates at Wellesley, where Rachelle's weight had fluctuated radically. She was either gaining or losing while acquiring no fixed shape of her own. At present she was in her hefty mode.

'You look great,' Elsa said.

'No, *you* do. I know exactly what I look like. What did you want to see me about?'

'My writing.'

'How did I guess?' Rachelle was an editor at Little, Brown. 'I'll give you my standard speech. The bare bones of all stories have been rattled since we first began spinning tales. It's language that keeps stories going, that refreshes and renews them. Language is a breathing thing, forever changing, shifting meanings, creating hues, adding nuances. That's your strength, Elsa. You write beautiful prose.'

'Then why did you reject my manuscript?'

'Let me finish. I read every word of it. You compose a sentence in the shape of a woman, full of grace and charm and flashes of intuition. A masculine sentence delivers the force of the obvious, but yours carries the delight of the unexpected.'

Elsa dabbed her mouth with a napkin. 'I'm waiting for the other shoe.'

Rachelle pointed. 'Are you going to finish that?'

'It's yours.' Elsa shoved her plate forward. 'Okay, let it drop.'

'This is delicious.'

'Rachelle. Please!'

'Your stuff is too introspective, too airtight. How to put this? Your stories are like hothouse tomatoes. The outdoor taste is lacking. Am I offending you?'

'No. Go on.'

'There's no plot and little movement. And too many of your stories have a vague father figure lurking in the background, more a ghost than a character.'

'Anything else?'

'Now you're angry.'

'No. I anticipated the criticism.' Elsa reached into her bag and extracted a folded sheet of paper. Unfolding it, she passed it over to Rachelle. 'Read this. It'll take only a minute.'

'What is it?' Rachelle donned glasses.

'Synopsis of something I've started.'

Rachelle started scanning it and stopped halfway down. Returning to the beginning, she knitted her brow and read it slowly and carefully to the end. Then she shivered. 'Jesus, Elsa, where did this come from?'

'I could make it a short story or work it into a novel. Whatever would feel right.'

Rachelle said nothing.

'It's about the unthinkable.'

'I can see that.'

'Would Little, Brown be interested?'

Rachelle folded the paper and returned it. 'I don't think so, Elsa.'

Behind the wheel of her seldom-used red Toyota, Elsa drove under the speed limit on I-93, with an eye in the rear-view. Any glimpse of a state police cruiser terrorised her. The trip to Haverhill, usually under an hour, took longer than she had planned. The rehab clinic was located near Lake Saltonstall, known to natives as Plug Pond. Flowers, some slain by careless feet, followed a walkway to the entrance. Inside, she knew her way around. Her uncle had a private room with a wide window overlooking a garden. At the open door she could hear the noon news. Peering in, she said, 'Hello, Uncle Edward.'

Pivoting in a bedside chair, he said, 'Come in, come in, Elsa. It was just on the news. Count Basie died. He was one of your father's favorites.'

'I know.' She looked down at a large round man wearing a Japanese robe of calligraphic patterns. 'My mother told me.'

He used a remote to turn off the television. She knew he expected a kiss on the cheek, but she could not bring herself to do it. Instead she drew up a chair and said, 'How are you doing?'

'Hard to say. We're all temporary, Elsa. It's mortality that gives life value. Immortality would flood the market and I'd be a poor man.'

'But you're not, Uncle Edward. You're rich.'

He smiled with a sigh. 'But how much control do we have over our lives? Even the wealthy worry about cancer.'

'You beat yours.'

'It could come back. Your aunt thinks I'll live for ever, stroke and all. That may not suit her.'

'She's not my aunt.'

'A shame you two never got along. Your father's fault. You look too much like him and Marion couldn't get past that. It was a love-hate thing with her. Jack had that effect on people. God, I miss him.'

Elsa experienced a wave of anxiety. Her uncle had some time ago given her a graduation picture of her father, Haverhill High, class of 1950. In the picture her father stood tall and smiled broadly, as if his world would never end. Quickly she said, 'Are you comfortable here, Uncle Edward?'

'I'm home. Haverhill's home. I never wanted to move to Brookline. Shifting my office to Boston, I never wanted to do that either. Marion's idea.'

'You enjoyed going to the symphony.'

'I liked the Pops, never the symphony. Symphony was Marion putting on airs, pretending she wasn't Haverhill.'

Elsa stared ironically at him. In Boston he had eaten lavishly at the best restaurants and grown fatter. His belly billowed from his loose robe, the robe a gift from Marion several birthdays ago.

'You know why I'm here, don't you, Uncle Edward?'

'Your aunt called me.'

'Please don't call her that.'

'You think I'm stealing from you. Why would I do that, Elsa? I've plenty of my own money.'

A quiet anger heated her face. 'I don't need to be a CPA to know I've been cheated. All these years I've trusted you. Is it just you, Uncle Edward?' Her tone turned insinuating. 'Or is it the three of you? The same old *ménage à trois*.'

'Don't be disgusting.'

'They control you, Uncle Edward, don't tell me they don't.'

His color rose. 'I'm my own man.'

'My father was a man. I'm not sure you are.'

'I don't deserve that,' he said as the air seemed to go out of him. 'And I've done nothing wrong.'

Elsa leaned forward in her chair, her voice low. 'You betrayed me. I can understand Robert and Marion doing that, but you and I, we're the same blood.'

Tears came into her uncle's eyes. Crocodile? She didn't know and didn't want to guess. He said, 'You're the only family I have.'

She started to soften and stopped herself. 'I'm taking charge of my own affairs. I'm hiring a lawyer to see how much has been taken from me.'

'You can't win, Elsa. They hold all the cards.'

'What do you mean?'

A burly man in starched whites appeared. It was time for her uncle's physical therapy, lunch to follow. The attendant helped him from his chair.

'Tell me what you mean.'

'Thank you for the visit, Elsa. It's always nice seeing you.'

She parked the Toyota on the street and strode to the front door of the stately brick house where a monarch, then another, hovered near rose bushes not yet in bloom. After a pause, she rang the bell and waited a full minute before the door was opened by a woman with the bluest eyes she'd ever seen. Each gazed at the other.

'I'm Elsa West.'

Sally West gripped the door's edge to steady herself. Her voice trembled. 'I'd recognise you anywhere. Please. Come in.'

'I should have phoned first.'

'No, it's all right.' Sally led her through the entrance hall, past a grand staircase and open airy rooms to a large kitchen full of sunlight. 'I was just making myself a liverwurst sandwich. Will you have one?'

'I'd love one.'

'And German beer?'

'Oh, yes.'

Sally moved swiftly toward a marble counter. 'Please, Elsa, sit down. I hope you don't mind eating in the kitchen. I spend most of my time here.'

'I can't think of a better place.' Elsa sat at a table, her hands clasped. 'This is where I was supposed to live.'

'I know. Jack – I mean, your father – wanted to make a home for the three of us, but especially for you. I wouldn't have been a substitute mother, but I could've been a big sister. I desperately wanted to meet you after what happened to your father and me.'

'Marion said it would upset you, but I often walked by your house on the chance I'd see you. Then we moved away.'

Sally placed two steins on the table. 'Your father brought these from Germany.' She poured dark beer from tall bottles and moments later, joining Elsa, served liverwurst on rye, slices of pickle on the side.

'Thank you,' Elsa said and for the first time clearly saw the plastic surgery performed on Sally's face. The bullet had gone into one side of the jaw and out the other. 'It must have been hell.'

'It all happened without warning. Your father and I had no time for goodbyes. I've gotten over much of that, but I still have nightmares. My doctor calls them re-enactments.'

'Horror shows.'

Sally looked away. 'Yes.'

'You never remarried?'

'No. I live in this big house by myself, though my two sisters lived here with me till they got married. I'm well provided for. My lawyer saw to that.'

'Robert?'

'Yes. Your uncle brought him to me. You and I shared in the settlement. I still can't believe we got so much, can you?'

'There were two settlements. You should have got more.'

'No, no, Elsa. You came first.'

'I didn't get shot.'

'But I'm alive. You lost a father.'

Elsa usually had a hearty appetite but could eat no more than half the sandwich. She drank the beer. 'I'll tell you what I'd like to do. Will you go somewhere with me?'

'Where?'

'The cemetery.'

Sally flushed with pleasure. 'The two of us? I'd love to.'

When they climbed into Elsa's Toyota, Sally said, 'I have one just like it.'

Elsa was not surprised. She ran the Toyota on to the road. 'Did Robert make the arrangements?'

'Yes. He's a wonderful person.'

'Is he also handling your money?'

'I trust him with everything.'

Elsa tightened her grip on the wheel. 'You might want to be careful. He's a charming man, but he's not a saint.'

'He'd never cheat me,' Sally said and went silent. They crossed the bridge spanning the Merrimack and stopped for the lights, a long-abandoned Woolworth's on the left and a high-rise for the elderly on the right. 'I remember when downtown had four movie theaters,' Sally said wistfully. 'My favorite was the Paramount, the biggest. That's where your father took me on our first date.'

The lights changed and Elsa turned right.

'I'll never forget the movie,' Sally went on. 'Dustin Hoffman pretended he was a woman. It was so funny. But I can't remember the name.'

'*Tootsie*,' Elsa murmured.

Within minutes they approached Linwood Cemetery, the gates thrown open, as if the dead craved company, theirs in particular. Sally pointed the way, a tortuous route, though Elsa knew it well from annual visits.

'I wonder, Elsa. Do the dead know they're dead?'

Elsa shook her head. 'For them, it's as though they never existed.'

'I don't want to believe that.'

'You don't have to.'

The Toyota drifted to a stop and the two women climbed out. Jack West's headstone, beside that of his parents, was an impressive piece of marble, his brother's doing. At the base were pots of geraniums.

'Those are mine,' Sally said. 'I put them there three days ago. I should have brought some for Hank and Milly, though I never knew them. Jack's father was murdered too, did you know that?'

'Marion gave me the history. Like father, like son, she said.'

'Marion is not kind. Your uncle is nicer.' Sally looked down at the ground. 'I loved your father more than he knew, more than he ever could know. I used to stand here obsessed. *If I think of you hard enough, Jack, will you come back?* I still do it at times. I'm doing it now. *I'm standing here with your daughter, Jack. Here we are.*'

In a voice not meant to be heard, Elsa said, 'He had no right getting himself killed.'

Sally must have heard. She said, 'If the trooper had done it right, I'd be with Jack.'

Elsa touched her arm. 'Are you all right?'

'Yes. Perfectly. I'm sorry.'

'Perhaps we should leave now.'

'I usually say a prayer.'

'Go ahead if you like. I'll wait in the car.'

Sally's eyes glistened. 'No. I feel like I've already said it.'

Each was quiet on the drive from the cemetery. Sally wore a small smile, as if she valued her grief and treasured her hurts. The surgery on the one side of her reconstructed jaw had left a shallow pocket, a less noticeable one on the other side. Almost playfully she began twisting her wedding ring as they approached the intersection at the bridge. The light was green.

'Go right,' she said suddenly, and Elsa obeyed. Seconds later Sally pointed excitedly. 'That's where it was! The Paramount! And afterwards he took me next door to the Paramount Tea Room. We had cheeseburgers.'

Elsa saw only the ugly edge of a strip mall.

Farther up the hill, at another set of lights, Sally pointed out the old high school, from which Jack had graduated, she from the new one. 'I have his yearbook,' she said. 'Do you know what they wrote under his picture? "Get thee behind me, Satan."'

Elsa made more turns.

'Go slow,' Sally said and pointed to the tenement house in which Jack and his brother had grown up. 'Take a left now. Let's go back downtown.' Downtown, they passed the Whittier, no longer a hotel. 'Your father used to take me there for a drink. He knew all the regulars, World War Two guys. I was their pet.' Farther up, nearing the railroad trestle, she said, 'Please, stop!'

Elsa pulled into a restricted space.

'Look! That's the diner where your father and I met. He was in for breakfast and I was his waitress.'

394

64

'Enough!' Elsa blurted out, as if her mind had blown open.

Each impacted in silence, they recrossed the river into Bradford. Sally peered through the windshield at the sky, as if answers were somewhere, possibly up there. Slowing the Toyota, Elsa pulled up at the brick house and immediately apologised. 'I shouldn't have shouted at you like that. Please forgive me.'

'Nothing to forgive. I'm sure I got on your nerves. Can we be sisters?'

'We already are.'

'You mean it?'

'Of course. And we'll stay in touch.' She leaned over and kissed Sally's cheek. 'But promise me something. Never sign anything unless you bring it to a lawyer.'

'Robert's my lawyer.'

'Not Robert. Anybody but Robert.'

'But I told you he would never cheat me.'

'Sally, look at me. He already has.'

In a world of wheelchairs, walkers and canes, Edward West toddled into the crowded dining room on his own, with pride and satisfaction. A lot of old people here. He wasn't one of them. He liked seeing flowers on the tables, but grimaced at the smell of institutional food, an offense to his acquired sensibilities. He sat at the only table with openings, joining Miss Lincoln, who was in her eighties, and another elderly woman, who was potty.

'You're red in the face, Edward. Are you all right?'

'I'm fine, Miss Lincoln.' He was annoyed. 'Thank you for asking.'

Miss Lincoln, who did not look her age, was recuperating from a hip replacement. She had been one of his high school English teachers, but she remembered Jack the best and never failed to mention him.

'A shame, such a shame, what happened to your brother.'

She turned to the potty lady, another hip case, and said, 'I had him and his brother in my class. His brother was quick, very quick, but didn't apply himself. Edward here applied himself but was slow.'

'I've done all right,' Edward snapped as he was served tuna casserole. He stared at it. Tasting it, he said, 'I've had better.'

'Yes, you look it.' Miss Lincoln said. 'When did you put on all that weight?'

The potty lady, who wasn't eating, grinned. She was painting her nails red, which gave her the aspect of an old bird with lethal claws. Edward avoided her eyes.

Miss Lincoln said, 'Where did you get that funny robe? From a catalog? Do you need to wear it here?'

Eating, Edward refused to respond.

'A lot of the boys from your time made much of themselves. Herbert Phillips and Michael Mooradian are lawyers. Francis Grose is a college professor. And of course your brother, for the short time he lived, did very well.'

'I'm a CPA and a damn good one. I have my own accounting firm in Boston and I have a big home in Brookline, did you know that?'

Miss Lincoln began eating her dessert, a bread pudding.

'Did you know that?' Edward demanded.

'Know what?'

'What I just told you.'

'I always thought you worked for your brother.'

Exasperated, he shut his eyes and reopened them slowly. 'You never liked me, did you?'

'I tried, Edward. God knows I tried.'

He put his fork down, rose awkwardly and left without a word. The potty lady waved goodbye.

*

Nearly an hour of physical therapy left Edward ready for a nap. Returning to his room, he stretched out on the bed and almost immediately fell asleep. He dreamed a man vaguely familiar punched him in the mouth and broke his front teeth, which were crowns, a good thousand dollars' worth of damage. Waking with his hand over his mouth, he was relieved to find no blood on his fingers. He wondered whether his assailant had been one of those panhandlers he routinely ignored on the streets of Boston. Then he wondered whether it might have been his brother.

A few minutes later a nurse appeared and took his blood pressure. Always she annoyed him for a reason he didn't divulge.

She got a reading and wrote it on a chart.

'Is anything wrong, Mr West? You always look pissed off.'

He flinched. In his day, nurses never talked like that. 'I'm fine.'

'This your last day here?'

'That's what they tell me.'

'It's been nice having you here.'

'It's been good being home.'

Moments after she left, the bedside phone rang. He thought it was Marion and answered in a gruff voice. The caller was Robert, who said lightly, 'What's the matter, Tiger?'

'Did you know nurses don't wear white any more? No uniforms, no caps. They wear any goddamn thing they please, with a tiny name plate that says RN, but you got to squint to see it. The one who tends to me looks like kitchen help.'

'I understand you have a bigger aggravation. Elsa. How'd the visit go?'

'We could be hurt.'

Robert's sigh was audible. 'Marion figured you'd be rattled.'

'Do I sound rattled? I'm not rattled!'

'Calm down, Edward. You're hyper. I understand you're going home tomorrow. I'll pick you up.'

'Marion can come after me.'

'She asked me to.'

There was silence.

'Relax, Tiger. There's no conspiracy going on.'

'Don't call me Tiger.'

'It gives you and me a chance to talk. I am your lawyer, after all.'

'You're more than that, Robert. That's the goddamn problem.' He disconnected without a goodbye.

She didn't have an appointment, but Dr Wall took her anyway. She had an urge to plant herself in his lap. *Daddy, I'm here. Read me a story.* Instead she settled into the familiar comfortable chair, where she had a diagonal view of a picture on his desk, that of his youngest daughter. Eloise. 'Thank you for seeing me,' she said.

'It sounded urgent.'

'I didn't say it was urgent.'

'Maybe it merely sounded urgent,' Dr Wall said and saw her shiver. 'Are you cold, Elsa?'

'I wouldn't mind winter coming if the flowers could stay.'

'Winter isn't coming. It's spring.'

'It doesn't feel it. Earlier I was at a cemetery. That's where the living hide the dead.'

'Is someone you know buried there?'

'My father. He should be buried next to my mother in Germany. They belong together. Maybe they are. I believe if by some meager chance there's a heaven, it's a hangout where angels serve white wine and espresso. Dietrich sings.

My mother loved Dietrich, though many Germans didn't. My father liked Sinatra. Do you think they're happy, Doctor?'

'If there's a heaven, I suspect happiness is mandatory.'

Elsa smiled. 'That sort of takes the joy out of it, doesn't it? Actually I have no faith in an afterlife – only the here and now. How about you, Doctor? Do you buy into this religious stuff?'

'Let's put it this way, Elsa. It's just as reasonable – or unreasonable – to believe in Homer's gods as it is to believe the Christian deity sired a son with a virgin. That's an old story updated.'

Elsa raised her eyebrows. 'You've never responded so openly before.'

'You're too intelligent for me not to. You'd put me in my place. And I know my place, Elsa. I'm sorry I've been so transparent in my feelings for you.'

'I'm the one who made an issue of it. No harm done.' She rose from her chair with a folded sheet of paper in hand and, straightening it, placed it on his desk. 'Please read this.'

In their shallow sockets Dr Wall's large eyes grew larger when he donned glasses. He glanced with mock suspicion at the neat page of typescript. 'This isn't a suicide note, is it?'

'It's a story idea.'

'I'm not an editor.'

'If you're not going to read it, give it back.'

He read it. Then he reread it. 'Why would you want to write something like this?'

'Why not?'

Dr Wall removed his glasses. 'It doesn't seem to relate to anything in your experience.'

'Loss is loss. Horror is horror.'

He was slow to speak. 'Why did you want me to read it?'

'Answers. You don't have any. Nor do I.'

'Wouldn't I need to hear the questions first?'

'They're yours to raise.'

He rose slowly and walked around his desk with no noise. His shoes were rubber-soled, his smile contrite. He returned her story proposal. 'All I can say, Elsa, is there's no deed so dark someone won't do it.'

She peered into his face. 'That's an answer?'

'No, my dearest. That's the human condition.'

Sally West moved slowly in the morning, bumping into a chair, dropping a spoon, spilling sugar, as if everything in life were a difficulty and, worse, a danger. When the doorbell rang, she gave a start and for seconds stood frozen. Anything unexpected set her on edge. She opened the door on the second ring and saw Robert standing straight, correct, expecting admiration.

He smiled. 'May I?'

She stepped aside, he stepped in. Immediately he kissed her forehead, not her cheek, and then stood back for a long look at her, which unsettled her.

'I thought I'd stop by,' he said. 'I'm on my way to pick up Edward. He's being released today.'

She took a breath. 'Do you have time for coffee,' she asked, hoping he didn't.

'I'll make time.'

She led him into the large airy kitchen, where he immediately took a chair at the breakfast table and watched her busy herself with cups and saucers. When her back was turned, he moistened a finger and poked it in the sugar bowl for a taste of sweet. She dropped a cup on the tile floor. *Smash!* She reddened.

'I never used to be clumsy.'

'Let me,' he said.

'No, it's all right.'

He stayed seated and Sally swept up the pieces. Minutes later she served coffee and joined him at the table. He stared at her, his smile returning as if he could read her lips when nothing was on them.

'You look wonderful,' he said.

Lightening her coffee, she remembered Robert telling her to rise so that the jury could see her face. Then he touched her face with one finger and then another, showing where the bullet went in and out. Her teeth, he told the jury, were no longer her own, which shamed her.

'I know what I look like, Robert.'

'You're too hard on yourself.'

She remembered her head tightening when Robert asked her to describe the moment the state trooper fired his gun at Jack West, her husband of only a couple of hours. Instead of speaking, she lost control and screamed. Only later did she realise Robert had wanted her to scream. So much money became hers . . . and his.

She said, 'I had a visitor yesterday. Elsa.'

'Elsa West? First time you two have met, isn't it? What was the occasion?'

Sally hesitated, only for a second. 'She thinks you're cheating me.'

'Why doesn't that surprise me?' Robert said with a laugh. 'She's accused Edward of the same thing. Claims Edward and I are in it together.'

'It's not true?'

'Of course it's not true. She has more money than she knows what to do with. It's made her paranoid, poor thing.'

'Everything I have is in your hands, Robert. Emotionally, I don't think I could take another hit.'

'Look at me, Sally. Do you think I would ever do anything to hurt you? If you do, then you should consider getting another lawyer.'

Suddenly she began to cry and just as suddenly Robert was on his feet. He swept around the table, pulled her to her feet and held her in his arms.

'I'll always be here for you,' he whispered close to her ear.

The sound was unmistakable, as if a seal had been broken and a secret let out. Presently Edward, dressed for travel, emerged from the tiny bathroom with his thin hair slicked back. 'Hardly room to fart in there,' he complained.

'You seem to have succeeded,' Robert said without a smile.

Edward's bag was packed, except for his Japanese robe, which lay draped over a chair. A nurse wearing what could have been a pajama top over yellow slacks arrived to wheel him out, a clinic rule, which annoyed him. Robert reached for the robe.

'Leave it! I never liked it.'

The nurse wheeled him down the corridor to a set of opening doors as Robert trailed with bag in hand, the robe folded under his arm. Outside, Edward pulled himself from the wheelchair and walked on his own to the parking area, where Robert guided him to a Mercedes.

'This new?'

Robert nodded and, opening the passenger door, helped him in. The scent of Edward's aftershave was strong, an irritant to Robert's sensibilities. They scarcely spoke until they were well out of Haverhill and nearing I-93. 'You're not wearing your seat belt,' Robert said critically.

'Too uncomfortable. What are we going to do about Elsa?'

'Nothing.' Robert merged the Mercedes into the swift highway traffic. 'The ball's in her court.'

'She could cause a hell of a lot of trouble.'

'If push comes to shove, I can make a case for her mental instability.'

'I don't want her destroyed,' Edward said.

'We might not have a choice, Tiger.'

Edward bristled. 'You call me that to get my ass, don't you?'

'And why would I do that?'

'That damn superior attitude of yours.'

A quick learner, Robert had graduated from Haverhill High younger than most. The son of a tannery worker, he received scholarships that put him into Boston University and through law school, after which he set up a practice in Haverhill, a reputation to make.

Edward looked out the window. 'Wasn't for me, you wouldn't be where you are.'

'Really?' Robert glided the Mercedes into another lane. 'Where would I be?'

'Still in Haverhill, goddamn it. My brother's death made you a lot of money.'

'It made us both a lot of money, Edward.'

Edward stiffened. 'I loved Jack.'

'I'm not suggesting you didn't.'

'Jack was my hero and so was my father, though my father didn't deserve to be. My mother was my strength.'

Robert drove with a single finger on the wheel. 'Now Marion is.'

'It's not the same. Never could be.'

'No? Marion's the best thing that ever happened to you. And it doesn't hurt to have me in your corner, does it?'

Edward gave him an ugly look. 'I am what I am because of my mother. Not Marion, not you, not even Jack. You understand?'

'Calm down, Tiger. No one's taking anything away from your mother. A wonderful person, she was.'

'You never knew her.'

'My loss.'

Lapsing into silence, Edward closed his eyes and did not open them until they were approaching Boston. A haze mellowing the city's skyline muted the Prudential Tower and warmed the frigid attitude of the Hancock. On Storrow Drive he said, 'Why didn't you ever marry? You must've had plenty of women.'

Robert appeared amused. 'There's the answer. Too many to choose from. Besides, my life is comfortable the way it is.'

Edward felt himself growing red. 'You never should've laid hands on my niece. She was just a kid.'

'You never should have stolen from her. What's worse?'

When they were in the thick of traffic in Kenmore Square, Edward said, 'Maybe I'll give it all back.'

'Think it through, Tiger. Marion would never let you.'

Gordon, in familiar bow tie and blazer, sat in Elsa's reading room, his book bag at his feet. She had sidetracked him on his way up to his apartment and now was serving him a glass of sherry and one for herself, her second within the hour. Gordon glanced at his watch. He was meeting friends later for dinner.

'Okay, Elsa. What's so important?'

She thrust a sheet of paper at him. 'Read it, Gordon. I need your opinion.'

'What is it?' he said, searching his blazer for his glasses.

'A story idea. Read it!'

Finally he found his glasses, got them on his face and, with lowered head, focused in. Elsa, staring at the small bald spot on his crown, remembered the first example of her writing she'd shown him. Kittens littered with fleas, no homes available to them, were put to sleep for their own good, the finality of death deemed worthier than the uncertainty of life. She had entitled the tale 'The Big Sleep', after her mother's favorite American mystery writer.

Gordon finished reading but did not look up. 'Let me give it another scan.'

Elsa remembered the stillborn moment when she learned her mother had died. The school administrator took her aside and delivered the message in German and, when she did not react, repeated it in French. Her face frozen, she pretended the administrator's lips were lying to her.

Removing his glasses, Gordon looked up with concern. 'This is a Stephen King sort of thing.'

'Can't it be more than that? I want to do what the Greeks were so great at.'

'You want to do horrendous tragedy. It's been done, Elsa. Over and over again. What the Greeks did is now the stuff of tabloids. *Medea* would be front page.'

'My father could have been Greek, he died like one. The gods did him in.'

'You consider your father a hero?'

'My mother thought he was.'

Gordon sipped his sherry. 'My heroes were those Celtic warriors who sprang naked on to their horses and galloped into battle with swords and hard-ons.'

'That's very revealing, Gordon, but did you know Dorothy Parker had a canary she named Onan because it spilled its seed on the ground?'

'As a matter of fact, I did. Did you know Walt Whitman slept on his mother's pillow for years after she died? And Emily Dickinson wondered whether she'd be punished in heaven for being homesick.' He gestured at her sherry glass. 'You finished that off fast.'

'I miss my mother, Gordon. And my father.'

He spoke gently. 'I know you do.'

'They're gone for ever. They're dead. Do you know what

death is, Gordon? It's God murdering you.'

Viewing her with concern, he said, 'I can call my friends and cancel out.'

Elsa gripped her empty glass. 'I may need another.'

'If you have another, someone will have to put you to bed.'

'Hitler will never pay for his crimes, Gordon. Nor will God.'

'Would you like me to stay?'

'Maybe you'd better.'

Fresh from the shower, girdled in a fluffy white towel, Marion stood barefoot by a window and watched the Mercedes glide up the drive and ease to a graceful stop. Doors winged open. Robert hopped out while Edward needed time, the effort visible on his face. She hurried downstairs, positioned herself where sunlight would wash over her when the front door opened and waited.

'Come on, fellas, move it,' she said under her breath.

The door opened.

'Well, my boys are back,' she said. Edward lumbered forward like a huge child. His kiss was sloppy, and she stepped back, not quite pushing him away. 'Nice to have you home, dear.'

'You're not dressed,' he whispered.

'You caught me unawares.'

Robert placed Edward's bag on the floor, the robe on top, and with mock indignation strode to Marion. 'Are you naked under that?' His hand raced under the towel. 'By God, she is, Edward.'

Marion slapped his wrist. 'Behave yourself.'

'Was that necessary?' Edward said angrily.

'Probably not, my friend. Do forgive me.' Robert blew Marion a kiss and she gave him an ugly look.

'You're leaving?'

'Things to do.'

Tightening the towel around her, she walked Robert to the door on her chorus girl legs, were they a little longer. Unable to decipher their whispers, Edward turned abruptly and began a slow climb up the stairway. Partway up, he heard the front door close, then Marion's voice. 'Should you be doing that?'

Without looking back he said, 'I'm not an invalid.'

'While you're up there, take a bath. Get that nursing home smell off you.'

In his bedroom, he viewed a picture of himself when he was young and courting Marion, his eyes shut tight to her faults, hers open to every one of his.

God, he had loved her! And still did.

He ran a bath and took off his clothes. When Marion looked in on him, he was standing on the scale and trying to get a reading. The weighted arc of his abdomen made his sexual organs remote, raising the question of whether he had any.

'The doctor says I must lose weight.'

'Anybody could've told you that.'

'I have to stick to my diet.'

'All up to you, isn't it?'

'Where's your maid? Juanita, is it?'

'Juana. I had to let her go. She didn't appreciate me.'

He stepped off the scale. Tilting, he was mass warping space. 'What are we going to do about Elsa?'

'Does she worry you that much?'

He placed a cautious foot into the tub. 'Yes.'

'Leave her to me,' Marion said.

Staring up, Marion saw no lights in the apartment. Keys Edward had given her got her into the building and then into the apartment. In the dark she pawed the wall for the light switch, found it, and flooded the front room. Then she gave a start. On the sofa was a small man sleeping under an afghan.

'Who the hell are you?'

Gordon woke. An arm shading his eyes, he said, 'Who are you? How did you get in?'

'A key, you damn fool. Elsa's uncle is co-owner of this apartment.'

'Does Elsa know that?'

'Whether she does or not doesn't change the truth of it,' Marion said and watched Gordon rise out of the afghan. He was in designer underwear, his shorts monogrammed. 'Excuse me for asking,' she said, 'but are you a fag?'

'Excuse me,' he replied, 'but are you a hag?'

Marion lifted her chin. 'Precious little prick, aren't you? Where's Elsa?'

'Sleeping. Best not to wake her.'

'Whatever-your-name-is, do you live here?'

'No.'

'Then get out.' Breezing by him, Marion marched directly through an unlit corridor to Elsa's bedroom and threw on a light. 'You awake?' Elsa stirred under the covers. Marion waited a moment. 'We have to talk. I'll wait for you out there. By the way, I told Twinkletoes to leave.'

Elsa's head appeared. 'You had no right.'

Returning to the front room, Marion said, 'You still here?'

Gordon was mostly dressed. He stepped into tasseled loafers and retrieved his bow tie and blazer. Presently Elsa, looking groggy, appeared in tank top and underpants.

'It's all right, Gordon. I can handle it.'

Gordon left with obvious misgivings. Marion, settling into a wing chair, said, 'I won't ask about him. That's your business.'

'It's hardly yours.' Elsa sat on the sofa and folded the afghan over her lap. 'What do you want?'

'We're all sick of your slanders. Any more of them, your uncle and Robert will bring suits against you. Are you listening to me?'

'Every word, Marion. Please go on.'

'Your credibility will be zero. I'll testify you falsely and maliciously accused Robert of seducing you when you were a teenager. Actually you were obsessed with him, that's what I'll say. And your uncle will tell the court how vindictively jealous you've been of me ever since you came to live in our house. Are you getting the picture, dear?'

'You're playing a good scene, Marion.'

'There's more. You're seeing a shrink, right? Right away, that tells the court you're unstable. Runs in the family. Did you know your grandfather was murdered? Your grandmother was never arrested but should have been. Your uncle could testify to that.'

'Any more, Marion? I'd love to get back to bed.'

'Just a question, dear. Why in God's name don't you shave under your arms?'

Elsa tossed the afghan aside and stood up. 'My mother never did. Why should I?'

'You have lovely legs, dear. We're both lucky in that regard.'

Elsa stepped away. Over her shoulder she said, 'If you have a key to my apartment, please leave it on the table on your way out.'

When she crawled back to bed, the dark of the room seemed to double. The phone rang and she fumbled with the receiver. Knowing who it was, she said, 'Am I going crazy?'

'Absolutely not,' Gordon said. 'That woman's a piece of work.'

'I'm afraid of her.'

'I would be too.'

There was a flash at her window, seconds later a thunderclap.

'Did you hear that, Gordon?'

'I did. It was predicted.'

There came another flash, a louder clap. 'That used to scare me, but now I realise thunderstorms are echoes from the *Iliad*. Who did you root for, Gordon? The Greeks or the Trojans?'

'I tried not to take sides, but Hector was my hero. He had class. Achilles had none.'

'My father was Odysseus, but he didn't make it home. My mother and I both waited.' There came more lightning, louder claps. 'Gordon, if you were with me right now, would you tuck me in? Like a real daddy?'

'Absolutely.'

'You're always there for me. Thank you,' she said.

She could feel her heart pounding when she rang the bell. The minister answered the door himself and ushered her into the parlor. Sally West. Of course he remembered her. How could he ever forget? Seated, they stared at each other. He had less hair and a paunch, but otherwise he looked the same. She could only imagine what she looked like to him.

'Thank you for seeing me,' she said.

'I've thought about you so many times, Sally. I visited you at the hospital, but you probably don't remember. You were in and out of sedation.'

Frowning, she scrutinised the room. 'You've changed the drapes. They were maroon.'

'I believe they were.'

She felt the weight of the minister's eye and smiled. 'I had on a blue dress and I wore a pearl choker that Jack bought me.' She lifted her left hand to display her jeweled wedding band.

'I certainly remember that,' the minister said.

She blushed happily. 'Jack was always a big spender. We drove away in his new convertible.'

'Yes. A white one.'

'Jack never came back.'

The minister went on the alert, fearing she was breaking down. 'Forgive me, Sally. Would you like something? Tea, coffee?'

'Nothing, thank you. Last night I dreamed of the trooper. Why did he do it, Reverend? Was he evil?'

'I'm not sure I believe in evil, Sally. It may be only a theological concept.'

'My doctor says some people are explosions waiting to happen. Do you believe that about the trooper?'

The minister let out his breath. 'I'm going through a crisis of my own, Sally, so I'll tell you exactly what I believe. I'm amazed that God miswires so many of us. Even the brain of a genius is out of kilter. Brains that work right belong to mediocre folks. Like me, Sally. Maybe like you.'

She might not have heard him. 'My doctor says the trooper's manhood was threatened when Jack didn't show respect.'

The minister nodded. 'We put a young fellow in a uniform, give him a gun and expect the best. Occasionally we get the worst.'

Sally half heard the words. She had an itch down below and, as if a child again, gave it a solid scratch through her thin dress. 'If God made us, Reverend, shouldn't he share the blame for the bad we do? Couldn't he at least give me my husband back?'

For moments the minister saw her as a child, which intimidated him, for he believed that the enormous questions children ask weigh as much as the world. 'I don't have an answer, Sally, and I don't think anyone else does, though they may pretend they do.'

'Do you have any answers at all?'

With a profound sadness, he shook his head.

STORY IDEA . . .

Twin girls, not yet a year old, are asleep in their cribs. A boy, nearly three, is at play in his room. Downstairs at the breakfast table a man in a business suit says that being married is being manacled; his wife, wearing a stained robe, says, 'You can leave any time you want.'

He says that marriage interferes with his life; she says, 'Do you want to take the kids, or should I keep them?'

He soaks his gaze in his coffee and says, 'I'm incarcerated. A life sentence.'

She commiserates. 'Poor darling. You know I'd do anything for you.'

'That's sweet of you, real sweet,' he says sarcastically and leaves for work.

When he returns that evening, the house is dark except for a single light burning in the kitchen, where his wife, still in her robe, sits immobile. His coffee cup is where he had left it.

'What the hell's going on?' he shouts. 'Where are the kids?'

Looking up with blasted eyes and blood on her robe, she says, 'You're free.'

ELSA WEST

'Why the hell did she send that to me?' Robert said. 'She's weird, you know that.'

Marion returned the typescript to him. 'But if I had to guess, I'd say she was telling you what a woman, any woman, is capable of.'

412

They were lunching at Locke-Ober. Each had strict dietary habits and was eating lightly, Caesar salad for Marion and smoked salmon for Robert. Robert said, 'But why would she want to write a thing like that? It has nothing to do with her life. And it certainly doesn't touch mine.'

'Are you sure? Maybe she wants to do you in and she's warning you. Don't smile. I'm half serious.'

Robert's gaze, skirting her, went to other tables, to anyone who might be looking. He liked being seen with Marion, for much about her was still eye-catching. 'You're being dramatic,' he said.

'Did you or did you not take advantage of her when she was of a tender age? Think hard. It may come to you.'

He sipped mineral water. 'You're being extraordinarily sarcastic, aren't you?'

'I'm concerned for your safety, darling.'

'You may have noticed. I sleep with one eye open.'

'Do you mind?' She sampled salmon from his plate. 'Mmmm. Good.'

Robert glowered. 'You know I hate you doing that. It's vulgar.'

'That's why I do it, darling. It gives me the upper hand, even if only for a moment.'

He smiled reluctantly. 'You're a worthy adversary, Marion. Married, we'd probably kill each other.'

'Married, darling, we'd simply lose interest.'

With a sigh, he looked at his watch. 'I'm running late.' He signaled for the check.

Marion patted her lips with a napkin. 'Will I see you tonight?'

'If Elsa doesn't shoot me.'

'Her grandmother used a blade. So the odds are you won't see it coming.'

*

Elsa peeked into the sun room and saw her uncle napping in a recliner, his head tipped back, his feet up. Approaching on tiptoes, she peered at his face in the hope of glimpsing something of her father. Heavy and expansive, the face smothered any token resemblance.

'Uncle Edward!'

He woke with a snort and gave a start when he saw her, momentary fear in his eyes. 'Elsa. How did you get in?'

'No one answered the bell, so I let myself in. What happened to Juana?'

'Who?'

'The maid.'

'I never met her. Marion let her go.' Edward straightened the recliner and rubbed his eyes. 'I seem to sleep mostly during the day. The past keeps me awake at night.'

'Mine is beginning to,' Elsa said. She took a seat near him. 'Where's Marion?'

'She and Robert still like to romp. I thought they'd have gotten over it by now, but they haven't.'

'It doesn't seem the hour for romping, Uncle Edward.'

'You never know with those two.' He spoke in a feeling voice. 'Do you hate me, Elsa?'

'Why would I hate you, Uncle Edward?'

'I can think of several reasons, one having to do with Robert and you. I never should have let that happen.'

'What happened, happened,' Elsa said with a painful memory of staring into Robert's eyes with monstrous innocence and total infatuation. 'As much my fault as anybody's.'

'But Marion and I should've looked after you. We owed it to you.'

'What you owe me now, Uncle Edward, is an accounting. I've chosen a lawyer. I went through the Yellow Pages of the Haverhill directory and a name jumped out. Mooradian.'

'Michael Mooradian?'

'Yes.'

'Your father went to high school with him. A good man, a good lawyer.'

'That might not be good for you, Uncle Edward.'

He closed his eyes. 'I've handled cancer and a stroke. I guess I can handle this.'

Elsa rose and rearranged the strap on her shoulder bag. She stood, stylish and a bit formidable in a gray suit, the jacket fitted, the skirt narrow.

Her uncle opened his eyes. 'This may be hard for you to believe,' he said, 'but I love you.'

'I love you too, Uncle Edward.' She leaned over and kissed his brow. 'Good luck.'

Elsa, sitting on a bench facing Park Street, glimpsed a familiar figure and said to herself, 'Why am I not surprised?'

Moments later Sally West entered the Common, proceeded up the pathway, and, tilting her head, broke out in a smile. 'Elsa! What a crazy coincidence!'

After an embrace, Elsa made room on the bench. She felt she knew the answer but asked anyway, 'What are you doing in Boston?'

'I come in once a month to see my doctor. Then, if the weather's nice, I kill time in the Common before catching the train back to Haverhill. What are you doing here?'

'Usually I'm not. At least not at this time of day. The last time I was sitting on this bench I saw my uncle conducting the Boston Symphony.'

'Edward?'

Elsa smiled. 'It was in a dream. Do you repeat your dreams to your doctor? Yes, I think you told me you did.'

Sally crossed her legs. 'I stopped doing that a long time ago. It's always the same sort of dream.'

'Did my father suffer?'

'He didn't have time.'

'Thank God for something.'

Sally skewed her head and looked at Elsa full in the face, her voice almost a child's. 'Is God good?'

Elsa shrugged, with a glance at her watch. 'I'm sure he has his faults. We all do.'

'I want to believe in something. There must be something.'

'Believe in yourself, Sally. It's worth a try.'

'Where are you going?'

Elsa was on her feet. Gripping the strap of her shoulder bag she said, 'I have an unscheduled appointment.'

Staring up at the length of her Sally said, 'You look so smart, Elsa. You look so . . . so Boston.'

'I think I'd rather look Haverhill.'

'Then it wouldn't be you.' Sally's voice reached out as Elsa stepped away. 'Will we stay in touch?'

'That's a promise,' Elsa said over her shoulder.

'Do you mean it?'

Elsa's stride was swift and she may not have heard.

Edward went to his bedroom with a terrible weariness and fell into a troubled sleep. An hour later Marion entered hers, followed by Robert. Tall twin windows looked out on spruce and hemlock.

Marion said, 'He'll sleep till midnight, then stay up most of the night.'

'Poor bugger,' Robert said, shedding his suit jacket.

'He's happy, darling. He has his money and he has me.'

Robert unknotted his tie, regimental, from Brooks Brothers. Contacts had long ago replaced his eyeglasses. 'What if he had to choose?'

'It would be a close call.' Marion reached down and

loosened a pump by its heel. 'But he'd choose me, of course.'

Robert's fine English shoes were placed side by side, like soldiers. Marion's pumps, which she had kicked away, lay one way and another, as if estranged. Robert shed his suit, his shirt and his underwear, and drew a smile from Marion.

'You should keep your clothes on. You no longer look distinguished. But I love watching you spring to life.'

'You keep me on my toes, Marion.'

'I hope so.' She drew off taupe panty hose and displayed buttocks as shiny as if they had been buffed. Freed, her breasts took on a life of their own. A hand on her hip, she said, 'Well?'

'You'll do fine.'

Each looked forward to the bed. Marion viewed the sexual act as two bodies in exquisite trauma. Robert said it was a debate turned violent over who was giving the most, orgasms at stake, reputations on the line.

'How about me?' he asked, both hands on his hips.

'Pick of the litter, Robert.'

Each had no complaints, for each invariably performed with accuracies that left the other with no letdowns. Each in intensely immodest ways made the other feel valuable, and each in oblique ways loved the other.

Robert moved toward the lamp. 'Leave it on or turn it off?'

'Up to you.'

'Does that make me boss?'

'If you like to think so.' In bed, under lamplight, she stretched her legs. 'What would you do without me, Robert?'

'Die?'

She paused for a second. 'You don't have to go that far.'

*

Dr Wall was squeezing her in, as she and his secretary had known he would. The secretary said to her, 'I love your outfit.'

'Thank you.'

Smiles were exchanged. 'You can go in now.'

In Dr Wall's office, she stared at the picture of his youngest daughter and said, 'Is that me?'

'I beg your pardon?'

'Sorry. A crazy idea was running through my head. It happens.'

'True,' Dr Wall said. 'It happens to all of us.'

Sitting straight, she pictured him with his clothes off, a little man strutting like a rooster. She imagined it wouldn't take much to make him cock-a-doodle-do.

'Why are you smiling?' he asked.

'Am I? Sorry. My father's widow is your patient. Why didn't you ever mention it?'

'Not my place. And it wouldn't have been proper.'

'Who recommended you to her? Was it Robert? My uncle? Or was it both?'

'Please, Elsa.'

'I hope you're helping her. She's been hurt much too cruelly. Of course, many of us suffer fates we don't deserve. God's way of showing us who's boss.'

Dr Wall's eyes were feasting on her. 'You're looking especially attractive today, Elsa.'

'You're not listening to me, Doctor. Any moment now, you might turn a little foolish. I hope not.'

Dr Wall envisioned her standing nude with a hand limply on her hip. Modigliani would have cherished her on canvas and stretched her neck. Dr Wall said, 'I'll try to control myself.'

'I have another story idea. Late at night a man is snacking at the kitchen table when his wife creeps from the bedroom and plunges a butcher knife into his back. Somehow he finds the strength to call 911, which saves his life, but he is never the same afterwards, neither physically nor mentally. The lesson is you never know anyone's true mental state, not even your own.'

'The human psyche, Elsa, is the least peaceful place in the universe, but I'm not telling you anything new, am I?'

'No, and you're staring at me in that foolish way again.'

He saw her as Dietrich's Lola in *Blue Angel* and himself as an actor mouthing scripted lines. He couldn't help himself.

'I love you, Elsa.'

'It's the second time you've told me. Once was enough.'

He didn't want this. He wanted Plato's cave, his face to the wall. 'More than enough. I'm sorry.'

'I came to tell you this is my last visit. I've had enough of this country. America is cattle herded into an abattoir for the benefit of McDonald's and Burger King. It's a storm trooper executing my father. It's a country where *der Tod das Leben schandet.*'

'I'm sorry, Elsa. I'm not sure I know what that means.'

'Death mocks life,' she said.

She was on her feet. He shot to his, his voice wavering. 'I don't want to lose you.'

Elsa spoke from the door. 'Remember what you told me about my father? You can't lose what you never had.'

Edward West dreamed of his mother, Milly, who, with a frayed voice, led him to the potty. Constipated, he produced only a few hard pennies. He couldn't remember his father's name and started to cry. 'Hank,' his mother told him. 'It's Hank.'

He was sorry the dream ended and more sorry he was lying awake and alone, with the small hours looming ahead of him. Rising, he pushed his feet into leather slippers and reached for the robe he thought he had discarded at the rehab center. The nightlight hurt his eyes. Depressed, he avoided looking at himself in the dresser mirror. A light burned in Marion's room, but the room was vacant.

He shuffled down the stairs and saw Marion poised, bare-legged, in an outsize T-shirt, one of his, near the front door. The door clicked.

'Who was that?'

'Robert,' she said. 'He was just leaving.'

'Damn you!' he said.

She viewed him with disgust. 'Time you grew up,' she said and turned away.

He followed her down the hall. 'I won't put up with it any more. I want you to end it.' He was talking to the swing of her hips, to the hard flash of her legs and the balls of her feet. 'Do you hear me?'

In the kitchen she turned on him. 'Who are you to dictate to *me*?'

'I'm your husband.' He struggled to keep his voice strong and his robe from falling open.

Marion poured herself a small glass of water and drank it down. 'Robert and I share something you'll never understand.'

'Try me.'

'It's in the blood. Beyond that, I don't want to hurt your feelings.'

'It's never stopped you before.'

She hesitated. Did she really want to bare differences between him and Robert? Would he even understand? Robert was over-the-calf hose. Edward was ankle socks dribbling into his shoes. 'Go to bed,' she said. 'I am.'

Left alone, he felt devalued, a major portion of him looted. He missed his mother, his father, his brother. *Jack! Where are you?*

He shuffled from the kitchen and paused at the hall mirror, his robe flopping apart. Not a pleasing picture.

The climb up the stairs winded him.

'Where are you?'

A foot on the closed toilet seat, she was clipping her toenails. 'Stay out.'

An order he obeyed. 'Robert's a crook,' he declared.

She laughed. 'So are you. We all are, Tiger.'

'Don't call me that!' He trembled. 'I keep perfect records. I could bury him.'

'He'd crush you like a bug.' She began work on the other foot. 'Face it, Tiger, you were never your brother, and you're certainly not Robert.'

Edward stepped forward and saw her from behind, an unholy view, arse and thighs cut smooth. God, he loved her! 'What am I, then?'

'A nobody.'

'What?' His robe had reopened.

She knew he was behind her but didn't bother to look up. A razor passed so smoothly across her throat that she had no idea she'd been murdered.

AFTERWORD

A tabloid dubbed Edward a vampire because he had licked blood from the murder weapon. Attorney Michael Mooradian said his client had no clear memory of events and was undergoing psychological evaluation at Bridgewater State Hospital where, at his niece's request, he was under a suicide watch. Edward lay on a cot with a charged air of anticipation, as if his brain were a chrysalis in which his very first thought was stirring.

'I'm going home, Sally. Please come with me.'

'Where's home?'

'Germany.'

'I have a home.'

'But not a life.'

'Why are you doing this? I'd just get in your way.'

'No, you wouldn't. And it's what my father would've wished.'

Sally wavered. 'What about Edward?'

'My uncle? What more can I do for him? Tell me and I'll do it.'

Sally looked away. 'What about Robert?'

'He'll survive, believe me,' Elsa said.

*

Robert's license to practice law was suspended for five years. He avoided disbarment by agreeing to make full restitution to the West family, represented by Michael Mooradian.

Michael Mooradian. Born 1932. Haverhill High School, class of 1950. Suffolk University Law School, 1957. Died 2001.

ABOUT THE AUTHORS

Mark Billingham is the author of a series of novels featuring London-based DI Tom Thorne, the latest of which is *The Burning Girl*. The second in the series, *Scaredy Cat,* was shortlisted for the CWA Gold Dagger for Best Crime Novel of 2002. He has also worked for many years as a stand-up comedian which some regard as big and brave, while others think it just shows a child-like need for attention. Mark tells jokes for money far less frequently these days, as those that read the books are not usually drunk, and can't throw things.

Visit his manly, yet also boyish website at: *www.markbillingham.com.*

Lawrence Block has never been a short-order cook, an over-the-road truck driver, or a professional prize fighter, nor has he gone to sea. He has written any number of books, the latest of which is *All the Flowers Are Dying*, which, like its author, is set in New York City.

Andrew Coburn is the author of eleven novels. His work has been translated into nine languages, and three of his novels have been made into *films noir* in France. Grace Stassio, writing for *Under Cover*, says that while reading

Coburn, 'he goes down like neat Scotch, nice and smooth'. In real life Mr Coburn prefers skimmed milk stormed with Hershey Syrup, the harsher the Hershey the better. The *New York Times* says, 'Coburn writes in a brilliant style of chilly elegance and is merciless in probing tormented characters.' Mr Coburn is unlikely ever to disagree with this.

Michael Connelly was born in Philadelphia but grew to manhood while living in various parts of Florida, where his story in this volume is set. He has published thirteen crime novels and after a decade and a half living in Los Angeles has recently returned to Florida where he is busy regressing from man to boy with the aid of a fishing pole.

Former journalist, folk singer and attorney, **Jeffery Deaver** is the author of eighteen novels; he's been nominated for five Edgar Awards from the Mystery Writers of America as well as an Anthony Award, and is a two-time recipient of the Ellery Queen Readers' Award for best Short Story of the Year. His most recent book is *The Twelfth Card*, a Lincoln Rhyme novel.

Readers can visit his website at: *www.jefferydeaver.com*.

He acknowledges the excellent book, *Scarne's Guide to Modern Poker*, which was very helpful in writing the story in this collection.

John Harvey is the author of ten Charlie Resnick novels, the stand-alone *In a True Light* and four short stories featuring Jack Kiley, of which 'Chance' is the most recent. He has previously edited *Blue Lightning*, a collection of short fiction with musical themes. For more fax 'n' info, check out *www.mellotone.co.uk*.

For those who want to chase it down, the Townes Van Zandt recording referred to in 'Chance' is *A Far Cry From Dead* and is available on Arista 07822-18888-2.

Reginald Hill has written a lot of books and hopes to write a lot more. He has won awards but can't remember where he put them. He lives happily in the Lake District from which he can only be extracted by large sums of money or alien abduction. People with large sums of money, or aliens, should contact his agent.

Bill James has published nineteen crime novels featuring Assistant Chief Constable Desmond Isles and Detective Chief Superintendent Colin Harpur. Reviewers describe Isles variously as clinically mad, Satanic, terrifyingly violent and instantly recognisable as an A.C.C. Harpur's wife was murdered and he longs to be remembered as an inspired single parent. 'Like an Arrangement' is taken from the twentieth Harpur and Isles book, *The Girl With the Long Back*. James also published spy novels and another crime series set around Cardiff docks.

Dennis Lehane is the author of seven novels, including *Mystic River* and his latest, *Shutter Island*. He often sets his short stories in the American South, where he lived for eight years until he tired of people not getting his jokes and moved back to Boston. He continues to live in Boston with two English bulldogs, Marlon and Stella, who don't get his jokes either.

Author-drummer **Bill Moody** has toured and recorded with Maynard Ferguson, Earl 'Fatha' Hines, Jon Hendricks and Lou Rawls. *Looking for Chet Baker* is the fifth in the Evan Horne mystery series. Moody lives in northern California, where he plays jazz and teaches at Sonoma State University.

George Pelecanos never fully made the transition from boy to man. For more on his books and other obsessions – Westerns, action films, soul and punk, blaxploitation, *film noir*, musclecars, ladies' shoes, ladies' feet, etc – go to *www.georgepelecanos.com*.

Peter Robinson is the author of the Inspector Banks series. His short story 'Missing in Action' won the Edgar Allan Poe Award in 2001. Though he thinks he's a man, there are those who say he'll always be a little boy at heart.

Jim Sallis is a poet, novelist and all-round literary hired gun. Author of the acclaimed Lew Griffin cycle, Jim has also published books on musicology, multiple collections of poems, stories and essays, a biography of Chester Himes and a translation of Raymond Queneau's novel *Saint Glinglin*. His work appears regularly in literary journals such as *The Georgia Review*, in mystery and science fiction magazines (for one of which, *The Magazine of Fantasy & Science Fiction*, he writes a books column), and in major US newspapers such as the *Washington Post* and *Boston Globe*. He loves Mozart, Hawaiian and steel guitar, French literature and, most of all, his wife, Karyn.

John Straley is a former private investigator who lives in Sitka, Alaska. His poems and essays have appeared in various journals in North America. He is the author of six novels featuring private investigator Cecil Younger.

Brian Thompson was born in Lambeth, London, read English at Cambridge and now lives in Oxford. His most recent works are *Imperial Vanities* (HarperCollins, 2003) and *Nightmare of a Victorian Bestseller* (Short Books, 2002).

Don Winslow has worked as a movie theatre manager, a production assistant on documentaries and a private investigator. In addition to being an author, he now works as an independent consultant on issues involving litigation arising from criminal behaviour. His novels include *The Death and Life of Bobby Z* and *California Fire and Life*.

Daniel Woodrell is the author of seven novels, has twice been a finalist for the Dashiell Hammett Award, and won the PEN Center West Award for the novel *Tomato Red*. He lives happily in the boonies of America, which is a region beyond the sticks, out past Podunk and way downriver from Nowheresville. His house has a bedroom and a half and a flush toilet, and he is not above bragging about either luxury to his neighbours. He figures Roy Rogers said it best, 'When you take the boy out of the man, you haven't got much left.'

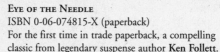

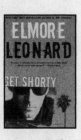